Praise for Elissa Soave

'One of the surest and clearest voices in Scottish fiction'
Andrew Meehan

'Humanity glows from every page'
Karen Campbell

'What a group of beautifully depicted, perfectly flawed and deeply engaging characters!'
Helen Paris

'A comforting story of coming together, friendship and the strength of community'
Catherine Simpson

'Funny, touching and wise, I loved it'
Kit de Waal

'Startling, sly and full of suspense'
Catherine Mayer

'Full of charm, insight and wit'
C. E. Riley

'Stingingly observed, expertly executed'
Claire Wilson

'Thought-provoking, acutely observed and full of compassion'
Helen Sedgwick

'By turns funny, dark and heartbreaking'
Louise Mumford

'A fiery, funny and fierce feminist read'
Emma Styles

ELISSA SOAVE won the inaugural Primadonna Prize in 2019. She is the author of two previous novels: *Ginger and Me*, which was shortlisted for the Saltire Society Scottish First Book Award, and *Graffiti Girls*. Elissa has been a judge on the Primadonna Prize and the Curae Prize. She currently lives in South Lanarkshire.

Also by Elissa Soave:
Ginger and Me
Graffiti Girls

COMMON GROUND

ELISSA SOAVE

ONE PLACE. MANY STORIES

HQ
An imprint of HarperCollins*Publishers* Ltd
1 London Bridge Street
London SE1 9GF

www.harpercollins.co.uk

HarperCollins*Publishers*
Macken House, 39/40 Mayor Street Upper
Dublin 1, D01 C9W8, Ireland

This edition 2026

1
First published in Great Britain by HQ,
an imprint of HarperCollins*Publishers* Ltd 2026

Copyright © Elissa Soave 2026

Elissa Soave asserts the moral right to be identified as the author of this work.
A catalogue record for this book is available from the British Library.

ISBN: 9780008673369

Typeset in Bembo Std by HarperCollins*Publishers* India

This novel is entirely a work of fiction. The names, characters and incidents portrayed in it are the work of the author's imagination. Any resemblance to actual persons, living or dead, events or localities is entirely coincidental.

All rights reserved. No part of this publication may be reproduced, stored in a retrieval system, or transmitted, in any form or by any means, electronic, mechanical, photocopying, recording or otherwise, without the prior written permission of the publishers.

Without limiting the exclusive rights of any author, contributor or the publisher of this publication, any unauthorised use of this publication to train generative artificial intelligence (AI) technologies is expressly prohibited. HarperCollins also exercise their rights under Article 4(3) of the Digital Single Market Directive 2019/790 and expressly reserve this publication from the text and data mining exception.

Printed and bound in the UK using 100%
Renewable Electricity at CPI Group (UK) Ltd

For my brothers, Joseph and Michael –
the best of men

Agenda of North Lanarkshire Communities Committee Meeting

Date: Monday, 22 April 2024

1. Sederunt/Present
    1.1 Karen McPhee, Jack McLaughlin, Neve Stewart, Fergus Cameron (Minute-taker)
    1.2 Councillors: James Murray
    1.3 Member of Scottish Parliament: Lewis O'Connor
    1.4 In attendance: Members of the public: None

All matters discussed to be regarded as highly confidential

2. Matters arising
    2.1 Armistice wreath: decision to be made on amount to be ringfenced from Q4 budget for this year's wreath; advance order from the Lord Hodges poppy factory to be agreed.
    2.2 Police report on Viewpark and surrounds to be reviewed and accepted. See attached.
    2.3 The cleaning of the underpass between Spindlehowe Road and St John the Baptist school. New contractors to be selected, and price agreed.
    2.4 Kenmar allotments: shortfall in funding identified following new local authority budget. Proposals for alternative finance/possible purchase and closure to be discussed.
    2.5 Any other matters arising.

1

Germaine Hounslow's father had raised his only daughter on a robust diet of baked potatoes, Sunday night baths, and the Hounslow family motto of 'an enemy a day'. He claimed that's how her mother would have wanted it. With scant memories of her mum, and her dad gone for almost a year, Germaine still loved a baked potato – always done in foil in the oven for at least an hour, never microwaved. She still indulged in a blistering hot soak in the bath every Sunday, sometimes even when she'd had one the night before and hadn't been digging or planting that day. Most importantly, Germaine still clung tightly to the family motto, making at least one and usually several enemies as she went about her business every day.

Take yesterday. With the early May sunshine splitting the clouds above her, she'd been getting on with the jobs of the day. She liked to break the back of her work during the week before the weekend folk descended and she might have call to be sociable. She'd sorted through the trays of seedlings she'd already sown indoors and was raking over the soft earth near the shed where she planned to transplant them.

She'd just pushed the spikes of her dad's old rake into the damp soil when she noticed a pair of ferrety little men coming in the main gates and stopping for a moment to take their bearings. Both wore sharp suits and shiny black shoes which were completely unsuited to a walk round the allotments, sunshine or not. The one on the left wore a red tie and carried a clipboard. The one on the right wore a green tie and was pointing towards the plots at the top of the hill with his stumpy fingers as he spoke, Red Tie noting down whatever it was he was saying.

Germaine leaned against the rake, watching them. One of the disadvantages of the allotments being funded by the council was that they had to be open to the public. Although most of the time no one was interested in wandering round the half-dozen plots, you did get the occasional busybody who wanted to see what they'd done with the land since the Flower Festival had closed, or to bring their annoying kids for a tramp around the fairy garden. This pair didn't seem the type for a meander across the muddy ground but, as her father used to say, 'There's nowt so queer as folk.'

'Hello, can I help you?' she called, just before they reached her.

Red Tie looked up in surprise, while Green Tie regarded her through narrowed eyes as though she were the intruder and not them.

'Thank you, no,' he said, in a nasally voice that matched his proportions exactly. 'We are just . . . surveying the land.'

'Surveying the land, yes,' repeated Red Tie, smoothing down the page on his clipboard.

It wasn't until later that Germaine reflected this was an odd way to put it – *surveying* the land, rather than admiring the plot holders' plants and floral displays, or visiting the fairy garden, or taking the air, or even tutting at the state of some of the plots, No 6 at the top on the right-hand side, for example. But at the time, she was happy they didn't need anything from her and she could go back to raking. She watched them shake their shoulders as a gentle spring drizzle started, Red Tie shielding the paper on his clipboard with his arm as they went about *surveying* the land.

It took them some time since the land on which the allotments were located was a fair size, taking up the whole of a huge field at the side of Viewpark nursery where they used to hold the village's annual Flower Festival. The cuts had seen to it that the Flower Festival was long gone but the field had been partitioned off from the main nursery, and split into six substantial plots, three on each side of the path that eventually led to the community centre at the other side of the old playing fields behind. Each plot came with a large shed and was demarcated with a small wooden fence round the perimeter.

The two men made their way up the hill, stopping at intervals to point at this one's shed or that one's path. Germaine looked on in surprise as Green Tie took out a measuring tape at Allotment No 5 halfway up the hill, and called out something to Red Tie who noted it down. She wondered whether she should go up and ask what they thought they were doing, measuring stuff, when Green Tie flicked the tape away from him and put it back in his pocket. The pair carried on to the top of the hill where they inspected the crumbling brick wall, which Germaine was pretty sure was only standing thanks to a combination of dirty white paint gluing the bricks together and the partially broken fence propping it up on the other side.

Weirdos, she thought. *What are they playing at? There's no plants to see up there.* She watched as the pair took in the playing fields behind the wall, Red Tie slightly behind Green Tie as he swept his arm in an arc over the fields, both nodding at the open expanse of green before them. Germaine was about to drop her rake and ask what on earth they were doing up there when the two men turned and headed back down the hill towards her.

Germaine's own plot, and her shed which doubled up as the management office, were near the entrance to the allotments, next to a communal area with a few picnic tables and some benches. On the other side, close to the entrance, there was an outbuilding for storage. Most of the plot holders stored their bigger tools there so that their own sheds could be used for relaxing in with cups of tea and keeping any personal items. Germaine kept the key hanging up on the wall of her office/shed, guarding it as though the ancient shovels and rusty rakes were worth something.

Further on from the picnic area was the fairy garden – Germaine had just learned to say this without a snort – built with the lottery funding they'd received a couple of years earlier. Again, one of the conditions for this was that the general public be allowed to come in and use the facilities whenever the place was open, so Germaine could hardly object to the two men moseying around that morning. But in the short time she'd been manager here, very few people had ever come to visit. It occurred to her that perhaps these guys were from the council and wanted to check she was providing a warm enough welcome to the odd individual or two who did wander in.

'No,' Green Tie said when they finally reached her allotment and she asked him as much. 'We're not from the council, perhaps we weren't making ourselves clear.'

Definitely not, thought Germaine, trying not to smirk as the man lifted his foot up and muttered something about his dirty shoes.

'That'll be the muck,' she said. 'Annoying, I know, but kind of crucial at an allotment. Ask the council.'

'Indeed.' Green Tie was looking at her with the same distaste he appeared to feel for the mud. 'We are not from the council,' he repeated.

'But I think we can say, on the basis of this morning's visit, you will be hearing from the council in due course,' added Red Tie, looking up from his clipboard momentarily and towards his partner for confirmation.

'We've got everything we need,' was all Green Tie was prepared to say. He glanced towards the picnic area, where two of the benches were covered in rectangular trays of curly kale, cabbage and spring onion seedlings, all grown from seed and awaiting their forever home in the soft mulchy earth of Germaine's allotment. No one ever sat on those benches though so she wasn't about to apologize for that.

'Right then. Thank you, Miss Hounslow,' said Green Tie, and the two men finally left her kingdom. She stifled a laugh as Red Tie lifted his right foot high into the air and made a face at the mud on his shiny unsuitable shoes. The fact that they'd known her name hadn't registered with her at the time, though the significance of it would not be lost on her some weeks later. But as soon as they left, she forgot all about them and went back to raking the dank and yielding earth.

Now it was Saturday, a new day and time for a new enemy. Not that there'd be anyone around to annoy her for a couple of hours or so yet, she thought, as she set about sowing the last of the spring onions, her fingers reaching into the earth and the smell of moist dark mulch reaching her nostrils. Apart from Stanley, that is, who was already doddering around his allotment when she arrived. Of course Stanley was there – probably had been since the crack of dawn.

Germaine glanced over to the first plot up the left-hand side of the path. Stanley was shuffling between shed and flower patch, like a slow and steady human crane picking up and depositing what seemed like an endless number of empty rectangular plastic boxes which had been filled with seedlings. As her dad had taught her to do, the old man had protected them from the frost over winter, waiting for some spring sunshine before judging the soil ready for germinating his tender young plants.

She guessed he'd be about the same age as her dad had been when he died, but his laborious movements and scruffy dress made him appear much older. When he took his bunnet off for a moment, she saw that his head was covered in freckles, or big brown spots anyway, rather than hair. The only hair on it was round the tops of his ears, and a bit more sprouting from the ears themselves. Thank God he covered it up with his bunnet again quickly. Although she couldn't see them from this far away, she knew from previous brief interactions with him that his eyes were soft and sad, with too much blood in the rim so he resembled the grizzled old bloodhound that used to live next door to her when she was growing up.

She thought she'd spotted the two weirdos from yesterday trying to have a word with him as they'd walked up the hill. The old lad had given them short shrift, quite right too. Like her dad, Stanley looked like he'd be quite happy to make an enemy or two a day. Still, she'd better make an effort to go and make small talk with him later, she was supposed to be the allotment manager after all and the poor old bugger probably wouldn't speak to anyone else all day. And maybe he could shed some light on what the two men had been doing on her allotments, with their clipboard and fancy shoes. That could wait though – there was planting to be done.

2

As most days, Stanley had been at his allotment since dawn, when orange light was beginning to streak the still-lilac sky. The deep silence of the other empty plots and the gentle May sun seeping into his bunnet and warming his head as he worked made him happier than he'd been in a long time.

He'd spotted but hadn't acknowledged the allotment manager when she came out of the office after doing whatever it was she did in there. They'd spoken before, of course, she'd even told him her name – Hounsfield, was it, Hutton, maybe, something like that. She wasn't Viewpark born and bred, he knew that, she was a newcomer from some big city or other. In his almost fifteen years as an allotment holder, Stanley had seen numerous managers come and go, some better than others. The Houndstooth woman didn't seem the worst by a long shot, at least she wasn't the type to lean on the fence and gossip, which suited Stanley fine. Like her, he wasn't given to chatter, preferring instead to give all his attention to the things that mattered to him in life, namely his seedlings, saplings and bulbs, the state of his soil, and the jewel in the crown of his allotment – his treasured rhododendron bush – which was currently at its magnificent purple best.

He'd spent the morning sifting out the weak from the strong. The sturdy pansies and primroses could fend for themselves but the more fragile geraniums had to be handled with care. He carried them, one pot at a time, from the shed out to the relative warmth of his allotment where they could spend the day leaning into the sunshine. The barest sparkle of frost would kill them though so even in May, he had to be prepared to bring them back in at night. He worked till his hands were stiff and stained with dirt. The palm of the left one, which trembled a bit these days, was striped with blood where a spiky thorn from the rose bush had grazed him.

As usual, he'd done most of his day's work before his fellow plot holders had set foot in the place. They started to arrive mid-morning and Stanley carried on working. He ignored the 'Good morning, my friend' from Mohid, his neighbour on Allotment No 2, and refused the offer of a Tunnock's teacake from that woman with the mad hair on Allotment No 4. She'd had her gormless-looking husband in tow, and the scrawny lad he took to be their son drifted in behind them. Stanley felt like telling her to give the biscuit to him instead, God knows he looked like he needed it. He worked on, wishing he still had the place to himself. It could be his imagination but it seemed to him that other people were becoming even more annoying than usual.

Yesterday, for example, he'd been minding his own business, pulling up some stubborn dandelions from between the paving stones, when two chaps, overdressed and one of them clutching a clipboard of all things at an allotment, had interrupted him while he was busy with his weeding. The one closest to him had asked him something about the wall at the top of the hill but Stanley had shrugged disinterestedly. What did he know about brickwork and the age of the wall, he was only interested in his own little slice of land. They'd soon taken the hint and moved on.

Stanley grimaced as a fork of electricity shot up from the base of his spine and through his shoulder blades. He straightened and reached up to massage his neck, pressing the knobbly bones there to try and get some relief from the pain. He must have been sleeping like a pretzel again, when he finally managed to get over to sleep, that is. Funny, for years he'd been one of those people who could sleep any time, anywhere. It used to annoy Mabel how quickly he'd fall asleep at night. 'How do you do it?' she'd say. 'Jump into bed, turn over and conk out in less time than it takes me to put down my Erica James.' He'd shrug and think nothing of it. That seemed so long ago; now he was lucky if he slept a couple of hours a night. It had started when Mabel got ill and he'd got used to sleeping on a knife's edge, alert to a missed breath, a moan in her sleep, every crackle of her besieged lungs.

'That's going to be quite the display of violas.' It was Mohid from the next allotment, stopping on the way into his shed to have a nosy at the fruits of Stanley's labour.

'Pansies,' hissed the old man under his breath in annoyance but he gave Mohid a half-wave in response so he wouldn't think he was being rude. It wasn't that Stanley didn't want to be friendly but another thing his long tenure at the allotments had taught him was that people came and went. Most of the time he didn't care, as long as he had Mabel, but after she died, he also lost his two old pals, Archie and Eddie, within a year of each other. They hadn't lived in each other's pockets by any means – Archie was more into his kayaking and wild swimming than his allotment, and Eddie was usually with his daughter, Maggi, and occasionally his wife Dorothy had deigned to put in an appearance. You couldn't miss either woman, they both dressed outlandishly in Stanley's opinion, but what did he know about fashion? Anyway, both men were gone now and even if it was stretching it a bit to call them friends, at least he'd had something in common with them – there was no common ground with these young folk. The professional types especially came in full of enthusiasm with their books and plans but before too long, usually after one hard winter, they'd realize it wasn't for them and the plot would be given to the next sucker on the list. No point in getting too invested. Mohid took the hint and closed the door of his shed behind him.

Stanley sighed. Sometimes, he thought it might be nice to have someone to chat to and his neighbours at No 2 did seem friendly. Then again, would they really want to be friends with an old goat like him? Stanley slid his bunnet to the back of his head, gave his massive earlobes a quick pull and got back to work.

The sky was glowering now, releasing sharp beads of rain that pinged off the paving stones running between the allotments. The trio from across the path had left after lunch, having achieved nothing of note on their overgrown allotment as far as Stanley could tell. They were followed by Mohid and Farah at around fourish. At Allotment No 3, the poor boy with the messed-up face had apparently been in his shed all day and had raised his hand vaguely in Stanley's direction as he left half an hour after his neighbours, so that left him and the manager. And since she was as taciturn as he was, he could relax and— No, wait. He'd spoken too soon, she was coming over.

'Still got some veggies to plant, I see.' Germaine was eyeing one small row at the back of the patch, prepped but empty, the top soil oily with the rain.

She seemed to be expecting a response. 'I've been working mostly on the flowers. Too tired to do a lot of digging today,' he said, wondering why he felt the need to explain himself to her. 'Didn't sleep much again last night.'

'"Old age doesn't come alone", as my dad used to say.'

'Did he? That's helpful, thanks.' Stanley did not look up from his primroses.

'Well then . . . I'll be heading off, unless you need me for anything?'

What on earth would he need her for? Stanley stopped himself from snorting. He pushed his bunnet back, scratched his head and carried on working, calculating that he had about twenty minutes to finish sweeping up the path before the rain began pelting down too hard even for him to be out.

It was less than ten minutes after Germaine left that the sky darkened alarmingly, till it was black as the sea floor. Rain drummed hard and fast on the shed roofs and fat pellets of water landed on Stanley's bunnet, which he ignored until the moisture started to seep through to his scalp. The thought popped into his head – Mabel wouldn't be putting out the washing today – instantly followed by the recollection that she wouldn't be putting the washing out again. Ever. He pulled off his sodden bunnet and resisted the urge to throw it on the ground and stamp on it in pure undiminished rage.

3

It was 11.50 p.m. and the navy night sky was filled with stars, sparking and shimmering and occasionally shooting their way across the moon. At least that's how it appeared to Mohid.

They could have used their key to unlock the front gate but the main gardens were closed at nine and he was worried someone would see them making their way into the allotments after hours. He and Farah had been there most of the day, leaving in the late afternoon and making a show of setting down their tools and packing up like they always did when they planned a midnight expedition like this.

The old man from the next-door allotment had ignored them as usual. It was a shame, Mohid could tell Stanley was an expert on plants and soil and no doubt many other things Mohid's school years and subsequent medical degree hadn't taught him. He would have loved his neighbour's advice on what to sow and when, how far apart to plant things, and which varieties of seeds did best indoors or out. Still, he couldn't make him be friends and if it ever occurred to him that perhaps the old man was of a generation that wasn't comfortable with people who didn't look exactly like him, he pushed the thought away and certainly never broached the subject with Farah.

They'd waved an ostentatious goodbye to the allotment manager, Germaine, on their way out of the main gates – 'We are leaving now and definitely not coming back after hours to light a fire and play music and dance,' their expansive waves were saying – but she'd barely acknowledged them. Mohid had spoken to her a handful of times since they'd taken on their allotment. She seemed nice enough, even if she preferred to wave at him from the office at the bottom of the path rather than getting to know him and his wife. He had observed at least that she treated all the plot holders the same way so he didn't take it personally. He could tell she was not the type to put up with any nonsense though so better to sneak in through the back, more thrilling in any case.

'If that snarky manager could see us now,' whispered his wife behind him, as though she'd read his thoughts.

He shone his torch at the gap in the fence, making sure she could see clearly enough to get through and over the crumbling wall without ripping her beautiful red sari. 'Why did you wear one of your best saris? I told you there'd be mud here after all the rain.'

Farah laughed and Mohid could see her teeth gleaming in the funnel of light thrown by the torch. 'Not one of my best, husband, *the* best. It's our anniversary, after all.'

Mohid shook his head but he wasn't annoyed with her. How could he be? One of the things he'd first loved about Farah was her flashy sense of style, with the twenty gold bracelets jingling up her arm, and lipstick, pillar-red, slashed across her mouth.

It had been almost ten years since his father's cousin Sarmed had first invited him to their home to meet her. He'd been reluctant to go, having been accepted into university by then and looking forward to meeting Scottish girls his own age, staying out all night partying and indulging his love of dancing and loud, loud music and whatever else came his way. But, as he sat between his parents on a huge green and gold couch in a living room surely heated beyond safety levels, he'd spotted her for the first time. She was in the kitchen, helping her mum to prepare the sweet gulab jamuns and milk cake, and he'd watched as she glided – there was no other word for it – between cooker and fridge and back again, her neck slender and fragile as she bent towards the worktop, her hands never still as she ground almonds and shelled cardamom pods. She must have felt his eye upon her because she looked up and rolled her eyes at him as if to say, what a fuss, we should leave them all to it, and with that, he was gone. He gave the impression of listening attentively to everything Sarmed had to say but his mind was elsewhere, making plans to talk to this beautiful woman alone, away from the prying eyes of their relatives. Two months later, they were engaged.

Farah took the supplies into the shed while Mohid prepared the fire outside.

He began by making a circle of the stones he kept in a pile behind the shed. He dug a hollow in the middle and placed smaller flat pebbles in the bottom. Smiling as he heard Farah humming to herself, he made a lattice from the kindling and carefully placed a couple of fire lighters between the twigs. He lit the wood and added some more small branches to the edges, poking at them with a stick. The flames began to rise.

'We have lift-off,' he called to Farah, who was still in the shed heating their chai tea on the little burner and arranging the samosas and spicy pani puris on a large oval plate. There was a smaller plate with Mohid's favourite milk cake for later.

'I've done too much as usual,' she said, bringing out the food and setting it down on the wrought-iron table Mohid had set up a little distance from the campfire. 'Looks pretty.' She indicated the pale pink cloth he'd used to cover the table, and the rose petals he'd scattered over that, in a late burst of inspiration. 'Thank you.'

'You're welcome, madame,' said Mohid, pulling out her chair for her like he was a waiter at a posh restaurant. He loved to make her happy and that hadn't always been easy in the last couple of years. Thank God their names had come up for an allotment. They both needed something apart from work, a joint project, to take their minds off the other stuff. But he knew it was never far from Farah's mind. As though on cue, he saw her eye drawn to the three artificial candles she'd placed on the step in front of their shed.

Before she could say anything, he said quickly, 'Music?' and brought out the small cylindrical speaker from under the table.

'Oh I think so, don't you?' said Farah, coming back to him.

Mohid scanned his phone for the playlist of their favourite songs he'd spent hours making earlier in the week. The music played and they tucked into their anniversary feast, the hot crumbly pastry of the samosas landing on their laps and their fingers sticky with chutney. They toasted each other with steaming chai tea. The fire was sparking now, their faces glowed in its orange light. Mohid prodded the branches to keep the flames licking the wood and Farah handed him a paper tissue and motioned to him to mop his brow.

Later, they danced in front of the firepit, swaying gently to the Eagles, Mohid breaking away occasionally to add more wood to the red hot ash bed, trying to make it last for ever.

At dawn, the dark purple sky gradually lightened to reveal soft pastel stripes, starting from low on the hill behind them and stretching across the horizon. The fire was almost out and Farah reached across Mohid to douse it with what remained of her tea.

'Time to get rid of the evidence, dear one?' Mohid smiled sleepily at Farah and shook himself awake.

She was looking over at the three candles on the step, still flickering but their pale flames less obvious now in the growing light. She turned to her husband and said in a low, urgent voice, 'They can see them, can't they? They can see them from wherever they are, and they know we're watching over them, thinking about them, don't they?' She was tired, her eyes heavy, but the glow of the fire's last embers was still reflected in them so that the look she gave her husband was glittering, hopeful.

Mohid pushed aside his years of scientific studies and all he knew to be true, and he drew his wife back towards him and whispered into her thickly plaited black hair, 'Definitely, my queen, I am certain of it.'

4

When Germaine arrived at the allotments the following morning, the door of Stanley's shed was open though Stanley himself was nowhere to be seen. She was surprised to see the couple on Allotment No 2 were also there already and apparently hard at work. Mohid was washing down the path that led up to the door of their shed, a pile of what looked like ash neatly stacked at the bottom of the path, and Farah was rinsing out their mugs at the tap, no doubt getting ready to make their first cup of tea.

It wasn't that Germaine didn't like Mohid and Farah exactly, it was more that she found it difficult to know what to say to a couple like that, who were so closed off, and in any case, were all work and no play. They were just . . . a bit boring, she supposed.

Mohid looked up and raised his hand in greeting. 'Getting an early start to beat the rain,' he called down to her, gesturing to the thick clouds gathering above them. Germaine waved back but went into her shed without bothering to reply.

She looked round her office and gave a quiet sigh of satisfaction as she took in the clean, dust-free desk with its chair positioned at a precise right angle beneath it. The desk was almost empty, holding only her laptop and a couple of books on potato blight from Viewpark library. Above the desk, and pinned on to the wall, was an A4 sheet of paper with a diagram she'd made on her first day here. She'd been working at the allotments long enough that she probably didn't need it any more but it was reassuring to have it there.

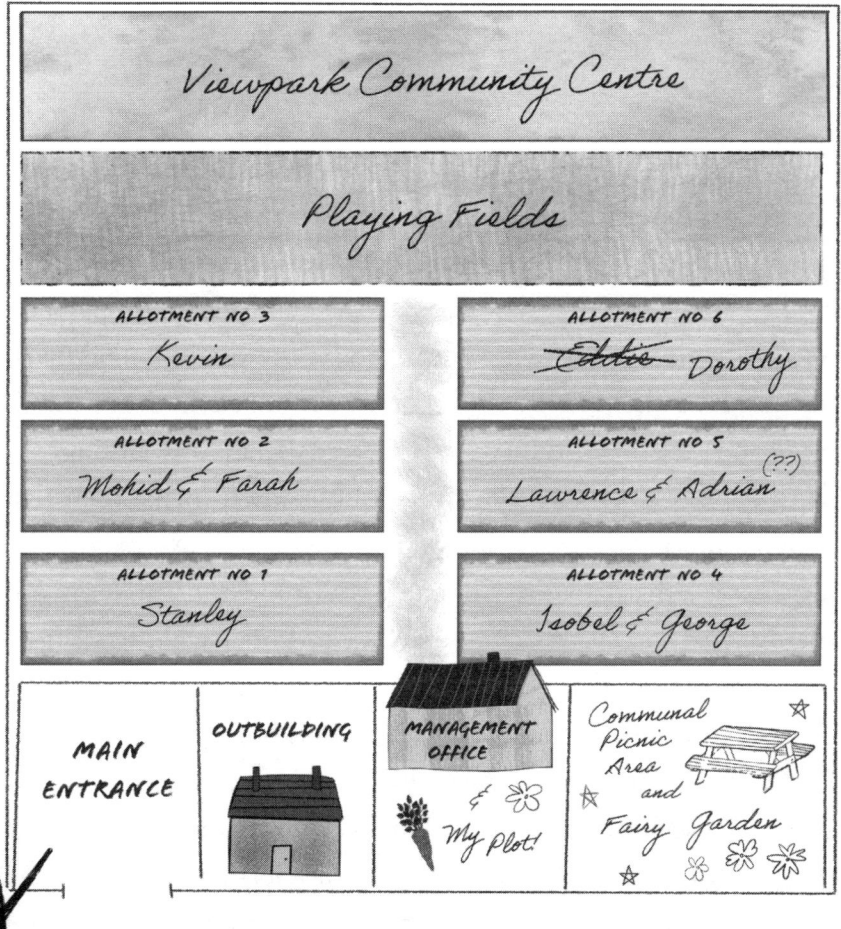

All was in order as Germaine sat at her desk and checked her task list for the day. The only way she could stay on top of things was to make lists. Trouble was, all the things on her list were admin-type tasks she really didn't want to do so she kept putting them off. Maybe if she could set herself one a day. She closed her eyes and pointed her finger at the list, opening them to see what task she'd landed on. Oh God, some huge questionnaire from the busybodies at the council about running costs for the previous six months, including the council charge – they'd know that better than her, surely – any drainage issues on the land, security, and on and on. Half of the questions related to the period before Germaine had taken over and what did they need to know all that for? Councillor Murray had already been on the phone twice last week chasing a response, and his assistant, Karen, had followed up with an email asking her when they could expect to have the information they needed. Harassed, she'd promised to make it a priority this week but it would take her hours to go back through her predecessor's records, which, by all accounts, were none too comprehensive, part of the reason Germaine herself had been brought in to replace the lazy old codger. And now it was going to be up to her to root about for facts and figures when all she really wanted to do was wage war on the slugs and snails that had the audacity to keep popping up on her allotment like whack-a-moles.

She groaned and thought maybe there was another task that would be easier. Closing her eyes again, this time her finger landed on the words 'Dorothy, Allotment No 6'. She was the one allotment holder Germaine hadn't met yet because she hadn't cared to put in an appearance since Germaine had taken over as manager and, judging by the state of her plot, not for a long time before that either. Now this was a task she could do, in fact it was something she could cross off her list right now. She reached over for her phone, gave the spotless screen a swift unnecessary wipe with an antiseptic cloth and called the number on the sheet. Either this Dorothy woman needed to turn up and do some work, or she'd be forced to give the plot to someone who really wanted it.

An hour or so later, Germaine stretched her back and closed over the lid of her laptop. Enough admin for one day, it was time to get outside. She looked up to the sky, trying to assess how long it would stay dry. She judged she had at least an hour or so before the drizzle started and decided the rest of the management duties that awaited her could carry on waiting a little longer.

All was quiet outside. None of the other plot holders had appeared while Germaine had been stuck in her office. Mohid and Farah's plot now looked empty, apart from the flames on those stupid artificial candles shimmying like a trio of tiny ghosts. She glanced over at Allotment No 1 and was surprised to see that Stanley too had gone already, his precious spade carefully stored away in his shed. Usually, she and Stanley were like two office workers vying for promotion, each staying later than the other to prove their commitment, regardless of the actual work requiring to be done.

Looked like today's prize for staying power was going to be hers. She picked up her own spade and started to dig over the rich soil at the back of the shed. Let the true work of the day begin.

5

THE BUS WAS ALREADY HALF-FULL when Dorothy got on at the first stop at the circle in Birkenshaw. Her new friends from the dancing, Irish Mary, Terry and Myra were in their usual seats, and had kept a seat for her beside them. Once she had her jacket off and her tote bag at her feet, Irish Mary called up to the driver, 'We're all settled, Wendy' and they set off.

'What about that Norah one winning again last night?' Myra was saying, as Dorothy moved along a bit to get comfy.

'Ah, not that again, Myra,' said Irish Mary.

'What, are you telling me it's a coincidence she just happens to be good friends with that nosy cow Pamela that calls the numbers?'

'Are you really suggesting Norah swindles the bingo cards to win – what was it last night – a bottle of Malbec?'

Myra sniffed. 'And she didn't share it with anyone.'

'She wasn't sitting anywhere near us,' protested Irish Mary.

'And you didn't share your win last month,' added Terry.

'How exactly you expect me to share a large set of Hoover bags I don't know. Hand them out one each?'

'Well, still . . .'

'That's me had it with the bingo. God knows what I've spent

on tickets in the last six months and what have I got to show for it – a dozen replacement bags for my old Hoover? Tsk.'

'I was reading somewhere that 90 per cent of gamblers give up just before their big win,' put in Dorothy, taking the opportunity to join in the conversation.

Myra considered. 'I'd better keep going then. It's an all-expenses paid weekend to Blackpool next week and our Donna'd kill me if I didn't give it a go.'

'There you go then,' said Irish Mary happily. 'Dorothy is the voice of reason.'

'Even if she is dressed like Old MacDonald.' Myra couldn't help herself. 'Where the hell are you going in a pair of dungarees – down to Lanark to pick strawberries?'

The others laughed but Dorothy didn't mind. She knew by now this kind of teasing was the way these women talked and they didn't mean any offence. On the contrary, if they were doing it to her face, it meant she was one of them.

'I'm going up to Eddie's allotment,' she said. 'Some rude woman from the management committee or somewhere phoned me up out the blue yesterday and—'

'There's supposed to be a waiting list as long as your arm to get one of those allotments,' said Terry. 'You know Margaret from the Friday club—'

'Is that the wee wifie with the glass eye, what happened—'

'That's the one.' Terry ignored Irish Mary's question. 'She told me her man was on the list so long he got dementia and died before his name came up.'

'It's the cuts.'

'Terrible.'

'I heard it's some woman from Aberdeen who's replaced

Frank Devlin as manager. Although how he was still there after what happened with the raffle money I don't know.'

'I thought they were closing down those allotments?'

'Who told you that?'

'Norah from the bingo, who else? But she's Frank's cousin and she said he wasn't bothered about losing his job because they were turning the allotments into flats soon and—'

Irish Mary rolled her eyes. 'He's saying that to save face. There's no way—'

'Mary's right. They'd never sell off those allotments. Folk'd be up in arms. Honest to God, rumours spread round Viewpark like margarine.'

'Anyway . . .' Dorothy found it difficult to navigate the fast-moving twists and turns of the conversation of her new friends but she was beginning to learn that you had to take your opportunity to break in and keep speaking or you'd never get the chance to talk. 'This woman said I had to come and do some work or they'd give the plot to someone else – and Eddie would hate that. Would have hated that,' she added softly.

'You're probably dressed all right for a bit of digging then,' even Myra had to concede.

'To be honest, I don't think I'm fit for anything else today after all that cider we sank last night. God knows what I look like. A face only a mother could love at the best of—' Terry nudged her and inclined her head to the other side of the bus.

Dorothy flushed as she shot a look at the young man across the aisle, ashamed of herself for caring about looks when other people . . . well. *Poor boy*, she thought, wondering whether anyone at the council had ever taken the rap for what had happened, and feeling angry at the way those schoolkids hounded him, calling him all sorts. She often saw him on the bus, and walking round Birkenshaw and Viewpark, but for someone who prided herself on talking to everyone, she'd never spoken to him. She told herself it was because he gave off don't-disturb-me vibes rather than because she found his appearance off-putting. He glanced over and caught her eye and she quickly lowered her gaze before turning back to her friends.

She pressed the bell at the stop after Aladdin's and told the other women to enjoy their coffee at St Columba's and she'd see them at the dancing tomorrow.

'Love your dungarees,' said the bus driver to her as she left the bus.

'Thanks, Wendy,' said Dorothy. At last, someone with some taste, maybe she'd even noticed the remnants of 'Greenham' stitched into the bib.

'Yeah,' Wendy continued. 'You look like the toddlers that come on the bus on their way to playdates. See you tomorrow.'

Dorothy dropped her shoulders and stuck out her chest, telling herself she didn't care what anyone else thought, she loved her old dungarees, they were part of history. Eddie had been so good about it all, even if he didn't understand what it was they were protesting. Being at Greenham Common was the highlight of Dorothy's life, even now. She'd been so young then, so full of life and what she could do to change the world. *What had happened to that young woman?* she wondered, until she felt the tears threatening again and shook the thoughts away. Maybe it was a good thing she had Eddie's allotment to keep her busy, and she could do with making more new friends too.

She waved goodbye to her dancing buddies and saw that the young man from across the aisle had got off at the same stop.

He was standing beside her on the pavement, patiently waiting for the clusters of speeding cars to pass and allow them to cross. She steeled herself to say something, when he darted across the road and marched down the hill towards the allotments. She wondered if he was a plot holder and promised herself she'd make a special effort to speak to him later if so.

Stanley's eyes narrowed as he took in the vaguely familiar newcomer, wondering what on earth she hoped to achieve in her patch this late in the day. Nearly lunchtime, for goodness' sake. Still, at least she was dressed for it, not like some he'd seen recently. Mabel would have approved of this woman's no-nonsense dungarees and thick red sweater.

Stanley watched as she stood at the edge of Allotment No 6 at the top of the path. Ah, he thought, Eddie's widow – Dorothy, that was her name. Nice enough woman, though he hadn't seen her since his old pal's funeral months back now. He knew he should go over and ask how she was coping. Mabel would have been right up there, with offers of sweet tea and a gossip, and full of ideas as to how they could put right Eddie's allotment which, after months of neglect, now resembled the Borneo rainforest. Stanley had felt vaguely guilty about that as he'd watched the grass grow taller and taller, the spreading brambles tangling round the dying crab apple trees and strawberry plants that Eddie had loved so much. But dammit all, Stanley had his own plants to worry about, and his own problems.

He leaned against his trusty spade, careful to face away from Eddie's wife lest she engage him in conversation. What with Iris from Viewpark Church 'checking in with him' first thing this morning, and another phone call from Larry at his chess club, asking him when he was coming back to play, he'd had enough conversing with other people for one day, thank you very much.

He went back to his digging, trying not to be annoyed by his neighbours' trio of always-on orange candles in his eyeline. Stanley detested this new fad where folk would decorate their plots with that sort of thing – not even traditional gnomes and bird baths, now it was fairy lights and wind chimes and all sorts. Not Stanley, though. His allotment was filled with seed beds, the potatoes, onions and cabbages he'd sown in early spring just starting to shoot up, alongside nature's other early bloomers, the hardy and reliable daffies and snowdrops. And of course, there was his pride and joy – Mabel's rhododendron bush. He walked over to the rhoddy and pressed one of its smooth fresh leaves between his thumb and index finger. He knew Mabel would have been impressed by how much her favourite plant had grown. Two years now – how quickly the seasons had passed, and yet, how the hours themselves stretched and dragged without her. The annual flowering of the magnificent purple rhoddy, nature at its finest, was a marker of how long she'd been gone, but also his tribute to her. The flickering of his neighbours' candles caught his eye again and he tutted loudly. Some folk had no idea, he thought, and went into his shed to make another cup of tea before the Indian man who worked the next-door plot could look up and try to start a conversation with him.

Mohid sighed and went back to his own digging. Maybe people here just weren't that friendly. The man at the bottom plot across the path, for instance. He'd been here almost as often as Mohid, but he seemed to spend most of his time pottering about at the side of his shed or behind it, as though he was avoiding having to speak to anyone. His dishevelled wife with the crazy hair was friendlier, had offered him and Farah carrot cake once, and admired Farah's gold bracelets. Farah had struggled to be nice to her though, didn't think she cared for their young son well enough. It was true that the boy looked very thin and half-dressed for the weather, and he was often here on school days, hopping around the allotments and kicking up leaves. But it was hardly their business, they had enough to worry about.

He glanced up at the new woman on the top plot, who'd been hovering outside the shed of No 6 for the last five minutes. He wondered if he should go up and introduce himself but having been roundly ignored by Stanley already today, he didn't think his ego could take another such encounter.

Minutes later, Farah came out of their shed, with a smile wide enough to dispel any of his dark thoughts. They didn't need to make friends here, they had each other. How blessed they'd been to find each other, how lucky they were, he thought, as he often did. The twinkling candles on their step caught his eye, and he reconsidered. Not always lucky.

'You've made good progress there,' said Farah, indicating the little square of soil Mohid had turned over and fed generously with the organic plant food the man at B&Q had recommended.

'Getting there. I've another hour or so before I need to go home and shower for work. Are you heading out?' He indicated the large red shopping bag which was slung over her shoulder.

'I thought I'd nip up for a few things. I'll get some lamb for tomorrow, and more asparagus if it looks fresh, okay?' She touched each of the three sunflowers in turn on her way past.

'I'd rather have a cold Pils and some Doritos,' he replied,

reaching for his wife for a quick hug before she left to go shopping.

'Beer in the middle of the day, you're one of the allotment gang now,' she laughed.

Hardly, thought Mohid but said nothing as he waved her off, her unusually sombre navy blue sari blowing in the sharp spring breeze. He spotted Germaine outside her office, along with Karen from the council. The two women seemed to be deep in conversation, Karen with her arms raised in the air and Germaine pointing her finger in Karen's face. Mohid wondered briefly what they were getting so worked up about, then shrugged – it was none of his business – and went back to his digging, trying not to notice how much better Stanley's plot was than his own.

6

Kevin scrolled anime shorts on his phone as he ate his cornflakes. He heard his downstairs neighbours leave and knew it must be half past so he washed out his bowl and wondered if he still had time to give the living room a quick hoover before he left. It wouldn't take long, the room was small and square and he hoovered it regularly so that it was never too bad. He tried to keep up all the routines his mum had instilled in him so that the housework remained manageable. 'Don't leave it till it's a mountain to climb, Kevin,' she'd say, and he never did. In the kitchen, he checked the sticking fridge door was definitely shut and at the last minute, reached up to open the top window a fraction to let the air circulate while he was out. He often felt guilty about having his own flat – plenty of people had to work for years before they could say that – whereas he'd inherited his from his mum. He knew he was lucky and he tried to do everything right so he'd feel like he deserved it.

He jumped on the bus, having timed the walk from his flat to the bus stop perfectly so that he reached the safety of public transport before the schoolkids hanging around outside Naf's spotted him. His favourite bus driver – the tall woman with the black bob who kept everybody in line – said good morning and told him his usual seat was free. She waited while he got himself settled even though the bus was busy.

He took his seat three rows from the back on the opposite side to the driver, and rested his head carefully against the window, the damp pane fresh against his face, as comforting as turning his pillow over in the night and laying his cheek on the cool side. All around him, other passengers were jostling and shouting, laughing with their friends, calling to others to come and sit with them. No one sat next to Kevin.

The bus jolted and set off. Kevin sat very still, as had become his habit since the accident and being forced to lie prone for months on his lonely white hospital bed, wrapped in bandages like a priceless jewel waiting to be unveiled. He rubbed a spyhole in the window's condensation and peeked through it at the row of shuttered houses and drawn curtains speeding past, all their edges blurred, and the cars crawling along at the side of the bus. Every so often, he pushed his long blond curls away from his eyes, thinking again that he badly needed a haircut. He'd been putting it off for ages, the idea of sitting in front of a mirror in a public place for the time it took to have his hair clipped filling him with dread, even eight years on.

His mum would say he was imagining people's stares, and that plenty of people had scars and limps and burns and all manner of imperfections and nobody really cared. He'd tried to explain it to her – that moment when a stranger's eyes grew wide with disbelief at what they were seeing, their turmoil as they tried to process his singular appearance. 'You're imagining it,' she'd insist again, stroking his hands, or smoothing down his curls like he was still five years old and perfect.

Sometimes, he tried to save people from having to look at him by keeping his face to one side. There was a particular angle, he knew, that if he sat at, the unlucky people in his vicinity wouldn't know there was anything wrong with him. But that could be worse because then they'd catch a glimpse of him unexpectedly and stumble, or even, on one occasion, fall back into the road and almost get run over, so horrified were they at the damage to his face. It was hard to know what to do for the best.

'You're still Kevin,' his mum would say, cupping his cheek. 'Be patient, your time will come.'

The bus juddered to a stop. His heart sank a little as a group of schoolkids got on at Scotmid in Tannochside. They were the worst. Kevin knew they thought they were better than him with their Nike bags and Stone Island jackets. Quite apart from what they were thinking about his face, he saw them sneering at his joggies from Asda and his blond curls, worn in no discernible style. When they followed him down the street and shouted 'Gorgeous Kevin' at him, they thought they were being so funny, that they were better than him with their smooth skin and symmetrical faces, their girlfriends and their crew. But that was okay because they weren't. No one was better than anyone else, his mum had told him that years ago when he was down after the accident, and he repeated it to himself like a Gregorian chant, till he almost believed it.

'Everybody in their seats?' shouted the driver, checking for herself in the rear-view mirror.

'Everyone's sitting down, Wendy,' called the woman who always sat three seats down on the opposite side to him.

'Oy, speak for yourself, Mary, some of us are still getting

settled,' said the woman next to her, who was always moaning about something or other.

They were off again, the young boys thankfully too busy ribbing one of their own gang to annoy him. The usual passengers got on and off at their usual bus stops, the driver with a friendly word or a nod of her head for all of them. He liked her; unlike most people she neither avoided looking at him nor gaped at his face, she just accepted him for who he was – even if she did call him Gorgeous Kevin. He suspected she thought that was really his name and he didn't have the heart to enlighten her. But now that he was travelling back and forth to his allotment on the bus every day, perhaps he'd find the opportunity to tell her at some point.

His name had come up for an allotment at exactly the right time. He hadn't been able to go back to work after the accident – he'd been three months into his apprenticeship but with his impaired vision, there was no way anyone was going to let him near soldering equipment, even if they could cope with his changed face. Too bad because he'd liked it there, but he'd been happy staying at home and helping his mum too. The benefits he was entitled to may not have been much but they were enough for him and his mum to do the things they liked doing. And even after the compensation had finally come through, they'd still done all those same things. They'd take the bus to Bellshill and do their shopping every week; some days they walked round Drumpellier or Chatelherault, they had takeaway on Friday nights and listened to music on his mum's old CD player. On special occasions, maybe his birthday or hers, they walked down to Uddingston and had lunch in one of the restaurants on Main Street. They talked about using the money to move away, a cottage by the sea maybe, or going on a cruise or a city break to somewhere exciting, but in the end, they did none of these things before she died. Afterwards, he couldn't shake the notion that if they hadn't fought so hard to get the money, they wouldn't have used up all their luck and his mum would still be alive. The money and her death were entwined, the one causing the other, so he left it sitting in his account, interest piling up and weighing him down so that he stopped opening the bank statements and tried to forget it was lurking there, like a curse. He'd started having headaches that made him want to crack open his skull and yank out whatever the raging aggression was inside it. He'd wander around all day without a purpose, his life in danger of becoming a slick of anger and sadness and disappointment, and all the things his mum had warned him against. Thank God for the allotments.

The bus drew up at the community centre and Kevin thanked the bus driver as he left.

'No problem, Gorgeous Kevin. See you tomorrow.' She tipped her forehead as though she was doffing her cap to him.

What must it feel like to go through life without a care in the world like that? thought Kevin. That business with the red-haired girl who used to sit on the bus with her didn't seem to have affected her at all. She was probably going home to her big loving family after her shift, a home-made tea, and lots of chat and laughter about their respective days. He shook his head, it didn't do to be envious. He returned her wave as she drove off, weaving her way carefully through the early-morning traffic on Old Edinburgh Road and avoiding the drunks already gathering outside the Flying Tumbler.

Kevin ran across the road, narrowly avoiding a bin lorry that veered away from him at the last minute with an angry shriek of its horn. He ignored it and carried on walking through the lane at the side of the old folks' home. He passed JR Tyres and the chubby guy who ran the place waved over at him. Kevin waved back but turned away quickly when a customer standing beside him did a double take when she saw Kevin's face and instinctively placed her hands over the eyes of her gawping toddler.

He strode down the hill and past the gas flats on the right-hand side. He'd felt a bit guilty about taking one of the allotments when the people living in the flats closer than him deserved a share in the land more than he did. Karen from the council told him not to be silly. 'Your name's been on the list as long as anyone else's, Kevin,' she said, 'and don't forget, the council owes you after the accident.' He'd curled his fingers round the keys to his brand new shed on his own little piece of land, excited to have a purpose and somewhere to go. The next week, the cherry blossom had bloomed in all its glory on the trees lining the entrance to the allotments and Kevin had marched to his plot below the pink awning happier and more hopeful than he'd been in months.

He'd started off his allotment adventure with dreams of being a noble warrior, surrounded by the bounty of nature and living off his home-grown produce and the fruits of the land. He soon discovered it wasn't that easy to grow tomatoes or keep the flies from buzzing round his strawberry plants, even if the old guy at the bottom made it look like it was.

As he walked through the gates, he saw that Stanley was already there. Of course he would be. Even on the days Kevin set his alarm for the crack of dawn to get to his allotment at first light, the old man would still be there before him, spade in the earth, or his gnarled fingers pushed into a pot of soil, or snipping at the leaves of his massive rhododendron bush. He'd decided this would be the day he steeled himself to go over and say hello, but as he ambled towards the first plot, Stanley lifted his head, looked through Kevin, then returned to his digging. Kevin was used to people pretending he and his face didn't exist so he didn't take it to heart. He changed course and headed to his own plot instead, sauntering and whistling nonchalantly to indicate this had been his plan all along.

He half-recognized the woman in cool dungarees, staring off into space at Allotment No 6. She'd shown up yesterday for the first time and she must have planned to keep the allotment on because here she was again today. She had her work cut out – the weeds at the side of the fence were almost as tall as she was. She looked over and seemed to recognize him too. She raised her chin in acknowledgement but didn't speak to him.

Kevin had noticed that nobody really spoke to each other so he didn't fret over it. He'd been surprised last week when the younger of the two men from No 5 had stopped for a chat. Probably because he had no option as they'd come face to face on the path, Kevin heading up towards the community centre and Lawrence walking down towards his own allotment.

'Hello there,' he'd said in that overly loud voice people used when they were too embarrassed to acknowledge his face. Kevin didn't mind, he understood. And anyway, he was doing his own double taking and surreptitious glancing at the other man, who seemed to be wearing – no, he was definitely wearing – make-up. Kevin had never seen a man with make-up on before, not a lot but it did make him wonder – what sort of man couldn't leave the house without first refining his features with mascara and blusher? He raised his hand in greeting, aware of the irony of being the one trying not to stare for a change.

'I thought it w-w-was you,' the man had said, as he stopped him at the top of the path.

'Me?'

'Kevin, isn't it? I'm Lawrence.'

Kevin was none the wiser.

'You were a couple of years above m-m-me at school.' He hesitated. 'There was that time, that day everyone was s-s-sledging at the gulley? You don't . . . remember me?'

Kevin shook his head. In truth, he remembered very little of his life Before The Accident, it seemed so insignificant now, his school days, the stuff he and his pals got up to, it had all merged into one amorphous mass of 'life BTA'. Even those he'd considered to be his good friends had either got fed up waiting for him to get better, or simply avoided him altogether. He honestly couldn't remember Lawrence at all.

'No point in me s-s-saying thanks then. Hopefully s-s-see you around.'

Later, Kevin had searched his memory for images of the impossibly good-looking man and found none. Still, he'd seemed nice and hadn't been put out by Kevin's face. Maybe he'd try offering him some of his dried mushrooms next time they met.

He was almost at the door of his shed when the man from No 2 stopped him.

'Hello,' he called from the bottom of Kevin's path. 'I'm your neighbour, I've been meaning to come and say hello for a week or so.'

Kevin swallowed and braced himself to walk back down the path, telling himself the man had approached him so he must want to talk.

'I can't stop for long,' the man said as Kevin drew closer. Kevin's heart tumbled a little and he wondered whether the man had seen his face and had a change of mind about being friendly. 'You're imagining it, Kevin.' He reminded himself of his mum's words and forced himself to be open to the man's approach.

'I have to dash off to work unfortunately.'

Kevin decided to give him the benefit of the doubt. 'Where do you work?'

'At Monklands, I'm a doctor in the Paediatrics unit there. In fact, could you tell my wife I've had to dash off? Don't want to be late.'

'Yes, I'll tell her.'

'Thank you,' said the man. 'Mohid Ahmed, by the way. And you're a newcomer to the allotments like us, I believe?'

Kevin was surprised that the man reached out his hand. Most people didn't, possibly wondering whether Kevin's hands were afflicted by the same misfortune as his face, and not stopping long enough to find out that they were perfectly normal hands. His best feature, in fact, his mum had often told him.

'Kevin,' he said, grasping Mohid's hand firmly and shaking it. And when the older man raised his eyebrows as though expecting more, he added, 'Just . . . Kevin.'

7

LAWRENCE SAT IN THE PASSENGER seat of Adrian's Mercedes, looking up and down their good-for-the-schools street and trying hard to stay calm. It was no good, he pressed the horn again, longer this time, not caring what his Kylepark neighbours thought of his chutzpah in making so much noise in this most noiseless of neighbourhoods. He looked towards the house again but their front door remained resolutely closed, with no sign of Adrian.

Every single time, thought Lawrence, sitting back and fuming. One of the things he'd so admired about Adrian when they'd first met was his always meticulous appearance – from the tip of his slicked-back City trader's hair to the toes of his well-polished Manolo brogues. The only thing stopping him from being aftershave-advert handsome was his sharp nose, long enough to be noticeable, though of course Lawrence never said so. In any case, Adrian made sure his nose was the last thing people noticed as he breezed in on clouds of Issey Miyake, Gucci watch glinting and the faintest touch of Fenty Beauty Pro foundation to cover the pale blue shadows under his eyes which, at forty, Adrian was beginning to notice. Even though it was Lawrence himself who had gently recommended this last touch to maintain his boyfriend's perfection, it had not occurred to him just how long it would take to achieve the overall look. Every single day.

Finally, the pinks and creams of their new Charles Rennie Mackintosh glass pane shimmered as the front door opened and Adrian came sauntering down the path, smoothing his tie and smacking his Vaselined lips together as he did so. *Not even a conciliatory quick step*, thought Lawrence, as he leaned over to open the driver's door, knowing there'd be no question but that Adrian would want to drive.

'What's with all the honking? Is there a fire somewhere?' said Adrian smoothly, closing the door behind him and settling himself into the white leather interior of his pride and joy.

'All right for you to s-s-say.' Lawrence hated the whining tone to his voice and the way his stutter would get worse when he was flustered or upset. 'If it's going to take you another ten m-m-minutes to get ready, why can't you s-s-say so? Don't tell me you're ready to leave then have me sitting in the car f-f-for hours.'

'Hardly hours, Lawrence. And I *was* ready till I saw the state of that pink tie against my white shirt. Why didn't you tell me I resembled a stick of Blackpool rock? Obviously I had to go and change it.'

He started the engine, and took a quick look at the empty street behind them before drawing away from the kerb. Lawrence steeled himself for the daily diatribe against the neighbours and their selfish parking. They had both fallen in love with their house instantly — how could they not, with its classic red sandstone frontage, the massive high-ceilinged rooms with the original cornicing and roses round the chandeliers, most rooms boasting golden oak floors and elegant marbled fireplaces. Very like the flat they'd sold in the West End, but much bigger. The downside was the postage stamp proportions of the back garden, even if it was almost as well-manicured as Adrian himself. But the lack of garden was something that bothered Lawrence more than Adrian and he'd already made up his mind to put his name down for an allotment. He could tell Adrian was impressed and pressed his advantage by speculating on how they could buff and varnish the plain wood, how well their six-foot-tall bookcase would fit in the vast hallway, the things they could get up to in front of those open fires . . .

'But . . . the parking,' Adrian had said, glancing out at the street lined with cars, and then at his pristine white Mercedes and trying to imagine leaving his baby in the street overnight.

'Oh come on,' said Lawrence, squeezing his arm. 'It's got to be better than trawling for a parking space in Hyndland and at least here, we don't need to worry about it getting stolen. It's Uddingston.'

And he'd been right. In a way. There was no issue with cars being stolen or vandalized, but the parking itself was problematic. Neither Lawrence nor Adrian could believe how selfish some of their neighbours were. Most of the houses were terraced so on-street parking was for everyone but even those who had a driveway used the street, keeping their driveways nice and clear while effectively booking their own space in front of their house each evening. It drove Adrian in particular mad, and by extension, Lawrence, as his boyfriend commented on it every single time they parked or moved their car.

'Street's not too b-b-bad this morning,' he said, pre-empting it.

Adrian humphed. 'It's tonight we'll have a problem, trying to get back in. I mean, look at that. Sandy's parked over two spaces!'

Lawrence was silent, waiting for it to pass. For once, Adrian seemed disinclined to interrogate the vagaries of his neighbours' minds and forgot about the parking as soon as they drove off.

'What's the rush anyway?' He spoke again once they were headed towards Uddingston Main Street. 'You're only going to the allotment.'

'I've got a lot to do these next few weeks. May is a key time for planting so I want to make the m-m-most of my day off. And I could have walked, it was you that insisted on giving m-m-me a lift.'

Adrian didn't reply, reaching over to put on Classic FM instead. Lawrence peeked at him from under his eyelashes, still in awe that this beautiful man had chosen to spend his life with him. Thirteen years younger than Adrian, Lawrence had recently graduated when they'd met at an after-party at the Tron. Confidence and success wafted off Adrian in perfumed ripples, and although he'd told Lawrence he was very happy in Glasgow, for the first year of their relationship, the younger man worried constantly that Adrian would dash off to New York, or somewhere else fast and exciting, and forget all about him. He'd discovered later that Adrian was equally worried that Lawrence would be tempted by a job at one of the big London theatres, and was delighted when Lawrence had been offered the permanent role of lead make-up artist at the Citizens and loved his job with a passion otherwise reserved exclusively for Adrian.

They'd moved to Uddingston the year before, having found the house, and Lawrence having painted a very convincing picture of the happy life they could lead in the suburbs where he'd been brought up. It had worked out well, and as they drove along Main Street, with its spring baskets and coffee shops,

Donald the butcher and Danny the barber, Stefano's bistro and the new Japanese place, and the well-maintained train station with its twelve-minute ride to Glasgow town centre, both gave small sighs of satisfaction with the place they now called home.

'You can drop me here,' said Lawrence suddenly, as they drew up to the traffic lights at the cross.

'But this is miles away from the allotments. Unless there's a shortcut? Is there?'

Adrian had not shown the slightest interest in their allotment, despite his name too being on the application and Lawrence's initial attempts to involve him in his plans. 'Small-town life in the back of beyond is one thing, Lawrence, I draw the line at sticking my shovel in an allotment' was his last word on the matter. After a few weeks, it occurred to Lawrence that he didn't mind at all. The allotment was his place, somewhere he didn't need to worry about the tautness of his stomach muscles and how many miles he'd run on the treadmill. Yesterday, he'd even had a Mars bar with his coffee, an indulgence Adrian would never have sanctioned.

'Hardly miles, and the walk will do me g-g-good. I can add it to today's steps,' he said, tapping the state-of-the-art Fitbit Adrian had bought him for his birthday. He turned to Adrian and gave him a quick kiss on the cheek, breathing in the expensive spicy scent of his skin.

Adrian reached over and gave Lawrence a hug. 'Text me if you need anything? Promise?'

'Of course.' Lawrence got out the car as the lights were turning green. Adrian put the car back into first gear and was about to drive off when Lawrence called after him, 'Linguine alle vongole and spinach salad tonight, make sure you're home on time.'

He watched as Adrian eased the car away from the kerb, and gathered speed as he headed towards Hamilton, where no doubt he had an appointment with some of his fancy clients. Lawrence didn't really know what his boyfriend did all day when he was at work and, if he was honest, had as little interest in learning more as Adrian did in the best colour palette for redheads, or indeed in Lawrence's allotment.

Lawrence straightened his shoulders, pushed his leather satchel further round his body so that the thick strap was a diagonal over his chest, and began the walk towards Viewpark. After all the rain they'd had recently, at last it was a bright morning, already quite warm at not yet nine, and not a cloud in the sky. He strode past the Tunnock's factory, eyes automatically to the ground as he passed a small group of men in white outfits, vaping, but no one noticed him, too busy with their conversations about the game on Saturday and whose team would get ahead. He occasionally recognized the odd face from primary school, but either they didn't recognize him or they were too embarrassed by the way they'd treated him when they became part of the mob at high school to acknowledge him now. Lawrence didn't blame them – he knew it was join in and survive, or break away and suffer the same fate as him.

He peeked into the library as he passed by. Inside was still dark though he could see the shadowy figures of the librarians padding around, putting away books and preparing for the day's visitors. He'd read in the local paper a couple of weeks back that the council was planning cuts to local services but Lawrence was sure the libraries would be safe – what was a community without a library after all? It had been a haven for him all through his school days, a safe place to hide from his tormentors. He'd always found bookish people to be the least judgemental – something to do with empathy for all the different characters they read about maybe? No, there was no way the council would close the library, he was sure of it. Some public services were too important to lose.

He left the library behind and carried on past the new housing estate opposite the doctors' surgery. He marvelled at the way Uddingston had grown in the time he'd been away. All these housing estates popping up all over the place, he wondered where all the people came from and how the village was accommodating them. A glance at the packed car park outside the surgery hinted at the pressure public services were under, and yet, it was still a beautiful place to live.

He passed the industrial estate on his left and felt the usual trepidation when a huge lorry trundled past him. He tensed, anticipating the beep of the horn and a comment about his tight jeans or his satchel worn bandolier-style over his chest, slung out the window from the beefy man at the wheel. Nothing. Lawrence looked to the sky, thought what a glorious day it was, and carried on up the hill to the allotments.

What does he think he looks like? Stanley took a break from wiping out the biggest of his flower pots. He'd have to use his secateurs later to poke a few holes in the bottom for drainage, it didn't matter how many times he told the folk at the gardening centre about that, they still sold pots with no holes. But at least he was dressed right for these tasks – not like that boy. Light blue jeans and a pink jumper? At the allotments? Stanley shook his head. He knew Mabel would have called out, 'I love that colour on you' or something nice anyway. What was it they said these days – good cop, bad cop? She'd been the good cop, all right, but that was why they'd worked so well all those years, surviving after they'd lost Brian, thriving even, which was something neither of them had thought possible at the start. Now there was just him. And his allotment. He could feel the tears rising again – they seemed to come all too often these days – and he swallowed hard and told himself to get over it and carry on working.

Across the path, the scruffy-looking man from No 4 looked up from rubbing the algae off his fence with a vinegar-soaked cloth. He spotted Lawrence coming and remembered the word he was looking for was 'hello', which he practised under his breath a few times as the young man approached. He opened his mouth, then shook his head at his inability to retrieve the word and say it out loud before Lawrence had disappeared into his shed.

8

Isobel had called in sick again today, she couldn't face it. It was all very well that social work lady, with her face like a soor ploom, saying she only worked three days, it was good for her to get out the house. She wasn't the one coming home to a sad and defeated husband, weak with hunger and disoriented with dehydration, having forgotten to eat and drink, and apparently blind to the small white plate with cheese and cucumber sandwiches under clingfilm and a carton of Ribena left for him in the fridge by Isobel the night before. He couldn't manage on his own any more, Isobel was sure of it, no matter what the so-called professionals said.

And it wasn't that she didn't love her job, she did. She only had eight kids in her class this year because one of them, wee Bobby, had needs so severe she had to spend the majority of her time making sure he didn't bite her or his classmates. That was not easy, a fact to which her own left wrist could attest, still bearing as it did the circle of regular indents from the troubled young boy's sturdy molars. But for all their problems, the kids were sweet and adorable and eager to learn, and she knew they all adored her too. Such a nice change from her own son, who she felt increasingly these days not only did not adore her, but positively hated her.

She sat at the cluttered kitchen table and pushed aside the debris from breakfast. Of course Isaac had refused to eat his Weetabix, no doubt in favour of a Tunnock's caramel wafer on the way round the corner to school. She did not know, and momentarily did not care, where her husband was and what havoc he was wreaking while being left to his own devices.

She dipped her head on to her forearms, thinking she would rest for a moment before taking up the reins again. She felt the hard edges of a little square package dig into her elbow and lifted her head to see the carrot seeds she'd bought in a fit of enthusiasm when the council had phoned to say there was an allotment free for them. Like the teacher she was, she'd started doing her research immediately. Sometimes she wasn't sure whether the internet, and the Google search function in particular, was a blessing or a curse. But perhaps not everyone lost hours of their lives starting off with a simple search on the humble carrot and ending up reading articles on the history of purple carrots, which was fascinating but hardly essential reading when you were trying to find out how to grow vegetables on a somewhat dry and lumpy-soiled allotment. And, as was usual these days since George had been diagnosed and Isaac had become a teenager a couple of years early, she hadn't actually put what she'd read into action. Still, she supposed all these endless facts, or factoids as the kids in her class would say, were stored away haphazardly in her brain, awaiting being called into action when required. At least she liked to think so, though she had no evidence to back up the theory.

She wondered occasionally whether her brain was going the same way as George's. Her poor husband had been losing words for months, and they'd had such good conversations over the years, putting the world to rights as they sat in front of their wood burner, the toddler Isaac safely tucked up in his attic bedroom two floors above them. George would pour the whisky and they'd toast ridiculous things like the local Tory MP getting voted out, or their lousy next-door neighbour selling up at last, or Isaac's thirty-second word. And the laughter. They'd laughed into the night, long after they should have been in bed, both teaching the next day. And that's how she knew something was wrong. They both did. Gradually, he couldn't tell her the ending to a joke, couldn't find the word to describe the fake orange skin of the young man who'd taken over at Anne's Pantry, couldn't tell her how much he loved her, couldn't say how it felt to lose parts of himself, his memories, his opinions, week after week. Till finally it was official. Early onset dementia, and it was getting worse, fast.

After he couldn't work any more – how could he teach children English when he now had so few words himself? – he was lost during the day. He'd roam the woods of Bothwell golf course gathering branches for the burner, or spend hours trying to put their back garden in some sort of order, but the task was too big. It was company he needed, Isobel had argued, for once articulate and to the point, when Karen from the council had asked why they needed an allotment. It was about finding somewhere close and safe and welcoming for him to go during the day when she was at work, somewhere he might be able to find friends who would understand these new limitations. If she was honest, it was also about finding somewhere he could go away from the house to give her and Isaac a break and allow them to spend some much-needed time together.

'There won't be anyone looking after him at the allotments, you know,' had been Karen's next objection.

But George didn't need that – not yet – what he needed was the security that comes from being part of a community of like-minded people, and the stimulation of having some kind of interaction, limited as it may be, with other human beings besides her and the increasingly taciturn Isaac.

They'd added their names to the list and prepared themselves for a long wait. But how lucky for them that the determination of some old bloke called Archie to try something new every year had not matched his ability to swim when he'd landed in the ocean after a bungee jump. Not so lucky for Archie, of course. But the allotment had been a godsend. George had taken to it like a duck to water, heading off there most days. There was a lot to do – Archie may have been keen on getting the most out of life but that didn't seem to have extended to making the most out of his allotment.

When they'd turned up on the first day, Isobel had gulped when she'd been led by Karen to their unruly plot at the bottom of the hill, unfortunately close to the most pristine and well-ordered plot in the place.

'Wow,' said Isobel, glancing over at the nearby plot and taking in the expanse of fine crumbly soil, its neatly trimmed borders of sage and rosemary, and the cloche-covered strawberry plants. 'That one's clearly run by a professional.'

'Yes,' said Karen. 'That's the new manager's, she's completely transformed that plot and started getting everyone else in order too since she took over in February.'

'Sounds terrifying,' Isobel joked, turning pale when Karen said, 'Yes, she is.' Seeing Isobel's face, she added, 'Her bark is worse than her bite,' and 'Almost certainly' under her breath.

★

Isobel turned the seed packet over and strained to read the minuscule text on the back. Definitely too small for her fifty-four-year-old eyes; maybe they'd just put the seeds in the ground and hope for the best.

She'd thought they were already too late to do any planting by the time they'd managed to get the soil into a condition where plants might grow, but the old man on the plot opposite theirs had reassured her. He said they could still sow the carrot seeds and be sure of a reasonable harvest at the end of the summer, Scottish weather notwithstanding. Although initially unforthcoming, the man had talked quite expansively when it came to plants and gardening. In the end, he'd been really helpful and she'd wondered whether he might be a friend for George. What was his name again – Arthur? Stanley? – God, her memory was getting as bad as George's these days. Which reminded her, where was her husband, and what was he up to?

Then she remembered he'd gone to the allotment early this morning, a flash of the old George appearing as he'd kissed her on the top of her head and indicated his gardening jacket.

'It's too early, George,' she'd said, but he'd patted the pockets of his jacket again and mumbled something that sounded like 'plants' so she'd let him go, and slept until her alarm went off to get Isaac up for school.

She glanced up at the clock now and calculated he'd been gone around three hours. He'll be fine, she told herself, and she had to trust he'd be okay by himself sometimes, he wasn't a child. She picked up two greasy-rimmed mugs from the table and a bowl of pistachio shells from the night before. She'd eaten most of them after George had poured some out for himself and started eating them but forgotten about them halfway through.

She checked the clock again, pressed her lips together, then grabbed her car keys and headed off to the allotment to check he was okay.

Twenty minutes later, Germaine peered out of the window of her shed, her head to one side to keep her phone balanced between ear and shoulder. The council had kept her on hold for almost eight minutes now, but if they thought that would be enough to put her off, they were very much mistaken.

She watched as the scruffy couple from No 4 sat on the step of their shed, the woman unscrewing the cup from a giant tartan thermos flask and filling it up. Germaine clicked her tongue. *Half of them are here for a day out*, she thought. *No wonder the council isn't taking my requests seriously.*

She'd been concerned about the safety of that wall at the back of the allotments since she'd taken on the job. Initially, she'd been told the council was aware of the issue and that someone from Facilities Management would be round to assess the structure and do some repointing. But when she'd broached the subject again with Karen last week, the woman had been decidedly evasive with her.

Germaine was not one to be fobbed off. 'It's quite simple, either you get somebody to come and fix that wall or there's going to be a serious accident one of these days.'

'Oh come on, those playing fields behind are never used so there shouldn't be anyone near the wall.' Karen seemed determined to make light of her concerns.

'That's as may be but I'm telling you, people do use it as a shortcut between here and the community centre and someone's going to come a cropper if that brickwork isn't patched up.'

'It's . . . a question of money, Germaine. I'm not sure the council's in a position to authorize any spending on the allotments at the moment—'

'It's going to cost them a lot more to compensate some poor old bugger for broken bones. Or worse. But if you're not going to listen to reason, please make sure it's noted that I did my duty as manager and flagged the problem. Right?' Germaine wagged her finger in Karen's face to emphasize the point and the woman had almost ended up in Germaine's chilli plants.

'Yes, of course,' she'd said finally. 'It's . . . You're right. Let me see what I can do. I'll speak to Councillor Murray, I promise.'

'And it isn't only the wall, you know. That old lock on the tool shed really needs replacing, you could shake that door open the lock's so rusty. Then there's the fencing . . . A place like this needs to be maintained properly if—'

Karen pushed her bag up her shoulder, preparing to leave. 'Okay, I've promised I'll do my best and I will. I'll speak to Councillor Murray this week.'

'Is there a problem?' Germaine narrowed her eyes. 'Some money issue, or something else I should know about?'

'Leave it with me,' said Karen, backing away before Germaine could push it any further. 'I've said I'll deal with it.'

And yet here Germaine was, still trying to pin someone down to a date to do the repairs. She held her phone away from her ear to give herself a break from the tinny rendition of 'Für Elise' that was playing on a loop in the background. The tune changed suddenly and even Germaine couldn't stand 'Nobody Does It Better' for longer than a minute. She swiped the screen and put the phone down. Something her dad used to say flashed into her mind – *what was it?* – if something smelled fishy, it probably was – something like that. Tapping her fingers against her neatly ordered desk and considering the almost-completed council questionnaire on her screen, she hoped that this was one saying she hadn't remembered correctly because as far as the council was concerned, she was beginning to detect a distinct whiff of fish.

9

It was Monday and Dorothy was back at the allotments. She hadn't been for couple of weeks because her first foray into horticulture had left her in serious back pain for days afterwards – she could hardly walk, never mind work the allotment. But she wanted to avoid another nippy telephone call from that new manager so here she was again, ready to give it her all.

A little self-consciously, as though she had no right to be there, she sauntered through the main gate, dawdling for a few minutes to admire the fairy garden, before heading up the main path to her allotment. She called out hello to Stanley, but he had his back to her and seemed to be gazing somewhere in the middle distance. Of all the plot holders, she'd expected Stanley to be friendly towards her when she came back, he and Eddie had been good friends, she thought he might even have been crying at Eddie's funeral. But he'd hardly spoken two words to her last time she'd been here. Perhaps he'd forgotten who she was.

She noticed a skinny boy of around nine or ten sitting outside the shed at No 4, enthralled by whatever was happening on the screen of the electronic thingy he had balanced on his knees. Dorothy glanced round but there were no responsible adults in the vicinity. 'Should you not be in school, son?' she called over, but he ignored her.

She walked up past the next allotment. The well-turned-out chap was also perched on his step, alternately blowing on the contents of an impossibly teensy coffee cup and gazing up at the horizon. It seemed rude to break into his thoughts – even though they were probably about how to prevent his clean white trainers getting dirty as he swept the path, or other such nonsense, she thought uncharitably and carried on walking. There was no one at No 2 across the path – the nice young Asian couple – probably both working. She hoped she'd see them at the weekend if they were here then, they at least had seemed friendly. At No 3, Dorothy tried not to feel slightly relieved that the poor young man with the face was nowhere to be seen.

She reached her own allotment at the top of the path without having had a single conversation. Really, she thought, for somewhere that called itself a community service, there wasn't much sense of community.

After ten minutes or so of jiggling the key up and down in the rusty lock, Dorothy managed to shoogle open the door of the shed on their— *her*, she supposed, allotment. Part of the reason she'd been avoiding coming here was that she dreaded the shed. This had been Eddie's place, he'd loved it here, they'd joked about him spending more time on his allotment than at home but both knew that was how they preferred it – Eddie pottering about with his plants and shrubs, while Dorothy did the things she liked doing. But now that he'd gone and she really was on her own, she wasn't sure any more what they were.

She clicked the door shut behind her and took a deep breath as she looked around at Eddie's stuff, collected over his many years as an allotment holder. There were piles of old newspapers and his back copies of *Gardeners' World* – perhaps there'd be someone on the allotments who'd want those, she thought, as she picked up the top few copies and put them down again. She opened the drawer nearest to her and ran her fingers over empty seed packets, old instruction manuals for the lawn mower and cordless pruner he'd purchased almost a decade earlier, endless elastic bands, pen lids but no pens, a schedule of council refuse pick-up times from 2008. *God's sake, Eddie*, she thought, at least she'd have no problem in sweeping the whole lot into a bin bag and— Then she saw it. She lifted it gently from the bottom of the drawer – the rosette he'd won for his courgettes at the last Flower Festival, inscribed in fancy gold letters with '1st Prize Steady Eddie'. They'd gone for a drink that night at the Rolling Barrel to celebrate, Eddie had been so chuffed to win. *This deserves to be seen*, she thought, and rooted round the drawer for a couple of drawing pins.

She stepped outside to hang it on the shed door, in pride of place. Standing back to admire it, she heard heavy footsteps and a woman clearing her throat loudly behind her.

'You must be Mrs Mackie?' said the woman, with short gun-metal grey hair and a ruddy face, free of make-up.

'Ms,' said Dorothy reflexively. 'Actually, just Dorothy is fine.'

The woman flapped her massive mud-stained hand. 'Right. Glad to see you here. You were about a month away from losing your allotment. It was me that called you, and I take it the council was also in touch to let you know that?'

Why was Dorothy starting to feel like she was back at school and scared to talk back to the male teachers, or in the antenatal clinic, queued up against the back wall with other women, their tights rounds their knees and dignity left at the front door? She straightened up suddenly. She was Dorothy Mackie, ex of Greenham Common, long-time women's rights campaigner, and worth a modicum of courtesy and respect.

'I was here earlier in the month. A couple of weeks ago. I came for two days in a row. I . . . made a start.' They both observed the tangle of weeds and long grass, and the frayed rosette she'd pinned to the door blowing behind them in the breeze.

'Yes, I see that,' sniffed Germaine.

Dorothy decided it was best to change tack and distract her. 'So – you never said when you phoned, are you the new manager now? Eddie never mentioned you.'

'I am.'

Dorothy waited for her to offer her condolences about Eddie but when nothing more was forthcoming, she said, 'And your name is . . . ?'

There was a pause. 'Germaine,' said the woman in a voice that suggested she was offended at being asked to offer up such information.

'Great name!' said Dorothy.

Germaine narrowed her eyes at her, wondering if she was taking the mickey. 'Is it? It was my nan's name, my . . . dad's mum, that is.'

Dorothy contemplated telling her about that time in Greenham when the superstar Australian feminist had turned up out of the blue, Amazonian in stature and brown curls gleaming. She'd had a BBC news team in tow and Dorothy was sure she'd been in the background of one shot but Eddie told her later he'd watched it and hadn't seen her. 'Once, when I was at—' she began, but she could tell by the way Germaine was looking back at her own allotment and fidgeting with her nails that she wanted to get on.

'That's me back now. I'll soon get Eddie's— that is, *my* allotment up to scratch.'

'Let's hope so or else . . .' The threat remained unspoken and the women parted ways. Dorothy watched as Germaine tramped straight across her allotment – okay it was unkempt but still – and thought that if she was looking to the allotments to make new friends, she'd probably be looking in the wrong place.

Stanley watched the exchange in silence. He thought about going across to say something to the woman in dungarees, maybe something about how much he'd liked her husband, missed him even, or about how the new allotment manager was pleasant enough once you got to know her, but in the end, he couldn't be bothered. He wasn't having a good day.

His eyes were tired and nippy, he hadn't slept again. He'd spent the evening watching a documentary about architecture, the kind of thing he usually loved, but there was one scene that had kept him awake all night. A tower block in the city centre – once a model of all that was new and exciting, now a monstrosity – had been declared unfit for purpose and razed to the ground, demolished, blown up by huge amounts of explosives in what the presenter described as a 'controlled explosion'. As Stanley had watched the old building, tall and slinky like a church spire, first being suffocated in graphite grey clouds, before succumbing to gravity and falling under its own weight, he'd been aware of the heavy weight against his own chest, his eyes unexpectedly pooling with tears, a feeling of exhaustion covering him, so great was the sadness he felt at watching the proud old building topple. Afterwards, as he replayed the scene over and over in his mind, trying to work out why he had been so affected by it, it came to him. This was how Mabel's death had made him feel – like he was being smothered in clouds of sadness and the ground beneath his feet had been blown away, his foundations shattered, and the rest of his life falling to the ground in huge puffs of smoke and rubble around him. He couldn't sleep for thinking about it, and for once, even his beloved rhoddy and his allotment were not making him feel any better.

He glanced up at the woman in dungarees again; she was gazing forlornly round her overgrown allotment as though she didn't know what to do with herself. But since Stanley felt exactly the same way even two years on, he didn't think there was much he could do to help her. Besides, he'd already done enough socializing for one day. It seemed to him that hardly a day went by these days without some busybody or other disturbing his peace.

Earlier that morning, when he'd been trying to forget about the tower block and focus instead on the peace and the solitude, some young chap, trussed up in a cheap suit and stinking of hair gel, had crept up on him and started on about some community meeting or other they were holding in a fortnight's time. 'All the allotment holders are invited, of course,' he said, his voice cracking like a schoolboy's and his fringe falling into his eyes. 'Although it's entirely up to you if you're not bothered about having a say.' It had occurred to Stanley that if Mabel were still around, he'd be saving this voice up for later, ready to mimic him over their tea. Mabel would laugh along with him, protesting, 'Oh don't, Stanley. That's not nice.' Instead, the man's squeaking grated on his bones. He'd straightened up in laborious instalments, hands on his knees and spine creaking.

The young stranger appeared to be waiting on a response so Stanley had employed his usual method of getting rid of people, which was to stand very still and say nothing at all. Most people couldn't stand even a minute without inane chatter about this one they'd been at school with, or that one whose son had gone to uni, or Mrs WhatsHerFace who'd won big at the bingo – really, who cared? – before they gave up. Sure enough, the youth sighed and said, 'No doubt the other allotment holders will keep you up to date with the plans. And you'll see some big posters up round the allotments too – once we've . . . decided.' *Great*, thought Stanley, *big posters now to add to all the other stupid ornaments and decorations all over the place.* He'd slid his bunnet to the back of his head as he watched the boy pick his way across the mud in his unsuitable faux leather loafers. It was a pity the new manager was nowhere to be seen at that point, she would have told him exactly where to put his posters.

Thinking about the encounter again, and the boy's ridiculous voice, his mood lifted for the first time that morning. Maybe he should go up and say hello to— Ah, no need, Dorothy had disappeared into her shed. Stanley's radiant rhododendron caught his eye, and he said to the nearest purple bloom, 'What? I was going to,' and went back to work.

10

KEVIN PRESSED HIS FACE CLOSE to the window, gauging how much activity was going on outside before he left the haven of his shed. He'd spent a pleasant half an hour or so drawing up a list of chores for the day, tapping his fingers in time to his mum's old Earth, Wind & Fire CD as he did so. He planned to start by deadheading the faded yellow rose bush at the side of his newly laid path. He was proud of the path, the first thing of note he'd achieved since taking on his allotment. He'd made it himself from the slabs his downstairs neighbour had given him. They weren't best friends or anything – he suspected the reason he'd never been invited to one of their summer barbecues was in case he frightened their toddlers, which was fair enough – but they were on neighbourly enough terms that Kevin could ask them for half a dozen of the small hexagonal slabs – three pink, three grey – stacked up in the back garden after their new path was finished. He'd taken his time to arrange them neatly to form a micro-path of his own leading up to his shed.

He watched the comings and goings and waited until Germaine had left Dorothy's allotment before judging it safe to come out. He squeezed himself sideways out of the barely opened shed door and stood on the path, stretching his back, his face upturned towards the sky. The morning was cool and cloudy but he braved the temperatures in a light grey T-shirt, planning on working too hard to feel the cold. From the corner of his eye, he could see Stanley shuffling across his allotment at the bottom of the path. Dorothy had already gone back into her shed, but she'd looked a bit miserable to Kevin and he wasn't sure if now was the right time to go over and make his offer to help her clear the overgrown plot. He rolled his shoulders. *That can wait*, he thought, *time to start gardening*, and all other concerns evaporated as he pruned and snipped and communed with his shrubs.

Then he saw her.

In fact, he heard her before he saw her – clumpy red Docs thumping down as she jumped over the crumbling wall behind them – but once she came into view you couldn't miss her. She was wearing what he knew was called a pinafore dress over a mustard polo neck but her thighs were so chubby it had ridden up and functioned as something between a long tank top and a mini dress instead. She had topped that with a floor-length faux fur leopard coat which she wore with ease like it was an old anorak, black fishnet tights over those strong thighs, and the clashing red Docs to complete the look. She had a red satchel strung diagonally across her chest, and her blonde hair was swept up into a high bun held up with a rose corsage accessory. Kevin did a double take. Then another one.

'Hello!' she called over to him, holding aloft a giant Greggs cup and brandishing it at him.

Kevin raised his chin in response, wondering automatically whether she had a good view of his face from where she was, and if not, whether her friendly attitude would change when she did. God, she was coming over!

'Hello,' she said again, her voice still cheerful.

Surely she could see his face by now, he thought. When was she going to squirm and excuse herself?

'I'm here to see Dorothy,' she said, spinning round on the path to take in all the allotments. 'So weird to be back in Dad's kingdom,' she added, her eyes resting on Dorothy's plot.

She turned back to face him. 'I'm Maggi. No e. Named after some artist who turned up at Greenham Common apparently, not Maggie after God forbid, you know who.'

Kevin looked at her blankly.

'Maggie the milk snatcher.'

'Oh, right, your parents were into politics then?'

Maggi snorted. 'Dad, no. Mum, yes, you could say that. You definitely could say that.' She looked at him closely and Kevin thought he saw the familiar ripple of confusion then revulsion pass over her face as she took in his appearance. *Any minute now*, he thought, *she'll make her excuses and go*.

'And you are?' She held out her hand, the nails topped with glittery chipped nail polish.

'Er, Kevin,' said Kevin, carefully placing his secateurs on the path and looking at her outstretched hand. He held out his own hand but withdrew it immediately as he became aware of the streaks of dirt, the half moons of black under each nail. 'Sorry. I've been working on my roses.'

Maggi's lips curved into an expansive smile. She smiled a lot, he noticed, and not in a half-hearted polite sort of way, she smiled in a way that made you want to smile back, that made you feel happy that she was bestowing her smile on you and you alone. Her lips were very red and shaped in a little bow, like the kind of mouth you see in antique paintings, or remember from cartoons in your childhood. She had a spot of colour high on each cheek, like she was permanently excited, or flustered maybe. Except she didn't seem flustered at all, she seemed happy, full of life. If Kevin had to use one word to describe his first impression of her, there could be only one choice – vivacious.

'So I see,' she was saying, through that smile. 'Reminds me of how my dad's hands used to be, after a day on the allotments.' She stopped. 'Am I shouting? Sorry, I'll take these out.' She reached up and pulled the earbuds from her ears, the right one jangling against her giant hoop earring as she did so.

'What are you listening to?'

'Donna Summer. Retro, that's me.' She performed a Mexican wave as she spoke. 'Are you a music fan?'

Before Kevin could answer, a loud sing-song voice called, 'Maaaggi.'

They both turned to see Dorothy waving over at them.

'I'll need to go, that's my mum calling. She who must be obeyed.' She laughed and Kevin could see the red lipstick on her bottom front teeth. 'Nice to meet you.' She waggled her chubby fingers at him, each adorned with a chunky coloured-glass ring, including her thumb.

'And you,' he said under his breath, watching her coat flap as she strode back down the path. He was aware of a strange feeling in his belly, like nerves, or anticipation, or . . . something anyway. He wondered what age she was, a little older than him maybe, although it was hard to tell with the wacky clothes and the make-up and everything. He caught himself suddenly: what did it matter what age she was, she was hardly likely to look at him. *Stay in your lane, Kevin*, he thought, shaking his head as he went into his shed to boil the kettle for his noodles.

11

Dorothy watched her only daughter take in her surroundings in silence in the cluttered shed, like she was marking Dorothy's efforts out of ten.

'It's . . . I've just started clearing out. After, you know, your dad . . .'

When Maggi still didn't speak, Dorothy could feel herself getting annoyed. She hadn't seen sight nor sound of her daughter since the funeral, and already she was making her feel like she'd done something wrong, or hadn't done enough, or something that made her not the world's best mother anyway.

The relationship between Dorothy and Maggi had always been this way. She'd tried to say as much to Eddie, attempted to describe the dislike she felt spilling out of Maggi like a cruel secret she couldn't quite hide from her mother. Eddie had told her not to be silly, and maybe dislike was too strong a word for it – after all, who really disliked their own mother – and yet . . .

'Dad had all this stuff for years.' She tried again. 'He was even more untidy than me and that's saying something,' she said, attempting lightness. 'Looks like he never threw anything away—'

'I know what Dad's shed looks like, Mum. I used to spend all my weekends with him, remember? When you were away, campaigning' – Dorothy told herself she was imagining the sneer on that last word – 'so I know exactly what he had in his shed. We used to love listening to these records after a day's weeding.'

She picked up an old LP, whose name on the front Dorothy didn't recognize. She'd forgotten that was another thing her husband and their daughter had had in common. A love of all that eighties music. 'You can have those records if you want? Take any that you like.'

Her daughter didn't answer, carried on picking up records, turning them over and placing them back on the tottering pile on the floor. Dorothy remained still.

'What happened to that guy's face?'

'Whose face?'

'That guy in the allotment across from you. His face is like . . .' She gestured with her hand and rubbed one of her own smooth-skinned cheeks.

'Oh, I think his name's Kevin. Do you know, I'm not really sure what happened to him. I know there was some sort of accident a few years back. At the fireworks display, I think, you know the one the council puts on in the park every year? I don't think your dad ever met him, he came after Dad's time. I haven't spoken to him yet. It's a bit, you know . . . off-putting.' She shrugged apologetically but she should have known her daughter would never let her get away with that.

'Mum! That's not on, you can't judge people on their appearance. You, of all people.'

She was right, Dorothy knew. Half of her had wondered if she would have been a bit more forthcoming with her allotment neighbour if he hadn't been so tough to look at. It was the eye more than the facial scarring, she had this thing about eyes.

'You know, for someone who prides themself on taking action for the underdog, you're quite fussy when it comes to defining who that underdog is, aren't you? Maybe they have to be put-upon old women for you to be interested.'

Now that wasn't fair, thought Dorothy, and she was about to say as much but thought better of it. No, she hadn't seen her daughter for months and she wasn't going to let it turn into one of their usual slanging matches. 'You're probably right, I'll go across and say hello if he's still working when you've gone.'

'Want rid of me already?' Maggi said, with a definite smirk.

God, she was impossible!

And it seemed to Dorothy like it had always been this way, starting from before she was even born. She'd been at Greenham for her second three-month stretch, having the time of her life, when she'd started to feel sick in the mornings, bloated at night, and exhausted in between. Of course Eddie had insisted she come back home – even though plenty of women on the Common had children with them, newborn babies even. But she'd come back to Viewpark and settled into family life. It wasn't that she resented it exactly, but they hadn't planned on her getting pregnant so soon into their marriage. Or at least she hadn't. Eddie was older than her and quite happy to have her back at home, looking after baby Maggi and having his meals ready when he finished work at the yard. She'd wondered over the years of their fractious relationship whether Maggi had felt her reluctance, her disinterest in the weaning and nappies talk that she was suddenly expected not only to participate in, but to find utterly fascinating. It hadn't fascinated her at all, motherhood hadn't come naturally to her in the same way fatherhood seemed to appeal to Eddie. He and Maggi had spent hours, days even, together when Eddie's name came up for the allotment, even though Maggi was well into her teens by then. She'd asked sometimes what they did there but, to be honest, she wasn't that interested and perhaps it showed.

She'd thought Eddie dying might draw them together, but since she hadn't even seen her daughter in the months after the funeral, Dorothy had had to make a life for herself. She'd tried to get back into activism but the confident young women at Feminists First didn't seem to want women like her – thought they'd done their bit. 'I'm fifty-eight, not ninety-eight,' she wanted to say, 'and the reason you have all the freedoms you enjoy today is because women like me fought for them,' even as they suggested that if she *was* staying maybe she could make herself useful making the tea or perhaps delivering leaflets – could she walk that far? One even referred to her as 'Great-Aunt Dot here' and when she told her in no uncertain terms she'd never been Dot in her life, the mood in the room had iced over and she hadn't felt able to go back. So she'd joined the dancing instead and though she did enjoy it, she felt she was capable of doing more, contributing somehow – surely all her years of experience as a woman in this world counted for something?

She tried again with Maggi. 'You're looking well.' Uncontroversial surely.

Maggi glared at her. 'What do you mean by that?'

'I—'

'You're right, I have put on more weight.'

'I never—'

'I always eat too much when I'm stressed out, and unlike

some people' – she swooshed a hand up and down Dorothy's sticklike frame – 'I put on weight if I so much as think about a piece of lemon tart. Thanks for pointing it out.'

Dorothy was about to protest but knew there was no point. Her daughter had always been spiky as a sea urchin and it seemed nothing was going to change. Still, it was only the two of them now and they had to try. 'If you're stressed, why don't you spend some time with me here at Dad's allotment? We could do some weeding, the fresh air would do us both good.'

'You haven't asked me what I'm stressed about.' Maggi pouted.

'Because I thought you'd tell me to mind my own business,' countered Dorothy, throwing her hands in the air. 'Is it work? How's the singing going? Are you getting plenty of bookings?'

'It's going fine,' said Maggi. And it was fine – as long as her aspirations didn't reach any higher than singing along with faded pianists at dilapidated hotels on a Saturday afternoon to the dozen or so folk who stopped in after their shopping and had as little interest in listening to her sing Neil Diamond's back catalogue as she had in singing it. It wasn't where she'd hoped to be at almost thirty-seven. 'It's fine,' she said again. 'Everything's . . . fine.'

'So how about it then? Will you help me restore Dad's allotment to its former glory?' Dorothy hesitated then took the plunge. 'Might be nice for us to spend some time together for a change.'

Maggi gave a dramatic sigh. 'Okay,' she said. 'I'll help you do some weeding. Make me a cup of tea first though, it took me almost an hour to get through that traffic on Uddingston Main Street.'

Dorothy decided not to tell her she could see where the

kettle was, and said instead, 'Biscuit?' as her daughter pulled off her ridiculous coat and tucked her legs under her on Eddie's favourite tartan garden chair.

'Tsk. No wonder I'm fat.'

Dorothy pressed her lips together and said nothing, wondering if all children were this difficult or whether she was, as she'd long feared, the world's worst mother. *But really, who'd take the role on voluntarily?* she thought, as she set about making tea for her daughter.

12

FARAH PEEPED OUT OF THE window to check and the boy was still there. Having spent his energy kicking up the leaves patiently raked into a pile by Lawrence the day before, he'd been sitting on the hard step outside the shed on his parents' allotment for the best part of an hour, staring down at his iPad. She didn't teach on a Monday but the boy should be at school, surely. The allotments were busy and someone should be looking after him, he couldn't be more than nine or ten.

She wondered whether she should go over when her phone rang. She squinted at the screen and saw a number she recognized and dreaded. Her fingers hovered over the screen for a moment then she decided not to answer. There was nothing her GP could tell her that her much more experienced husband could not, and besides, she knew her own body better than anyone. It was not good news again this month, she already knew that.

She wasn't sure when getting pregnant and having the family they'd always wanted had become an issue, when they knew for sure it wasn't going to be a question of simply deciding the time was right and planning maternity leave, redecorating the spare bedroom, and researching prams and Moses baskets. She recalled the joy of that first pregnancy test – she'd been in Asda when she'd seen the kits and couldn't resist. Weighed down by four heavy bags of shopping, she dashed through the café and into the toilets to do the test, she hadn't even waited till she got home. And when she saw the second blue line, she celebrated with a cup of tea – no more strong coffees for her! – and a giant empire biscuit, excitement mounting as she planned how she would give Mohid the news.

'Well done, daughter,' Mohid's mother had said, and immediately made her sit on the sofa and plied her with ladoos, gulab jamuns, twirls of orange jalebis and sweetened milky chai. At last, she had done it.

When the blood appeared two months later, seemingly in torrents and with no regard for the fact she was in class teaching her third years, the joy was snatched away as quickly as it had been given. She remembered the stretching feeling in her lower tummy, a feeling that had become familiar to her over the years and which she now knew was the lining of her uterus coming away and leaving her unborn child homeless. She'd never forgive her body for that.

'We'll try again, my love, don't worry, our little family is yet to come.' Mohid was sweet and understanding, his breezy optimism lifting her too. And he was right. She'd got pregnant again six months later. But her uterus had stretched and snagged, and said no.

'Not yet,' Mohid had translated for her. 'It wasn't our time yet.' He smoothed her hair and stroked her cheek as she mourned her second lost child.

By the third loss, Mohid had changed tack. 'A holiday,' he'd announced, as she lay in the bath, struggling to love her treacherous body with its unfriendly terrain. She didn't want to leave Scotland, she had this half-baked notion that the three lost babies needed them here to care for them, and also that no new babies would come if they weren't on home turf. Of course she couldn't say this out loud. 'Oh no,' she'd said instead. 'I'm far too busy and what about your work? We can't just pick up and leave.' But Mohid had insisted. A trip to Capri was booked for the last two weeks of the school holidays.

They'd been on Signor Aprea's boat on their way to the island, the plane journey having been something of an ordeal with the turbulence and the twin babies seated across the aisle. Although not a linguist like Farah, Mohid had practised his Italian enthusiastically with Signor Aprea. Farah heard him say how lovely it was to be in 'la bella Italia in agosto' and it came to her from nowhere that if she jumped into the ocean, she wouldn't need to think about anything else. Ever. She stared at the endless tide, half-blinded by the sheen, then deeper into the water, catching the metallic flash of sea bream and the clusters of briny seaweed beneath the boat. She heard Signor Aprea say they'd be welcome to join them at that evening's celebrations for the Feast of Madonna Assunta and suddenly the need to jump off the boat was overwhelming. She'd tried to explain it to Mohid over a glass of limoncello later – the lure of the water, the irresistibility of the waves closing over her head, a glimmering blue nothingness enticing her in. But she'd told him about it as she would an anecdote from school, with a self-deprecating chuckle and a shrug of her shoulders. He'd said calmly, 'Everyone feels that way. It's a well-recognized phenomenon. The same thing happens on bridges. You feel this urge to throw yourself off, but you don't though, do you?' He'd hugged her and poured her another thick sweet limoncello. She was glad she'd told him because he made her feel better immediately, as he always did. It seemed, that first night, that the holiday would be exactly what they needed.

She wished he was here with her now, and checked her phone to see how long it was till he came off shift. Not even eleven o'clock. Ages yet. She went back to the window and frowned to see the boy was still there, sitting on his own and glued to that iPad he carried with him everywhere like a lifejacket. His parents' shed was closed up and empty, there was no one looking after him, checking to see whether he was cold, or hungry, or needed a drink. Farah sat back down, tapping her fingers in annoyance. That poor boy had been left to fend for himself, like the little sunshine girl in Capri.

It was halfway through the second week of their holiday and they'd spent the morning shopping for fresh lobster and nutty-smelling coffee beans at the local market. A dazzling sun was streaming through the pine trees, hot enough to quiet the birds. They'd stopped for shade on their way back to the cottage and spotted an alimentaro, still open, even at lunchtime. It was much cooler in the shop, and darker too so that it took a moment or so for their eyes to adjust from the brilliant sunshine.

'Ooh look, Mohid, ziti, let's buy some for tonight.' Farah picked up a couple of packs of pasta and looked around the empty shop for someone to serve her.

'Ecco me,' came a small voice from somewhere below the counter.

'Hello?'

'Sono io,' squeaked the voice.

Farah bent over the counter and saw a little girl in a red pinafore over a stripey red and white T-shirt, her hair a glistening blonde cap, the fringe held back from her face with a red clasp. 'Hello, I mean, buon giorno,' said Farah, a huge smile spreading across her face.

The girl said, 'Ciao. Posso?' indicating the packs of pasta in Farah's hand.

Farah handed them to her and she rang them up in the till, standing on her tiptoes to press the old-fashioned buttons.

A stocky man with a half-beard came rushing through from the back, wiping his mouth on his apron. 'Ah, excuse please. I not hear door.'

'Oh, no problem.' Farah's eyes did not stray from the child. 'Your little helper has been excellent.'

The man didn't understand.

'Your daughter? Tua figlia?'

'Ah yes, my daughter, Maria Sole.'

Farah turned to Mohid, beaming. 'Maria Sole, Mohid, Maria Sunshine.'

Mohid waved to the girl, who gave them a gap-toothed smile in return, before picking up her squashy yellow banana from the counter and skipping into the back room with it.

Farah's eyes followed her and she said in a faraway voice, 'Che bella ragazza. Bellissima!' She moved a little closer to the counter to get a better view.

The man met Mohid's eye.

Mohid stepped forward and tapped Farah's elbow. 'We should get going, don't you think? Let these good people have their lunch and we'll head home for ours.'

Reluctantly, Farah allowed herself to be guided out of the shop. She turned at the door to say goodbye but the man behind the counter had already gone back to his lunch.

In the afternoon, as she and Mohid lay together on the bed, the blinds shut tight against the heat of the sun, she'd been sharp with him.

'What are you thinking about?' he'd asked her, running his fingers across the curve of her stomach. She lay on her back, not acknowledging his touch as she focused on the fan whirring round above them.

'Nothing really,' she lied. She turned to face him. 'I was wondering what age Maria Sole might be?'

'Maria . . . ?'

'Maria Sole. Little Sunshine. From the shop? She was adorable, wasn't she?'

'I suppose,' he said tentatively.

She glared at him.

'I mean, yes, she was very cute.'

'What age would you say?'

'I don't know. It was quite dark in the shop. Maybe about five or so, I'd say? Some of my patients at that age—'

'Do you not think that's too young to let her go into the front shop on her own?'

'Maybe, but her father was right behind her and—'

'No mother though, did you notice that? No mother following her through to check she was okay. Strange, don't you think?'

'Well—'

She hadn't waited for his response, instead, flouncing off the bed, she complained about the heat – as though that were Mohid's fault – and slammed the bathroom door behind her as she went for her second shower of the day.

Later that evening, she'd gone outside to brush the dust

from the flagstones in the front yard. A sudden breeze swooshed through the trees and the dirt flew up and made her mouth crunchy with grit. The weather was turning. Farah wondered if someone had checked the little sunshine girl had a jumper on.

A flash of something green going past the window of the shed caught her eye, and Farah looked over again to make sure the boy was okay. Maybe she should offer him an oatmeal cookie and a cup of hot chocolate; he always looked half-starved. She slipped her cardigan round her shoulders and opened the door. The boy was gone. *Probably for the best*, she thought. Now she could make the most of her day off and get some gardening done to surprise Mohid when he joined her later.

13

IT WAS LATE MORNING, THE sun hard and bright, when the boy finally sidled over to Stanley's allotment. Stanley had been busy with his potatoes all morning, carefully covering the nascent stalks with fresh soil as they peeked out at the world for the first time. He glanced over at the boy every so often, wondering what he was doing there on his own. His scrawny legs were curled up under him on the cold step, he'd been staring at Stanley from under his ginger fringe, the ever-present electronic device balanced on his knee. He tried to remember what Karen had called him when she'd told him a new family was coming — Isaac was it? — a decent name anyway, not Jaiden or Max or Rocky, or whatever they called children these days.

'Shouldn't you be at school?' he said, shielding his eyes from the sun and looking down at the boy.

Isaac held up his tablet. 'I learn more from this than I do at school.'

Stanley looked at the boy with interest, since he was equally sceptical about the benefits of reciting times tables or learning capital cities by rote, or any of the other useless things he'd been forced to do himself at school. 'Maybe so but I don't think your mum would be happy if she knew you were skipping school, would she?'

Isaac sniffed and rubbed his nose with the back of his hand. 'You won't tell her, will you, mister?'

'It's Mr Seddon to you.'

The boy said nothing, and Stanley took in his pale face, with its dusting of freckles across his nose, cheekbones like knives and blueish hands poking out from his shirtsleeves, fingernails bitten to the quick. But there was something about him that appealed to Stanley – his stillness maybe, his willingness to sit quietly without indulging in the kind of chit-chat that Stanley detested.

'Are you hungry, lad?' he said. 'Did you have breakfast?'

'No. Have you got any sweets?'

'It's not even midday yet – too early for sweets.' He hesitated but the boy looked like he could do with some warmth. 'What about some nice hot tea?'

'Okay.' Isaac left the path and crossed through the middle of Stanley's allotment.

'What do you think the path's for?' Stanley said. 'Mind my seed beds.'

The boy ignored him and pushed open the door of Stanley's shed. Stanley indicated a fold-up gardening chair for Isaac to sit on. 'I prefer this one,' he said, settling himself on Mabel's wicker chair with the faded blue cushion, next to the old portable gas heater. 'Can we put that on?'

'I suppose so,' said Stanley, 'but mind you don't get too close.'

Isaac warmed his hands at the heater, while Stanley boiled the kettle and searched for an extra mug.

'Who's that old woman?'

Stanley turned to see Isaac pointing at a picture of Mabel,

taken when she'd won second prize for the cha-cha-cha at her dance club. 'You should come to the club and dance with me sometime,' she'd say. Of course Stanley didn't go and dance with her, and now he never could. 'Less of the old,' he said to Isaac. 'That's Mabel. She was only sixty-seven there.'

'Sixty-seven? Wow!'

Stanley was about to tell him off for his cheek, but something about the way he sat there, open-mouthed and shaking his head at the impossibility of reaching such a grand old age, made him laugh, a real belly laugh like he and Mabel used to enjoy together. It occurred to him that talking to this boy was cheering him up. Isaac had transferred his attention back to his tablet.

'You should do something other than spend all day on that thing,' Stanley said.

'Like what?'

'Well, like . . .' Stanley scratched the top of his head and thought for a moment. 'You should get a hobby,' he said finally.

'What's your hobby?'

'My hobby? I mean . . . I like to . . .' Stanley was stumped. The truth was, apart from spending all day on his allotment, he'd done nothing much at all since Mabel had died. She'd been the one who signed them up to things. She was the one people warmed to. She hadn't minded chatting about the small stuff, was interested in everyone's kids, their grandkids, their sick relative. 'People's lives, Stanley,' she'd say, 'what else is more important than that?' before picking up the phone to chat with one of her friends. He'd stopped going to their Thursday morning coffee club at the church because it was hard when everyone kept asking him how he was coping after Mabel, and worse if they didn't mention her so it was like she'd never existed at all. He'd even stopped going to his Tuesday afternoon chess club and he'd loved that.

It came to him with a start that he missed playing chess, with its rules and strategies, all the stuff that had kept his mind agile and alert. 'My hobby's playing chess,' he said. 'Would you . . . fancy a game one day? Might keep you off your iPod thingy for a bit?'

Isaac shook his head.

'Ach no, why would you want to play with an old man like me?' Stanley glanced down at his hands, veins pushing through the paper-thin skin and mud ingrained around the nails. He felt conscious suddenly of the way his hair seemed to have migrated to his chest, the thick wiry curls the colour and texture of steel wool poking out of his shirt collar. He thought of how unappealing he must appear to the boy. 'I understand, don't worry.'

'It's not because you're ancient.'

'Good to know,' said Stanley.

'No, it's because' – Isaac looked up at Stanley from under his orange eyelashes – 'I don't know how to play.'

'Don't you ever play with your dad?'

Isaac snorted. 'My dad can't play chess. He couldn't, even before . . .' He gripped the arms of the comfy old chair. 'He's useless.'

Stanley put the kettle down. 'Don't say that, lad. I'm sure he loves you very much.'

The boy shifted, now folding his arms so tightly his hands were gripping his waist and he was leaning back against his own fingers.

'You know, it's not that hard to play chess. I could teach you. If you want . . .'

The boy brightened. 'If you like. I'll be rubbish though, I'm rubbish at everything.'

Stanley brought over the tea. 'We'll see, shall we? Here you go.'

'Thanks. Got any biscuits?'

14

It was a slate-grey Tuesday and Germaine was sitting on the bench in the communal area, sorting through her seeds. She put packets of the vegetables she loved so much – beetroot, French beans – to one side for planting in a week or so. May was such a seductive month for gardeners, she knew, a thin early sunshine and all the rookies were out with even the most delicate of seeds, sowing and planting them far too early. A month later and they'd discover all their work was for nothing as half the seeds failed to germinate in ground that wasn't yet warm enough, or else they'd be killed off by the icy fingers of late-spring frost or a deadly attack of slugs in the night. Germaine knew better. She'd done most of her outdoor planting but the most tender of her young seeds were still undercover – snug and protected in their trays and kept inside her shed as shelter against the still-bitter Scottish spring. They'd be ready to come out and find their forever home in the soil in another few weeks. Meanwhile, she was keeping a close eye on the hardier seedlings at the back of her patch – the robust brassicas, as well as rows of potatoes and spring onions.

'Don't forget to cover over the stalks, love, or they'll drag the potatoes up too early. And spread out the sowing, remember, that's what's going to give you the best chance of a successful harvest.'

Germaine stopped what she was doing as her father's words came back to her. She could picture the scene so clearly – it was almost fifty years ago, she was eight or nine years old, standing in the frost-hardened ground of their small but thriving garden in Aberdeen. Her dad, in his faded green cords and the bunnet he rarely took off, showing her how to handle the seedlings like babies, talking to them in a soft voice, caressing them almost. She was content to be out in the brittle sunlight, blowing on her nippy fingers and spending time with him after another unhappy week at school. Sometimes she imagined her mum was still with them, beckoning them in with her big yellow rubber gloves from the kitchen window, holding up a mug of tea for her dad to come in and drink while it was hot. But she was long gone by then, and a sudden image of her dad, soft-eyed as he muttered, 'Life's a wee look out the window, Germaine, that's all it is,' came back to her.

She bit her lip despondently, reminding herself that she'd left Aberdeen and all that had happened there behind her when she'd started her new life here in Viewpark. She piled the seed packets together and looked up to survey her kingdom. With May almost over, the allotments were busier than Germaine had ever seen them.

Stanley had been there since before she'd arrived, and probably since dawn. His rhododendron was coming into its own, and his flowers and fresh veg patches were rivals to her own. Almost.

No 2 next door were also starting to see some pay-off for their hard work, the tender young spinach leaves and spring cabbages in particular were looking bright, she'd noticed, as she'd inspected the plots yesterday checking everyone's progress.

No 5 was going round his shed with a damp cloth, sponging off dirt spots visible only to him. He was resplendent in a striped cardigan and white jeans, dark sunglasses propped redundantly on his head. Germaine couldn't fault his allotment though. Perhaps more flowers than she would have chosen, but even Germaine had to admire the vivid profusion of plant life that was thriving there. Arranged in colour clusters were the pinks and reds of the last of the tulips, then the brilliant whites of the early geraniums, carefully nurtured indoors and beginning to flourish, and lastly, the fragile-looking yellow primroses, slightly past their best now but still strong enough to contribute to the colour palette. *He should be deadheading some of those tulips and primroses*, she thought, encourage them to multiply. The bonus blooms, her dad called them, she'd tell Lawrence that later. Set back behind the flowers, his baby turnips and radishes in the smaller patch dedicated to vegetables were almost ready to pull. In front of the shed was a zigzag path, crystal clear and not a weed in sight, Germaine noted with approval, and the shed itself was gleaming white, having been repainted immediately by the young man – whatever his name was – as soon as he had taken possession of the plot. All in all, it was quite an achievement considering the other chap whose name was on the allotment with him rarely deigned to put in an appearance so that this male model – despite appearances to the contrary – had knuckled down and put in all the hard graft himself.

No 3, with the unfortunate face, had waved to her as he'd arrived around nine, and he was in his shed, doing whatever it was he did in there. Listening to his music mostly, she thought, but his land had improved too since he'd taken it over, perhaps not as much as No 5's but these things took time, Germaine understood that.

No 4 was digging, as usual. He was a strange one. Some days he'd greet Germaine with a big hello and ask after her plants; other days, it was like he couldn't talk at all, hardly gave her the time of day. Still, Germaine wasn't one to talk either so, if anything, she preferred the days he didn't speak. Better than that wife of his who couldn't stop talking when she came by. And Germaine was not interested in fashion, God knows, but at least she was always neat and tidy. The woman at No 4 was permanently rumpled. Her blouses were creased, she wore shabby leggings, and everything looked like it had been worn two or three times and needed a good wash, even when she came straight from work. And why she felt the need to mollycoddle her husband the way she did, dropping him off and picking him up again like he was a kid at school, Germaine couldn't imagine. Really, some people made it all too easy for her to make an enemy a day.

Which reminded her of No 6 and the still-tangled wilderness of the top plot which seemed to be getting denser by the week. The woman in dungarees was making little progress and Germaine feared something was going to have to be done about her. But that could wait till another day.

No 6 aside, they were all working on their separate plots and what some might view as lack of engagement, Germaine appreciated as the complete tranquillity that comes from human beings engaged in their own endeavours and not bothering each other. Her eye caught on the crumbling wall at the top of the hill and she tutted. She still hadn't been able to contact anyone at the council about the repairs, despite leaving several grumpy messages for first Karen, then eventually Councillor Murray himself. She couldn't shake the niggling feeling that something was going on behind the scenes but with limited interest in the admin of the place, she didn't dwell on it. As long as the plants and flowers were flourishing, she didn't give anything else much thought. And the place *was* thriving. There was harmony in the air, a cool breeze, birds singing, insects humming, and the sweet scent of raspberries from the hedges blowing over the allotments. Germaine breathed in deeply and exhaled loudly with contentment before returning to her shed, feeling for the first time in a long time, that perhaps all would be well.

Rap rap rap.

'Ignore it,' said Mohid, but Farah told him not to be silly, and opened the door to a red-faced Dorothy, who was waving the *Bellshill Speaker* in her hand.

'Good, you're here. Come with me.'

Farah poked her head out of the shed and was surprised to see Kevin and Lawrence looking sheepish at the bottom of the path.

'What's this about?' she asked, as she and Mohid joined the little group following behind Dorothy like the von Trapp family traipsing down the mountain after Maria.

Kevin raised his hands and made a face to indicate he didn't know. Lawrence said, 'No idea, we were s-s-summonsed same as you were,' and pointed to Dorothy, who was at that moment striding down towards Germaine's plot, her lips moving as she chuntered away to herself and gestured with her hands, clearly agitated by something.

They passed Stanley at the bottom of the path. He was minding his own business as usual and didn't even look up as he tenderly polished the bigger leaves at the bottom of his rhoddy with a soft cloth. 'Come with us please,' Dorothy called to him as she passed, and the others were astonished to see that he did as he was told, putting down the cloth and joining their merry band. 'You too.' Isobel left her tea to go cold on the step and grabbed George by the arm to join them.

They reached Germaine's office at the bottom of the path. Dorothy rapped on the door, then walked over to the window to rap on that as well before Germaine even had the chance to open the door.

Germaine was sitting at her desk, her eyes skimming the words one more time as though a reread might alter the offending communication on her screen for the better. She scowled at the email from Councillor Murray instructing her – *instructing*, if you please – to complete the detailed questionnaire covering all manner of issues relating to the allotments as a matter of urgency. Her hands were high in the air, poised to strike back at Councillor Murray with the power of her keyboard, when she spotted the white moon of Dorothy's face peering in at her through the shed's small rectangular pane. The woman was mouthing something at her and pointing to the door. Germaine ignored her for a few seconds but when she looked up again, the apparition was still at her window, mouth open like Viewpark's own version of *The Scream*. There was nothing else for it.

'Doroth—' She stopped, as she opened the door wider and saw what appeared to be the entire complement of allotment holders bunched together at the bottom of the path. At least Mohid and a couple of the others had the grace to look embarrassed about the interruption.

'What's going on?' She stepped out of the shed, pulling on her green Trespass jacket as she did so.

'That's a very good question. And this tiny article buried in the middle of the local paper begs a few more.' Dorothy held the pages of the *Bellshill Speaker* above her head as she spoke. 'And here's another one for you – when were you going to tell us about the contents of that notice?' She indicated the A4 sheet stuck on to the community noticeboard with giant red tacks, like the kind they used at primary school.

'Who put that there?' said Germaine, walking across to inspect the usually empty noticeboard.

The entire group followed closely behind and they all gathered round the noticeboard like schoolchildren looking to see who had secured the lead role in the nativity play. Behind them, Isaac was hopping across from allotment to allotment, scattering leaves and thinking how much better it was to be at the allotments than at school.

Germaine scanned the notice quickly and stepped back onto Lawrence's foot in surprise.

'Ow,' he said, and Stanley wondered if now was the right time to tell him that soft top plimsolls, Gucci or otherwise, were not the best footwear for gardening. He thought not as he watched the boy screw his face up in pain.

Germaine was too distracted to apologize, or even notice she'd hurt him. 'Who put that there?' she repeated. 'It certainly wasn't here when I opened up this morning.'

'Does that matter?' said Dorothy impatiently. 'It's what it says that's important.'

'What does it say?' called Kevin from the back of the group. 'I can't see it from here.'

'Read it out, love,' said Stanley. 'My eyes are struggling with the small print as well.'

Dorothy took a couple of steps closer to the noticeboard and read out the contents of the notice in the loud voice she'd cultivated during her years of campaigning.

> Tenants and residents of Viewpark, Birkenshaw and Uddingston, including and especially plot holders at the Kenmar Allotments, Viewpark, are invited to the next North Lanarkshire Communities Committee Neighbourhood Board Meeting. Find out about events and projects, including but not limited to the proposed closure of the Kenmar Allotments, and discuss issues with your local councillors, officials and other residents on Monday 3 June at 7 p.m. in Burnhead Community Centre.

She stepped back. 'Now do you see the problem?' She glared round at her fellow allotment holders as though they were at fault.

The stunned silence was broken by Isobel. 'What the—?'

'Language,' warned Germaine, though Isobel hadn't said anything offensive yet.

'What are they talking about, "proposed closures"?'

'What does that mean?'

'Why didn't you tell us, Germaine?'

'We've just moved our stuff on to the allotment. Does this mean we'll need to move it all out again?'

'*Quiet!*' Germaine raised her hands in front of her chest as though she was fending them off physically. 'I can't answer you all at once. Point of fact, I can't answer any of you at all because I haven't got a clue what's going on. No one's said anything to me.'

'But that can't be right, surely?' Lawrence surprised himself by speaking up, and again by not stuttering as he did so.

'No, it cannot,' said Germaine in the stern voice she usually reserved for her frequently late postman or those dog walkers who did not pick up their dog's mess right outside her block of flats. 'They want us to attend and ask questions? That's exactly what we're going to do.'

There was a great deal of indignant chatter from the group as they gathered round to read the notice again, and made plans to attend the meeting en masse. Dorothy looked around and realized that this was the first time the whole lot of them had been together, united as the community they were supposed to be. Perhaps things would be okay after all.

15

'Come on, George,' said Isobel, not liking the hectoring tone in her voice but pushed to the limit at this point. 'You had them at lunchtime, I gave you them so you could lock up after you left for the woods.'

George stood in the middle of the kitchen, surrounded by chaos. The half-empty spice jars, hardened paint brushes and Tesco receipts all seemed to be multiplying on the table whose surface no longer had even an inch of scored wood visible. The remains of their hastily prepared egg and chips lay on top of days-old newspapers, the yolk-smeared plates turning Isobel's stomach as she lifted and dropped them, wondering if by some miracle the keys could have landed underneath.

'Gggrrr,' he said, pointing to the door. 'Nnnnggrrr.'

Isobel looked to where he was pointing. 'Yes, the keys, it's the keys I'm looking for.' 'Idiot,' she whispered under her breath.

George pressed his lips together and opened the back door. On the other side, still in the lock, were Isobel's door keys.

'Oh George, thank you.' She took the keys from him.

He smiled at her, revealing the gap in his lower gum.

'I'm sorry, George, for . . . getting upset. I'm a bit harassed because the meeting starts at seven and it'll take me twenty minutes to walk up there. I shouldn't have taken it out on you though.'

George patted her arm, forgiving her easily.

Isobel looked down at his hand, with its weather-roughened skin and calloused knuckles, and was reminded of the many times that simple gesture – his hand on her arm – had calmed her and made everything better. She still remembered the first time. They'd been in Rome, she'd been early to meet him and had gone into the bar to wait for him. How elegant and European she'd felt as she sat in a booth at the back, her large red wine in front of her as she scanned the bustling bar, thinking how impressed George would be by her sophistication. She hadn't known what to say when those two guys came over, bearded and reeking of beer and menthol, and asked if they could join her. They'd sat on the same side of the table as her, one on either side, blocking her in so she couldn't move. There were people all around, but she'd been so young, hadn't known she could cry out, scream even, she hadn't wanted to draw attention to herself so she'd put up with it for what seemed like hours, their fawning, their smoky breath in her face, the way they stroked her bare arms insistently, but gently, so it was hard to complain they were doing anything wrong, pressing their warm thighs closer and closer to hers till she felt like she couldn't breathe. And then, George had arrived. The two men – younger than her, still half-formed and ignorant, she realized suddenly – scarpered and George sat beside her, providing instant reassurance, his huge hand patting her arm like balm on a wound.

'Gggrrrnnn.'

'Everything will be fine, George,' she said in a softer voice. 'You remember I told you I'm going to this meeting about the allotments. Isaac's at Hayden's house, his mum's dropping him off later. He's got his own key so I'm going to lock the door after me. Understand?' She performed a locking motion with the key, before settling him in front of Netflix.

She took a final backwards glance at him, already engrossed in a documentary about the rain forests, a glass of beer and a bowl of honey roasted nuts at his elbow. He'll be fine, she told herself, trying not to feel like his jailer as she locked the door behind her.

They'd set up a long narrow table on the slightly raised platform at the front of the hall, as though the people from the council – whenever they deigned to turn up – were going to perform a comedy sketch or a sharp political play for their audience.

Not that there was much of an audience, thought Mohid, glancing round the echoey hall. There were about ten rows of chairs, the uncomfortable wooden ones he remembered from school, laid out in neat rows on front of the stage. Sitting a couple of rows in front of Mohid and Farah were an old couple in their seventies or so, passing a tube of sweeties between them as though they were indeed at a theatre and waiting for the show to begin. On the front row was the lollipop lady from Old Edinburgh Road, still in her high-vis vest, her big yellow and red STOP sign propped up against the wall. Across the aisle, and sitting in splendid isolation on the third row back, was a tall woman in a grey windcheater, her straight black bob falling into her eyes as she read the book on her lap. She looked up suddenly and caught Mohid's eye. She waved and Mohid waved back though he was pretty sure they didn't know each other. Perhaps she'd been a patient, he thought, they often remembered him.

'It's supposed to start at seven,' grumbled Farah by his side. 'That's five past now.'

'And where are all the others? I thought we agreed, we'd all come out and show support.' Mohid was beginning to wonder why he and Farah were giving up their evening to sit in a draughty community centre when no one else had bothered.

'Maybe they couldn't get babysitters and things, not everyone is footloose and fancy-free like us.'

Only Farah could make that sound like a disadvantage, thought Mohid. 'They've had plenty of time to organize things. If I can manage to swap shifts, so can they.'

Farah knew he had a point and she laid her hand on top of his to show she agreed.

The back doors swung open and Isobel, Germaine and Dorothy came bounding in. Germaine gestured to the back row but Dorothy said in a loud voice, 'Oh no, we're sitting at the front. Where they can see us.'

They acknowledged Mohid and Farah as they passed, Dorothy calling out, 'Thanks for coming' as they made their way to the front of the hall.

Stanley arrived next, puffing as he took off his bunnet and found a seat. He was here for Mabel, he told himself, it's what she would have wanted. He sat down in the second row from the back, hoping it would be over in time for *Lewis*.

The door opened again, softly this time, but heads turned and almost everyone did a double take. Kevin mooched into the hall, eyes to the ground.

'Gorgeous Kevin.' Kevin looked up to see the girl who drove his bus in the mornings gesturing at the seat beside hers. 'Over here,' she called. 'Come and sit beside me.'

Kevin did so, thinking again that he'd have to find some way of telling her his name was just Kevin. She seemed so pleased to see him though, he knew he couldn't do it tonight.

The hall began to fill up row by row. The rain must have started again as folk were coming in in damp pairs, trailing limp umbrellas like broken birds along the ground. Mohid waved over at their local GP, and again at Scott from the library, and one of the lovely women who served him his daily Americano at Greggs.

'Turnout's pretty good after all, considering it's a rainy Monday,' he whispered to Farah, as he spotted Lawrence slipping into his seat. He leaned forward and called hello, noticing Adrian was not with him. He was about to beckon Lawrence over to come and sit with him and Farah when there was commotion at the front of the hall.

A grey-suited man bounced on to the stage, leading the way for two smaller and altogether better-dressed gentlemen. The first man was beaming and thrusting his chest out pigeon-style. He seemed not to notice the rows of people gawping up at them as he pulled out a chair each for the expensive-looking duo, who condescended to take the seats that were offered. Last onto the stage was a reluctant-looking Karen, her oversized cardigan wrapped tightly round her like a shield. Her cheeks were red and although she scarcely glanced at the audience in the body of the hall, she seemed to be the only one of the group who was aware of every eye upon them as they took their places behind the long table.

'That's the two blokes that came rooting around the allotments a few weeks ago,' said Germaine. 'Measuring things and all sorts. Wish I hadn't been so nice to them now.'

'You were nice to visitors?' said Dorothy, shaking her head at the tube of Werther's originals Isobel was wiggling under her nose.

'Of course I was—'

'If we could have a bit of order please,' came a patronizing voice from the top of the hall.

The hum of chatter and scraping of seats faded until there was total silence. The pigeon-man on the stage was bursting with his own importance as he took the microphone from its stand and strode to the edge of the stage with it, throwing the long wire out of his way and taking a good look at his audience.

'I didn't know we were here to see Rod Stewart,' said Isobel to Dorothy, and they both laughed until Germaine glared at them.

'Ahum,' said Pigeon-Man. 'Thank you, everyone, for coming along this evening. And I'd like you all to extend a big thank you to Messrs Joseph and Michael Biggart who have agreed to attend tonight's meeting to give us a presentation on their proposal for an utterly wonderful new housing development right here in the heart of Viewpark.'

'Completely unbiased approach from the council then,' whispered Dorothy sarcastically to Germaine, amidst the half-hearted applause from the audience. At the back, Stanley did not participate. *Like turkeys cheering for Christmas*, he thought. *No, I won't be clapping for that.*

'As many of you will know, my name is Councillor Murray, and I am proud to represent the borough of Viewpark and its residents.'

A snort from Stanley loud enough to draw attention and some shushing from the two women sitting to his left. The councillor gave a lengthy introduction to the evening's business and Stanley managed not to cringe audibly when the man announced the developers as 'two young Wishaw boys made good' and asked the audience to 'put their hands together for the fabulous Biggart Brothers' – as though they were a pair of trapeze artists in sequins and tights from the Greatest Show on Earth.

There was a spattering of applause as the two dapper men stood up to peddle their wares. A PowerPoint presentation flashed into life behind them and there was a sharp communal intake of breath as the land currently containing the allotments appeared, but with the sheds and plots mysteriously wiped out from the picture, as the brothers described in some detail the land on which the allotments were situated, the extent of the playing fields behind, and why it was all ripe for development.

Germaine could hardly take her eyes off the screen, especially the part of the map where her own little office and lovingly tended plot should have been. It was like seeing her own grave, with the final date on the tombstone carefully etched onto the marble, before she had died. She saw that Dorothy too was silently fuming. Beside her, Isobel's eyes were shiny with tears, her knuckles white as she gripped her Werther's.

Completely unaware of the emotions they had triggered, the duo onstage were talking over a new slide that was being beamed into the hall. This time, the audience found themselves staring at a picture-perfect development of four huge houses, each with a balcony on the front, looking down at Uddingston, and a square of perfect green at the back which Germaine supposed was meant to represent the garden.

'And of course,' the taller of the two men was saying in his curiously high-pitched tones, 'each residence will come fully carpeted' – an odd slide showing plush mushroom-coloured carpeting appeared – 'and with state-of-the-art' – the other man repeated '*state*-of-the-art' – 'kitchen appliances for the kitchen-diner which will run the full length of the house, and bathroom fittings for each of the four bathrooms.' He looked to his brother who held up four fingers, presumably in case the audience didn't grasp the import of having four lavatories in their house.

'If all goes to plan, these residences will be available to buy in the middle of next year. We are happy to take any questions,' he finished, putting his arm round his brother and both of them returning to their seats, as though the very last thing they expected from this audience were any questions.

There was a stunned silence round the hall.

'Okaaay then,' said Councillor Murray. 'If there are no questions, we'll thank Messrs Biggart and Biggart for coming and move on to—' He spotted a hand up in the audience and performed an exaggerated double take. 'Oh. You wanted to ask something?'

'Yes.'

Everyone in the hall swivelled their heads round to see where the voice was coming from and Mohid knew from the reactions of those turning round who the speaker would be. He was right.

Kevin cleared his throat, but stood up, determined to say his piece. 'Thanks to the developers for coming. But I wanted to ask why they think Viewpark would benefit more from houses that no one from Viewpark could ever afford, than the current allotments which provide an invaluable space not only for the allotment holders, but also for the whole community to enjoy?'

He got the whole lot out in one breath and sat back down on his uncomfortable chair with a thud, pleased with himself for saying what he'd wanted to say. He felt the woman next to him pat him on the shoulder approvingly.

The brothers glanced at each other and the smaller one muttered something about focus groups and market research and house prices in the area being positively impacted by the development.

There was a murmuring from the audience, who did not appear convinced by this reply. Encouraged, the woman beside Kevin raised her hand.

'Yes?' The councillor's tone had become decidedly snippy.

'Wendy. Local bus driver and resident.' The woman pointed to her own chest as she introduced herself. 'These houses are very big. Bigger than any other house already in Viewpark, in fact. My question is: Why?'

On the stage, Karen sat forward in her seat. This was more like it.

The councillor gave Wendy a blank look. 'Why?' he repeated deadpan, as though simply echoing her question would be enough to satisfy her and spare the investors from the need to reply.

'Yes,' said Wendy. 'Why does anyone need a house with four bathrooms when there are people who haven't even got one? My dad was homeless. One of these houses would be big enough to house a lot of men like him.'

There was silence from the stage and Councillor Murray's chest deflated a little. 'It's . . . I . . . Perhaps the developers could answer that,' he said, rather ungallantly passing the problem on.

The brothers exchanged another look, then the taller one said,

'All our research shows that there is more . . . ah . . . return for houses like this than' – he lowered his voice – 'more affordable housing.'

The woman who ran the Viewpark Church Open Space stood up. 'Iris Maclean. Did you know we've got a food bank in Viewpark?'

Councillor Murray paled. 'I don't think—'

Iris wasn't about to be shut down. 'It doesn't seem right to me that on the same road, practically, as we have a food bank – that's people who can't afford to feed and clothe their families coming to us for the basic essentials – we also have a development of houses for the ultra-rich.'

There was a ripple of applause round the hall which grew loud enough that the councillor was forced to stand up and gesture with his hands for everyone to quiet down.

Emboldened by the applause, Dorothy stuck her own hand in the air, determined to bring matters back to the allotments.

'Dorothy Mackie, plot holder at the *Kenmar allotments*.' She shouted the last two words and was rewarded by a thunderous round of applause and a cheer from Isobel next to her, while Germaine ducked her head and hoped no one thought she was actually friends with either of them.

Dorothy continued. 'Are the council and the developers aware that these allotments have been part of this community for over twenty years? They've been home to the village garden festival, they've hosted any number of school and nursery trips, and they've provided fruit and veg for that food bank Iris mentioned. In fact, as my late husband used to say, they're at the very heart of anything good that every community should strive for. Are the people of Viewpark really being asked to give all that up so that a tiny number of rich folk can live it up, quaffing their Prosecco from a "state-of-the-art" fridge freezer' – the quote marks she attached to the phrase were palpable and the audience clapped – 'and peeing against a different toilet pan every day of the week? I mean, come on.'

There was a roar of applause and several people actually stood up and raised their hands to clap louder. Germaine looked up at Dorothy with grudging admiration.

The two developers had decided to cut their losses and were already making their way out of the hall. Councillor Murray watched them go with dismay and sank back into his own seat so quickly that he ripped the leg of his cheap grey suit on the wooden chair. Karen remained seated, inwardly delighted by the audience reaction, and watching approvingly as they got up from their seats in disgust and filed out of the hall.

'Mum.' A voice called in the dark from a blue Mini that was parked in front of the community centre.

Dorothy turned to see Maggi getting out of her car, her face quickly turning pink in the evening air.

'Maggi. What are you doing here?'

'You asked me to come and pick you up. Don't you remember? You wanted me to take you to Aldi as soon as the meeting was finished?'

'Never mind Aldi,' said Dorothy, turning to catch the other allotment holders before they could get away. 'Mohid, Farah, stop right there please. Stanley, thank you. Germaine and Isobel, where are you headed off to so fast?'

'I've got to get home for George. I've left him on his own.' Isobel glanced at her watch.

'He'll be fine for another half-hour,' said Dorothy briskly. 'He's got your number, hasn't he?'

'Of course he has but—'

'Well then. Eh, excuse me, Kevin, I don't know where you're sloping off to, and you, Lawrence, stay where I can see you, thank you.'

The group huddled awkwardly together under the awning outside the hall. Farah shivered in her light jacket but in the face of Dorothy's insistence, leaving didn't seem to be an option.

'Right,' she said. 'What are we going to do about this?'

'Do?' Germaine's fleeting admiration for the woman had already been replaced with something bordering on dislike.

'Yes, what's the plan? How are we going to make sure we keep what's rightfully ours?'

Germaine was at a loss and looked to the others for support.

But before anyone else could speak, Dorothy took charge. 'Right. Rolling Barrel, everyone. Follow me.'

16

THE PUB WAS FIVE MINUTES' walk along the road, but to Kevin, it felt more like twenty, with Germaine grumbling every step of the way.

'I don't go into pubs,' she was saying, but Dorothy was having none of it and pushed aside all objections. Isobel didn't dare bring up George and Isaac again and in any case, part of her was thrilled to be going out with other adults on a Monday night.

Kevin didn't go into pubs either. Without his mum to remind him he was imagining things, he felt like an exotic animal in a zoo, sure that everyone was staring and trying not to stare. But maybe it would be all right if he stayed in the middle of the group. He kept glancing at Maggi, who was marching a few steps ahead of the rest of them, the orange chiffon scarf she'd tied round her hair lighting the way for everyone. He tried to think of things he could say to her but all he could come up with was 'I like your scarf', which didn't seem to cut it. Lawrence walked beside him, saying Adrian wouldn't like him having alcohol on a week night.

'Adrian's not here, is he?' said Stanley gruffly, limping slightly as he walked on Lawrence's other side. 'Besides, you're a grown man, you can make your own choices.'

Lawrence hadn't thought of that.

'Remember you're on an early tomorrow,' Farah was whispering to Mohid, her hand clasping his tightly as they walked at the back of the group.

'We can leave after one drink,' he said, putting his arm round his wife to shelter her from the sudden breeze as cars whooshed past them on the top road.

The Rolling Barrel was dead, even for a Monday night.

Germaine insisted on accompanying Mohid and Dorothy to the bar, to make sure they got her drink right, she said. Mohid felt sure he could manage to get her the glass of Coke she wanted but she insisted. She seemed nervous, or jumpy, not her usual domineering self anyway, so he hadn't argued the point.

A young girl was lolling against the bar, scrolling down her phone, her hand reaching into the sharing bag of Doritos beside her on the counter every few seconds, her eyes never leaving the screen.

Germaine was not impressed. She stood for a few moments saying nothing, hoping her laboured breathing and strong presence would do the trick. Nothing. The girl kept scrolling and crunching and reaching and crunching and scrolling.

Slap.

The palm of Germaine's large hand, still faintly earthy after the day's digging, whacked the counter top and made the girl jump.

'Are you serving or just decorating the place?'

The girl sniffed, seemingly not in the least put out by the distraction. 'Welcome to the Rolling Barrel, my name's Chelsea, what can I get you?' Her voice was monotone, as she glanced behind Germaine to see Mohid and Dorothy bringing up the rear.

'A pint of Coca-Cola for me. In a long pint glass, not the one with a handle, ice, two slices of lemon, no pips, and proper Cola please, none of that disgusting diluting syrup which has as much in common with Coca-Cola as I have with Cindy Crawford.' Germaine turned to Mohid and Dorothy. 'That's me ordered, you can get the rest,' and left to take her seat with the others at the large oval table at the window.

'No wonder she wanted to come and order her own,' said Mohid but Dorothy didn't reply as she was busy checking the list on her phone which had everyone else's order on it. Mohid was impressed. 'Very professional.'

'Someone's got to take charge.' Dorothy scanned her list for a moment longer before giving Mohid the side-eye. 'I hope you don't mind me saying this but – I always thought your lot didn't drink. Part of your religion, I thought?'

Mohid gave Dorothy one of his slow smiles. 'Many of us don't, but some of us do,' he said simply. 'Bit like your lot,' he added, with a wink.

Two bottles of icy Pils appeared on the counter, followed by Isobel's vodka, two small glasses of rosé for Farah and Lawrence, and a pint of cider and black, a murky concoction which Mohid hadn't seen since his student days.

'That's for me.' Dorothy lifted the pint glass and took a quick swig.

Mohid put the rest of the drinks on a tray. 'You take these over, I'll bring those two.' He indicated the pints of Guinness for Stanley and Maggi, sitting under the taps settling before being topped up.

He carried the last drinks over to the table and squeezed in at the corner, next to Farah. 'Give these to Stanley, will you?' He handed the bag of cheese and onion to Germaine to pass down the table to Stanley. He had to shout because the noise coming from their table was reaching school disco levels. Given their relative strangeness at the allotments during the day, Mohid was surprised by the gusts of laughter and unrelenting chatter round the table.

He took a sip of his Pils, refreshingly cold, and sat back, his hand on Farah's knee as they both looked round the table in silence. On Mohid's left was Germaine, who was shouting down to the bottom of the table where Dorothy sat, Kevin to her left. Next to Farah, and between her and Kevin, was Lawrence, and the two men were deep in conversation. Mohid was surprised, thinking the pair had little in common. Opposite Kevin, and casting small frequent glances in his direction, was Dorothy's daughter, Maggi. *Nice of her to come,* Mohid thought, *must be here to support her mother.* Isobel sat next to Maggi, quietly sipping her vodka and enjoying being out.

'Okay?' He nudged Farah on the shoulder, noticing she wasn't talking to any of the others.

'Oh yes.' She treated him to a rare gleaming smile. 'I'm enjoying listening in.'

As though this was her cue to put a stop to the hilarity, Dorothy banged her hand on the table and began the proceedings. 'Now that we're all settled in, let's talk about why we're here. And thank you, all, by the way, for agreeing to come and talk—'

'Didn't know there was an option.' Stanley wiped the Guinness froth from his top lip.

Dorothy ignored him. 'That meeting tonight was not a

consultation. There was no discussion, those rich guys want the land and they're going to take it, and never mind us and our poxy allotments. They think they're poxy, not me, to be clear.'

There was a silence, except for the sound of Stanley crunching his crisps. 'Sorry,' he said, looking up to find everyone staring at him.

'Never mind your crisps, Stanley, let's hear your ideas. You've had — what — ninety years on this planet, give us your wisdom on how we fight the bigwigs at the council.'

Stanley snorted and was going to carry on eating his cheese and onion when he realized they were waiting for him to come up with an idea. For the first time in, who knows how long, it seemed that a group of people actually wanted to hear what he had to say. They might not be quite so keen when he told them what he thought.

'Money,' he said slowly, putting down his crisps.

Dorothy gestured with her hand for him to continue.

'Money's the only thing that matters,' Stanley elaborated. 'Money trumps everything else — what people need, especially folk like us, what a community can benefit from, what even makes a community — it all crumbles to dust in the face of money. And that's what these guys have got, and that's why it doesn't matter what we do, or what we say, or what we want, those guys with money will win every time. That's what I've learned in my almost *eighty*' — he gave Dorothy a glare — 'years on this planet.' He picked up his crisps again and carried on crunching.

There was a silence as the rest of the group thought about what Stanley had said. Meanwhile, he finished his crisps and tied the empty packet into a tight tiny bow and placed it on the table.

'You did ask,' he said finally.

'I've got something to say.' Dorothy stood up suddenly to make her point. 'For background, let me tell you about Greenham Common.'

Maggi gave a theatrical sigh and rolled her eyes at Kevin. 'Here we go,' she mouthed at him across the table.

Dorothy ignored her daughter. 'It was about forty years ago now that I was driving to work when I was listening to a discussion about what the Greenham Common women were doing. Now, like everyone else, I knew these women were doing great things – giving up their jobs, going weeks, months some of them, without seeing their families, putting themselves in danger, I mean some of these policemen were absolute brutes, but these women, they put up with it all because they were determined to secure a better world for their children, one where nuclear weapons were not tolerated. Like most people, I supported them from afar. Sure, I dropped a few pence now and then into buckets at the supermarket to support their campaign, I signed any petitions that were put in front of me, I think one even made it to Downing Street—'

'Is there a point to this story, Mum, because I can't for the life of me see how this affects the allotments?'

Mohid and Isobel exchanged a look of agreement, Kevin busied himself shredding the label of his beer bottle, and Stanley looked round for more crisps.

'Yes, there is a point, I'm coming to that.' Dorothy reached down for a quick gulp of her pint of impossibly sweet cider and blackcurrant. 'So – what I couldn't believe on this radio station was this one man, Tory, naturally' – there she did get some signs of approval and a 'hear hear' from Stanley – 'who was basically ridiculing these women, saying it was all a waste of time and what was the point because the little people like them could never win over whatever it was the establishment wanted. Now, that could be nuclear weapons or closing down community facilities, right? Same point.'

'And?' Maggi still couldn't see where this was going.

'The point is, that attitude, that attempt at the complete obliteration of our right to complain, to campaign, to try and make things better, to refuse to hold nuclear weapons just because the powers that be wanted the country to hold them, that made me angry enough to go and join the Greenham Common women, and trust me, being part of that uprising was without a doubt the best experience of my life.'

'Apart from motherhood obviously,' said Maggi to no one in particular, and again, Dorothy ignored the interruption.

'A fine speech, Dorothy, and we're all very happy for you,' said Germaine drily, 'but again, how does that relate to the allotments?'

'The point is simply this,' said an exasperated Dorothy, sitting down at last and reaching again for her glass, 'the Greenham Common women didn't give in, they wouldn't be cowed and now we have no nuclear weapons!'

There was a small silence round the table until it was broken by a round of applause initiated by Isobel. The others joined in reluctantly, even as Farah leaned over and whispered in Mohid's ear, 'Nobody better tell her about Faslane.'

'Okay, I do understand where you're coming from, Dorothy, but what does that really mean in practical terms? We're hardly going to start a campaign to save the allotments.' Germaine looked round at the others and laughed.

No one else laughed with her.

'Oh come on, you're not serious?' she said.

'Never more so,' said Dorothy. 'Now for God's sake, are we going to let them walk all over us and shut down our allotments, or are we going to rise up and fight?'

Without waiting for an answer, she stood up and signalled to Maggi with the raising of her index finger that she should come and help her bring back more drinks. 'Nobody go anywhere,' she called back over her shoulder. 'There's a lot to discuss.'

Half an hour, and a great deal of chat and laughter later, Dorothy was sitting with a pad full of scribbles in front of her, several of the items on the list underlined.

'Order, order,' she called to quieten down their little group. In some ways, she wanted to let them carry on, they'd all swapped seats as this one got up for the toilet, or that one went back to the bar, and threads of conversations were twisting and snapping and knotting together again all around her. She'd never seen her fellow allotment holders getting on so well – Stanley was pointing his finger in Kevin's face as he made some point or other, Isobel was laughing at either one or both of them and making extravagant gestures with her hands, Mohid was discussing the meaning of 'revolution' with Germaine, and Farah and Maggi were deep in discussion about, well, lipstick it appeared, but never mind, at least they were all talking.

She raised her hand and they quietened down. 'Time for us to get back to matters in hand. I think we've all agreed the first thing we need to do is set up a petition. Agreed?'

The others nodded. Stanley said, 'Aye-aye, Captain' and Dorothy ignored him.

'I'll make up a rota of who can collect signatures and how

far they can travel. Not Stanley with all the walking involved, or Kevin obviously.'

'Why not Kevin?' Maggi frowned.

Kevin picked up his wheat beer and occupied himself by throwing his head back and finishing his drink in one.

There was a silence.

'Because of his . . . I mean because . . .' Dorothy blustered and the others shifted in their seats and fiddled with their drinks until Mohid supplied, 'I think she meant because Kevin can't drive, didn't you, Dorothy?'

Dorothy shot him a grateful look. 'Exactly! Exactly that. Thank you, Mohid.'

'We don't need to drive, these routes are all local, that's the point, isn't it, to get local people to sign.' Maggi was not willing to let her mother off the hook so easily.

'I'll go round the back of Birkenshaw if you like? Round where I live.' Kevin was too used to being dismissed, however well-meaning that dismissal, to be insulted.

'Perfect,' said Dorothy quickly. 'That'd be . . . great. Thank you, Kevin.'

Maggi winked at him and he blushed right down the unscarred side of his face, all the way into the collar of his *Chainsaw Man* T-shirt.

The others were also given their routes so that between them they were covering Birkenshaw, Viewpark and slightly beyond, up to the Bellshill roundabout, and most of Uddingston, including the new housing estates up the Bellshill Road, and along Main Street to Bothwell in one direction and the big Uddingston sign on Glasgow Road in the other.

'That's a lot of ground to cover.' Mohid hesitated. 'Just a

thought, and of course you know better than me, Dorothy, with your campaigning experience and everything, but would we not be better putting this online – you know, Facebook, Twitter, or X, or whatever they're calling it these days? Maybe Instagram too, all that sort of thing?'

'Thanks for the suggestion, but this is how we did it at Greenham. People prefer the personal touch, you'll see.'

Mohid exchanged a glance with Farah, but said nothing more.

'In terms of raising money—'

'What do we need money for?' asked Isobel.

'Well, for . . . I mean, all campaigns need money,' said Dorothy uncertainly. 'I thought maybe a Tesco bag pack? Same weekend as the signature collecting, what do you think?'

'G-g-great idea,' said Lawrence before Mohid could formulate his objections, and another item on Dorothy's ever-growing list of things to do was given a big tick.

At half past nine, Dorothy declared that the initial planning work was complete.

'Thank goodness for that.' Isobel was already searching for her anorak. 'Isaac and George have been alone together this past hour, I don't know who's supposed to be watching who. I'd better get back.'

The group took this as their cue to leave, and everyone gathered their things.

'Good work tonight,' called Dorothy, watching them pick up their jackets and bags and leave the pub one by one. 'The campaign to save Kenmar allotments is under way.'

Mohid had a sinking feeling that the plans for a petition and a bag pack were woefully inadequate and felt sure they were going to be disappointed. But he didn't want to be the one to burst everyone's bubble for the second time that night so he joined with the others in a general atmosphere of optimism and unusual community spirit. He helped Farah put on her jacket and hoped he would be proved wrong.

17

THE WEEKEND CAME ROUND AND a damp and overcast Saturday morning found Farah and Mohid meandering round the garden centre at the back of B&M, Mohid pushing an unfeasibly large trolley and Farah trailing behind trying to summon up some enthusiasm for the bare-root perennials and summer bulbs. Neither she nor Mohid had mentioned the night before, each skirting round the subject and neither willing to be the one to raise it again.

They'd gone to Mohid's brother's in Bellshill for dinner. Farah had always got along well with her husband's family, especially his brother Mustafa and then later, his young wife Priya. The two women would chat and confide in each other as they cubed potatoes and chopped garlic for supper, while the brothers talked about football. They had so much in common, both young Muslim women, traditional to a point, but also trying to navigate a new path for themselves that included a career and friends, and a life of their own. Although Farah suspected Mohid was more progressive than his younger brother in many ways, she loved and admired her brother-in-law nonetheless.

But things had changed since the babies had come along. Mustafa and Priya were now the parents of twin boys, two gorgeous, healthy toddlers – *surely more than any one couple deserved* was a thought that swirled at the back of Farah's mind and that even she had not examined closely – and it was hard sometimes to keep her boiling-hot jealousy from bubbling over. She'd watch as Mohid's brother ruffled the hair of one darling boy, or blew raspberries on the chubby belly of the other, delighted for the chance to show them off to his older brother who, in every other respect, had been the first to achieve, their whole lives. Farah would sneak glances at Mohid as he tried to walk the line between delight for his brother and care not to upset his wife, but the idea that he was deliberately not watching father and sons bond in order to spare her feelings was somehow worse than his being openly envious of Mustafa.

And of course it affected her relationship with Priya, whose life was now completely different. Farah understood the children needed all her sister-in-law's time and attention, but it was like she'd become a different person. She'd given up her job as a nurse immediately – 'But dear one, who else would take care of my darling babies?' she'd said when Farah questioned her choice – and her every waking hour was spent tending home and family.

'You need a night out occasionally,' Farah had chided gently.

'I've never been happier,' Priya insisted, keeping one eye on her husband as she said this.

'Yes, of course, I can see that, but even so, you need some life of your own too. I'm sure Mustafa still leaves the house when he feels like it.' Farah gave a small laugh.

'Farah.' Mohid shot her a warning glare.

Too late, Mustafa put down his samosa and said quietly, 'Please, Farah. Keep your envy in check, I beg you.'

Farah sat back as though she'd been stung. Later, her own kind Mohid had tried to smooth things over but his whispered 'She's tired, overwrought, the IVF has taken a lot out of her, failure again this month' only served to make her angrier than Mustafa's nasty barb.

'Farah, what about this one?' Mohid called to her from the potted plant display. He was holding up a blue begonia for her to consider.

'Blue? No, no, it would clash with my sunflowers, for one thing.'

Mohid was pleased to see her expression lighten for the first time that day. He wanted to apologize for his brother's behaviour the night before but thought it better to say nothing and hope for it all to blow over. 'You might be right,' he said. 'A pink one then?'

But Farah was no longer listening. Her eyes were fixed on the perfect family walking up the path opposite them. Mohid glanced at the woman in a floaty flowery skirt to his left, and the small waistcoated man walking arm in arm beside her. Farah had no time for either of them, her gaze was fully taken by the little girl, chuntering away happily to herself as she skipped up the path in front of the couple, a neon pink Dora rucksack hanging off one shoulder, a small yellow plastic pony in one hand and a cloth book, stained with blackcurrant juice, in the other. Her hair was a white-blonde bowl, a strong fringe reaching almost to her eyes. Of course, any child of theirs would look nothing like that but as Mohid watched Farah's eyes track the girl's every move, he knew she was visualizing her own babies at the same age, dressed in outfits carefully chosen by her, their hair worn in gleaming plaits like her own perhaps. He dropped the begonia back on to the shelf, knowing already the day would end in the same way it had in Capri, with the little sunshine girl.

Later, as they sat in the café, having purchased nothing in the end for their allotment, Mohid tried to persuade his wife to have a cake. 'Go on, have a Belgian bun, you know you want to.'

She sighed deeply and loudly.

'Farah—' he began.

'Don't. The thing is, it's always been bearable before, when there was the possibility. Even just that *possibility*, however infinitesimal, meant we could still hope, but now . . .'

'Anything's possible,' said Mohid, which was true but completely unhelpful, he knew.

They drank their tea in silence for a few moments and Mohid wondered how he could bring up the idea that had been on his mind for months now, when it had become clear, at least to him, that they weren't going to be able to have their own children, or not without some sort of miracle. Every day at the hospital, he saw things that he would never be able to unsee – terrible cruelties inflicted on children, babies sometimes. He and Farah, they had so much love to give, why couldn't they give some of it to children like that? Children whose lives they could transform, save, even, in some cases. He glanced across the table, taking in Farah's clenched shoulders and the tightness of her jaw. Today wasn't the day for that discussion.

She stood up suddenly, adopting a determined cheeriness which made her look like Mohid imagined she did when she was being stern but fair with her pupils. 'Right, that's it. Now we know what we're dealing with, let's put that behind us and get on with everyday things.'

'Are you sure?' he said. 'We could go home now and—'

'No.' Farah was firm. 'Let's get on with the jobs of the day, let's keep things moving, Mohid.'

Mohid stood up and gave her a small kiss on the forehead. 'I love you.'

'I love you too, husband. We are lucky.'

They went straight to the allotments and were surprised to find no one was there, except perhaps Stanley in his shed. It wasn't until later that Mohid remembered they were all supposed to be out collecting signatures for Dorothy's petition. He checked out of the window to see what his wife was doing and saw she was watering and feeding her precious sunflowers.

One of the first things she'd done when they were given the allotment was to plant those three sunflowers. Having done her homework – she was a teacher after all – she'd sown the seeds in little clay pots at the start of April, and stored them on the window ledge in their kitchen to keep them safe from slugs and snails until they could be planted outside. She'd watered them daily, and together, they'd watched as the slim green shoots shot up through the moist earth. When they were strong enough, she'd carefully transported them to the allotment and planted them lovingly in a row of three in the narrow strip of soil in front of their shed. On sunny days, they leaned their faces towards the sun and Farah worried the soil would dry out. When it rained, she was concerned they'd become waterlogged. She fussed and fretted, but watched with delight as they thrived, and Mohid's heart ached for her.

Let the others collect signatures for the petition, he thought, putting on the kettle to make his wife a cup of her favourite green tea. He and Farah would stay here, tending their plot, until the council told them otherwise.

18

It was almost lunchtime and Stanley plodded round his shed, boiling the kettle for the third time that day. He'd been at the allotment since before first light, following another sleepless night. Except it couldn't have been completely sleepless because he'd started awake at one point, sweating and crying out after a vivid and disturbing dream about Mabel. They'd been sitting on their favourite bench down by the Clyde, enjoying an ice cream from Anne's Pantry, when he'd glanced over at her and found she was entirely blue. He'd reached out to touch her and she'd slid down the bench and toppled off the edge onto the cold hard ground, stone dead, her strawberry ice-cream cone lying uneaten beside her. He still couldn't get the image out of his head hours later.

His stomach was sour. He hadn't had breakfast and was beginning to feel light-headed with lack of food. Perhaps a Tunnock's teacake was what he needed, he thought. He was searching for the half-full box he'd brought with him yesterday when there was a small rap on his shed door. Stanley clicked his tongue against his teeth. There was an unwritten rule at the allotments that once a person was in their shed, you did not disturb them. At least that was Stanley's rule and if it was up to him people wouldn't be allowed to engage you in conversation while you were on the land either. Unfortunately, these things were never up to him and the gentle knocking sounded again.

It was the boy from across the path. He hadn't seen much of him since they'd had a go at playing chess a couple of weeks ago. The boy had been surprisingly good, learning the ways the pieces moved round the board very quickly and even trying out a couple of basic opening moves. Stanley had liked the boy's attitude. He'd been quiet, but listening, trying his best, he'd reminded him a lot of Brian at the same age. Stanley thought he could end up being a worthy opponent in time. But from his absence, he gathered the boy wasn't as keen to keep on learning as Stanley had been to teach him.

'Lad,' he said, in a tone that he hoped made clear he was not in the mood for company.

The boy sniffed. His hands were behind his back, holding something Stanley couldn't see.

'Have you not got a handkerchief?' he said, as the boy continued to sniff and move his mouth around as though that could keep the mucus safely where it was.

'Can you help me with this?' He produced a shoebox from behind his back. It had been painted a lurid green.

'What is it? I mean, apart from being a shoebox, what's it supposed to be?'

'We've to make an Anderson shelter? From the war? You're old so I thought you'd know all about the war.'

Stanley laughed. 'I'm not that old, son, I don't remember the war.' He thought about it. 'Not really, but I do know what an Anderson shelter is. There was one still standing near where the allotments are now when I was a boy.'

'So will you help me? They're going to tell my mum if I don't hand this in. I haven't . . . been going to school much so they're kicking me out if I don't start doing the work. Not that I care,' he added defiantly, with a toss of his head so that his long wispy fringe fell away from his forehead then back into his eyes.

Stanley hesitated, then stood aside to let the boy in. 'I suppose so.'

He sat on Mabel's chair again, like it was his, so Stanley sat opposite, drawing the little card table between them and watching as the boy placed the box on it. They both studied it.

'Doesn't look much like an air raid shelter, does it?'

The boy stuck out his lower lip.

'Tell you what it needs – a roof.'

'Can you make a roof?' Isaac was already impressed and Stanley couldn't back down now – besides, he'd thought he was no use to anyone and yet here was this boy, asking for his help. 'Give me a minute to think,' he said. 'Here, have a teacake while I fetch the tea.' He got up, adding, 'And I said one, mind' just as Isaac was stuffing the first teacake whole into his mouth, and reaching his skinny hand out for the second.

An hour later and the thing was finished.

'How about that then?' Stanley stuck his chin out as he admired what they'd made.

On the table between them was a miniature version of the old Anderson shelter Stanley remembered from his childhood. They'd taken the lid off the box, which Isaac had already painted green, and used that for the base. Stanley had cleaned out an old coffee container and then helped Isaac to cut it in half – that was Isaac's favourite bit, the destruction, kids never changed –

and they'd stretched that across the lid and attached it so that it became a dome on top of grass.

'We could pick some old twigs and leaves and attach them to the lid so it looks like the shelter's sitting in the ground?' suggested Isaac, his cheeks pink and his eyes brighter than Stanley had ever seen them.

'Excellent idea, son,' he said, and drank another cup of tea while the boy gathered up what he needed from the path and round the shed, and stuck them on with some ancient Gorilla glue Stanley had found at the back of his tool drawer. The results were perfect.

'This reminds me of the time I tried to make a banner for Mabel's fiftieth.' Stanley was gluing a small dried beech leaf to the model.

'Do you still have birthdays at fifty?'

'Oy! What do you mean – do you still have birthdays – of course you do. Fifty's no age, still young, half your life to go, if you're lucky . . .'

'So what happened? To Mabel's banner I mean?'

'I wanted to make it special, you see, so I painted on this huge white sheet – "Happy 50th birthday Mabel" – to drape across the window. I thought she'd wake up and I'd go ta-dah and she'd be so pleased. But . . .'

'Did you forget to do it?'

'No, I didn't forget. But by the time she went to bed, it was that late it was too dark for me to see. I stuck the ladder into the ground outside the front window and climbed up it. I hung the sheet, it covered the whole window, looked great in fact, but . . . when I came down and tried to take the ladder away, it slipped from my hands and crashed into the front window and smashed it.'

Isaac's mouth fell open.

'Exactly.' Stanley shook his head at the memory. 'I can laugh now but at the time, can you imagine – middle of the night, Mabel's out in her nightie shouting what the hell, Stanley, sheet flapping between us in the wind, the neighbours called the police thinking we'd been burgled. Complete disaster.'

'Was Mabel angry?'

Stanley thought for a moment. 'Do you know, she was at first but after we'd patched up the window with a bit of cardboard, we sat in the kitchen, freezing, and she made us a hot chocolate to heat us up and we ended up having one of the best nights ever, we never laughed so much. She said it would always be a birthday to remember and—' The tears arrived so unexpectedly that Stanley didn't realize he was crying until the boy fished out a crumpled tissue from his pocket and handed it to him.

He wiped his eyes. 'Memory can be a cruel master, son.'

'What does that mean?' said Isaac, rubbing his nose and reaching out for a third teacake.

'Ach, don't mind me. And how many of those biscuits have you had?'

The boy grinned and didn't answer.

'What are you doing now then?' It was past Stanley's usual lunchtime and he was ready to go home and snooze in front of the telly but the boy seemed so happy he didn't want to leave him on his own.

'I don't know. My mum's . . . not feeling well today.'

'You could go and help with the bag pack?' Stanley suggested. 'I think that's today. Or is it the petition?' Despite the fuss created by the notice that remained pinned to the noticeboard about the threatened closure, Stanley couldn't bring himself to seriously consider the allotments being closed down. They were too important to too many people, not least Stanley. Sometimes though, when he couldn't sleep at night, he'd remember that they'd already closed down the youth club, the men's mental health shed, and even one of Mabel's beloved dance clubs. Why should the allotments be any different?

Isaac broke into his thoughts. 'I don't want to talk to people doing their shopping.'

Stanley was inclined to agree. Dorothy and the others were on top of things, he reasoned, and he was too old to stand about a supermarket helping people younger and fitter than him to pack their shopping. And he certainly wasn't going to weave his way round the neighbourhood asking folk to sign a petition to save what was already rightfully his. He could see the boy felt the same way. 'No, you're right, lad, what's the point? Let's leave it to the rest of them, what will be will be.'

'Could play chess?' Isaac said quietly, not meeting Stanley's eye as he picked fluff off his sleeve.

Stanley was about to ask, 'Are you sure your mum won't mind? Does she know you're here?' when it occurred to him that maybe he could do the poor woman a favour and take care of the boy for a few more hours, let her enjoy a day of peace. She could go shopping, or bake a cake, have a coffee and a natter with her pals, or do any of the things Mabel used to enjoy doing. He'd be helping her out. Feeling the pleasure of being needed for a change, he said, 'So we could, son', thinking too that if he did without an afternoon nap he'd be more likely to sleep for a change tonight. He reached up for the chessboard. 'Okay, the winner gets that last— Oh, for goodness' sake, Isaac.'

The box of teacakes was empty.

19

AT AROUND THE SAME TIME as Isaac was polishing off the last of Stanley's teacakes, Isobel was at home pulling on the same nylon stretch leggings she'd had on the day before, trying not to notice their frowsy smell or the faded coffee stain extending most of the way down one of the legs. She picked up a sweatshirt from the pile in the corner by the door, sniffed it under the arm and decided it would do. Without facing the mirror, she ran her hand through her unruly hair – she really should get it cut, she thought, but when? – and decided she would brush her teeth later.

She climbed the few stairs to the half landing to do a quick check on Isaac. The tiny room, with its ceiling sloping under the eaves, was empty. Isobel had a faint memory of hearing the front door slam shut while she slept and felt momentary guilt at not knowing where her son was. But then she reasoned, he was eleven, and had probably gone round to one of his friends' houses. As to who those friends might be, she had no real clue as her son no longer shared that sort of information with her. Still, it was the weekend and better that he spend it outdoors having fun than shut in here with her and George.

She sat on the edge of Isaac's bed, throwing the duvet back

in some semblance of order. She knew she should change his wooden Thomas the tank engine bed for something more age-appropriate, even if Isaac was small enough still at eleven for his legs to fit into this bed for much younger children. No wonder he never brought any friends home – how could he have them up here? she thought, taking in the long-discarded toys – the dusty fort, once much-prized and played with, now home to a long-forgotten army of knights and wizards, a dirty old SpongeBob plushy, and two decapitated bobblehead figures. There was broken plastic everywhere. She had to get on top of this, make time to clear out all his old toys and replace them with whatever it was that interested him these days.

She glanced out of the small window under the eaves, the rain leaving slug trails down its greasy panes. It was a dreich, dreary day of the type at which Scotland excels, everywhere damper than a used teabag, rain dripping off gutters and the sun making the odd appearance to be put back in its place half an hour later. So much for June, Isobel blew out her cheeks in despair. Maybe it was the night out with other people who could talk and communicate and laugh, reminding her of everything she was missing with George, but she'd been in a grey mood ever since that evening at the Rolling Barrel with the rest of the allotment holders. In fact, she hadn't summoned up the energy to go to the allotments since. And what was the point if the council was intent on closing the place down and throwing them all off the land? Even George hadn't wanted to go, hadn't wanted to leave the house at all as his speech was becoming more and more garbled, his vocabulary diminishing by the day. Isobel took another look round the messy little room, smelling the damp and aware of the lack of loving care reflected by the outdated décor. No, today was not the day for clear-outs and fresh starts.

She heard a sudden thud from somewhere else in the house. George.

Isobel heaved herself off the bed and trudged down the stairs, dreading what was going to greet her in the kitchen.

George was standing by the open fridge, a box of eggs in his hand.

'Are you hungry, George? Do you want me to make you something?'

George turned, his eyes searching her face urgently, and she knew he was running through a list of possibilities in his mind. Who was this woman in the doorway, he was wondering, his mother maybe, he often forgot she was dead, or the nice lady who served him in Scotmid, or one of the annoying social workers who treated him like he'd lost his mind as well as the ability to communicate? Isobel flushed as she saw the recognition glimmer in his eyes. He'd remembered it was his wife, who was always angry with him and never had time to talk.

'Break,' he said, pointing to the eggs. 'Break.'

'Breakfast, for goodness' sake.' Isobel grabbed the box from his hand and pushed him towards the chair at the kitchen table.

She bustled around, getting out the butter for toast and putting teabags in cups in front of the kettle. She didn't speak to George as she watched the eggs poaching in the big frying pan with the white handle they'd bought on that trip to Skye one time. Must have been their last holiday before Isaac came along, she thought, watching the eggs turn white and a pale skin shroud the yolks. She remembered how they'd walked for hours across long deserted beaches, going back to make love in their overheated hotel room in the middle of the afternoon before heading downstairs late every evening for dinner in the cosy dining room. Her hand gripped the pan as she dished up the eggs.

She put the plates on the table and placed her hands on George's shoulders before she sat down beside him. 'Sorry, George, I'm sorry for snapping at you.'

'Break. Nng.' George turned his head to kiss his wife's fingers, delighted to see her smiling again.

After they'd eaten their eggs, Isobel got up to clear the plates and suddenly remembered she'd agreed to help Dorothy and the others collect signatures for the petition. She was about to suggest to George they could use it as an opportunity to go out and get some fresh air when she heard the post land on the hall floor.

She feared the worst when she saw her school's insignia on the envelope and ripped it open, reading the brisk paragraph standing in the hall, among the piles of scraggy winter coats and cracked old wellies. The headmaster informed her, on behalf of South Lanarkshire council, that if she called in sick again with no doctor's note, they would have no option but to suspend her without pay.

'George, wait till you hear this – can they do that?' she called to her husband. She heard a crash and when she returned to the kitchen, George was standing by the open fridge, saying 'Break' and what remained of the eggs lay smashed in a jeering yellow puddle on the floor.

'For God's sake, George!' She slammed the fridge door shut,

pushed him back into his chair and told him to stay there while she cleared up the mess.

Throwing the letter from the school on to the surface beside the kettle, she thought the petitions and bag packs could go to hell. Let the others who had easier lives than her do all that stuff, she had more important things to worry about.

20

Lawrence was finishing off his muesli at the breakfast bar while Adrian was upstairs exercising. Adrian had left the oats soaking in the fridge overnight, so all Lawrence had to do this morning was add some chopped nuts and raisins, pour the soya milk, and top it with Greek yoghurt.

'And don't forget to take your moju shot,' he'd said before he went up to do his forty-five minutes on the rowing machine in their spare room. 'That's what's going to raise your energy levels and maybe even help you get rid of your little pot.'

He'd bent down and kissed Lawrence's midriff to show he was joking and that he loved Lawrence's not-quite-flat stomach really, but Lawrence wished he wouldn't feel the need to point it out quite so often. They couldn't all have abs like supermodels, or Adrian himself for that matter.

He chewed his cereal diligently, trying not to think about a Greggs cappuccino and pain au chocolat which was the breakfast he'd much rather be having. He flicked through his phone, checking the news – boring; his bank statement – terrifying; the *Daily Mail* celebrity news page – embarrassing that he was interested; and finally, sat back and kicked his feet until Adrian came back down to chat.

Right on cue, forty-five minutes later, Adrian came into the kitchen with a white Dolce and Gabbana towel round his neck and a tall glass of water in his hand. He tensed his six-pack when he saw Lawrence glance over, and laughed when he was abashed at being caught staring.

'What are we doing today then?' he said, as he sat down to his own bowl of the dreaded muesli.

'Don't tell me you've forgotten?'

Adrian raised his plucked and dyed eyebrows. 'Enlighten me.'

'We're going to collect signatures for the petition. We've got the Moorlands estate and the houses in front of Muiredge Primary.'

Adrian put his spoon down. 'Lawrence, sweetheart, I did not agree to spend my Saturday doing that.'

'You did! Remember, after I came back from the Rolling Barrel that night, I told you, we all agreed we would fight the closure and Dorothy—'

'Is that the mad woman in the dungarees or the other old biddy with the hair like an outsized brillo pad?'

Lawrence laughed but quickly followed it with, 'That's not nice, they're our friends.'

'Oh come on, that's pushing it, we hardly know them.'

'You mean *you* don't because on the very odd occasion you come to the allotments you never make the effort to speak to anyone.'

'That's not true, I'm always perfectly nice to them.'

'Who do you chat to?'

Adrian thought for a moment. 'I said hello to the young guy the other day, from the top allotment, you know the one with . . .' Adrian made a vague gesture towards his face.

Lawrence did not help him out.

'You know who I mean,' said Adrian impatiently. 'What do you think happened to his face? It's quite horrific, isn't it, the eye and everything, it's—'

Lawrence couldn't bear to hear any more. 'Don't, Adrian. He can't help it.'

'I'm not saying he can, but come on, you can't seriously claim you don't find it off-putting.'

As a make-up artist, Kevin was used to imperfections but he'd never seen a face so imperfect as Kevin's, and yet, in all honesty, he didn't find it off-putting. There was something about Kevin – his sweet nature, the calmness of his manner, the way he pottered around his plot seemingly oblivious to life's constant trials and struggles. And when you saw him almost every day, the way Lawrence did, you hardly even noticed his face. Perhaps that's why he'd been so shocked the previous week.

He'd been walking along Main Street to pick up some sushi for lunch when he heard the rumpus on the other side of the road. There was a small group of kids, teenagers not children, all dressed in sports gear though Lawrence doubted any of them had seen the inside of a gym in their life. Kevin was coming out of Marini's – how did he stay so slim if he ate chips for lunch, a mystery to Lawrence – and he'd almost bumped into them on the pavement.

'Oy, freak, watch where you're putting that face of yours, it could scare young kids,' the stocky lad in the red Nike shouted, his face close enough to Kevin's face for it to feel threatening.

Lawrence stopped, considering whether to cross over.

Kevin put his head down and carried on walking.

'Oy!' shouted the boy again to Kevin's retreating figure.

Lawrence wasn't sure whether he always walked that fast or whether he was half-sprinting to get away from his tormentors. 'Folk like you shouldn't be allowed out the house.'

The others laughed and cheered, and Lawrence could hear the cries of 'Gorgeous Kevin' following Kevin down the street. He knew he should go over and say something, he almost did, then the leader of the gang caught his eye. Lawrence was suddenly aware of the delicate way he walked, the high voice in which he talked, the brightness of his Armani sweater, the tightness of his jeans, and so, to his shame, he said nothing and walked on, still half aware of Kevin, taking the steps up to the bank two at a time and dashing towards the park.

Of all people who should have stepped in and helped, Lawrence owed it to Kevin. Even if Kevin didn't remember, Lawrence did. That time at school, when they'd all been sledging at the gulley. He'd been much heavier then, and for some reason, his parents had allowed him to dress as he pleased which in this case meant his bulky frame was squeezed into a skintight white and silver snowsuit. Really he was asking for all he got. Except – Kevin wouldn't allow it. When he'd come upon those thugs pushing him and jeering at him and his ridiculous outfit, he'd marched right into the circle surrounding him and let them have it. Bigger than the rest of them and angry too, he'd made short work of any pushback, and as they scarpered, he'd shouted after them not to bother coming back. 'Okay?' he'd asked Lawrence, as he helped him up from the slushy wet ground. 'Ignore them, they're assholes. Maybe get a new tailor though,' he'd laughed and Lawrence eventually had to laugh too. Kevin had stood up for him that day and he'd never forgotten it.

And yet, he'd stood by and done nothing as those kids had

tormented Kevin in exactly the same way. He'd been thinking about it ever since, but there didn't seem any way to explain how he felt to Adrian. 'He's not off-putting,' he said instead. 'It's just the way he is. Not everyone can be perfect like you, you know.'

Adrian looked up sharply, unused to criticism from Lawrence, however faint. 'Off-putting or not, I am not spending my Saturday traipsing round some godforsaken new housing estate, begging strangers to sign a petition for a cause I don't even believe in.'

'I love our allotment,' said Lawrence, but in a quieter voice, and biting the nail on his index finger uncertainly. 'I don't want the council to close it down, I'd really miss it.'

'I know.' Adrian swiped Lawrence's hand away from his mouth. 'But all those other plot holders feel the same way and they've got nothing better to do than go door to door collecting signatures. Don't worry about it, they'll make sure the petition is done.'

'You're probably right about that,' said Lawrence, brightening. 'The others will all show up. Let's you and me do something together then.'

'Right decision. I'll buzz Mark and see if he and Simon are up for lunch at Rosso's. Then I'm going to head to the gym for a sauna this afternoon.' Adrian paused. 'You should too, keep that little belly of yours in check,' he said, joking but also not.

Lawrence sighed, as he watched Adrian grab the bar on the door frame and lift himself up to do his daily one hundred pull-ups.

21

GERMAINE HAD BEEN FEELING OKAY all week, had scarcely even thought about her dad and everything that happened before she moved here. The uncertainty surrounding the allotments and Dorothy's plans to fight the council had taken up all her energy and given her other things to think about.

It was the jam that pushed her over.

She was having a slice of toast before heading out to knock on doors on Old Edinburgh Road, starting with the new estate opposite the community centre, as instructed by their self-appointed campaign leader, Dorothy. Germaine's allocated area wasn't far from the allotments so she'd decided that when she'd collected a hundred signatures, or when she was fed-up being pleasant to people, whichever came first, she would head down to her allotment. She planned to get on with weeding that little area of no-man's land between her plot and the fairy garden which was getting overgrown enough to annoy her. It wasn't her responsibility but she had this vague idea that if the allotments were kept pristine and thriving, the council might think twice about bulldozing over their efforts. She could only try.

And that's when she noticed the jam pot was empty. It was finished, gone – the last of the last batch her dad had made with his home-grown strawberries. He'd made twelve jars every year, one jar for every month until the new batch was made the following year. Germaine's job was to label each pot, always the same – 'Bernard's Strawberry Delight' and the date – but both had become smudged and difficult to read.

Something snapped. She threw the lid of the jar against the kitchen wall then stood up and pushed over the kitchen chair so that it landed on the floor behind her with a clatter. What was the point? She might as well— She placed the palms of her hands flat against the kitchen table and breathed deeply, waiting for the surge of anger to pass, as she'd been taught. Gradually, her breathing returned to normal and she picked up the chair and replaced the sticky lid on to the empty jar. 'Come on, Germaine,' she whispered to herself. She'd been doing so well for the last year and finishing her dad's jam wasn't going to be the thing that broke her.

She found the nearest meeting online but her heart dipped a little when she saw how close it was to the allotments. The Tannochside Senior Citizens' Club, right next to the paper shop where she often bought rolls and milk on her way to the allotment. What if anyone saw her? But it was either take that risk, or spend the day travelling up to Aberdeen to the meeting she'd been attending before she moved to Viewpark. She tapped her fingers off the edge of the kitchen table for a few seconds then made up her mind. She grabbed her jacket and walked briskly along to Tannochside.

The hall looked shuttered from the outside but the main door was open. 'Hello?' she called from the doorway. No answer. There was a noticeboard to her left along the narrow passage so she walked towards it to check if the meeting was still on.

'Line dancing in the main hall at half past,' she read. 'God, as if. Wait, there it is.' Beneath the brightly coloured posters variously advertising dancing clubs and toddlers' groups, giving the times of a mothers and babies Zumba class in Bothwell, and one proclaiming that God's way was the only way, she spotted the scrappy grey notice headed 'Birkenshaw Fresh Start', and yes, there it was, they were meeting in the small committee room in ten minutes. Glancing all round to make sure no one had seen her, Germaine made her way slowly along the corridor to the open door at the end.

The room was empty when she walked in but the semicircle of chairs in the middle of the space reassured her she was in the right place. She perched on the edge of a wooden chair at the very end of the circle nearest the door and took some deep breaths.

In the end there were six of them, including the group's leader, Yvette, a tiny woman with a shaved head and tie-dye kaftan. The chap sitting next to Germaine had introduced himself as Pablo Escobar, presumably on account of his ridiculous moustache, or perhaps as a nod to the unmistakable skunky scent of weed which grew stronger as the room heated up and he started to sweat. The meeting began and she tried to ignore the smell and concentrate instead on the scruffy young man at the other end of the semicircle, who'd said his name was Tam. He was skinny, the way drinkers often are, but he might have been handsome once. It was hard to tell behind the thick-rimmed glasses and the sneer. He was looking fixedly at the floor as he talked about the guilt he felt at not taking better care of his niece.

'We need to let go of guilt after a while, don't we, Tam – we were talking about that last week, do you remember?'

The man said he had been drinking less and keeping better company.

'That's very positive. Keep building on that,' said Yvette, smiling encouragingly round the room. 'Anyone else care to share today? Simon?'

Pablo Escobar/Simon grunted and glared at the wooden floorboards. He was clearly not feeling it today, Germaine thought, probably still high on—

'What about you – you're new to the group today, aren't you? Would you like to share anything with us?'

Germaine snapped her head round. 'Me?'

'Only if you'd like to?'

Germaine pursed her lips. 'My name's Germaine.' She paused. 'And . . . and I've got a drink problem.'

'We're all here to support you, Germaine,' said Yvette softly.

'I mean . . . I haven't had a drink for a year and a day.'

'Well done. Everyone, I think that deserves a round of applause.'

Pablo, Tam, and the two washed-out women in the middle of the circle clapped their hands together with varying levels of enthusiasm. The woman closest to Yvette struggled a bit as she was clutching a small fidget spinner which she whirred round between index finger and thumb the whole time but Germaine was touched to see she did her best to clap along with the others. She scratched her head and continued, 'Thing is, I don't really deserve praise or anything. It was something I had to do – quit after my dad died – because . . . I killed him, you see.'

She could tell she had even Pablo's attention now, as he looped his arm over the back of his chair to face her, the sweat patch under his thin cotton shirt big as an autumn puddle.

'I mean, not actually kill him' – she could sense Pablo's disappointment but carried on – 'what I mean is, he asked me to pick him up from an OAP darts tournament he was at, and I said I would but . . . then I started drinking, one cider I thought, but then I had a few more and . . . you know how it is' – Tam and the two women grimaced in shameful solidarity – 'and . . . I forgot to pick him up.'

'You did the right thing not to drive though if you'd been drinking,' said one of the women, her skin creased like paper with all available bodily fluids apparently having migrated to her rheumy drinker's eyes.

'Yes, that's true but I forgot all about him, I didn't tell him I wasn't coming to pick him up so he had no option. He was eighty-two, how else could he have got home? He took a lift from one of his mates who'd also been drinking. Maybe not as much as me but enough that he shouldn't have been driving and they . . . they crashed.' Germaine put her hand on her leg to stop it from shaking.

The room was silent, except for the low purr of the whirring fidget spinner.

'That wasn't an easy story to share, Germaine, thank you. And a year into your sober journey is an achievement you should be proud of.' She rewarded Germaine with a wide smile. 'We're going to take a quick coffee break and then we'll talk more about coping strategies that have already worked for some of our members.'

Germaine joined the queue at the counter, then took her small plastic cup back to her chair and sank the oily black coffee like her life depended on it.

When they were putting their jackets on after the meeting had finished, she suddenly remembered she hadn't collected any signatures for the petition. She pulled the blank sheet from her bag and asked the others if they'd mind signing it. 'Make the most of every opportunity,' her dad's familiar voice hummed in her ears, as they all appended their names, hardly caring what it was they were signing.

She was putting the sheet back into her bag and heading out the door when she spotted her next-door neighbour, an annoyingly friendly woman named Sue, with a passionate overenthusiasm for life which caused Germaine to avoid her whenever possible. She put her head down and hoped for the best.

'Germaine!'

Too late.

'Hello! I thought it was you. I've hardly seen you at the weekends since you moved in, aren't you usually away at the garden centre or something?'

'My allotment, yes,' said Germaine. 'If you'll excuse me . . .'

'But what are you doing here? Apart from us, there's only the AA meeting in here on a Saturday so that must mean . . .'

Germaine could feel her cheeks burning and she waited for her neighbour to put two and two together.

'. . . you've finally decided to take me up on my offer of joining us at the line dancing?!'

'Line dancing?' said Germaine faintly. 'I . . .'

Her neighbour's grin was now wide enough to appear demonic. There was nothing else for it.

'Yeeees. Line dancing, that's it. I came to . . . try out the line dancing. Can't wait,' she said, her heart tumbling as she saw a group of twenty or so women gathered in the main hall, some in cowboy hats, others holding lassos and already practising their Yee-hahs. 'How long does it last, out of interest?'

'Only two hours, you'll be fine, don't worry, your fitness levels will soon improve after you've been two or three times. Brilliant! Everyone, this is my next-door neighbour, Germaine! She's here to join our line dancing club!'

'Yee-hah,' muttered Germaine under her breath. 'Thank goodness all the others will be out in force collecting signatures for the petition because there is no way I am going door-to-door after this.'

Billy Ray Cyrus gave it his all, and Germaine took a deep breath and prayed her own achy breaky heart would last the pace.

22

HE'D BEEN UP FOR HALF an hour and already Kevin felt the need of a strong coffee. It wasn't just that the thought of knocking on strangers' doors and asking them to sign their petition to save the allotments was giving him heart failure – although it was and he'd been dreading it all week. It was also down to his having necked three bottles of Lidl's fake German beer the night before. Lidl's beer was every bit as good as Warsteiner's, in Kevin's opinion – and he knew a thing or two about beer – but the problem was that each (large) bottle was 7 per cent proof, much higher than Kevin liked and guaranteed to give him a hangover like the one he was currently fighting. Which was why he was prepared to stand patiently in the dozen-long queue at Greggs for his extra strong Americano – twice as good as Starbucks and half the price. Again, coffee and the strength and price thereof were things he felt sure he knew as much if not more about than the next person and he was quite prepared to stake his reputation (known solely to him) on that fact.

They'd had a refit in Greggs, he noticed, as the queue inched towards the counter. The sitting-in area had been removed in favour of a station for JustEat drivers to come in and collect their orders. *Who on earth would call JustEat for a coffee?* thought

Kevin, but the presence of the area and the fact that there were two drivers standing there waiting to fill their hot bags with orders indicated that many people did. This was part of what was wrong with teenagers today, he thought. On the bus, he'd listen in to the conversations between the old women who went back and forth to their dancing clubs, the bingo, coffee mornings at the church, you name it, and they had to be seventy if they were a day and yet, the vitality! Their non-stop chatter about this one who'd had their hair restyled – 'It's not everyone that can carry off curls as tight as that, mind' – and that one whose husband had 'shuffled off to meet his maker', and what they'd had for dinner last night – 'a gorgeous wee one-pot stew, looked exactly like that Jamie Oliver's, maybe better' – and what they were having for dinner tonight – 'leftovers, what else?' – and the routines and minutiae of their daily lives were fascinating to Kevin. The laughter, the ribbing, the general hilarity that accompanied each of their trips. And you knew, just knew for a fact, that none of those women would dream of calling up Greggs or Domino's or Starbucks or McDonald's to have food and drink delivered. Their food and drink went hand in hand with human company, which was their real sustenance and why they'd lived the long happy lives they had. Kevin always eyed them enviously as he made his way to the allotments.

'Next . . . *Neeext!*'

'Oh sorry,' said Kevin. 'That must be me.' The girl behind the counter didn't bat an eyelid when she saw him, he was in three or four times a week after all, but the young lad in front of him did a double take, then pretended to be examining the contents of the fridge instead when Kevin caught his eye.

Kevin gave him a small smile of reassurance though he'd

often wondered when he practised facial expressions in the mirror whether maybe the ruched skin and trembling eyelid as he attempted his lopsided smile might make things worse but since he could hardly ask anyone that, he had no way of knowing. He thought the boy moved further along the counter than was strictly necessary to give Kevin room to order – he practically stood on the JustEat man who was leaning against the wall – but remembered his mum telling him he was imagining such reactions.

'An Americano please,' he said, shaking off his doubts. 'No, actually, I'll go for a cappuccino this morning please, large, and a roll and bacon as well.'

'Two minutes for the bacon,' said the girl in her sing-song voice, indicating he should stand to the side. 'Neeext.'

The boy had grabbed his steak bake and left, and Kevin took his place, keeping the scarred side of his face to the wall for the benefit of the group of teenage girls who'd walked in, squealing with laughter at something one of them had said.

He focused on the picture of coffee beans on the wall behind him and thought about the tasks waiting for him on his allotment. Probably about time he started bedding in those new geraniums, and he'd some more sweet peas to plant too. Part of him did wonder if it was worth starting work on anything new when the allotments might be closing down soon. He shook his head, he couldn't think about that today, he loved his allotment so much already.

'Chocolate on the cappuccino?'

'Yes please,' Kevin answered at the same time as the young woman being served after the group of girls.

'Sorry,' they both said, again at the same time.

The woman laughed. 'You were first, it must be yours.'

Kevin's heart did a little leap as he recognized Dorothy's daughter, Maggi, and wondered how he could have missed her. She was wearing thigh-hugging white jeans that flared at the knee and a black silk blouse beneath a white waistcoat à la Barry from the Bee Gees, circa 1979.

'Kevin, isn't it?'

Kevin couldn't believe she'd remembered his name. They both said, 'From the allotments' at the same time, then laughed as Maggi added, 'Jinx'.

'I hate to interrupt the love fest,' said the boy who was manning the coffee machine, 'but could we have the definitive decision on chocolate powder on the cappuccino some time before my shift finishes?'

Kevin was mortified but Maggi laughed again and said, 'Chocolate on both please' before turning to him and saying, 'You'd have to be a psychopath to go for full-fat cappuccino and save a few calories on the chocolate dust on top, am I right?'

Holding their paper cups of coffee, they left the shop and stood together on the pavement. Two young boys in Uddingston rugby strips passed them and the one closest to Kevin gave an audible low whistle when he saw Kevin's face and nudged his pal, both turning back to give Kevin's face a second look.

Sensing the girl's silent fury at their reaction, he whispered to her, 'Leave it' and kept her gaze until the pair walked on.

'Did you not . . .' she began, her eyes blazing as she glared at the boys until they disappeared into the shop.

'It's just kids being kids.' Kevin shrugged his shoulders. 'If I got angry every time someone rubbernecked me, I'd be angry *all* the time. What's the point?'

They were both quiet for a bit. Kevin contemplated the milky bubbles frothing over the lid of his coffee.

Maggi spoke first. 'Are you— Do you have to be somewhere or shall we go and drink these coffees while they're hot?'

Kevin thought about saying he never had to be anywhere, but guessed correctly that that wouldn't project the right level of nonchalance and said instead, 'Nowhere special. As long as I go and collect signatures for your mum's petition at some point.' He looked up at the sky, considering. Light was filtering through the clouds, the sun wasn't far away. 'Should we . . . how about having our coffee in the park?'

'That'd be great,' she said. 'You lead the way, I don't know Uddingston any more.'

They crossed Main Street, took the cut up by the bank, and crossed the road again at the Rowantree, heading into the swing park beside the Tunnock's factory.

'What a lovely wee park.' Maggi pulled her rucksack from her back and sat cross-legged on the damp grass, seemingly unperturbed by the prospect of grass stains on her white trousers. Kevin followed her lead and sat down next to her.

The park was quiet – very different from weekdays when Kevin wouldn't dream of running the gauntlet of the schoolkids running around, pointing and jeering until their parents or childminders came over, embarrassed and pulling them away, telling them to please be kind – but rarely acknowledging him, he noticed. There was no one around today, thank goodness. The caramel-sweet gusts coming from the factory made the air thick and cloying, and seemed to take the air from Kevin's lungs. His hangover had magically evaporated though and he sipped his coffee carefully, placing the bag with his bacon roll on the ground beside him.

'Are you not going to eat that?' Maggi pointed to his roll. 'Don't let it go cold on my account.'

Kevin licked his lips and lied that he had bought it for later. She didn't seem in the least put out by his face, but he wasn't sure she was ready to watch him eat. They'd told him that his injuries might make eating, and chewing in particular, difficult but they hadn't been explicit about how awful he looked when he was doing those things. When he'd first left hospital, he used to watch himself eating in the mirror, dismayed to discover that he now resembled a turkey, gobbling and chomping gracelessly, unable to make the lips on the scarred side of his mouth meet so that his masticated food was always visible. He'd grappled with different ways round the problem, and had even considered putting the food into his mouth in tiny chunks and then swallowing it intact rather than go through the rigmarole of chewing and swallowing with his bottom lip distended and pushed out to one side. However, he'd discovered that that made him look like nothing more than a snake swallowing its prey whole, so there was really no way round the problem.

'I bought it to have for lunch at the allotment later.' He pushed the greasy bag further away from him.

'I wondered if you were going to the allotments,' she said. 'I love it there, so many happy memories. I'd go and sit in the fairy garden more often except . . . my mum's always there these days.' Maggi took a sip of her cappuccino, leaving chocolate smears at the corners of her mouth.

'Do you not get on with your mum then? She seems . . . nice.'

'I'm sure she does to you. Very helpful?'

'Well, yeah, she gave me some home-made scones last week.

Said one of her dancing buddies had given them to her and she can't stand them.'

'That'd be about right,' said Maggi, her tongue reaching for the chocolate on her lower lip. Kevin tried not to stare. 'Too homely for her, home-made scones.'

He waited for Maggi to say more, part of him not quite believing he was having such a long conversation with . . . well, anyone, never mind a woman.

'My mum's great with causes,' she went on. 'You saw her in action yourself the other night at the Rolling Barrel.'

'I thought she was brilliant. The way she got us all in order.'

'Oh yes,' said Maggi, her eye caught momentarily by a stray black Labrador lifting its leg at the grimy slide. 'If you need someone to run a campaign for you, collect for charity, march to Downing Street, stay away from home for months on end if she thought it would help, she's the woman for the job all right.'

'Is that not . . . a good thing? Public-spirited?'

'Yeah, I suppose it is great if you're a stranger in need of charity. Not so great if you're her daughter wanting to be taken care of, like other kids in your class are.' Maggi forced a laugh. 'Dad and me managed. Water under the bridge now.'

Kevin wanted to say that it clearly wasn't if she was still talking about it but she'd already moved on. As quick and talkative as Kevin was slow and quiet, he was having trouble keeping up with her. He licked his lower lip again and concentrated hard.

'What about your family? Do they ever come up to the allotment?'

Kevin swirled his coffee round the cup. 'I don't have any family now. My dad died when I was a baby, so there was only me and Mum. But we got on great. She was brilliant, but' – he could feel his eyes growing shiny – 'she died. Almost a year ago now.'

'I'm sorry, Kevin.'

'What for?'

'Sorry for . . . asking.'

'No, it's fine. I like talking about Mum.'

Maggi had finished her coffee and was using her finger to wipe round the inside of the cup. She noticed he was watching her and said, 'Be a shame to waste the chocolate, am I right?'

'You are right.' Kevin turned his own cup on its side and did the same thing, buying himself some time as he thought about something to say to keep her here with him on the grass.

No need, she was off again. 'And do you work?'

'No, I . . . not since . . .' Kevin gestured vaguely to his face but before she could ask him about that, he took his cue from her and added quickly, 'What about you – what do you do?'

'I'm a singer.' She snorted. 'Supposed to be.'

'Wow!'

'Don't be too impressed, it's mostly fiftieth birthday parties and weddings, you know the kind of thing. Not what I'd hoped for but then I'm hardly Taylor Swift.' She wafted her hand up and down her figure as she said this.

Kevin was about to say he thought she looked amazing but she was talking again. Really, Kevin had never met anyone like her – the speed with which she spoke, her jerky movements like she was giddy all the time. He tried to keep up.

'What sort of music do you like?'

Kevin wondered whether he should lie and say he also liked Taylor Swift but then she might catch him out and ask which songs were his favourites. 'I like mostly eighties music. It's . . .

disco and dance and all the stuff my mum used to play. I've got her old CD player in my shed.' His eyes met hers to gauge her reaction.

'Me too! That's the stuff my dad used to play all the time. Mum hated it. Obviously.'

'Oh, obviously,' said Kevin, laughing, thrilled when she laughed too.

'You're right, I should be kinder to her, she's not that bad.' Maggi tipped her head to one side as she thought back. 'She and Dad got on, I think. When she was home. They used to play the Gypsy Kings on an old record-player in the living room and pretend to do the flamenco together.'

'Records were weird, weren't they?' *Seriously, Kevin? Where did that come from??*

'Weird how?'

He ploughed on. 'I mean, B sides, what other art form could you get away with saying, eh well, it's sort of second rate, certainly not the best work we can do, that's all on our A sides, but it's good enough to be a B side.' He'd started so he had to keep going: 'You'd think they could work on it some more and make it an A side, wouldn't you? Like writers have to do with their constant editing and rewriting. A writer wouldn't dream of saying, "This story isn't quite good enough so I'll just make it the B side of a really good story", would they?'

'Do you know, I've never thought about that before, but you're right.' She mulled it over. 'Or: I'm so sorry this steak is somewhat overdone, I usually cook much better than this, but let's call it lunch rather than dinner and I'll try harder next time.'

Kevin took the baton. 'Or: I beg your pardon, the paint has streaked round the edges of this seascape, it's not my best work but never mind, I'll paint something better on the other side and let you choose which one to display.'

They were both laughing hard by then, Maggi clutching Kevin's arm as she fell back on to the grass, saying, 'Brilliant, that's hilarious!'

Kevin felt the warmth on his arm even after she'd taken her hand away.

She sat up again. 'But seriously, what do you do all day, if you're not working?'

Kevin panicked – what *did* he do all day – but then he remembered his allotment. 'I'm mostly at the allotment these days. It's been really good for me. I would hate it if they closed down.'

Suddenly, Kevin realized it was true. In the short time he'd had his allotment, he'd met more people than he had in the whole time since his accident. They weren't great friends or anything but slowly, people were beginning to open up to each other. Whatever Maggi felt about her mum, she'd been very nice to him, even more so recently. Stanley usually said hello to him now too. Last week he'd offered him cuttings from his geranium and told him the best place on his plot to plant them so that they would be sheltered from the wind. He'd had a few good chats with Lawrence from No 5, who'd been at the same school as him, he said. Last week, he'd asked him if he wanted a coffee from the fancy machine he kept in his shed. It had turned out to be a tiny cup of black poison, bitter as medicine and strong enough to keep him awake that night, but he'd enjoyed sitting on Lawrence's step, chatting about tomatoes and mulch and slugs. Mohid, the doctor from No 2, had given him something called feverfew for his headaches that had really helped. And now look, he'd spent the morning talking to a woman! Kevin wanted the allotments to stay open.

'We need to fight to keep your allotments out of the developers' hands then,' said Maggi. 'Not to sound like my mum, I suppose we should get started collecting signatures. Maybe we could double up and cover some of the ground together?'

'That would be . . . yes, I'd like that.' Kevin was beaming as he got up from the grass, reaching out his hand to help Maggi. The sun was fully out now and a glorious rainbow curved over the park. This was shaping up to be one of the best days he'd had in—And then he saw them.

Sauntering in past the wrought-iron gates at the entrance to the park, a group of three teenage boys, all swagger and knock-off Nike and vape clouds. He recognized them immediately, and froze. Most days, he didn't care, he could ignore them, but he desperately didn't want Maggi to see the way they treated him. He couldn't bear her to know what they called him, didn't want to be Gorgeous Kevin to her, or Scarface, or Freakster. He wanted her to see him as just . . . Kevin.

'Kevin, what's the matter?' She turned to see what had unnerved him.

'Nothing,' said Kevin quickly. 'Nothing, it's . . . sorry . . . I've got to get home. I completely forgot I've got to . . .'

She waited for him to explain.

The group of boys drew closer.

'I'm too busy today. Sorry,' he threw over his shoulder as he headed out of the park in the opposite direction. 'I'll see you at the allotments.'

'But . . . the petition?' Maggi's eyes followed Kevin out of the park and she wondered what she'd said wrong. Perhaps she'd misread the signs as usual, talked too much, laughed too much, *been* too much.

'Fat slag,' jeered the thickset boy in red Nike as he passed her on the path. The other two laughed, as he blew his cheeks out to illustrate the point.

Maggi ignored them, glad that Kevin hadn't been around to hear their comments. She wandered back to her car, deciding to give the petition a miss after all. With all the others out collecting signatures, no one would miss her, especially not her mum.

23

ACCORDING TO KAREN, THE NEXT meeting with the developers would take place at the council headquarters the following Wednesday afternoon. Germaine had made the mistake of telling Dorothy this in passing and Dorothy insisted they go along to hand in their petition personally.

'Not quite sure I see the point, Dorothy, we've got – what – fifty signatures?'

'Fifty-two, to be precise. And don't blame me for that. You and I were the only ones who actually got any signatures, and you only managed five, sorry, four since I don't think we can count Mr Pablo Escobar Esquire.'

Dorothy was still smarting from the spectacular lack of success of her plan to show support for the allotments by compiling a huge petition full of signatures from local people demanding that the allotments remain in public ownership. She'd done her bit, of course she had – traipsing all round the Springfield estate, fighting off unaccompanied toddlers who'd clung to her legs, gigantic brutes of dogs she could hardly believe lived in people's houses, and standing at door after door, almost always unanswered even though she could see the householders going about their business behind the dimpled glass. She'd done well to get the forty-eight signatures she had got, and most of those were from the staff she'd seen smoking on the corner outside the Tunnock's factory, and a few from the girls at her dancing club. Irish Mary had said couldn't we all sign it a dozen times with made-up names but Myra had pouted and said her Jason worked at the council and she'd need to tell him about any fraud so that put an end to that.

They'd all had an excuse for why they hadn't participated. But it was just . . . so disappointing. After they'd had that great night bonding at the Rolling Barrel too, and they'd all been enthusiastic about the plan, it wasn't her getting carried away as usual, she was sure of it.

'What about the bag pack?' said Germaine. 'I couldn't do it because I was . . . busy, but did any of the others turn up to that?'

Dorothy blew her lips out in a manner that said it all. Despite her lack of success on the Saturday, Dorothy had turned up at Tesco in Uddingston raring to go at 9 a.m. the following day. She'd waited for the others at the entrance for ages, continually checking her phone and glancing round the car park. She wasn't even surprised this time when no one showed up and she did the bag pack on her own. She didn't need any help as it turned out. The teeming rain and a gala day in East Kilbride meant very few customers at Uddingston Tesco. At half past two, and having packed half a dozen bags for a total of £5.70, she nearly kissed a pair of teenagers who dropped fifty pence each in her bucket and stopped to sign the petition. Six hours later and the bag pack had raised £172.37, with a fifty-pound note donated by the guy who owned the ice-cream shop on Main Street and said he was old enough to remember when a community allotment meant something. At closing time, she'd put her pen back into the pocket of her dungarees, grabbed the bucket full of change and trudged home, thanking the spotty-faced youth who ran the shop for letting her stand there all day.

'No use crying over spilt milk,' said Germaine briskly. 'We'll have to work with what we've got. Not that I think it'll make a blind bit of difference, mind.' Germaine was now resigned to the allotments closing. Stanley was right, all that mattered was money. She was going to tell Dorothy about her dad's saying about money making the world go round – or was it the root of all evil – she couldn't remember now. But Dorothy seemed so crestfallen, sitting on her shambolic allotment in her ridiculous dungarees, that agreeing to accompany her to the council offices in Hamilton seemed the least she could do.

The meeting had already started when Germaine and Dorothy arrived but it didn't matter as it wasn't open to the public this time and the sniffy receptionist on the ground floor had been quite insistent they were not allowed to go upstairs.

'But what about our petition?' Dorothy swooshed the couple of sheets of scraggy A4 lined paper in front of the woman's overly made-up face.

'Look, doesn't matter,' said Germaine, taking charge. 'The meeting started half an hour ago, you said. We'll wait here until it's finished and hand our petition over to the developers ourselves.'

The receptionist protested she had no idea how long the meeting would last but Germaine simply put her hand up and led Dorothy over to the row of hard seats by the lift.

'That's right,' called Dorothy back over her shoulder to the receptionist. 'We'll be right here waiting.' The receptionist had already put her headphones back in and was making every show of being engrossed in whatever was on the screen in front of her.

Twenty minutes later, they were still sitting there and Germaine had bitten her fingernails almost to the tips of her fingers.

'I didn't know you were a nail biter.' Dorothy watched in fascination as Germaine gnawed on the edge of her thumb, though there was surely no more nail to devour.

'I'm not.' Germaine took her hand away from her mouth and drummed her fingers against her thigh instead.

The receptionist was now signing for a package that had been delivered.

'God, I hate it when women simper, don't you?' Dorothy watched as the receptionist flirted outrageously with the delivery man.

'Simper?'

'Yeah, you know' – Dorothy inclined her head, and did something weird with her eyelashes while pushing her lips together and outwards.

'Well if that's simpering, then yes I also hate it when women simper. Right, that's it, we've been patient long enough.' Germaine stood up and pulled Dorothy by her elbow up on to her feet.

'Where are you going? We've to wait—'

Germaine was not waiting any longer. While the receptionist continued fluttering her eyelashes and being enchanted by whatever the guy in motorcycle leathers was saying, the women crept up the back stairs and headed for the meeting rooms.

'This way,' whispered Germaine, as they skulked along the top corridor.

'Why are you whispering? There's no one here.'

Germaine ignored her.

Before they reached the end of the corridor, a door opened and Karen came out, a gentle smile on her face as though she was enjoying some private joke.

'What are you doing here?' she started, when she caught sight of Germaine and Dorothy inching their way along the corridor on tiptoes like middle-aged ninjas.

'We've come on allotment committee business.' Dorothy stuck her chest out to indicate the official nature of their visit.

'Listen,' said Karen, taking each woman by the elbow and leading them back the way they'd come. 'This is not a public meeting and what I'm going to tell you can't go any further but' – she shot a look back at the door she'd come out of – 'things are not going well for the developers. They've told the committee there's a problem with financing . . .'

'Woohoo,' shouted Dorothy, before being quickly shushed by the other two women. 'Sorry, but that's good news for us, isn't it? If they haven't got the money to buy the land, I mean?'

'Yes, it does look that way but—'

'That's fantastic! You understand what this means, Germaine – we win, the developers lose.'

Germaine turned to Karen. 'Is that what this means?'

'Not exactly, it means that—'

Dorothy wasn't listening. 'Of course it does. Listen, give them this petition, to seal the deal sort of thing, and Germaine, come on, let's get back and tell the others the good news.'

'I think it'd be best to wait, though,' said Karen. 'I've just nipped out for the toilet then I need to go back into the meeting, but stay here so we can—'

Too late, Dorothy was practically skipping down the corridor, dragging a reluctant Germaine beside her.

Karen watched them leave and wished she'd kept her mouth shut. Still, it did look very much as though the developers were going to pull out and the allotments given the reprieve they deserved. She heard Councillor Murray guffawing from the committee room behind her and she decided to skip the toilet break and put her game face back on before returning to the fray.

24

THE INTENSE COBALT BLUE SKY that a mid-June evening in Scotland occasionally provides was just beginning to fade as dusk fell. Three sparrows were sitting companionably on the wall, preening themselves and observing the land like it was their own kingdom. *Little do they know it all belongs to me*, thought Germaine smugly as she stood at the top of the path, admiring the scene before her.

The strings of fairy lights weaving in and out of the trees were already twinkling and the dozen or so lanterns placed at intervals along the path gave off a warm glow. The picnic tables in the fairy garden had been draped in long white sheets, with pink and yellow petals strewn across them by Isobel, who, despite appearances to the contrary, turned out to have a designer's eye for detail. Kevin had brought in a stack of vintage floral dishes which he said had been gathering dust at home since his mum died, and they now contained party snacks purchased by the money raised at Dorothy's bag pack.

Germaine sighed with satisfaction. Everything looked good, especially since it had been organized on the spur of the moment. It had been Dorothy's idea, of course, suggested to Germaine as soon as they'd left the council premises on Almada Street the previous afternoon.

'How are we going to celebrate?' she'd asked as they crossed the road at the Water Palace and headed back towards Uddingston.

'What do you mean?' Germaine checked along the road to see if the bus was coming. 'We'll tell the other plot holders the good news when we see them on the allotments.'

Dorothy stopped and placed her hand on Germaine's arm. 'You're kidding, right? We *have* to celebrate. This is a historic victory – us against them and we won! The allotments are staying within the community, big business lost and—'

'God's sake, you sound like you're on one of your women's marches or something. Greenham was over years ago, you know. And we won by default, one of the very few occasions we can say thank God for an economy that's nosediving.'

But Dorothy's mind was made up. As soon as they got back to Viewpark, she spoke with all the other plot holders and plans were made for a celebration. And now here they were, Thursday night at Kenmar allotments and it was time to party.

'There's more room on the table at the end,' called Germaine to Lawrence who had arrived with more crisps and nuts, and a long tube of plastic tumblers under his arm. 'More money than sense, as Dad would say,' Germaine whispered to herself, when Adrian followed on behind with not one, but two, magnums of Champagne. But Isobel had shouted, 'Three cheers for Lawrence and Adrian' when she saw them and Lawrence was glad he'd persuaded Adrian to bring the second bottle.

Farah and Mohid arrived, Mohid carrying the big pot of pasta his wife had spent all afternoon making.

'Put it in the middle of the table, Mohid. It'll stay warm enough for a while yet.'

'Ooh,' said Adrian, eyes wide at the size of the pot, 'what's in there – curry?'

'No,' laughed Farah. 'It's pasta with home-made sugo. You'll love it.'

'Pasta?' He frowned.

'Yes, what – do you not like pasta?'

'No, I just assumed it'd be something, you know, from where you come from.'

'I come from Hamilton.'

'No, but originally.'

'I was born in Hamilton.'

'Yes, but . . . but . . . ah, Lawrence, there you are. I'll need to go and . . . refill my glass,' he said, darting away from the drinks table with a full glass of Champagne.

Farah winked at Lawrence to show she wasn't offended, and took the glass of Champagne he offered her.

'I like your s-s-sari,' he said, shyly.

'Thank you, dear. This one was made for me by my cousin, Malaika. Such a talent, see the detail?' Farah twirled and the gold thread of the rose petals shimmered beneath the fairy lights.

'Gorgeous,' agreed Lawrence. Now they were here, he wished he'd stuck with his original plan to wear his statement Ted Baker floral shirt with the mandarin collar, paired with his white Armani jeans and a shiny black leather belt.

'Is that what you're wearing?' Adrian had said, when he'd walked into the bedroom while Lawrence was treating himself to a sneaky spray of his boyfriend's Issey Miyake.

Since the shirt was buttoned and on Lawrence's back, he didn't feel the need to answer that.

Adrian saw his face fall and added quickly, 'I just mean it's very . . . colourful. But it's up to you, of course, you look great whatever you wear.' He checked himself out, standing side-on to the mirror, his head cocked to one side and his mouth pouting a little as he did so. 'I think these body conditioning classes are finally starting to pay off. You should try them. Right, I'll start putting the stuff in the car. See you downstairs.'

Lawrence had changed into a plain white Dolce and Gabbana shirt but was still debating his outfit when the impatient screech of Adrian's horn from the pavement below made his mind up for him.

Stanley turned up half an hour later than everyone else, wearing the same cords and cardigan he wore to Mass on a Sunday. He couldn't understand why they had to have a party to celebrate keeping what was theirs but Isobel had begged him so hard to come he didn't have the heart to say no. 'I'll stay an hour,' he said, 'then I'm going home to watch some David Attenborough.' 'An hour will do fine,' Isobel had said happily, rushing back to tell George, who would forget ten minutes later but that didn't matter.

'Hello, Maggi.' Dorothy walked over to greet her daughter, who was standing awkwardly by the main gate.

'Why do you sound surprised to see me?' said Maggi, already irritated and pulling at the strands of her half-up, half-down chignon, with its tartan ribbon. 'Were you not expecting me to accept your invite?'

It was true that Dorothy had assumed her gregarious and popular daughter would have far better things to do than attend a quickly arranged bash at the local allotments but she shook her head and kissed her on the cheek. 'Of course I was expecting you to come. Hoping you would, so don't be prickly, I'm delighted to see you.' She didn't add that she couldn't miss her in her scarlet flares with a red, white and blue striped T-shirt which had the word 'OUI' scrawled in huge yellow letters diagonally across her chest. 'Come and have a drink. Everyone's brought wine and beer, and I think Adrian and Lawrence have even brought Champagne.'

Mohid had produced the speaker that he and Farah used when they came to the allotments on their middle-of-the-night dancing trips. 'Any requests?' he called out, but no one was listening. 'Okay, it's my choice then.' He turned up the volume. 'Let's try this one on for size.'

Chaka Khan started singing how much she felt for them and Mohid sidled over to Farah and whispered something in her ear that made her give him a friendly slap on the shoulder and exclaim 'Please, Mohid, someone might hear you!'

'These sausage rolls are good,' said Stanley to Isaac, who was sitting alone on the low bench in the fairy garden, the screen of his iPad reflecting a blueish light on to his face.

The boy didn't answer but he did put his iPad down beside him on the bench. He drew his hands around his knees.

Stanley hesitated for a moment, wondering where the boy's parents were; he was always on his own, it seemed. 'You look cold, lad,' he said, sitting beside him on the bench although his knees felt the strain. 'Here, have one of these.'

'What is it?'

'It's a sausage roll, for goodness' sake, it won't kill you.' The child was exasperating, thought Stanley, but maybe it had been so long since he'd talked to an eleven-year-old boy that he'd forgotten how annoying they could be.

'Here.' He wrapped the warm sausage roll in a napkin and handed it over.

'Thanks,' he said gruffly and took a tiny bite. His eyes lit up and he took another larger bite.

'Good?' Stanley was surprised by how happy it made him to see the boy eat.

Isaac said nothing but kept eating, and he hadn't run away, Stanley noticed, so he tried again. 'What happened about the Anderson shelter, did they like it?'

'I was top!'

'Top? Well done, son, your mum must have been pleased about that.'

'Didn't tell her. She'd have asked me more about school and I haven't been going much.'

Stanley remained still, as though Isaac was a kitten he was trying not to frighten away, and waited for him to say more.

'You wouldn't understand.'

'I'm seventy-nine years old, son, there's not much I haven't heard before. Try me.'

'They all talk about their dads, playing football with them and . . . gaming and stuff. My dad can't do anything. He's useless.' He threw the greasy napkin on the ground. 'My mum's useless too.'

'They're both doing their best, son. And have you ever thought about how they might feel when you talk about them like that? When they're doing their best.'

'My mum, maybe . . . but my dad is definitely useless. He can't even speak right.'

Stanley thought for a moment. 'See that fence there, all round the allotments?'

Isaac looked over where the old man was pointing.

'Your dad did that. He mended that whole fence, all by himself. I watched him, every day he came and repaired it, plank by plank. That takes a lot of skill and patience, don't you think?'

The boy grunted but his eyes widened as he took in the extent of the fence.

'And this party? See all the decorations and the homemade food, maybe even that sausage roll you enjoyed so much? Your mum helped with all that, she was here all day setting it up. Takes a special kind of person to spend their day making sure things are nice for others, doesn't it?'

The boy blew a soft raspberry. 'S'pose.'

'They love you very much, your mum and dad.'

'Pppfff.'

'There's no pppfff about it, lad, all parents do – most of them anyway – and your mum and dad are lucky to have you, they know that and they want you to be happy.'

'Will my dad ever get better?' he asked Stanley suddenly.

Stanley wasn't sure how to answer. 'Honestly, Isaac, I don't know. But what I do know is that you'll get used to the way things are, and if you keep talking to him, keep reminding him of the folk that love him, that will help you all feel better, won't it?'

'S'pose.' Isaac kept his eyes to the ground and picked up some dry earth, throwing it across the path.

'I hope you're going to sweep that mess up later.' Stanley paused then took a chance. 'Here's something else I've learned – we've got to be more like plants.' Isaac made a face but Stanley carried on. 'What I mean is, plants are resilient and adapt when they need to. Some days rain falls when they need sun, too bad, that's the way it is. They have to adapt or die. Do you understand, son?'

'I think so.' He turned and put his hand on Stanley's knee. 'I'll play chess with you tomorrow if you like?'

'You will? I'll hold you to that.'

The boy flashed his lopsided, blink-and-you'll-miss-it grin, and the pair stayed on the bench, comfortable in the silence as the party fluttered and sparkled around them.

The sky was blue-black now and pierced with stars. Kevin was lying on his back in the field behind the allotments, the strains of Phil Collins feeling something in the air tonight and the comforting buzz of the mingled voices and laughter of his fellow allotment holders in the background. Kevin had his usual sense of being on the outside looking in but he didn't mind. The air was warm and sweet with the scent of summer flowers and he was enjoying the light breeze. Still not too chilly to be lying there in his T-shirt and cargo shorts, or at least, he never seemed to feel the cold the way other people did.

Soothed by the peace of being alone in the field under the night sky, he counted the stars and it reminded him how nothing anyone was doing down here mattered – none of it and none of them.

'Hello? Hello, Kevin, is that you?'

Kevin sat up, his hand to his face as he waited to see who would come from between the hedges.

'Here you are,' she said. 'I've been looking for you.'

Kevin's eyes widened. 'You've been looking . . . for me?'

Maggi sat down next to him. 'Can I join you?'

'Okay.' Kevin watched as she stretched her legs on the grass and sat back on her elbows. He lay back down and scanned the sky.

Maggi took her elbows away so that she too was lying flat on her back. They were silent for a few moments till Maggi said, 'Erm, what is it we're doing?'

'Just . . . enjoying the sky.'

'The sky?'

'Yeah.'

Maggi looked up. 'It is beautiful. We don't often lie and just look, do we?'

Kevin did, all the time, but he didn't say so in case she thought that was odd.

Minutes passed, the air grew sticky and Kevin could hear Maggi breathing next to him. He closed his eyes briefly but missed the sparkling stars too much and opened them again. Directly above him there was a group of round, extra-bright stars clustered together like the popular kids at school but suddenly a smaller star spun across the sky, taking their attention. Maggi pointed at it. 'Look at that one doing its own thing!' She was aware of the grass beneath her fingers, reminding her of long schoolgirl summers, and the music of the party floating in the space between them and the stars, but gently, requiring nothing from them. For once, she didn't feel the need to keep talking.

Kevin said softly, 'Do you ever feel like you could . . .'

Maggi waited.

'No, it's stupid . . .'

'What? Say.'

Maggi staring up at the sky and not directly at his face was giving Kevin confidence. And she was here, wasn't she, lying next to him, not going anywhere. 'Do you ever feel like you could reach up' – Kevin stretched his arm and made a starfish of his hand, and Maggi thought how long and slim and perfect his fingers were – 'just reach up and tear open the sky so that all the stars within it, they come tumbling down on you? Like glitter.'

'Or confetti at a wedding.' Maggi reached her own hand up so that it was inches away from Kevin's, stretching towards the diamond-studded sky.

'Yeah, like sparkling confetti.'

Maggi turned to face him. 'Kevin—'

'Maggi! *Maaaggi!*'

Maggi sat up suddenly. 'That's my mum,' she said, putting her finger to her mouth to indicate they should keep quiet and she might go away.

No such luck.

'There you are. I've been searching everywhere for you. Everyone's asking where you've got to.'

Not him though, Kevin noted. No one had missed him.

'Why? Why do they need me? I'm not even an allotment holder.'

'Well.' Dorothy glanced back at the allotments, stalling.

'Mum?'

'Well. I might have said you would sing for them. Just one song, it's a celebration.'

'Oh for God's sake, Mum. No one wants to hear me sing.'

'I do,' said Kevin, sitting up quickly.

Dorothy peered into the darkness. 'Kevin? I didn't see you there. Are you two taking a rest from the party?'

Kevin knew it would never have crossed her mind that there could have been anything else to it.

'Don't blame you, mind you,' continued Dorothy. 'Isobel's

had far too much of Adrian's Champagne and is giggling like a fifteen-year-old. George is talking nonsense — not that he needs booze for that. Stanley's still here and telling me all about his sowing methods, in some detail mark you, and meanwhile Germaine is stone-cold sober and standing sentry in front of her shed with a face like fizz, as if she'd rather be anywhere else but here. Come oooon, Maggi, we need some entertainment.'

'I'd love to hear you sing,' Kevin said to Maggi quietly.

'I'm not that good.' She grabbed a handful of grass on each side and felt the cool spiky blades between her fingers.

'Don't listen to her, Kevin. She's got a voice on her that Dolly Parton would give her best brassiere for.'

'Muuum.'

'Ladies and gentlemen,' announced Dorothy, standing on the path at the top of the hill, between her own plot and Kevin's. The others were dotted all over the allotments, holding half-empty bottles of beer and paper cups of rough red wine or warm Champagne. Mohid had his arm draped round Farah, Lawrence and Adrian were standing by the messy buffet table, talking together, heads close, the wee lad was beside Stanley — was he holding his hand, Dorothy couldn't see, but she was glad someone had taken charge of him as Isobel was swaying from left to right and trying to focus on George who was talking nonsense nineteen to the dozen by her side. Germaine remained at the bottom of the hill, in front of her shed. They all looked towards Dorothy as she spoke.

'My very talented daughter' — she ignored Maggi snorting behind her — 'is going to sing us a song.' She turned to her daughter. 'What will you sing, Maggi?'

Maggi made a face to indicate she had no idea but, undeterred, Dorothy turned back to the others who were now approaching the top of the hill to be able to hear better, and asked for any requests.

'Anything except Billy Ray Cyrus,' called Germaine. 'I'm still traumatized.'

'Blossom Dearie,' shouted Stanley. 'Mabel's favourite,' he told Isaac who was still sticking to his side like glue, even though his mother was gesturing at him to come and stand with her.

'No idea who that is,' said Maggi. 'Sorry.'

Mohid stepped forward with his speaker. 'If I may? I've got some background music here – you could sing along?'

'What have you got?'

'Let me see . . .' Mohid scrolled through his playlist while Maggi tapped her feet nervously, acutely aware that Kevin had come from behind her and was now standing with the small cluster of people at the top of the hill, waiting to hear her sing.

'What about this?' said Mohid, and when she heard the opening bars, Maggi told him that would be perfect.

The music was turned up loud and the small appreciative audience swayed and danced together on the hill, so that when Maggi sang in her clear confident tones, 'I Will Survive', it was easy for each of them to believe that they would.

What a ragtag bunch they were, thought Germaine, looking around her at the very different individuals whose only common ground was the ground on which they were currently standing. Between them, they hadn't been able to come up with a single other person who wanted to join them in their celebrations, but maybe that was okay because, however much she might deny it, slowly but surely they were forming their own community. And it was her allotments that had done that for them. Germaine hummed along quietly to the music and took another sip of her flat cola. Thank goodness everything had worked out for the best.

25

Farah was still gathering up empty squashed paper cups when everyone else had left. There was a hush over the allotments that Germaine loved so much more than the surprisingly raucous noise of even such a small party. She was anxious now for Farah and Mohid to go home too and leave her to her domain.

She walked over to Farah, stooping to pick up a crushed napkin full of sandwich crusts on her way. 'Leave everything else now, Farah. I said to the others, we can all clear up tomorrow. It's been a long day.'

Farah carried on scooping up the debris from the picnic tables and dropping it into the already-bulging black refuse sack in her hand. 'Oh no, I couldn't go home and leave a mess, honestly, you go home and I'll keep—'

'Farah.'

Farah stopped and saw that Germaine was weary of company and meant what she said. 'Okay.' She signalled over to Mohid who was busy scrunching up crisp packets from the area around the fairy garden and amusing himself by trying to land them in the bin. 'But listen.' She put her hand on Germaine's arm. 'Don't do any more clearing up yourself, this is a job for all of us tomorrow. Promise?'

Germaine promised she'd leave everything as it was, and said goodbye as the couple walked down the hill and left by the main gate. She heard Mohid say to Farah as he put his arm around her, 'Are you warm enough, my queen?' She didn't wait for Farah's reply as she went back into the management shed to do a final check before leaving herself.

'Hello? Is someone still here?'

Germaine heard the front gate jiggle a few moments later and shouted, 'We're closed', instantly aware of her vulnerability as a lone woman on the now dark and silent allotments. She stuck her head out of the shed and saw that it was Karen from the council, and breathed more easily. 'Goodness' sake, Karen,' she said as she unlocked the gate. 'You gave me the fright of my life there. What are you doing here at this time of night?'

Karen wrapped her cardigan closer to her chest. 'Sorry, I thought . . . I know you're here till all hours, and it's important, I thought you'd want to know.' She stepped into the allotments and her mouth opened wide as she clocked the litter left over from their celebrations.

'What on earth—'

'Don't worry,' said Germaine quickly. 'We're going to clear it all up tomorrow. We had a little party, to celebrate, you know?'

'Oh, Germaine.' Karen's face fell. 'That's what I've come to tell you. There's nothing to celebrate.'

'What do you mean? The developers backed out, didn't they? And there was our petition, okay, there weren't as many signatures as we'd have liked but—'

Karen put up her hand to stop her from saying any more. 'I tried to tell you but you weren't listening. That Dorothy woman you were with wasn't *letting* you listen. You left before the meeting finished. Sit down a moment and I'll tell you what else was said.'

Germaine sat with Karen on the swing seat under the fairy lights which twinkled annoyingly as they talked. Or at least, Karen talked and Germaine's face grew longer by the second. It seemed the council had reconvened after the tea break – Karen had tried to make Germaine and Dorothy stay till the meeting was finished but Dorothy wasn't having it – so the meeting had gone on again after they'd left, and an agreement on the price had been reached.

'So the upshot is, the developers still get the allotments but now for even less money than before?' she said, when Karen had finished talking.

'I'm afraid that's about the size of it. I'm so sorry for getting your hopes up before the thing had been decided. I did try to say. But . . . the developers know they've got us over a barrel. They only said they'd pull out to drag the price down lower.' She shook her head in disgust. 'People like them? You think they didn't know the reason they were called in in the first place was because the council can't afford the upkeep? We'd need to find at least another eight grand in the budget this year alone, that's to cover ground rent, council charge, ongoing maintenance, not least of which is knocking down that dangerous wall at the top of the allotments, the list goes on. The council doesn't have that kind of money, Germaine, that's why the developers' proposal was so appealing in the first place. We need to find cost savings somewhere.'

'But why does it have to be us that suffer?' Germaine swept her hand across the allotments, a gesture that encompassed the well-tended plots, the love that had gone into the sowing, the planting, the weeding, the painting, the sheds with their decorations and ornaments, all of it. For the first time since her dad had died, she felt like crying.

'I know, and I'm sorry. If it makes you feel any better, it's not just you – the Pensioners' Club is being stopped, the library's having to go to half-day closing two days a week too. It's . . . times are hard, Germaine.'

For the people who already have the least, Germaine wanted to add, but she knew it wasn't fair to take it out on Karen, she was on their side. 'Thanks for coming to tell me.' She looked down to the ground and dragged her toes along the dirt.

'I'm sorry,' said Karen, getting up to leave. 'There'll be an official letter telling you all this next week, with a proposed closure date and arrangements to terminate your position and . . . you get the idea.'

Germaine watched Karen close the gate carefully behind her. She looked up sadly at the allotments, still bearing the signs of the evening's celebrations, and thought about the community they'd started to build and how they would all cope without it. Stanley, who'd been here for years and would have to leave his rhododendron tribute to his late wife. Isobel, who'd been so happy to have somewhere for her husband to be occupied and feel safe while she was at work, even somewhere for that boy of theirs to hang around when he wasn't at school. Mohid and Farah, who'd worked so hard on their plot and were beginning to open up to other plot holders. Kevin, who she was pretty sure had nothing else in his life bar his plants and his shed. Dorothy, who'd no sooner found the place than was being turfed out of it. And shy Lawrence with his speech problems who was starting to open up and talk to people. Of course, she would be fine, it didn't matter to her, she didn't need anyone else, she told herself.

How on earth was she going to break it to them? The community they'd started to build was over before it had begun.

26

AFTER A SLEEPLESS NIGHT, GERMAINE was back at the allotments before even Stanley had set foot in the place. She dreaded the task that lay ahead of her but she was still the manager here and she owed it to the plot holders to give them the truth – the development plans were going ahead, the allotments would be closed down and sold, and there was nothing they, or anyone else, could do about it.

She gathered them all round the entrance to the fairy garden, trying to ignore the party debris at their feet, and broke the news to a hungover and stunned silence.

'What about my rhoddy?' Stanley spoke first, pushing his bunnet to the back of his head as he did so.

'I've just planted tomatoes,' from Kevin.

'But why, I don't understand? I thought we'd won,' said Farah, her face crumpling. Mohid put his arm round her shoulder but she shook him off.

'But . . . we had a p-p-party to celebrate.' Lawrence looked round at his fellow plot holders and caught George's eye. Even he seemed to understand what they were being told and he threw Lawrence a half-smile in sympathy.

'They can't do this!' Dorothy stamped her foot and glared at Germaine.

'I'm afraid they can,' said Germaine, not meeting anyone's eye as she spoke, 'and no amount of screeching and crying about it is going to change things. The decision's been made.'

The group was silent again but remained huddled together, unwilling to let the matter end there.

'Okay,' said Dorothy finally, in a calmer voice. 'That's what the council's told us, but we need to talk about this, make plans.'

'What do you mean?' said Kevin. 'The allotments are closing, aren't they? I thought that was the final decision.'

'That's the case, I'm afraid,' said Germaine. 'Nothing else to be done. And we've been down this road before, Dorothy. We all did our best with the petition and everything.'

'Did we though?' Dorothy pushed through the others to the front of the group, kicking aside an empty wine bottle from the evening before as she did so. 'Can we really call a pathetic wee petition with fifty-two—'

'Fifty-four,' said Germaine. 'Remember we stopped in at Greggs on our way to the council and those two nice women signed it and asked us if—'

'Germaine, come on. Fifty-four, ninety-four, a hundred and four, whatever. It's hardly Churchill telling them we'd fight them in the fields, or Yeltsin standing on that tank, or even Tommy Sheridan saying no to the bloody poll tax.'

'I'm afraid you've lost me.' Germaine sniffed, longing for the quiet and privacy of her shed.

'What I mean is, it wasn't a strong stand in the fight for justice. It was more like, I don't know, a wee hiccup or a half-cry into the dark: "Please don't take away our allotments."'

This last plea was said in a baby voice and George mumbled something like 'Bay . . . if what if if nothing . . . baby.'

'Exactly, George, thank you,' said Dorothy, as though he'd confirmed her point.

'What are you suggesting?' said Germaine.

'A campaign, a proper campaign this time, take action like we mean it, like we won't be pushed aside while they knock down our allotments that we've worked so hard over.' She was raising her voice again and Germaine gestured to her to keep it down. Dorothy ignored her. 'These allotments belong to all of us. We've got to show them who they're dealing with.'

'Lord, here we go,' said Maggi.

'Yes, exactly. Exactly. Here we go.' Dorothy gave her daughter a stony look before extending it to the whole group. 'Let's *get* going. Let's show them these are our allotments, for people like us who need them, dammit. They want a fight? Let's give them one.'

Dorothy's words hit home. Saturday saw them all gathered at the foot of the hill, a group of disciples simultaneously awaiting instruction and wondering what exactly it was they'd signed up for. Dorothy, sporting a pair of pinstriped dungarees to reflect the seriousness of the situation, said an online petition would be critical to their new campaign – Mohid caught Farah's eye and nodded an 'I told you so' – but there was plenty more to be done. 'I've organized another bag pack for next Sunday. Scotmid Viewpark said we could have it there and – to prevent a repeat of the last fiasco – I'll be handing round a list of time slots that I've already allocated.'

'Someone means b-b-business,' whispered Lawrence to Kevin, who didn't dare interrupt Dorothy's flow with a reply.

'Iris from Viewpark Church has very kindly agreed to help us organize a jumble sale and she's got a group of volunteers from the Sunday Prayer Club going round picking up donations. And the Village Messy Crafts group has offered to donate items – pottery, embroidery – you know the sort of thing. Tannochside Boys' Brigade is organizing a competition to design the best campaign poster which will then be displayed in all the local shops and Tony the caretaker from the Birkenshaw Sports Barn has agreed to hand out leaflets to everyone who comes through the door. The community is on our side! If we all stick together, we can pull this off. And this time' – she fixed her eye on each of the plot holders in turn – 'there will be consequences for anyone who says they'll do something then doesn't follow through.' Precisely what those consequences would be was not spelled out but the stern look on Dorothy's face as she stood, hand on hips, at the top of the allotments and gave them their instruction sheets, was enough to make them all toe the line.

'Any questions?'

They all looked at each other then back towards Dorothy.

'Right then,' she said. 'The new and improved Operation Save Our Allotments campaign is under way.'

They were each allocated a partner and a task to fulfil together. Mohid and Lawrence were to go to the printers at the industrial estate to pick up what Dorothy referred to darkly as 'equipment'. The two men weren't quite sure what they were collecting but apparently it would take two of them to carry the stuff. Mohid gave Lawrence an awkward little wave when their names were called, and the younger man blushed.

'Now, Maggi and Kevin, you can pick up the paint and brushes from Kreative in Blantyre. Maggi, I know your sense of direction is even worse than your dad's was so you can drive your own car but let Kevin help you with the directions, okay? And do your best to get us a deal on the brushes. I don't know anyone who works there so as it stands, they're charging us full price.'

'Germaine, you're with me and Isobel, we are going to head to the council offices and see whether *someone* from the council will speak to us because they sure as hell aren't giving out any information over the phone, bastards.'

'I can see why your mum's going,' whispered Kevin to Maggi. 'Diplomacy and tact are definitely her strong suit', and was rewarded with a huge grin from Maggi.

'Sshh, no talking please,' shouted Dorothy from her position on top of the Mount. 'Farah, you are going to get online and keep pushing the Facebook and Twitter accounts which my clever daughter here set up for us last night.' Lawrence clapped and said, 'Well done, Maggi.' 'It was easy, you just—' but Dorothy shushed them again and continued addressing Farah. 'If you have time to start a blog and let everyone know what's happening with the campaign and how they can support us, please do.' She glared at everyone. 'What are we waiting for?'

They all got ready to leave. Everyone, that is, except George, Stanley and Isaac, who were staying on the allotments until the others returned that afternoon. As to which of these was looking after the other it was not quite clear, but the general feeling was that between the three of them, they would all be safe.

'You will make sure Isaac stays on this side of the wall, won't you?' Isobel asked Stanley, before she left with Germaine and Dorothy. She was actually talking to Stanley's back as he stooped to pick out the persistent weeds growing round his beloved rhoddy. He wasn't using a tool for the job, Isobel noticed, though she was sure that, of all the plot holders, he must have a tool for every possible occasion. Instead, he was taking each stubborn weed between his two fingers and, using a pincer movement, pulling each blade out separately by the root.

'That's very effective.' Isobel couldn't hide her admiration.

'Hmph.'

'You will keep an eye out for them, won't you?' she said again. 'Especially George. I know he's a grown man but I do worry about leaving him here on his own.'

The silence continued and Isobel began to think that Germaine and Dorothy might have to go on their own, when Stanley straightened up suddenly, throwing a handful of spiky weeds straight into the black plastic bin bag at the side of the path. 'He's not on his own, is he?' he said, finally. 'I'm here.' He took off his bunnet, his bald head glowing in the sunshine.

'That's . . . thank you, Stanley, I really appreciate that.'

Stanley replaced his bunnet and stooped to the ground again before adding, 'And make sure you tell them we need these allotments, right?'

'We will, we definitely will do that.'

'Any time this week,' said Germaine to Dorothy, who seemed to be taking hours faffing around in her shed.

'Come in and wait.' Dorothy rooted through the tumble of jackets on the floor, trying to find her anorak. She thought again that she must donate Eddie's stuff to charity but she couldn't seem to let go of it all, not yet.

Germaine peeked in at the mess, and stepped right back out again. She couldn't understand how people could function in such chaos. She glanced over at her own pristine shed – a place for everything and everything in its place, as her dad would say. 'Hurry up,' she called again. 'The council offices will be closed by the time we get there at this rate.'

'Give me a minute,' said Dorothy. 'I can't find my anorak and it'll probably rain later, summer or no summer.'

'I'm not surprised you can't find anything in that mess.' Germaine couldn't help herself.

Dorothy laughed. 'I've never been a homemaker, I'm not going to change now.'

Isobel appeared suddenly behind Germaine and poked her head round the open door. 'Ooh, Dorothy, I love what you've done with your shed – so bohemian.'

Germaine snorted. When she was surrounded by folk who thought having the Shatin calendar from 2017 hanging on your wall and so much crap on your floor you couldn't find your own jacket was bohemian, no wonder she had no difficulty in making an enemy a day. But then Isobel said, 'Isn't this great – a lovely day out for the three of us?' and even she had to admit it was better than sitting at home with a chicken curry for one, avoiding Sue from next door lest her new-found line dancing skills be called back into action.

'Come on,' said Dorothy, finding her anorak at last under a pile of yellowing copies of the *Guardian*. 'What are we waiting for?'

Mohid knocked on the door of Lawrence's shed a little impatiently. He'd much rather be partnering up with Farah but Dorothy had said she was the campaign manager and in her judgement, it would take two men to cart back the huge rolls of paper and pieces of thick card promised to them by her friend Irish Mary's cousin, Keith.

'H-h-hello.' Lawrence peeked his head out of the shed. 'T-t-two minutes and I'll be w-w-with you.'

Mohid was embarrassed on the young man's behalf and wondered what it felt like not to be able to express yourself when you wanted to. He'd never actually had a conversation with him on his own before, and had no idea what they would find to talk about all day as they went about their allotted task.

Lawrence came out wrapping a mustard-coloured scarf round his neck. 'S-s-sorry.'

'You won't need that,' said Mohid then wished he'd said nothing as perhaps it was part of the man's armour, like the cuddly toys the sick children on his ward clung to when they saw him approaching in his white coat.

The men walked to the bottom gate in silence and turned right out of the allotments.

'This Keith's place is at the back of the industrial estate opposite Capo's so I thought we'd walk up Spindlehowe, along the top road, then cut down at the Royal Bank, okay?'

'Fine by m-m-me.'

They walked in silence for a bit, stepping aside for dog walkers, the traffic keeping a constant flow beside them.

As they turned right at the top of Spindlehowe, Mohid said, 'It's further than I thought. I hope we'll be okay to carry whatever it is back with us.'

'We can make two journeys if n-n-not. I need the exercise.'

'You look pretty trim to me.'

'Thanks. I wish s-s-someone would tell Adrian that. I think he's worried I'm going to go back to how I was before we met. I was f-f-fat. Very f-f-fat,' he added, not sure why he was telling Mohid this, it wasn't something he usually shared. Perhaps it was down to the man's doctorly manner, his way of saying very little so that you felt you had to fill in the silence. He shot him a sideways glance and was glad to see he didn't seem perturbed by the information.

'We can't all be perfect,' said Mohid smoothly. 'As long as you're fit and healthy, that's all that matters. People probably shouldn't be so pass-remarkable about the appearance of others, especially not those who are supposed to love us.'

'Oh, he does love me, I'm sure he does. It's just . . . he's a p-p-perfectionist, you know? He thinks we should all measure up to his high s-s-standards. He's perfect himself so . . .'

Mohid laughed. They waited for a gap in the traffic and crossed at the bank before he spoke again. 'Like I said, we can't all be perfect, can we?'

'I don't know, you and your w-w-wife seem to have a pretty much p-p-perfect existence, from what I can see.'

Mohid looked at Lawrence in surprise. 'Is that what you think?'

'Well, yeah. You're a doctor, she's a teacher, you l-l-love each other a lot, I can tell. What's not perfect about that l-l-life?'

'We do love each other. Very much.' Mohid hesitated but suddenly thought how good it would be to say some things out loud. He couldn't talk to his own family about their issues – having children, trying to have children – these were not matters he could share with his mother and father, it would be tantamount to talking about their sex life, for goodness' sake. No, definitely not. And he was so busy at work that he'd never taken the time to cultivate relationships with colleagues with whom he could trade confidences. It struck him that since they'd taken on their plot at Kenmar, his fellow allotment holders had come closest to being his friends than anyone else. How odd that he hadn't noticed that happening, the slow morphing of a group of completely separate and very different individuals into a community of people with a shared goal. It had happened so gradually he hadn't registered the change. He was aware of Lawrence by his side, attentive to whatever it was Mohid wanted to confide, and it occurred to him that perhaps this was how friendships were made – not just giving out advice to others, but revealing one's own weaknesses and asking for advice in turn.

He took the plunge. 'We've been trying to have children, a family of our own, for almost six years. Farah—' he corrected himself, 'that is, *we* – it's not Farah's fault, of course – keep losing the babies.'

'I'm so s-s-sorry, I didn't know that.'

'No reason why you should, we keep ourselves to ourselves, it's true.'

They carried on walking, past the big cash 'n' carry and the plumbing supplies, and beyond the Devitt's burger and hot chicken van, which had a queue right along the pavement.

'Those candles that are always lit on your s-s-step. Are they—'

'Yes,' said Mohid quietly before Lawrence could formulate the question.

'I'm sorry.'

'Thanks.' He touched Lawrence lightly on his forearm. 'So you see, no one's perfect, you tell Adrian I said so. And I'm a doctor.' He laughed and looked away to indicate he'd had enough sharing for now.

'This is it,' said Lawrence ten minutes later, stopping at the huge sign advertising 'Keith's Printing Supplies – Trade Only'.

'Let's see what Dorothy's managed to swing for us.'

Back at the allotments, Stanley had been digging over his rose bed for the best part of an hour. Across the path, George was busy painting a huge square of cardboard green. He was doing it with great concentration, apparently oblivious to the paint splattering over his joggers and occasionally on to the path. Stanley wondered whether he should go over and ask him to stop but he was so engaged in the task, it seemed to Stanley that a few paint stains on the path were worth it. He'd been at it all morning, disappearing once and coming back ten minutes later with another piece of cardboard, ready to begin the whole task of covering it in green paint all over again. It seemed an utterly pointless endeavour to Stanley but it was keeping George happy so he'd let him carry on.

He stood up and took off his bunnet, wiping his hot forehead with the back of his hand. He glanced round the empty allotments and wondered where the boy had got to. He felt a vague irritation at being asked to keep an eye on him because this was the quietest the allotments had been for weeks and he'd have liked to enjoy the calm. Between newspaper reporters barging in and asking all the plot holders their views on the closure, locals who'd never even heard of the allotments before last month coming in for a nosy after they'd read about it in the local paper, and the allotment holders themselves seemingly more engaged in their plots than they'd ever been, Stanley was having to come so early to get a minute's peace, sometimes he was here before his paper had even been put through the door in the morning.

Still, he had promised the boy's mother so he put down his spade and strolled to the top of the allotments to see if he could spot him.

'Isaac,' he called over the back field. 'Isaac lad, are you there?'

No answer.

Stanley returned to the main path and tried to think where he'd last seen the boy. He'd been sitting on the step in front of the shed with his electronic thing on his knee as usual when his mother and the others had left. Stanley stood and thought for a moment. That's right, he'd seen him walking round the back of the shed on his own allotment, carrying a box of something under his skinny arm.

Stanley walked past George with an 'All right, George?' as he passed. The man carried on painting, but he was content, happier than Stanley had ever seen him in fact.

Glad one of us is happy, he thought. *Now where is that damn—*

Oh.

Isaac was crouching behind the shed, his back to Stanley and so engrossed in his task that he didn't notice the old man behind him. His ginger hair was on end and the tips of it were covered with red paint. His elbow was raised and swirling in a wide circular motion as he covered the bright green canvas on the ground with huge red bubble letters.

Stanley crept a little closer and looked over the boy's shoulder. He was completing the bottom curve of the letter 'S', making the word 'ALLOTMENTS' stand out in red on top of the vibrant background, painted earlier by his dad. Propped up against the fence was a similar canvas on which the word 'SAVE' was scrawled in the same bright red.

'It's a big sign for the entrance,' Isaac explained when he became aware of Stanley standing there. 'That old woman – Dorothy – she said we need to let everyone know.' He pulled his fringe uncertainly, smearing his forehead red and transferring more red paint on to his hair.

'Well done, son,' said Stanley. 'Even Dorothy will be pleased with that.' Isaac's shoulders dropped and the corners of his mouth curved upwards.

There was a scraping on the gravel behind them and they turned to see George, his arms outstretched so that he was holding a third green canvas, still darkly wet, away from his sweatshirt.

'Weh,' he was saying, pointing to the canvas. 'Gggnnn, tsk, twe,' and finally, clearly, 'Wet.'

'Thanks, Dad.' Isaac stood up and took the large painted canvas from his father and leaned it against the fence next to the first completed panel.

George gave his son the thumbs up.

'Good,' said Isaac.

George shook his head, uncertain.

'Good,' said Isaac again.

'Good,' repeated George, his eyes lighting up as his son gave him a thumbs up in return.

At one o'clock, Stanley offered to make lunch for the three of them but Isaac said wouldn't a pizza be better and he'd nip down to Enzo's and get a large Margherita – as long as Stanley paid for it.

'You won't get a better offer than that, you know.' He flashed a grin.

'Chancer,' said Stanley but delighted to see the boy coming

out of his shell. 'Why not? Mabel used to love a slice of pizza with *Strictly*, I haven't had one for ages.' He handed over two ten pound notes. 'Get us a large bottle of Irn-Bru as well. And bring my change, mind,' he called after him as Isaac pelted through the allotments gate and down to Main Street.

27

WHILE STANLEY, GEORGE AND ISAAC were tucking into a 14-inch cheese and tomato pizza, Germaine, Dorothy and Isobel were arguing over who should go in and talk to the bigwigs at the council.

'I'm the campaign manager,' said Dorothy.

'Self-elected,' muttered Germaine.

'Still counts, doesn't it?' Dorothy looked to Isobel for support.

Isobel was staring at the newly whitewashed walls of the Almada Street offices. 'Wasn't this where they had all that graffiti up the wall last year? Those wimmin's libbers?'

Germaine swung round. 'Wimmin's libbers? What kind of phrase is that? Were you born in the Middle Ages? Wimmin's libbers, for God's sake.'

'Exactly, thank you, Germaine. It was a group of women who let this bloody council know what's what, and to be quite frank I don't know why they stopped, they were doing the women of Lanarkshire a public service, in my view.'

Germaine raised her hand in a high five, which Dorothy slapped enthusiastically. 'Well said, missus.' Isobel looked sheepish and said, 'Pardon me for breathing, I'm sure.' Germaine appraised Dorothy with fresh eyes. 'Maybe you should lead the way, Ms Pankhurst, and me and Doormat here will back you up.' Isobel tutted but followed dutifully behind the other two as they strode into the main reception area of the council headquarters.

The place was quiet. 'Are you sure they'll be here on a Saturday?' said Isobel.

'Let's find out, shall we?' There was no one behind the desk so Dorothy rang the bell and the three women stood in an impatient huddle. Moments later, a short plump woman with a helmet of curls and a dirty beige bodywarmer zipped up to her neck came out of the lift behind them and approached the main desk. She appeared not to see them at first and crouched down behind the desk, leafing through the sheaves of paper on the shelves.

Germaine cleared her throat loudly while Dorothy mouthed, 'Leave this to me.'

'Hello?' she called over the desk.

The woman popped up like a cork from a bottle, her sweet open face beaming at them. 'Hello,' she said.

'Hello. Again.' Germaine stepped forward, having decided not to leave it to Dorothy after all. 'We're from the Kenmar allotments and we are here to see— in fact, we demand to see someone about the closures.'

'Kenmar allotments? Was there a fatality?'

Germaine screwed up her eyes. 'A fatality? No, I . . . what do you mean, a fatality?'

'It means death, Germaine,' said Isobel helpfully, glad to be able to redeem herself after her earlier faux pas.

'Yes, thank you, Isobel, I know what the word means.' She turned back to the woman behind the desk. 'I meant, why are you asking us about deaths at the allotments? What are you talking about?'

Dorothy put her hand on Germaine's arm and said in a slow soothing voice to the woman behind the counter, 'We are here to speak to someone from the Communities Committee. Do. You. Understand?'

'Ah,' said the woman. 'I don't work for Communities. I'm in Bereavement. It's brilliant.' She beamed again.

'And we're all very happy for you and your death wish,' said Germaine, 'but if you could let someone from Communities know the . . . representatives' – Dorothy raised her thumb in approval – 'from Kenmar Allotments Save Our Allotments campaign are here, we'd be very grateful.'

Dorothy scanned the empty corridor. She checked the reception desk, which was now also empty, before rejoining Isobel and Germaine who were sitting in silence where she'd left them. 'Do you think anyone's coming to talk to us? That's been hours.'

'Eighteen minutes,' said Germaine, tapping her phone.

'Still . . .'

The lift door opened and Councillor Murray stepped out, his trench coat flapping around him as he checked his phone. Karen followed close behind.

'Finally.' Dorothy walked towards the lift.

'I'm sorry, do you have an appointment?' said the councillor at the same time as Karen said, 'What are you doing here?' in a shrill voice, keen to avoid any further confrontation between her boss and the Kenmar plot holders.

'Wait. Did no one give you the message?'

'What message?' Councillor Murray looked Dorothy up and

down as though he found her dungarees, if not her presence itself in his domain, distasteful.

'The message that we were here and wished to speak to you.' She stood her ground and the other two came to back her up. 'We are the representatives of the Kenmar Allotments Save Our Allotments campaign' – she ignored his snort of laughter – 'and we are here for an update on exactly what the plans are for the allotments.'

Karen stepped forward quickly. 'I think the council has been quite clear on its plans with regard to the allotments. And we will be informing all the plot holders in writing, we haven't had the time yet—'

'Never you mind justifying the council position to them, Karen.' He raised a hand so that his palm was directly in front of the three women, very close to their faces. 'I am not going to explain myself to a bunch of Karens . . . sorry, Karen, no offence. But I haven't got all day to stand around and talk to three old ladies who haven't even gone to the trouble of making an appointment about council business. On a Saturday, if you please. Now, if you'll excuse me.' With a last flap of his overcoat and a reassuring pat of his combover, the pompous little man swept out of the building and left the women standing in a semicircle watching him leave.

Karen flushed in embarrassment on her boss's behalf but said, 'You can't keep turning up here without an appointment and expect to be told all the details of council business. That's not how it works.'

'I know none of this is your fault, Karen, but we are not going to take this lying down.' Dorothy's voice was even louder than usual, her own cheeks red with fury. 'Old ladies indeed.'

Turning back to Germaine and Isobel, she glared at them until Isobel said faintly, 'Er yes, I mean, no, no we're not going to take it lying down. Are we? Germaine?'

Germaine licked her lips and stood tall. 'No, we are not. So – he won't talk to three women without an appointment, will he? Let's see how he feels about taking on an entire community, all of whom, I am quite sure, will be backing our new campaign. Something tells me Councillor Murray has no idea what people like us are capable of. Come on, Dorothy' – Germaine swished towards the door – 'Isobel, keep up. If Councillor Murray wants a fight, trust me, I don't need any persuasion to make an enemy out of him.'

Karen watched as the three women got stuck together in the revolving door and had to do a slow 180-degree shuffle so that the door finally opened on to the street and freed them. Probably not quite the dramatic exit they'd been hoping for but Karen couldn't help being impressed by them nonetheless.

'I don't think they were very impressed with us, were they?'

The day was almost over and Maggi and Kevin sat in Maggi's car outside Kevin's flat.

'Our bargaining technique wasn't what you'd call a resounding success,' Maggi agreed. 'I think they might even have charged us extra for those bigger brushes.'

'Sorry.' Kevin touched his face.

'Nothing to do with you, Kevin, they probably didn't like me. I should have talked less, I think. Mum's always telling me that. Though she's one to talk.'

Kevin wanted to tell her that he loved listening to her talk, that he was riveted by her stories about gigs she'd done at Angels and the Olde Club, or festivals she'd performed at up in Skye or the Isle of Lewis. He thought about it, almost got the words out, but too late, she was speaking again. 'Anyway, we've done what we were asked to do, I'll drop all the stuff off tomorrow. So – we're finished for the day . . .'

'I think we've done a good job.'

'Yeah.'

'Definitely.'

'So, I guess I'll be heading home – unless . . .' She looked towards his flat, then back to him.

Kevin sat on his hands – did she want him to . . . was she really waiting for him to . . .

Maggi gave an exasperated sigh and raised her hands in the air before dropping them back to her steering wheel. 'Okay then.'

'Yes, um, okay.'

'See you, Kevin.'

Dammit.

Later that night, while Kevin was brushing his teeth and getting ready for bed, he faced the mirror and turned his head left and right, inspecting his reflection. Maybe it wasn't that bad, he thought, in certain lights. He put down his toothbrush and licked his minty-fresh lips. 'You're the loveliest girl I've ever seen, Maggi,' he whispered and leaned closer into the mirror, closing his eyes and puckering his lips in an approximation of the kiss he dreamed about giving Maggi. Inches away from the glass, he snapped his eyes open to see what he looked like close up. He bent over the sink as though he'd been punched in the softness of his belly and recoiled from his own image, exactly as Maggi would have done had he actually tried to kiss her. He brushed a warm tear from his cheek. 'Stupid,' he hissed at his reflection, and punched the side of his scarred cheek with his fist closed tight as a bud, knuckles white. A small bruise bloomed on the corrugated skin, it would be pale blue tomorrow, like an early begonia from his allotment. Kevin shook his head at his audacity to dream, jabbing at the light switch and plunging himself back into darkness.

28

SaveOurAllotments@KenmarAllotments

Please sign the petition to reverse the decision to close Kenmar allotments. Get involved and help us keep our community spaces #SaveOurAllotments

HamiltonAdvertiser@AdvOfficial

Kenmar allotments to be bought over and developed into residential property, Biggart Bros announce. Local residents not happy

JennyT@UddyRules

Just what North Lanarkshire needs – luxury housing. NOT!!!!!! #SaveOurAllotments

SaveOurAllotments@KenmarAllotments

Don't forget the bag pack #Sunday30June @scotmid_viewpark. Ten o'clock onwards. #SaveOurAllotments

JohnBryan@Journo

Kenmar allotment holders vow to keep their allotments open. *Uddingston Speaker* learns of campaign plans

FrancisMcG@FitbaBhoy1888

Sign the petition to save Kenmar allotments. This is our community, don't let them take it away from us #SaveOurAllotments

FinlayM@Club1872

I live in Viewpark, those allotments are always empty. There's a wall at the back that's an accident waiting to happen. Better off knocking the whole place down IMO #MakeViewparkGreatAgain

FrancisMcG@FitbaBhoy1888

@Club1872 Talking crap as usual. My neighbour's an old bloke who lives for his allotment and he's not the only one #SaveOurAllotments

FinlayM@Club1872

[This post has been removed]

Scotmid@scotmid_viewpark

Show your support for the Kenmar allotments #BagPack #30June #SaveOurAllotments

SaveOurAllotments@KenmarAllotments

Help us make the council change its mind about selling Kenmar allotments. Please join us and make a difference in your community #SaveOurAllotments

Facebook post for Kenmar allotments

A huge thank you to everyone who's been sharing details of our campaign to save our allotments. Follow us on Twitter/X @KenmarAllotments and help us spread the word #SaveOurAllotments

SaveOurAllotments@KenmarAllotments

We are marching to the council buildings on #Saturday27July. Join us and help to save our community spaces #SaveOurAllotments

HamiltonAdvertiser@AdvOfficial

Allotment holder and community representative Dorothy Mackie tells *Hamilton Advertiser* that support to save Kenmar allotments is growing as online petition garners over 2,000 signatures

SaveOurAllotments@KenmarAllotments

Have you signed the petition to save Kenmar allotments yet? This is OUR community, don't let them take it #SaveOurAllotments

NeilMcB@NeilMcBride

Kenmar allotment holders are wasting their time, that council's a bunch of fannies #Moneytalks #Deluded

SusanHendo@Shenderson

@NeilMcBride Not helping! That's the attitude that lost us Motherwell Baths and our biggest library. Don't let them win this one as well #SaveOurAllotments

Facebook post for Kenmar allotments

Come along to our jumble sale and craft fayre at Viewpark Church! Quality clothing and bric-a-brac – Handmade items – Books – Pottery – Art – Jewellery – Street food – And much more. 6.30 p.m. onwards Tuesday 9 July

SaveOurAllotments@KenmarAllotments

Stand up and be counted! Every signature counts, every protestor counts. Save the date #Saturday27July #SaveOurAllotments

Billy@WilliamSeddon

Use it or lose it. Don't let them win #SaveOurAllotments

SaveOurAllotments@KenmarAllotments

Our petition now has over 2,500 signatures. Have you signed it yet? #SaveOurAllotments

ViewparkChurchEvents@ViewparkChurch

Come and help us raise funds for our local allotments. Jumble sale and craft fayre #Tuesday9July #SaveOurAllotments

DavidWilson@UHMonklands

Stand up to the Tory bullies. Help save our community spaces. Rise up and join the march #SupportOurNHS #SaveOurAllotments #Saturday27July

SaveOurAllotments@KenmarAllotments

Stand up and be counted. Come and march with us #Saturday27July #SaveOurAllotments

BigGordo@GordonH

WTF are the Kenmar allotments? #CelticFCForever

29

Kevin had set his alarm for half eight. It was Sunday but he'd promised Dorothy he would take the first shift at the bag pack. 'I can't make it myself because I'm leafletting first thing then I've to drop off more bags of donations for the jumble sale so I'm relying on you, Kevin,' she'd said. 'Ten till twelve. Do not be late.'

Kevin wouldn't dare.

The butterflies started when he finished his cornflakes. What if no one let him pack their bags? What if they were too disgusted by his face to even stop? He wondered whether he was brave enough to call Dorothy back and make his excuses. After all, what could she do to him really—

His buzzer rang.

Kevin was washing up his bowl and stopped mid-wipe. His buzzer never rang.

'Hello?'

'Kevin? It's Germaine. Buzz me up?'

'Germaine? How did you know where I— '

'Let me in, Kevin, will you? I'm standing out here like a stalker and it's not a good look for me.'

Minutes later, Germaine was standing in Kevin's small neat living room.

'Nice flat,' she said, running her hand along the top of the mantelpiece, as though checking for dust.

'Thanks.' Kevin frowned. 'Is there . . . is there something wrong? Has the bag pack been cancelled?'

Germaine perched on the edge of his sofa. 'No, nothing's wrong. Dorothy's got us both on the first shift and she thought . . . that is to say, *I* thought maybe we could walk to Scotmid together.'

Kevin felt a spike of embarrassment at the idea of the two women discussing him and whether he'd be too nervous to fulfil his promise without one of the others holding his hand. 'Thanks for thinking of me but I don't need—'

'It's a walk along to Scotmid together, Kevin,' said Germaine smoothly. 'Or are you embarrassed to be seen with me?'

Kevin relented. 'Okay, let me get my anorak.'

There was a steady stream of customers in the shop, even at ten o'clock on a Sunday morning. The store manager had put Kevin at the end of the first checkout and Germaine a couple of checkouts along so Kevin was able to keep an eye on how many customers they each had. He was pretty sure the same number of people had come through his checkout as Germaine's and they all seemed quite happy to let him put away their shopping and throw some coins into his bucket. He soon developed a system of stacking the tins neatly in a row at the bottom of each bag and carefully separating the leaking packs of meat from the vegetables before placing them on top. As the morning wore on and customers laughed and chatted with him as he packed their bags, he wasn't sure what he'd been so worried about.

He was finding it unexpectedly fascinating to see the items

that other people purchased on their weekly shop. He'd often wondered who'd bought the inferior Koka noodles when the original and best Pot Noodles were on display and he would not have guessed it was his old headmaster, Mr McLoughlin, who'd muttered something about the pleasures of the single life as Kevin packed his noodles and a bottle of Bell's whisky into his reusable carrier bag. He'd seemed pleased to see Kevin though and they'd had a nice chat about the allotments. Iris from the church had stopped by to pick up some bashed tins of tomatoes and beans that the supermarket was donating to the food bank. She also bought reduced-price butter and bacon and Scotch eggs. They were just on the sell-by date but perfectly good, she told him. Later, when he packed a bag with steak and porcini and three bottles of red wine for an expensively dressed couple who blew kisses at each other as he packed, Kevin wondered at such different lives being led in such close proximity.

Lawrence spotted him first and called out 'Hello' as he waited in line. He was dressed from head to toe in white and had a pair of shades on his head, holding back his hair like a girl's hairband. Adrian was standing next to him, also in white, and frowning at something on his phone. He looked up from the screen when he heard Lawrence say hello and gave Kevin a small wave.

They started to place the items from their basket on the belt and Kevin took the large hemp bag from Lawrence and reached for the groceries being flung towards him by the checkout boy.

'Wait a minute,' said Adrian, holding up a bag of rice. 'Did you know this rice isn't wholegrain? You carry on here, I'll go and change it.'

When Adrian was safely up aisle 9, Kevin said, 'You did know that, didn't you?'

'Course.' Lawrence winked. 'Worth a try, wasn't it?'

'How come you got out of the bag pack then?'

'Adrian said Sundays were for relaxing. So far today we've been for a run and done a spin class. Now we're shopping before I go home and mix the marinade for the chicken and prepare the vegetables.'

'Sounds very relaxing.'

'Exactly. I'm on the crepe stand at the jumble sale next week though. Are you going?'

'I don't think I've ever been to a jumble sale. Will there be a manga stand?'

'It's Viewpark Church, Kevin, so I highly doubt it but you never know. You should definitely come, it'll be fun.'

Adrian returned and took the bag from Kevin, dropping a twenty pound note into his bucket.

'I was saying to Kevin, he should come to the jumble—'

'Ready?' said Adrian, with a small dip of his chin to acknowledge Kevin's thanks for the donation.

Lawrence bit his lip then followed Adrian out to the car, lowering his head so that his sunglasses fell on to his face and covered his eyes as he did so.

They had almost finished their two-hour shift when Germaine came over to Kevin's checkout and whispered, 'Could we swap for five minutes?'

'Yeah, why? Is something wrong?'

'It's just . . .' Germaine inclined her head towards the queue at her own checkout. Kevin saw a skinny man lurching towards the till, thick glasses on at a squint. The assistant was ignoring him so he flapped his hands back and forth in front of her face.

'What's up wi' your face, doll?' he slurred as he dropped a six-pack of Tennent's on to the counter. 'Gawn, gie's a smile.'

The two girls who'd been queuing behind him laughed nervously and swapped queues to the next checkout.

'Stay here for now,' said Kevin. 'He can put his own beer in a bag.'

They watched as the man tried and failed to pull a bag from the hook at the end of the checkout. The assistant swivelled round on her chair and pulled it off for him. '30p,' she said curtly.

'Wha'? Wha's 30p? Just give me my beer.'

'The bag. They're thirty pence each. Do you want a bag?'

'I need a bag for my beer. But I'm not paying 30p for it.'

The assistant tried to grab the bag back from him but the man tightened his grip on it.

'Fine,' said the assistant. She rang up the price of his beer and said, 'Cash or card?' without looking at him.

'Right decision, he's clearly beyond reasoning with,' whispered Germaine, now standing slightly behind Kevin and hiding behind her hair, praying that Tam wouldn't see her and recognize her from the AA meeting.

Kevin agreed though he was surprised at the usually unflappable Germaine's reaction. 'He's had one too many, that's all.'

'He's a dirty drunk and he deserves all he gets.'

Kevin didn't reply until the man had paid up and staggered out of the shop, the stench of alcohol and despair billowing round him and poisoning the air. 'I'm surprised you'd say that, to be honest, Germaine. Some people have got problems no one else can guess at, reasons why they get like that. Could happen to any of us.'

Relaxing a little now Tam had left, Germaine relented. 'Sorry – that was harsh. But think about the effect that man's drinking might be having on others. Not just people he meets when he goes about his business, but his family, children maybe. He could be ruining their lives too.'

'Everyone makes their own choices. But . . . we don't always know what choices people are facing. And even if he is drunk, he can't be responsible for everyone else around him too. We're all responsible for our own decisions. That's what my mum— That's what I think anyway.'

Germaine thought about what Kevin had said and tried to store it for later, to turn over and consider when she was beating herself up about what had happened to her dad. 'You should say what you think more often, Kevin. You make a lot more sense than most of your fellow plot holders.'

Kevin blushed and mumbled, 'Thanks.'

'No, I mean it.' And she did. This was the longest conversation she'd ever had with the boy and she was beginning to understand why Lawrence, Mohid and the others were drawn to him. 'Tell me, is there a girlfriend you're keeping quiet about?'

Kevin shook his head.

'Someone you're interested in then?'

Kevin could feel his colour rising again as an image of Maggi in her red lipstick and wild outfits flashed into his mind and Germaine said, 'Ah-ha, I'm right.'

'I refuse to believe you're right about anything, Germaine Hounslow.' It was Dorothy, marching towards them in her dungarees, carrying a small white bucket like theirs, with a sticker saying 'Save Our Allotments' taped on its side. 'And by the way, I've stood and watched about half a dozen people pack their own bags while you two have been gabbing. Good job I'm here to take over the second shift.'

Kevin checked behind her. 'Is Maggi not helping you today?'

'Maggi? No. She did offer but I told her we didn't need her. She's far too busy with her own life to be bothering with us, Kevin. She'll be out with her pals or off singing somewhere. I'll manage fine till Farah gets here.'

Kevin's hands fell loosely by his sides but he tried not to let the skewer of disappointment show on his face. Dorothy was right. Of course Maggi would be far too busy with all her friends and her exciting career to bother with him and the allotments. He'd been mad to think otherwise.

'Are you two heading off now?' Dorothy was already packing an old man's shopping wheelie as she spoke.

'Yes, things to do,' said Germaine briskly, handing over her bucket of change and wondering how much Dorothy had overheard before they'd noticed her. 'I've done my duty here. I'm going straight to the allotments to wage war on that damn chickweed before it starts flowering.' She made to go then turned back and added, 'Thanks for your help, Kevin' before leaving them to it.

Dorothy raised her eyebrows in surprise.

'I'll be going as well if that's okay. I'm very busy too,' Kevin assured her. 'Loads of . . . things to do.' He paused. 'I might go and stock up on some Pot Noodles while I'm here though. Save me going out again.'

30

Dorothy had been at the hall since half past five. Iris and her volunteers from the church had done them proud, setting up large tables in a horseshoe round the hall and filling them with the many and various donations that had come in over the last three weeks. Everywhere Dorothy looked, she could see piles of coloured knitwear, jeans and shirts. Someone had brought in a couple of clothes racks and these were hung with heavy winter coats and musty-looking tweeds, scarves strung along the top and hanging over them like streamers. One stand was devoted to toys and it was already being swarmed by children with eyes large as plates, their hands reaching up to the multicoloured plastic as they pestered whoever was with them to buy the treasure on display. The crafts group had set up their own stand and it was a work of art compared to the rest. Ceramics skilfully interspersed with chunky coloured glassware, donated artwork from the Bothwell Art Club, and long threads of silver jewellery dangling from a rack above the stand, the gemstone pendants sparkling like diamonds as they caught the light.

A huge white sheet with the words 'Viewpark Girl Guides Say Save Kenmar Allotments' emblazoned on it in red paint was draped on the back wall and one of the enterprising young guides had set up a stand underneath it, charging 50p a go for anyone who wanted to autograph the sheet and have their name put in a draw to win it as a souvenir when the jumble sale was finished.

Dorothy was manning the book stand opposite the stage, where they'd set up the food stalls. She'd had plenty of customers since they'd opened half an hour ago and her cash box was pleasingly full. She was wondering whether she should take the proceeds back to Iris in the office for safekeeping when she spotted her dancing friends through the crowds.

'Myra,' she called. 'Irish Mary, Terry, over here.' She motioned to them and they approached her stand.

'You're looking very pleased with yourself,' she said to the habitually sour-faced Myra, who was clutching a large bottle and wearing a smug expression.

'Sure, wouldn't you be if you'd won a bottle of the Celtic centenary whisky.' Irish Mary dug her friend playfully in the ribs with her elbow.

'Signed by Tommy Boyd too,' said Terry. 'Still a handsome man,' she added, and Irish Mary said, 'He is indeed.'

'Course you'll be sharing that with everyone, won't you? Not like that Norah one from the bingo.' Dorothy couldn't resist.

'You can go off some people, you know,' sniffed Myra, wrapping the edge of her rain jacket round the bottle as though one of her friends was going to snatch it away from her.

'Ah, we're kidding you,' said Irish Mary. 'Now, Dorothy, what have you got for us here then? Sell us your wares.'

'Funny you should say that.' Dorothy reached below the counter for the CD she'd spotted and put aside for her friend the moment she'd seen it on the stand. She handed it to Irish Mary.

'Dorothy Mackie, I always knew you were a good one! Daniel O'Donnell live in Castlerea from 1982 – only the finest singer who ever stood in shoe leather.' She turned to the others and pointed to the cherubic manchild in a grey blouson jacket adorning the front of the CD. 'Keep your Tommy Boyds. Now that there is a handsome man.'

'I think that cataract surgery affected you more than you thought, Mary,' said Terry, and her friend laughed good-naturedly.

'What on earth are they selling?' Myra pointed at the stall a couple of pitches along. The table was covered in rocks and crystals, clusters of amethysts and tiny trees adorned with translucent stones.

'They're to aid healing.' Dorothy told her friends what Iris had told her earlier. For a small fee, local business owners had been offered the chance to show their wares at the event and the softly spoken young man from Quartz Moon had taken them up on it. 'You know, chakra trees and crystals, pondering your orb, that sort of thing.'

'Pondering your orb?' Myra repeated incredulously.

'Don't look now,' said Irish Mary. 'There's that weird Helen from the Friday club, checking out the crystals.'

'That's exactly the kind of thing she would buy,' said Myra tartly. 'Practically lives on probiotic yoghurt *and* she wore a beret to the last St Patrick's dance.'

'A beret? She never?'

'She did. Red.'

'A red beret on St Patrick's night? You're right, she's definitely the type to buy a crystal.'

'I'm shopped out,' said Myra. 'Anyone else ready to leave?'

'Wait, have you been to the food stalls yet?' Dorothy indicated the line of stands on the stage, waving to Lawrence who she'd just noticed was serving up crepes at the second stand along. 'They've got all sorts – hot dogs, Nutella pancakes, street food . . .'

'What's street food?' Terry asked Irish Mary, her eyes drifting over to the stage.

'It means you don't get a plate. Come on, you'll love it. See you later, Dorothy.'

An hour later and the crowds were starting to thin out, the heaving tables now mostly empty. Dorothy had stayed on the book stand all evening, saying hi to Farah and waving across the hall at Stanley, who'd taken one look at the place and plonked himself down on a chair at the entrance, allowing the eddies of people to swirl around him. Germaine had stopped for a chat, bought a couple of Agatha Christies then said she had to head, she had things to do. 'You've always got things to do,' Dorothy said. 'Why don't you leave them for now and stay and enjoy yourself?' but Germaine shook her head and left.

Dorothy checked the clock above the stage and thought it was almost time to start the clear-up when she spotted Maggi at the other side of the hall. She couldn't remember the last time her daughter had popped by the allotments though she had called her at the weekend and offered to help at the jumble sale. Dorothy hadn't wanted to take any more of her time, assumed she'd have better things to do with herself, singing gigs maybe, or nights out with her own pals. But as she watched her daughter wandering forlornly round the draughty hall, inspecting mismatching cups and chipped plates, and picking up a faded gypsy skirt (and laying it down again, thank God), she wondered whether she'd been right about that. Maybe she'd call her later and ask if she fancied helping them to paint placards on Saturday for the big march, they needed all hands on deck for that, especially the creative ones like Maggi and Isobel.

It crossed her mind that she hadn't seen Isobel for a couple of weeks either. Not since they'd been to the council offices with Germaine, in fact. Now that she thought about it, she couldn't remember the last time she'd seen Isobel or George at the allotments. Dorothy piled up the few unsold paperbacks from her stand and dumped them in the box at her feet, promising herself she'd call Isobel too the moment she got home.

Farah didn't stay long at the jumble sale. She wasn't a big fan of rooting through other people's cast-offs but Mohid was working and he'd persuaded her that one of them should put in an appearance in support of the campaign. 'Don't be so snooty, you might even find something you like,' he'd teased her. And he'd been right, as usual. She was holding a small ceramic pot, patterned with delicate blue birds, which would be lovely at their kitchen window, filled with cornflowers or blue violets.

She crossed at the lights and ambled along Old Edinburgh Road, enjoying the warm evening and the way the sunlight danced against the white brickwork of the neat houses on her left. *Another new housing estate for all the young couples with their growing families*, she thought enviously. She saw a group of teenagers outside Cakes and Shakes. Such a sweet tooth these people had, especially the young. She'd noticed with her own pupils very few of them stood at breaktime and ate an apple or a sandwich, and certainly not one of the previous evening's samosas wrapped in greaseproof paper, like she herself had done.

Their hands were always full of sweetie wrappers and cake. No wonder they had the worst teeth in Europe. One of the group spotted her and called, 'Hi, Mrs Ahmed' and the chubby girl beside her turned and waved, her high ponytail swinging. Farah waved back and felt guilty for judging them. They were happy and no doubt healthy enough. They'd survived beyond babyhood at any rate, a niggling voice wormed its way into her head and she chased it away. She was a lucky woman with her dear Mohid and she knew she should be grateful for what they did have and not mourn what they did not.

As the group of teenagers moved away, a small figure perched on the edge of the pavement came into view, his knees under his chin as he threw pebbles across the road and looked back longingly at the thick chocolate shakes and brownies being passed around the young people as they walked.

'Isaac?' she called.

The boy turned and gave her a reluctant smile.

'Hello.' She crouched down so that her face was level with his. He looked tired and she could almost trace the bone of his narrow jaw, so thin was his face. 'What are you doing here on your own? Is your mum—'

'My mum's not well. She's in bed. She's been in bed all week.' He threw a stone half-heartedly and it landed a few inches from his feet.

'I see. What about your dad? Or . . . is there someone else who'll be wondering where you are?' What age was the boy? she wondered, annoyed with herself for not knowing that by now. Surely too young to be sitting on a road by himself this late in the evening though.

'My dad's at the woods. Searching for . . . wood.'

There was a pause as Farah debated with herself whether she could, in good conscience, go home and leave the boy here on his own.

'Hello.'

'Stanley!' Isaac's face lit up and he leapt up from the ground.

'All roads lead to Cakes and Shakes.' Stanley gestured to the sugar temple behind them.

Farah looked down at the boy. 'Would you like something? If you don't need to rush home, I mean? We could go in and have a cake or . . .'

'Will you come too?' Isaac peeped at Stanley through his fringe.

Stanley hesitated. He'd already missed most of *Morse* to show his face at the jumble sale.

'Please.'

'Come on,' said Farah. 'My treat.'

This was the first time Farah had been in the café and now she wondered why she hadn't been before. The place was small, but warm and welcoming, with three or four round wooden tables and a squashy sofa by the window. The walls were covered in framed black and white photographs of old Italian movie stars and Stanley and Isaac sat beneath a huge print of Gina Lollobrigida sucking an olive seductively, while Farah waited at the counter for their coffees and cake.

'Good?' she asked Isaac, as the boy tucked into a slab of double chocolate fudge cake.

Isaac's mouth was too full for him to speak but his bulging cheeks and the speed with which he was hoovering up the giant dessert answered the question for him.

Farah sipped her flat white. 'No wonder they call it death by chocolate,' she said to Stanley.

'It's fine every once in a while. We used to let Brian eat whatever he wanted and he was fit as a fiddle . . . until . . .'

Farah checked Isaac's attention was completely taken up by his cake before she said, 'So sorry to hear about your son, Stanley. Mohid told me you'd spoken to him about it once, I hope that's okay.'

'Yes, it's not a secret. But . . . I don't talk about him much. Can still be painful, all these years later. Leukaemia.' Stanley answered her unspoken question. 'He was so brave about it too. He was just about to turn twelve.'

They both looked at Isaac.

'Life can be very unfair,' said Farah.

'He was a great boy, we were lucky to have him for the time we did. And I had Mabel too, so I was extra lucky.' Stanley smacked his lips together and put down his cup. 'Do you think you and Mohid will have children? You're good with them, I can see that.' He gestured towards Isaac, who'd left the table to go and get a straw for his milkshake.

'We'd love to,' said Farah. 'But . . . I'm not sure it's going to happen for us.' She hesitated but she did need to talk to someone about it. 'Mohid has suggested we adopt.' Her eyes rested on her coffee as she spoke.

'And you're not keen?'

'It's not . . . It's more that I really want a baby, not a toddler or a child Isaac's age.' She looked up suddenly. 'Sorry, but it's not as selfish as it sounds. A baby would need us more, we have all this love to give . . .'

Stanley handed her a napkin and she dried her eyes. 'Older

kids need love too.' He inclined his head towards Isaac who was now exploring the café, taking his time to study all the movie prints, his lips moving as he read the names beneath each one. 'You've done a good thing tonight.'

'Buying him double chocolate cake, I'm not so sure.'

'It's not about the cake, but you know that.'

Farah nodded.

'You've made sure he's okay, that someone's looking out for him while his parents are going through . . . whatever it is they're going through.'

'I suppose. But a baby needs parents more—'

Stanley leaned forward. 'Listen, when we first had Brian, I was surplus to requirements.'

'That can't be true.'

'No, it is. But I'll tell you something else, Mabel wasn't that special either.'

'What do you mean?'

'What I mean is, babies need to be fed, burped, kept warm. That's all there is to it. It doesn't really matter who's doing those things, can be Mum, Dad, whoever, right?'

Farah said nothing, not sure where Stanley was going with this.

'But when they get that little bit older, *that's* when you can really make a difference. Listening to them when they tell you about their day, what happened at nursery or school, sympathizing when they tell you no one wanted to play with them, this one or that one took their toys, wouldn't give them back their books. Their personality, it forms right in front of your eyes, you can't believe it, almost, when they become their own person. But they need help with that – direction, advice –

someone willing to give up their time, their own needs, to help them. That's when the real parenting's done, not when they're babies.' Stanley sat back. 'Just my opinion, mind.'

Farah's eyes were wide. 'That . . . makes so much sense, Stanley. Thank you, I—'

'Is that not the woman from the allotments?' Isaac had returned to the table and was pointing at the counter.

'Look who it is,' said Stanley. 'Cakes and Shakes is clearly the place to be on a Tuesday night.'

In fact, Germaine was to be found in Cakes and Shakes most nights of the week, not just a Tuesday. Now that she no longer had alcohol to treat herself with, she often popped in to buy a little something for after her dinner. And tonight, the thought of an illicit slice of apple strudel to enjoy with a cup of hot chocolate when she got home had been the only thing getting her through the jumble sale. But she didn't think they needed to know any of these things. 'What are you lot doing here?' She came over to join them when she'd been served. 'Were you at the jumble sale?'

'Yes.' Farah indicated the plant pot at her feet. 'Didn't see you there?'

'It was busy.' Germaine watched as Farah dipped the last napkin on the table into her glass of water and gently wiped the chocolate smears from Isaac's mouth. 'You're good with kids.'

'Thanks,' said Farah. 'I am a teacher.'

'Are you?' It struck Germaine how little she knew about the woman, or her husband.

'Mabel would have loved this,' said Stanley suddenly.

'Did she like cake?' said Isaac.

'Cake, yes, she did, very much but I meant this' – he gestured round the table – 'us sitting here together, chatting, having a laugh. She would have loved that.'

'Thank goodness for the allotments,' said Farah. 'We'd never have met otherwise.'

Germaine's eyebrow arched in surprise, she hadn't taken Farah for someone who wanted to make friends.

'But they're closing now, aren't they? My mum told me, that's part of the reason she . . .' Isaac slid his eyes to the floor.

'Maybe not, son. We've got the community behind us.' Stanley pointed over at the small poster pinned to the wall behind the counter, advertising the march and highlighting their campaign. 'What do you think?' he asked Germaine. 'Any chance the council will change its mind?'

'I don't think so,' said Germaine. 'I'm afraid whatever we've raised between the bag pack and tonight won't be enough to change the situation.'

'Don't forget the petition.'

'There is that, but still . . .'

'What a pity,' said Farah.

Germaine picked up the white bag with her strudel and stood up. 'I'd better get going. I've got . . .'

'Things to do,' Farah finished her sentence for her.

'Things to— Yes, that's right. But . . . I'll see you all at the community centre on Saturday.' As she left, she heard Farah say again, 'It really is a pity' and Isaac piped up, 'Any chance of another strawberry milkshake?'

31

Maggi hadn't been to the allotments for three weeks, she was too worried about bumping into Kevin. After their trip to the suppliers, she'd realized that Kevin wasn't interested in her. She'd given him plenty of opportunity to ask her in to his flat for a coffee and he hadn't, even though they were sitting right outside. Not to mention the fact she'd practically thrown herself at him that time they'd had a party at the start of summer. She'd lain on the grass right next to him and he hadn't so much as kissed her on the cheek. No point in kidding herself, she thought, and why should someone like Kevin be interested in an ugly whale like her? Maybe she should go on a diet and lose some weight. And think about getting a proper job too; perhaps the time had to come to accept that she was kidding herself that someone like her could be a singer. But what sort of job could she do? Singing was all she was interested in, she was useless at everything else.

The ringing of her phone cut short her musings. It was her mum.

'My help?' she said in an incredulous voice, holding the phone close to her ear to make sure she'd got it right.

'Don't sound so surprised, Maggi. You're the best artist I know and we need that kind of creative input to the campaign.'

'What do you want me to do?' Maggi was on the edge of her sofa as she listened to her mother's request. 'Yes,' she said finally. 'Yes, I'll come along on Saturday morning, first thing, and help. I'll . . . look forward to it.'

She'd been standing outside Viewpark Community Centre for twenty minutes before someone came to open the door and let her in.

'You're keen,' said Amanda, the caretaker. 'No one else is here yet. We've set up though.' She indicated the long table at the back of the hall, covered in the supplies Dorothy had managed to secure from her various contacts and pals in the community.

'Brilliant,' said Maggi. 'I'll make a start.'

By the time her mother arrived with Stanley, the latter grumping about being away from the allotments again but there all the same, and Mohid and Farah following on close behind, Maggi had already sorted the materials out into a conveyor belt of activities.

'Let me walk you through it,' she said, the sheen on her face reflecting the effort she'd put in. 'The first job is painting the big squares of card all over then leaning them against the wall to dry. Second, we paint the slogan, before moving on to add the finishing touches – glitter, crepe paper and so forth – then after another drying session, someone at the last station has to attach the card to these poles, which someone else will helpfully have cut to size. Meanwhile, there's a couple of hundred blank badges that need messages felt-tipped on them – Save Our Allotments – you know the sort of thing, and piled up on that other table. Got it?'

'Wow,' said Farah. 'I'm impressed.'

'Don't be daft, it was nothing.' Maggi bit her thumbnail as she waited for her mum's verdict.

'Well done, Maggi.' Dorothy took in the well-organized work stations. 'We'll make a campaigner out of you yet, am I right?'

Maggi's eyes lit up but she shook out her hair and made a face to let everyone know a compliment from her mother was no big deal. 'Come on,' she said instead. 'Let's get to work.'

Half an hour later, Lawrence arrived, in the middle of apologizing for being late and for Adrian's no-show when George and Isaac trundled in, even later, bearing three large bags of Pick 'n' Mix. 'My mum says these are to share,' said Isaac, grabbing a handful of caramel cups before dropping the bags on the nearest table.

'Where is your mum?'

'She dropped us off.' Isaac was busy peeling back the gold foil from a sweet. 'She said she's too tired to help today, she's going back to bed and I've to make sure Dad comes straight home after with me.'

Dorothy frowned. She'd called Isobel two or three times since the evening of the jumble sale and left several messages but there was never any reply. She wondered if something was wrong but she didn't have time to deal with that today. 'Right then,' she said to the boy. 'Go and ask Maggi how you can make yourself useful. Wait' – Isaac looked at her expectantly – 'give me a couple of those caramel cups before you go.'

The hall was a hive of activity for the next hour and a half, till a dozen or so placards were lined up against the back wall and a satisfying number of decorated badges were piled up at the end table, pins in the air like a tiny bed of nails.

'You're here at last, Kevin,' called Mohid. 'Come and join us.'

Maggi didn't look up from her cutting, her stomach muscles tensed. She felt, rather than saw, Kevin standing two stations down from her, and noticed he hadn't even bothered to say hello. She picked out four Everton mints from the bag nearest her. What did it matter what she ate, someone like Kevin would never be interested in someone like her anyway.

At the other side of the hall, Stanley straightened up and cracked the bones in his lower back. As he did so, he saw Isaac approaching him, his head down so his long fringe covered his eyes.

'Wanted to show you something,' he mumbled when he reached the old man. 'I've done a couple of badges so you can see the design.'

'Excellent, let's have a gander then, lad.' Stanley wiped his hands on an old towel as he waited for Isaac to show him his handiwork.

'I hope you like them,' said the boy shyly, hiding behind his fringe. He unwound his fingers so that Stanley could see the two badges sitting face up in the palm of his hand.

'Do you need your glasses or can you see what they say?' He bent and scratched behind his knee as Stanley said nothing. '"Keep Kenmar in the Kommunity". What do you think?'

Stanley studied the badges in stunned silence. The words ran in three lines across the centre of the badge, but the Ks of Keep, Kenmar and Kommunity were in thick black lettering, the rest of the words were in tiny letters between them, so that all you could see when you pinned the badge to your lapel were the three huge Ks.

'I . . . well . . .'

George pinned both badges on to the front of his hoodie.

'I spent ages on the design before I painted them. And I know that's not how you spell community but for the effect, you see it – the three big Ks?'

'Oh I see it, lad,' said Stanley, scratching his head.

'What's happening over here then?' said Mohid, heading towards them with Lawrence. 'What has Chairwoman Dot got us to do now?'

Stanley thought fast. He spun Isaac to face away from him and put his arms round him from behind, enveloping the surprised boy in a huge bear hug, the palms of his hands resting against the boy's chest and covering the badges completely. 'I think she needs a few more hands over on the big banner,' he said. 'There's a lot of background to be painted green.'

'Right-o,' said Mohid. 'Shall we?' to Lawrence, and Stanley heard Lawrence muttering as they headed towards the banner painting station, 'I hope she's got m-m-machine-washable paint, this is one of my best Guccis.'

Stanley moved to release Isaac from his embrace but to his surprise, the boy turned to face him and raised his skinny arms so that they were round Stanley's waist. Stanley felt the boy's face against the old striped jumper Mabel had knitted for his fiftieth, and held him tighter. After a moment or so, Isaac released himself and sniffed. 'Do you think they need more colour, the badges?'

'Yeah,' said Stanley, ruffling the boy's hair. 'More colour will do it, lad, and maybe we'll change the design ever so slightly – even though yours is brilliant. You keep those ones as whaddyacallit – prototypes, right? Come on, I'll help you make a few more.'

Kevin tried to apply himself to the task he'd been given, this glitter was fiddly stuff and he had more of it on his joggers than on the placards, but he couldn't help glancing towards the first station every so often to see what Maggi was doing. She hadn't been to the allotments since that Saturday they'd been to Blantyre to get the art supplies for Dorothy, and he knew that for sure because he'd been every day since – not looking for her *exactly*, but pretty sure all the same he'd have spotted her if she'd been within a ten-mile radius of the place. Kevin grew flustered as he considered whether her absence was because she'd figured out what had been going through his mind as they'd spent the day together. They might not have got the discount Dorothy had hoped for but it had been one of the best days of Kevin's life – from the minute he sat in the passenger seat of her car and she'd told him to suit himself about the heating, she never felt the cold (nor did he!), and to change the music if it wasn't to his taste (was there anyone who didn't like the Bee Gees?!), and to help himself to the Smarties, her favourites (his too, he could eat them without chewing!), and to tell her to shut up when he got fed-up listening to her stories (when hell froze over!), her company had transformed him into a bigger, brighter, better version of himself and his one regret about the day was that the arts supply place wasn't in New Zealand, or at least London so they could have carried on driving into the night. But.

She'd been nowhere near the allotments since. She was definitely avoiding him. She clearly hadn't enjoyed his company the way he'd enjoyed hers and was probably only here today because her mum had forced her into it. The tube of glitter slipped out of his hand, and he swore quietly to himself as the silver sparkles twinkled at him mockingly.

He could feel George's eye on him, so he gave him what he hoped was a reassuring smile.

'Ffffsssshhhn.' George was busy cutting circles from green crepe paper.

Kevin picked up the Pritt stick again. As he rubbed it back and forth over the cardboard, he wondered how he could have misread the signs, whether there had even been any signs. But she had come to find him that evening of the party, when they'd mistakenly celebrated the allotments staying open. Kevin couldn't believe it, that someone could have been thinking about him, Kevin, when he wasn't there, and come looking for him. When she'd driven away that Saturday evening after their trip to Blantyre, he'd started to wonder if maybe she thought about him other times too, when she wasn't even at the allotments. Thinking about his hands perhaps, his mum always told him he had good hands and he didn't think she was making that up to boost his confidence. He'd examined them closely as he poured the hot water on to his Pot Noodle, twisting them this way and that, and decided his mum was right, he did have nice hands, not scarred and spoiled like his face, anyway. Then he thought about how Maggi could have been on the bus into town, say, and heard someone laughing and that would remind her of him, and his laugh. That could have led her to think about things he'd said, funny things, he could be funny sometimes, he'd thought, maybe not laugh-out-loud hilarious but quietly funny, interesting, let's say. He certainly knew a lot about mushrooms. And maybe when she was making herself a cup of tea, she'd wondered about how he took his, sugar or not, lots of milk or black. That's what he'd been thinking at the start, but as the weeks wore on and it became clear she was avoiding him, he wasn't so sure.

Because wasn't it more likely that if she'd thought of him at all — and honestly, why would she be thinking of him? —

but if she was though, wasn't it more likely she'd be thinking about his face, the roughness of his skin and how it would feel under her fingertips, how it would be to gaze into his eyes but be distracted by the webbing on his eyelid, and across half of the iris. Wouldn't she have wondered what her friends would think if she took him along to meet them at a pub in town, or at one of her singing gigs. Let's be honest, he thought, if she was thinking about him at all, she would just be thinking all the time about his freaky, godawful, hideous face. Kevin heard a small mewling sound and turned quickly to see what it was, before he realized the noise was coming from him.

'Gaaadddd.' Kevin felt a hand on his arm and it was George, his concern clear from the hard straight line of his mouth. 'Ggggdddd?'

Kevin patted him back. 'Thanks for asking, George. I'm fine, thanks,' and he was, because none of it mattered because someone like Maggi would never be thinking about someone like him anyway. 'Let's get this finished, eh?'

'I see your teacherly skills are being put to good use over here.' Mohid leaned over his wife's shoulder, admiring the intricate calligraphy that she was adding to the top of the banner they were both working on.

Farah's eyebrows drew together as she traced the extravagant swirls of the last couple of letters. 'You stay focused on your own work,' she said, then laughed at how teacherly that sounded. She was about to say as much to Mohid when her eye was caught by the line of a dozen or so pre-school children walking in the front door. They were roped together like mountaineers, a harassed young woman, surely not much older than the kids Farah herself taught, calling from the front, 'Keep holding on to the rope now, everyone, we're nearly there.'

Farah watched as the boy at the front, his hair worn in a perfect blond bowl like a little Prussian aristocrat or a kid from an American sitcom, jostled the pretty girl next to him, both laughing and showing their milky white teeth, each with gaps between them that she knew would make them hiss their words as they spoke. She couldn't take her eyes off them as they marched past, their own eyes wide at the sight of the jumble of paper and arts supplies, the unusual number of adults crammed into what was normally an empty hall.

'Come on, everyone, up the stairs,' called the girl.

The line speeded up and the smallest boy at the back struggled to keep up, and let go of the rope, tripping over Mohid's foot as he did so. Farah glared at Mohid and dashed forward to help the boy. His teeth gleamed against his brown skin, the soft silk of his tunic sliding against Farah's palm as she picked him up and set him back on his feet.

'Okay?' she asked in a soft voice, and he gave her an unexpected dazzling grin. Farah reached her hand out to ruffle his hair when she heard the sharp voice from the stair. 'Hamza! Put your hand back on the rope please and hurry up. Everyone else is being held up on your account.'

Farah watched as the boy quickly grabbed the rope and walked as fast as his chubby legs would go to join the rest of the group, who were chattering loudly in the stairwell. He turned and said, 'Shukran' before disappearing up the stairs.

Farah stood for a few moments before turning back to the table, her tears blurring the almost-finished banner.

Mohid put his hand on her shoulder but she shook him off. 'Don't,' she said then quickly caught his hand with her own and apologized softly. 'What age would you say . . . ?' Her eyes darted back to where Hamza had been standing.

'About four maybe?'

Farah nodded thoughtfully, and carried on painting.

'You're quiet, love, are you all right over here?'

'I'm fine, Mum.' Maggi took a quick break from attaching the pins to the back of the little round badges Stanley had handed her. She'd tried to meet Kevin's eye a few times and he was definitely ignoring her so she'd kept her head down and absorbed herself in each task she was given. 'You know, I think I remember coming here when I was a toddler.'

Dorothy's face lit up. 'Do you? That was a long time ago.'

'Yeah. Dad used to bring me here to Rising 5s, didn't he?'

Dorothy shook her head. 'No, I did.' She paused. 'That's funny, I haven't thought about that for years. I used to drop you off to play with all your little friends, then when I picked you up after, we'd go round to the Bowling Club for lentil soup and a roll. Those were good times.' How could she have forgotten that, those *were* good times, some of the best times of her life, in fact. 'Maggi,' she said. 'I wanted—'

Someone tapped her on the shoulder. 'Are you the organizer?' she said to Dorothy.

'Who's asking?' Dorothy gazed down at the girl, who couldn't be any older than fourteen, surely, an old-fashioned camera, bigger than her own head, strapped across her skinny chest.

'Me,' said the girl, unhelpfully. 'Wait a minute.' She dug into the pocket of her jeans and took out a small, crumpled card which bore three lines of tiny black text saying, 'Lanarkshire Courier, Julie Malmont, Junior Reporter'. 'And photographer.' The girl pointed to her camera. 'I'm here to write an article about your campaign to save the allotments.'

32

JULIE FLOUNCED OUT OF THE editor's office and sat back down at her own tiny desk, wedged between the toilet and the towering pile of A4 paper they kept for the printer they never used.

'The wanted ads again,' she fumed. She'd been at the paper for four months now and had yet to contribute to a story, never mind have her own byline. But she'd felt sure her story on the bunch of misfits that were trying to save their allotments was a winner.

'What's the angle here?' Mr Gisborne had bitten his thumbnail enthusiastically while he was talking to her and placed the ragged yellow nail at the edge of his desk, where it joined a long line of similar trimmings. Julie tried not to notice.

'Angle? What angle do we need? This is a local paper and closing down the allotments is very much a local issue.'

'Yes, but from where I'm sitting, it seems like it only affects the half-dozen or so plot holders who will lose their right to grow their own strawberries and have a brew and a natter with their pals outside their sheds. So what, who cares?'

The same people who cared about last week's lead story of the ill-fated toddler who'd locked himself into the toilet at Scotmid and whose frantic granny had called the police, the fire brigade and anybody else she could think of until the unfortunately unphotogenic boy had emerged looking sheepish and, for reasons no one could fathom, covered in toilet roll – was what she wanted to say. She said instead, 'It's the thin edge of the wedge, isn't it?'

Mr Gisborne had raised an untidy eyebrow.

'It's the allotments getting the chop today, what's going to go tomorrow – Uddy library? The Matt Busby? We could do a whole feature on—'

Mr Gisborne's phone rang and he motioned to her with the back of his hand that she should vacate his office. 'The wanted ads please, Julie. And close the door, I'm on the phone.'

'But—'

'Hellooo, Councillor Murray, how can we help you?'

She'd resisted the urge to slam the door.

I'll show him, she thought, and started to punch her keyboard like the letter keys themselves had done her a disservice.

Has the council lost the plot? These plot holders think so

Local residents in Viewpark, Birkenshaw and Uddingston are furious about plans announced by North Lanarkshire Council to call time on the local allotments that have been a popular feature of the Viewpark community since 1995.

The *Lanarkshire Courier* understands that an extensive consultation process was followed, resulting in the acceptance of a proposal from Glasgow-based property development firm, Biggart Bros & Co. Plans were announced last month to close the allotments and use the land to build up to ten luxury villas on the site.

Speaking from their campaign headquarters in the Viewpark

Community Centre, veteran Greenham Common campaigner Mrs Dot McKie said, 'The Kenmar allotments are important to the whole community. They're an essential service.' The straight-talking leader of the #SaveOurAllotments crusade to halt the closure went on, 'We understand times are hard for everybody but why should it always be those who already have the least that have to suffer?'

The *Lanarkshire Courier* approached members of North Lanarkshire Council for a response and was given the following statement: 'The council has no choice but to make savings in their annual spending forecast because of successive real-term cuts in its budget from the Scottish Government. These cuts, coupled with increasing demand for services, have contributed to an extremely difficult financial year for the council in North Lanarkshire, as elsewhere, and tough decisions have had to be made. The council continues to work towards providing the people of North Lanarkshire with the services they require.'

Councillor Murray was not available for interview.

Local residents vow to fight against the closure, with a petition that has garnered in excess of 250 signatures and continued efforts to publicize their campaign to keep the allotments open. Recent fundraising events include an arts and crafts fayre at Viewpark Church, as well as ongoing efforts to raise funds within the community. As the longest-standing plot holder, plucky 95-year-old Stanley Sleddon, put it, 'These are our allotments, and we'll fight for our right to keep them.'

Local support for the allotment crusaders is strong and shows the importance of maintaining a loud collective voice in the community if we want to keep our public services. With a march and demonstration planned for the end of the month, time will tell if the fight for this particular public service is one the allotment holders can win.

Perfect, thought Julie, saving the document. She knew Mr Gisborne wouldn't say no to this, especially not if she had a great photo to accompany it. She pulled her phone towards her and scrolled through the images for the group shot she'd taken the day before at the community centre and downloaded on to her phone.

After sitting back and shaking her head, she dared to take another look. 'What a bunch!' She wrinkled her nose in distaste. 'What does that wee wifie think she looks like, wearing dungarees at her age? Campaign leader my arse. And even this younger one, I mean – SlimFast, hello? And whoever thought they could wear lime green next to their face like that and get away with it, size extra-huge or not? Some folk mistake looking different for looking ridiculous.' She sniffed and carried on looking down the line. 'How's that old man still alive, the eyes of a hungover bloodhound and big flabby ears like a rugby player. And even the wee boy, the one who might have saved it for them all and added a bit of cuteness, but there's nothing cute about looking like you haven't eaten for a week and your clothes come from a skip. Oh, loving the sari there though, that's the diversity angle covered at least. Wait a minute' – she zoomed in closer, then wished she hadn't – 'Jesus Christ, what is wrong with that man's face on the end? Nobody wants to open a paper and see that, we'll have to crop him out. Yeesh.'

33

GERMAINE WAS IN BED, TRYING to sleep after another draining week at the allotments. The campaign had been under way for a month or so now and the days were busy with leafletting, going door-to-door to encourage people to sign their petition, spending hours packing bags in Scotmid, handing out posters to anyone who would display them, counting and banking cash as it came in, and doing whatever else Dorothy asked of them. And despite the uncertainty hanging over their future, things had to be kept ticking over on the allotments in the meantime. In addition to feeding flowers, sweeping paths, netting peas and pruning berries, Germaine was still being paid to manage the place. Potential closure or not, the dour but dutiful Aberdonian in her felt compelled to do what she was being paid for and she'd been there all weekend sorting through the paperwork the developers had demanded on handover. She was exhausted, yet she still couldn't sleep.

The minutes ticked by and she lay awake in the dark, worrying about whether she'd booked the right date for the skip and how long it would take her to sort through the tools—

The tool shed!

She sat upright in bed and thought back through her movements that afternoon. She'd definitely moved Stanley's shovel into the main tool shed and a large levelling rake from the back of Lawrence's plot. That was almost brand new, she thought in a panic, her hand to her forehead as she tried to retrace her steps and remember if she'd locked the outbuilding before she'd left. In fact, now she really thought about it, had she even locked up the management shed? Her mind was all over the place these days, but she would have locked up, surely . . . Wait a minute, what about the front gate . . .

Ten minutes later, Germaine was dressed and marching up to the allotments. She pulled her fleece tightly round her against the 4 a.m. chill. *I must be mad*, she thought, as she walked towards New Edinburgh Road, and yet she was determined to do a good job managing those allotments, right till the end. No one was going to say otherwise.

The main gates were locked, the allotments sleeping peacefully. Germaine shook her head at her own stupidity. *I'm not mad after all*. She was about to turn on her heel when she thought she might as well check the tool shed and management office were locked too. After all, she was here now. The heavy iron gate scraped against the path as she pushed it open and closed it behind her. You could never be too careful—

'What the—?'

Germaine could not believe her eyes. Halfway up the hill, Mohid and Farah were standing beside a roaring campfire, Mohid clutching a bottle of beer and Farah with one hand over her mouth, the other gesturing towards a wrought-iron table creaking under the weight of their midnight feast, as though Mohid could somehow magic it out of sight.

'I suppose this means we're busted.' Mohid reached out for Farah's hand and shrugged his shoulders.

Germaine stood where she was for a moment or so, taking in the scene. Slowly, she made her way up the hill to join them. Mohid turned off the music that had been playing softly in the background.

'What's going on here then?' she said.

'It's just something we like to do. Come here during the night and light a fire. Eat, talk, dance to music.'

'We're not doing anything wrong,' Farah added.

'The allotments shut at nine,' said Germaine icily.

There was a pause. Germaine shivered and looked over at the fire – it was burning so brightly, the logs sizzling and sparking and casting a warm glow on Mohid and Farah's faces. And the food reminded her she hadn't eaten for hours and then a meagre snack of toast and butter. 'Is that . . . pakora?' She pointed to the plate nearest her.

'Yes. Would you like some?'

Germaine said nothing as Mohid brought out a third chair and Farah disappeared into the shed and came out with another plate. She placed a red napkin over it and handed it to Germaine. 'Please. Help yourself.'

Germaine licked her lips. 'This is really not . . . I mean, we can't be here. Not in the middle of the night like this. The plot holder rules clearly state—'

'What do the rules matter now when the whole place could be closing down? Might as well make the most of our last few weeks, don't you think?' Mohid had taken the plate from her and filled it with food she didn't recognize but the aromatic scents of ginger and garlic reaching her nostrils made it impossible to resist.

'Eat. Please,' said Farah, and all three sat down round the fire.

The pastry of the warm pakora melted in Germaine's mouth. Mohid offered her a beer but she shook her head.

'Tea?' said Farah.

'Thank you. How often do you come and do this?'

'Not that often. Now and then when the weather's reasonable. Sometimes on a special occasion.'

'And – forgive me, I should probably know this – but do you not have children? Family who must wonder where you are at night?' Germaine took a sip of the delicately fragranced tea Farah had handed her. 'Delicious.'

'Children, no,' said Mohid.

'If only.' Farah looked into the fire, quick tears making her eyes flash through the flames.

'I'm sorry,' said Germaine. 'I didn't . . .'

Mohid shook his head. 'Don't worry. We don't talk about it much.'

'I've never taken time to ask,' admitted Germaine, thinking of all the times she'd waved at the couple then dismissed them instantly. She'd never dreamed they'd be the type to break the rules and enjoy themselves while everyone else slept. She'd certainly never considered that they might be leading anything other than the picture-perfect family life.

'What about your family?' said Farah, refilling Germaine's cup with tea so hot and sweet and reassuring that it seemed to be loosening Germaine's inhibitions more than any alcohol might have done.

'I . . . don't really have a family. It was my dad and me for a long time but now it's just me.'

'Is that why you moved from Aberdeen?'

'Kind of. A new start.' And it struck Germaine that it had

been a good move. She'd always known she'd love the job but she hadn't anticipated the effect the small community would have on her. Outwardly, they might not have much in common but as she'd spent more time with this one or the other, she'd found herself less irritated by her fellow plot holders, certainly less keen to make an enemy a day. There had indeed been several occasions recently when it occurred to her that she might even miss some of them if the allotments closed down.

Picking up on her thoughts, Mohid said, 'How do you think the campaign's going? Is there any chance the council will have a change of heart about keeping the allotments open?'

'You're the second person to ask me that recently and unfortunately, my answer's the same. It does feel like we're making people in the community listen and understand but I'm not so sure about the council. I'm afraid Stanley got it right at the start – it's all about money. Dorothy says we've raised quite a bit but . . . it's a drop in the ocean really. I don't think the fundraising, or the petition, will be enough to make the council change tack.' She scrunched up her napkin and placed her plate on the ground beside her chair.

'There's still the march,' said Farah.

'Yes, that's true, we've still got the march,' said Germaine, her lack of enthusiasm leaving neither Farah nor Mohid in any doubt about her hopes for that.

'Such a pity.' Mohid sat forward as he spoke and nudged some smaller branches from the edge of the fire pit into the middle.

Germaine watched as the flames rose momentarily and they all three sat back from the sudden spurt of heat, laughing as Mohid batted away a small sparking twig. *Anything's possible.*

Germaine caught a fleeting image of her father through the plumes of smoke, whispering those words into the warm night air. 'You never know,' she said suddenly, raising her cup towards Mohid and Farah, and wondering why on earth she'd never thought to spend time with them like this before. 'Anything's possible.'

34

Germaine was on her way back to the allotments a couple of days later, still feeling cheered by her night round the campfire with Mohid and Farah. She was a little after her usual time because she'd had several unexpected encounters along the way. Two different women had stopped to ask her about the campaign and wish them well with it. Germaine didn't know either woman and had to fight against her instinct to ignore them and keep walking. But Dorothy had instilled in her, and all the plot holders, the need to spread the word and get the whole community on their side so she stopped and was polite to both women. Afterwards, she was surprised by how nice it felt to exchange pleasantries with people as they all went about their respective days. She turned down Spindlehowe and a tattooed guy being pulled along by a rottweiler shouted over from the other side of the road, 'See you at the march, love' and gave her a huge grin and a thumbs up with his entirely blue-inked hand. She walked into the allotments with a smile on her own face.

The bullish mood was fleeting; snuffed out by the sight of Isobel sitting on the step outside her shed, weeping.

What's happening here? thought Germaine. *I wonder if I can pretend not to have seen her.* She crept further towards her own shed, the key poised at the lock, her back to Isobel now. A loud sob made her pause. From the corner of her eye, she saw that Isobel's shoulders were shaking, her hair even more all over the place than usual, and her hands wiping her cheeks every so often.

Germaine looked round the rest of the allotments. The whole place had a morning after the night before feel and, apart from Isobel, there wasn't a soul to be seen. Where were they all? It was the middle of July, prime gardening weather and plants still had to be tended, threatened closure and campaign business to keep the place open notwithstanding. More importantly, there was not a bloody one of them on site to take over dealing with Isobel, a job she knew she was going to have to do herself. What was it her dad used to say – 'Misery loves company'. *Here goes nothing*, she thought.

She walked over to Isobel's shed and cleared her throat. Isobel raised her head and Germaine took a step back when she saw the other woman's face. Her eyes were half-shut, swollen with crying, her mouth loose and wet, and she hardly seemed to be in control of it. Her cheeks were mottled and the least said about her hair the better. Germaine felt completely out of her depth.

She dug into her pocket for a pack of tissues and thrust them at Isobel. 'Can I . . . Is there something wrong?'

Isobel gulped and sniffed and indicated that Germaine should sit on the step beside her.

Germaine swapped from one foot to the other like a naughty schoolgirl, she really did not want to sit down. 'Okay, great, sure,' she said, in a voice she didn't recognize.

They were both big women so there wasn't much room on the step but it felt churlish to ask Isobel to move over, so Germaine remained with one cheek perched on the edge of the concrete. She waited for the slurping and gulping to recede. It took a while.

'I'm sorry,' said Isobel finally, taking a breath. 'This is so humiliating, I never cry. And the truth is, I don't really know why I'm crying now, except . . . except . . .' and then she started off again.

Germaine fought the urge to get up and walk away. She scratched her scalp which felt itchy with embarrassment on Isobel's behalf but managed to stay where she was.

'Where's your husband today, George, was it?'

'Yeah, George, and I do love him, you know.'

Germaine squirmed. That Isobel might not love her husband had never crossed her mind nor did she wish to know one way or the other. 'Yes. I . . . I see.'

'No, but, I know some folk might think how can she when it's practically like being with a baby, but that's not it, you see. I love him for what he was, how he was when we met, when we fell in love, not . . . not the way he is now. Do you know what I mean?'

'I suppose so, yes. But' – Germaine hesitated – 'I've never had a husband so I don't really know how it works. How . . . relationships work.' She covered her face with her hand, noticing as she did so that the tips of her fingers were dirty, the half-moon at the top of each nail no longer white, turned greyish brown with old soil. They were like her dad's fingers.

'Did you never want—'

Germaine batted away Isobel's question before she could finish it. 'This isn't about me. You're sitting on your step breaking your heart, I had to— I mean, I *wanted* to check you were okay?'

'Thank you,' said Isobel. 'That's very kind of you.' She gazed across the deserted allotments. 'No one else about today?'

'No. I don't know why it's so quiet this morning. We've got to keep things going until . . . we know for sure.'

'Is Stanley not here?' Isobel nodded over to the opposite plot where the spade that usually stood sentry outside Stanley's shed was nowhere to be seen.

'Oh that's right, Stanley's not coming today, he did say. Apparently he's on a day out with his chess club.'

'Fuck's sake!'

Germaine nearly fell off the step.

'Sorry,' said Isobel. 'But honest to God, even Stanley is off having a day out to himself. When am I ever allowed to be off duty?'

'What do you mean?'

'Look, Germaine, I know you're not one to chat with the plot holders, and that's fine, but it probably means you are unaware that George is completely off his trolley.'

'Oh, I'm sure he isn't that—'

'Nope. There's no other way to say it, he's doolally, a sixpence short of the shilling, crackers. So, of course, he's completely my responsibility twenty-four hours a day, seven days a week. Except for a couple of hours twice a week when he's at the club.' She swiped her face ineffectually with the back of her hand. 'Which, by the way, is where he is now and look how I'm using my precious hours of freedom, crying on the step of my shed at a soon-to-be-shut-down allotment because . . . because I really don't have anywhere else to go. I've been cooped up at home looking after George for so many months now that there really is just me. And Isaac. Don't get me started on Isaac. He's on summer holiday from school now and he goes off every day and I've no idea where or who with, he refuses to talk to me.

Every day he disengages a little more so that I hardly see him. And he's eleven, Germaine, only eleven, and he's got to cope with the fact his dad's not the dad he used to be and is probably going to die an early death without a fucking clue who we are and . . . and . . . now even the fucking allotment's closing down. Pardon my language. But honestly, what's the point of anything any more?'

Before Germaine could say anything, Isobel had started crying again, big rough sobs racking her body.

'Isobel, you're here at last.' Dorothy appeared suddenly from nowhere, dropping the Tesco bag with her cheese and tomato sandwiches for lunch, and sitting on the step on the other side of Isobel. 'Do you not pick up your phone any more? I've been worried about you, wondering where you'd been, if everything was okay.'

Germaine felt a swift pang of guilt as, unlike Dorothy, she hadn't given Isobel or her problems a second thought, hadn't even noticed her absence. She'd been so caught up with the allotments, the campaign, her own problems. Relieved to have backup and keen to show she'd been doing her best to help, she said, 'Isobel's feeling a bit . . . overwhelmed, I think. That cover it?' She turned to Isobel.

Before Isobel could answer, Dorothy said, 'Of course she is, who wouldn't be, in her position?'

Isobel and Germaine both looked up, surprised.

'Oh yes, I've seen you hauling in bags of tools and seeds and whatever else for George, leading him in by the hand like he's your child. No, it's not his fault but that doesn't make any difference to the way you feel, does it? An unpaid carer at – what – sixty?'

'Fifty-four,' said Isobel.

'You're younger than me?' Germaine and Dorothy both said together. They all looked at each other, then Dorothy and Germaine both had to hide their surprise that Isobel was a mere fifty-four years old when she was so weary and worn down they'd both taken her for a lot older. Isobel was oblivious.

'Fifty-four then,' Dorothy recovered quickly, 'and before you've even finished caring for the child you did bargain for, now you're the full-time carer for your husband as well, which you definitely didn't bargain for. I see it all the time and, do you know what, it's always women. Women who give up careers to care for children, women who go part-time to look after elderly parents, and now what, women having to shoulder the burden of caring for demented relatives till they die. When is it our turn, is it *ever* our turn?'

She stuck her hands into the bib of her dungarees. 'Sorry. On my soapbox.'

'No. You're right, I know,' said Isobel. 'It's just . . . I feel I should be able to cope with this, that other women, better women than me, would manage better.'

'Ha!' Dorothy freed her hands again so she could gesticulate with them to make her point with the force it deserved. 'That's what they want you to think. With all their "You're doing brilliantly", "Keep going", "You've got this". God forbid you should stop and say, "I'm not actually", "I can't", and "'I haven't got this at all, please help". What would they do then? The economy would collapse without all their unpaid carers.'

Germaine considered Dorothy with renewed interest. She was saying all the things she herself had thought for years and yet she'd pinned the long-married Dorothy as being exactly the kind of woman who would put up with all that nonsense. Seems this was yet another plot holder whose character she'd had totally wrong.

'Thanks, girls,' said Isobel, wiping her nose. 'You've both made me feel much better, honestly. I will think about asking for some help. No, I mean it, I will.'

'You'd better if you want to stop feeling like this. But listen, I've got an idea. Why don't the three of us do something?'

Germaine squirmed on the step and longed for the comfort and safety of her own shed.

'Like what?' said Isobel.

'I don't know, but something that makes us feel good, something just for us. Nothing to do with the allotments or the campaign or the needs of anyone else.' She paused and thought for a moment. 'What about . . . what about a day out? The three of us.'

Germaine's immediate reaction was *hell no* and it showed in her face.

'Come on,' wheedled Dorothy. 'The three of us could have a great time together, leave everything else behind, just for the day.'

'What about George?'

'That response is the very reason you need a day to yourself. But he's at a club now, right? Could that be extended maybe by a couple of hours or so, and he's not completely incapable, is he? You leave him on his own while you're at work?'

'I suppose . . . But then there's also Isaac.'

'We'll be back by four and he's got a phone, hasn't he? Come on, what do you say?'

'We'd definitely need to be back by four,' said Germaine. 'I've got . . . things to do.'

'Ppff, we've all got things to do all the time. Sometimes you need to say to hell with it, the world can manage without me for a day.'

Dorothy was like a speeding train once she got going, there was no stopping her. Germaine was beginning to see how she'd managed to hold on to her allotment after her husband died – who would dare to say no to her? 'I can see the only way I am going to get anything done today is if I agree to this day out. But you're arranging it. All I need to know is where I've to be and when. And now,' she said, shaking out her leg which had gone numb from sitting on the cold step for so long, 'I need to get to work.'

When the women dispersed at last, Kevin, Lawrence and Mohid all peeked out of their respective sheds, trying to gauge whether or not it was safe to come out.

35

GERMAINE PULLED THE CURTAINS BACK on a dazzling midsummer day. Unfortunately, the brilliance of the sunshine shed more light than she would have liked on the dusty surfaces of her bedroom. As she straightened out her duvet, and picked up last night's empty water glass, Germaine thought that if she was going to have the day off the allotments, she'd much rather spend it catching up on her cleaning chores. Too bad she'd agreed to spend the day doing something else entirely.

It was the Friday after Isobel's breakdown at the allotments and Germaine was already regretting her acquiescence to Dorothy's plan. Too late now. She grabbed a faded blue bath towel from the wicker basket in her bathroom, and turned the spare room upside down to find the swimsuit she'd last seen circa 1984. She threw a carton of Ribena and an overripe banana into her old rucksack and took a last lingering look at the safety of her flat before she shut the door on it and braced herself for the day ahead.

Isobel stood at the bottom of the stairs and called up, 'Isaac! Isaac, come down and eat something so I can be sure at least you've had breakfast before I go.'

There was no response and Isobel trudged back to the kitchen to see what George was doing.

'George, no!' She pulled his hand away from the kettle before he could pick it up.

'It's why tea mmmzzzhh tea Geo Geo fuckssake.' George slumped at the table and pulled at his hair.

'Sorry for shouting, but that kettle's hot. *Hot.*' Isobel put her fingers to her mouth and made a hissing noise. 'Hot,' she repeated, but George had already forgotten about the kettle and was busy unpicking the frayed edge of a napkin that lay amidst the assorted dirty dishes and growing pile of gardening brochures, old Sunday supplements, and unopened letters from school on the table.

Isobel told herself she'd be on her own in twenty minutes, she could last till then. She heard the door slam as Isaac left the house without telling her where he was going, with no breakfast, and without saying goodbye again.

Dorothy was humming to herself as she buttered the bread and sliced ripe tomatoes – from her very own allotment – for their packed lunch. She could see the sun like a huge egg yolk spreading across the pale sky and knew they were in for a magical day. She stooped down to the bottom cupboard and pulled out three mini gins for later, she had an inkling they all needed them. She hoped the others were looking forward to their big day out as much as she was.

'I didn't even know you could drive,' she said to Germaine an hour or so later as they drew up to the car park in Gourock.

The sun was higher in the sky now and Dorothy was glad

she'd put on her one and only sundress, the orange straps falling down her shoulders and the skirt sticking to the back of her legs as she peeled herself from the back seat.

'I've not driven for . . . a while.' Germaine was already irritable, sweating profusely in her thick sweatshirt and jeans, and regretting her decision to come along. 'Though I'm probably going to have to get used to it again. I'm thinking of doing food deliveries and stuff, JustEat, whatever, you know, when . . . *if* the allotments close and I'm out of a job.'

'Ah-ah,' said Dorothy quickly. 'No allotment talk today. This is our day to enjoy ourselves, not to worry about all that.'

They made the short walk across the car park to the open-air pool.

'How lucky we are to have this on our doorstep,' said Isobel, fighting the urge to check that George was close by, that Isaac was not falling behind. She was feeling lopsided without George in particular by her side, and she had to keep reminding herself she was on her own, free to swing her arms and walk at her own pace.

'Gourock's not exactly next door,' muttered Germaine, pushing her sleeves up and wiping her clammy forehead. She thought of the cool comfort of her car, sitting under the shade of the trees.

'No, but it's hardly a million miles away and then there's this.' Isobel pointed towards the long and deep saltwater pool, with the Clyde estuary behind it, stretching out for miles. And even better, she was free to relax and enjoy it all day long.

They should have known the pool would be swarming with sunseekers on a day like this, weekday or not. Everywhere Germaine looked, there were spotty teenagers, lounging by the toilets vaping, taking up all the plastic sunloungers, splashing, jumping in at the deep end, slouching in pairs as they stood in the ten-deep queue at the ice-cream stall, catcalling each other, laughing, pointing, and being generally annoying. Frazzled parents chased their chubby red toddlers out of the baby pool and into the shade.

'We didn't think this through, did we?' Germaine huffed as the other two women started to lay out their towels. 'What? You're not thinking of staying, are you? Look how busy it is, we can hardly even see the water.'

That was a slight exaggeration but the pool was certainly busy. There were about half a dozen young men patrolling the sides of the pool, three of whom were scrolling their phones so what on earth they would do in an emergency Germaine could not imagine.

'Oh come on,' said Dorothy, indicating a small square of concrete next to her for Germaine to lay out her towel. 'Stop complaining and start having fun. Am I right, Isobel? Isobel, what are you doing, please tell me you're not checking up on that husband and son of yours already? This is your day, remember.'

'Sorry,' said Isobel, guiltily, quickly finishing off the text she was sending to the people who ran George's club. 'He was getting picked up much earlier than usual this morning and he doesn't like it if his routine gets changed.' She put the phone down on the towel beside her. 'Never used to be like that, he used to be a real adventurer, always heading up north or suggesting we took a trip somewhere. On the spur of the moment, if the sun was out, or if there was an extra bank holiday. *Up and at 'em*, he'd say and off we'd go. Now look at him, he can't even go to a day club an hour early without throwing a tantrum.' She added quickly, 'Not that it's his fault. I don't blame him.'

Dorothy reached out and patted her hand. 'Where did you meet him?'

'In Rome, of all places, can you believe it? We were both TEFL teachers, I was starting out, barely in my twenties. He's a few years older than me, you see. Never seemed to matter until . . . it did,' she finished lamely.

'At least you've got your boy – Jacob, is it?'

'Isaac. Yes, at least I've got Isaac. Oh, I know some people think it was bad luck falling pregnant when I did – I was forty-three – but the truth is, he was our lovely little surprise. We felt so lucky to have him. But . . . it's been hard on him, all this happening with his dad. One time, before we knew what was wrong with George, he went to pick up Isaac from the swing park and the other mothers there thought George was drunk. He was starting to slur his words then, lose a few here and there, forget his thread. Like a drunk, I suppose; you can't blame them.'

'Ha,' said Dorothy. 'Playground mums – worse than the kids themselves, as I remember it. If you didn't fit in, and I never seemed to fit in, you had to stand in the corner on your own. Norma NoMates, that was me.'

'I'm sorry,' said Isobel.

'Oh, don't be, I didn't want to fit in. Who wants to be in with the playground gang?'

'Certainly not me,' said Germaine, who'd given every impression of not listening up till that point. 'Never interested me, the whole motherhood thing. I'm too selfish, I suppose.'

That wasn't quite true. There had been a time when she'd desperately wanted children, when she'd been with Cameron, but he'd used her like a rag before leaving her high and dry, though not dry for long because it was at that point that the drinking had really taken hold. And then of course no one would have wanted to have children with her, the state she was in, but these women didn't need to know that. One of the reasons she'd moved to Uddingston in the first place was to get away from the past and everyone who knew what had happened.

'Having kids isn't for everyone,' said Dorothy. 'And some of us aren't cut out for it, it seems.' She thought of her own strained relationship with Maggi.

'That sun is scorchio.' Germaine was tired of all this serious talk and keen to get into the pool. 'Anyone fancy dipping their toe in?'

Dorothy sprang up from the ground and pulled her sundress over her head, revealing a floral Marks and Spencer's one-piece that clung to her skinny frame everywhere except her non-existent chest. The stiffened cups of the swimsuit were large enough to bake potatoes in and certainly far too roomy for Dorothy's fried eggs. Unperturbed, she shoogled her hips a little, pulling at the sides of her costume and pushing the gigantic cups down in a vain attempt to make them sit flat against her chest.

Germaine pulled down her jeans, feeling better about her own poor effort at swimming gear now she'd seen Dorothy's. She might not be Naomi Campbell, but she wasn't as scrawny as Dorothy either.

'I think I'll sit it out for a bit,' said Isobel.

'Okay, but promise us you won't be on the blower to that husband of yours, or checking up on Isaac the minute our backs are turned?' Dorothy wagged her finger.

'Promise,' said Isobel, and she meant it. She lay down against the already sun-warmed bath towel and prepared to relax for the first time in months.

'Come on then,' said Dorothy to Germaine. 'Race you to the deep end.'

A couple of hours later and the day had turned into a Monet painting, the midday sun a buttery rub against the blue, its rays shimmering on the water. The pool was quieter now, everyone having gone for their lunch, or to sit in the shade of the trees for a while and allow their Scottish pigment to recover from the unusual onslaught. Germaine was enjoying one of the Tunnock's caramel wafers Isobel had brought with her, and Dorothy was lazing on her tummy reading a book by some new writer or other called Andrea Dworkin that neither Germaine nor Isobel had heard of. Isobel could feel the sweat drying on her face at the same time as fresh perspiration oozed at the back of her knees. She decided it was time for the pool.

Germaine and Dorothy watched as Isobel hauled herself off the ground and rearranged her cleavage. Her thighs had stuck together in the heat and there was a sound like Sellotape peeling from a wall as she placed her feet on either side of the towel to ease them apart. Germaine raised a single eyebrow to Dorothy. 'Aye-aye, here comes Esther Williams.'

'Who?' Dorothy sat up and leaned on her elbows.

'Swimmer,' said Germaine. 'One of my dad's favourites. She was a movie star too, bit like Isobel here could be if she wanted, with that pose.'

They watched Isobel leaning over to one side, stretching out her chubby arm, then repeating the exercise on the other side.

'Come on, Isobel, you're not swimming the Channel, you know.'

'Leave her alone,' said Dorothy. 'Not everyone can be good at everything; as long as she enjoys splashing about, that's the thing. You dip your toe in and enjoy yourself, Isobel.'

Isobel ambled over to the water, oblivious to the smirking and nudging of the teenage supermodels as they watched her clamber down, with all the grace of a walrus, into the enticing blue water.

'Oof, it's chillier than I thought,' she said, bouncing against the side at the shock of the cold.

'Goodness' sake,' muttered Germaine, and was about to pick up her new issue of *Gardeners' World* when something surprising happened.

Isobel pushed herself away from the side and started to swim – beautifully. Her arms were no longer chubby, they were long and purposeful, casting into the water and propelling her through the waves. There was hardly a ripple behind her as she sliced through the water effortlessly, with the grace of a dancer and the speed of an athlete. She tore down the length of the pool like it was a step across the floor, and back again, and repeat. Her progress was mesmerizing, other swimmers flopped out of the way as she came upon them like a seal, the skin of her shoulders sleek and gleaming in the sunlight. The lucky few who'd nabbed sunloungers looked over their sunglasses and beneath their caps to watch; kids queuing at the ice-cream stand turned to admire her. She kept it up until Germaine lost count of the laps she'd completed and Dorothy was on her feet cheering her on.

Finally, Isobel raised her face from the water – it was glowing pink now — and scrambled awkwardly out of the pool, her feet once more made of clay.

'You kept that quiet.' Dorothy handed her friend her towel.

Isobel grinned. 'I've always been a good swimmer,' she said, rubbing her chest and standing on one foot then the other as she dried her knees. 'Funny, I'd forgotten that.'

'Sounds like you need to do a bit more remembering of the things that make *you* happy and stop worrying about everyone else all the time. And speaking of things which make us happy . . .' Dorothy dipped into her bag and brought out the three tins of gin. 'Here we go, girls.'

Isobel laid her towel back on the concrete and sat down. 'Alcohol? Are we allowed that at the pool?'

'What do you mean, are we allowed it? That's another thing you need to stop thinking about, what you're allowed to do and what you're not. The patriarchy's worked its spell a bit too well on you, missus.' Dorothy turned to Germaine. 'Here, one for you too. They're warmer than they should be but they'll still go down nicely.'

Germaine didn't take the tin Dorothy offered her. 'Not for me, thanks,' she said quietly.

'Och, go on, you only live once.'

'No, I . . .' Germaine hesitated, then made up her mind. 'Not that you need to know this,' she said, 'but I'm an alcoholic, okay? It's . . . I can't have alcohol.'

Dorothy and Isobel both stopped what they were doing, mouths gaping.

'See, this is why I don't tell people, now you'll feel all awkward about drinking your gin but you shouldn't. Go ahead, I don't mind, I just can't have any.'

Isobel opened her can and wasn't sure if it was her imagination but it sounded like the loudest ring pull ever. Dorothy did the same and took an awkward gulp which left her spluttering and coughing up the fizzy sweet-sour drink. She turned to Isobel. 'Do you know what? I think I'd rather have a white Magnum instead, what about you?'

'Definitely.' Isobel put down her can.

'You don't need to, honestly—'

'Sshh,' said Dorothy. 'We're having white Magnums and they're on me, so there.' She turned and made a face as she headed off to join the queue at the ice-cream stand. 'See you at closing time.'

After lunch, a bell rang out to signal they'd opened the diving boards.

'Are you going to tell us you're also a world-class diver now?' said Germaine to Isobel.

'Not me, I'm afraid of heights, you wouldn't catch me up there.'

The women watched as a queue of young men formed at the bottom of the diving boards. There were no women in the queue, they were all bunched up at the side of the pool waiting to be impressed by the men.

'See, this is what's wrong with the younger generation of women,' said Dorothy over her sunglasses to her companions. 'Oh, they think they know it all, you should hear the stuff Maggi says to me, lecturing me on this and that, and how she knows better, but look at them – lined up watching the action, rather than being part of it, rather than showing off their own skills. Makes me sad, honestly it does.'

'I think you're reading too much into it,' said Germaine lazily. 'The boys want to dive, the girls don't, so what?'

Dorothy sat up suddenly, pulling her sunglasses off her face. 'But do you never wonder why that is?'

'No doubt you're going to tell us.'

'Yes, I will. It's because all their lives, and I mean from the minute they come out and get settled in their frilly pink prams, they're praised for how they look. "So pretty!", "Look at her lovely tiny hands", "Her hair is so thick", I mean you must have heard it. But not the boys, oh no, they get told how strong they are, look how fast he's learned to walk, that's it, get in there, rough and tumble. Another thing that makes me sick, honestly. I certainly never praised Maggi like that.' She paused; now that she thought about it, she couldn't remember having praised her daughter at all. But she must have, surely—

'Germaine's right though. There's more to be annoyed about than that. I wish that was all I had to worry about,' said Isobel, envious of the carefree young women, swooshing out their hair and reapplying their lip gloss. Was she ever that young, that free, with endless options and potential?

'You've got to get some verve back, you know. You deserve a life of your own, too, as well as being everyone else's carer. I did all sorts when Maggi was still a baby, I never stayed at home sticking things onto paper and counting blocks . . .'

'And how's that working out for you and your daughter now?' chimed in Germaine, regretting it immediately when she saw Dorothy's face fall. 'Sorry, I didn't mean to offend.'

'No, you're right that me and Maggi don't get on. Never have. And yeah, I do wonder sometimes if it's because she's resentful but' – she slapped the ground – 'dammit all, women have to have a life too and no one ever wonders if the kids are messed up because Dad went out to work or followed his own interests, do they?'

'Anyway,' added Isobel, 'I've been at home with Isaac most of his life. I gave up work till he went to school and even now he's nearly at big school I still work part time, and I don't think he's any the better for it.'

The other two women waited for her to say more, watching as she bit her bottom lip but carried on, free at last to express how she'd been feeling for months. 'Seems like I can't reach him at all these days. And we used to be so close. But ever since his dad got ill, it's like he can't accept what's happening and would rather switch off completely than deal with it. It's so hard.'

After a moment or so, Dorothy said, 'I understand that you feel responsible for everyone, it's how we all feel, how we're brought up to feel. Women do so little for themselves though, don't they? As young women, it's all about fading into the background. Not attracting the wrong sort of attention, and no attention at all as mothers, and of course we're all expected to become mothers.'

Germaine sniffed, thinking that at least she hadn't succumbed to that, and judging by what Dorothy and Maggi had to say, she'd dodged a bullet.

Dorothy was still talking. 'Then we get older and there's the looking after of parents to be done, or in your case, Isobel, a demented husband. Where's the break? When is it our time?'

'Maybe we just take it,' said Germaine wryly. 'Maybe we're honest and say, I'm doing this now because that's what I want to do.'

'I think you're right,' said Dorothy.

The women were quiet as they mulled over their conversation.

Dorothy basked in the sunshine, wiggling her toes and admiring the glistening blue vista of the Clyde estuary stretching out as far as the horizon. 'On a different topic, did you know Gourock open-air pool, right where we're sitting, was on the cover of Blur's latest album?'

Isobel shook her head, and Germaine said, 'Er, no. Why would we know that? How do *you* know that?'

'Maggi told me, she's in the music business, you know.' She sat up again and leaned forward conspiratorially. 'But she told me like she'd discovered them or something. Me and Eddie had Blur on in the car before she was even at school, that's what she forgets when she claims these "old" bands for herself.' She bent down to scratch a bony knee before adding, 'You know, Damon Albarn's about the same age as me? Might even be older than you, Isobel.'

'Who?'

'Damon, the lead singer?'

Germaine looked at her blankly, Isobel shrugged.

Dorothy couldn't believe they'd never heard of him. Where had these women been in the eighties and nineties? Had they slept through Cool Britannia? 'Wait, I'll show you.' She took out her phone and googled Damon Albarn.

'There, that's him.' She tapped on the screen as she handed her phone to Germaine.

'He's the same age as you?' She passed the phone to Isobel.

Isobel shook her head in disbelief. 'No way!'

'Unbelievable,' agreed Germaine, looking again at the image on Dorothy's phone and back at Dorothy, and shaking her head.

'Okay, thank you,' said Dorothy, snatching her phone back. 'A girl could get offended, you know.'

'Sorry.'

Dorothy threw her head back and laughed. 'I'm kidding, I couldn't care less what I look like, and neither should you.'

The other two laughed with her, and when Dorothy said, 'We need to do more of this, we all need to start putting our own interests first sometimes,' Isobel agreed wholeheartedly, and jumped back into the cool clear water.

36

They passed the Uddingston sign and headed along Main Street. Nearly home.

'Thank God for that,' said Germaine. 'If I had to listen to another verse of "Parklife" or the pair of you harmonizing on "Wonderwall" one more time, I would not be responsible for my actions.' But her unusually chipper manner told her passengers she'd enjoyed the day out, and perhaps even the singing all the way home, as much as they had.

'Thanks for the lift. And, you know, the whole day. It's lifted my spirits no end,' said Isobel as Germaine slowed down at the address she'd given her and parked outside her house.

Neither Germaine nor Dorothy said anything but Isobel knew what they were thinking. 'It was George's childhood home,' she said, saving them the trouble of asking. 'We moved in with his parents when we got back from Rome. It was supposed to be temporary, then . . . they died, and we never moved out.'

Dorothy blew a low whistle. 'Some house! Lucky you.'

Yes and no, thought Isobel. From the outside, the large two-storey sandstone was impressive, but when you went indoors, you could almost sense the decay, certainly you could smell it – the damp, the pervading scent of long-dead cats. It was permanently cold, since they'd never installed central heating and the old wood burner only heated up the living room, while a fast wind whistled up from the spaces between the floorboards in all the other rooms. The kitchen wall was being held up by a broken-down conservatory, or vice versa, Isobel was never sure, and the upstairs toilet was out of bounds nine months of the year due to various blockages and drainage issues.

She said none of this to Dorothy and Germaine though. 'Yes, I suppose so.' She picked up her bag and patted down the back seat to make sure she hadn't left anything behind.

'Do you always leave the front door open like that?' asked Germaine, looking towards the front of the property.

They all followed her eyes and Isobel shivered slightly, and said in a small voice, 'George,' before stepping out of the car and running towards the house.

Germaine looked at Dorothy.

'We'd better stay till we know everything's okay,' said Dorothy, and Germaine turned off the engine.

Inside the house, Isobel dropped her bag amidst the pile of other bags, jackets and tossed-aside trainers at the front door. She called up the stairs to Isaac but there was no reply. She stood uncertainly at the bottom of the staircase, but decided to check downstairs first.

Throwing open the door to the living room, she could feel from the heat of the room that the burner had been on recently and had just gone out, the orange embers still fizzling in the range. But where was her husband? He should have been home a couple of hours ago. She could feel panic rising in her chest as she ran through to the kitchen, calling 'George? George, where are you?' The kitchen was freezing – and empty. A pot of cold beans sat on the stove, and when she touched the kettle, it too was stone cold. Something caught her eye in the garden and she ran out of the back door. 'George?' but it was the next-door neighbour's old black cat, rooting around their dwindling wood supply.

Isobel ran back through the kitchen, slipping on the greasy floor, and headed through the living room and up the stairs, calling 'Isaac, Isaac?' as she ran.

Isaac's bedroom door was shut tight, as usual. Even in her panic, Isobel remembered to tap her knuckles on the door before pushing it open. There, seated on the floor of his under-the-eaves bedroom was Isaac, back to her and headphones on, as he engaged in a fierce onscreen battle for glory.

Momentarily relieved to see her son at least was alive and well, she tapped Isaac on his bony shoulder and he jumped and dropped his controller.

'Isaac, thank goodness you're okay.'

The boy didn't reply.

'Where's Dad?'

Silence.

Isobel snapped. 'For goodness' sake, Isaac, where is he? Did he come home after the club?'

Isaac pursed his lips, seemed about to say something, then grabbed his controller from the floor instead, turned and resumed playing.

Isobel could feel the tears of frustration welling up behind her eyes and had to leave the room before she walked over and shook her son by his scraggy shoulders till he spoke to her.

Outside, Germaine was tapping her fingers on the steering wheel.

'Should we go in?' said Dorothy.

Before Germaine could answer, Isobel came running back out of the house. 'George has gone missing!'

Ten minutes later, Kevin was walking home from Scotmid, wondering whether he should have chicken or spicy beef noodles for his tea, when the car horn beeped at him on the top road. He ignored it, he was well-used to random cars and lorries catching sight of him and beeping. What they got out of it Kevin couldn't imagine but it no longer affected him. He kept walking.

This one was persistent though, and finally he turned round to see a dilapidated red Corsa, packed with what seemed like far too many people, all calling to him frantically.

He recognized Dorothy first, hanging out the passenger seat window. 'Have you seen George?' she called. 'Isobel's George.'

'He's gone missing,' shouted Isobel from the back seat, and Kevin noticed for the first time Maggi was sitting next to her, her blonde hair high on her head, and tied up in a huge purple bow.

'No, I haven't seen him today,' said Kevin. 'He wasn't at the allotments. I was there all day clearing out my shed for when . . . if it closes.'

Isobel started crying. 'This is completely my fault. I left him all day and went bloody swimming. Like I'm a teenager without a care in the world, for goodness' sake. And now look!'

'Don't blame yourself, Isobel, everyone's allowed a day off, you haven't done anything wrong.'

'And we haven't lost him yet,' chimed in Germaine from the driver's seat. 'We're bound to see him if we drive round for a bit.'

'What about Bothwell woods?' said Kevin suddenly. 'Did you

not say he goes there a lot to fetch branches for your wood burner?'

'That's right!' said Isobel. 'Why did I not think of that? Oh, I'm hopeless . . .'

'Never mind that, let's get going.' Germaine was turning the engine over again when a large white Mercedes stopped opposite. It was Adrian and Lawrence, dressed in their pristine gym kits.

'Is s-s-something wrong?' called out Lawrence from the passenger seat, while Adrian, at the wheel, kept the car purring over and looked straight ahead at the oncoming traffic.

'George has gone missing. Kevin will fill you in,' shouted Germaine, signalling to Kevin to get into the men's car and follow them down to Bothwell.

'Wait, what?' said Adrian. 'We're going to the gym and—'

'The gym can wait,' said Lawrence. 'Open the d-d-door for K-K-Kevin, Adrian. We're going to help.'

Kevin glanced down at his blue plastic bag with his Pot Noodles, gathered it up in his fist and crossed the road to jump into Adrian and Lawrence's car. He clambered into the back seat, pretty sure this would be the first time the sleek saloon had ever been home to a Pot Noodle, and trying his best not to dirty the white leather with his boots.

37

The woods behind Bothell Golf course were quiet in the late afternoon. Most of the golfers had gone, either back home for an aperitif or into the clubhouse for a gin and tonic in the bar overlooking the flat lush greens. Dog walkers and speed walkers tended to come in the morning so that by this time in the day, as the light was beginning to fade and the gnarly trees and dropped branches conspired to give the place a spooky feel, Isobel and the others had the place almost to themselves.

'Right,' said Dorothy, as Adrian drew the Mercedes up at the side of the road. 'There's' – she did a quick head count – 'seven of us. The three of us' – she pointed to herself, Dorothy and Isobel, who was stepping anxiously from foot to foot and biting her thumbnail – 'will go down by the front of the clubhouse.' She pointed to Adrian and Lawrence. 'You two follow this path round to the back of the clubhouse, down by the stream, because George sometimes gathers sticks down there, right, Isobel?'

'Mmhhmm.' Isobel was distracted, her head on a swivel as she cast about the woods for her poor missing husband.

'And you two' – she pointed to Kevin and Maggi – 'you take the side path, and go right the way down by the new housing estate, okay?'

Kevin checked Maggi's reaction at being landed with him again, but he needn't have worried – she was too busy trying to get her mum's attention, raising her hand like she was back in class.

'Maggi?'

'Would it be helpful for us to know what he was wearing? Like maybe if he had a bright-coloured anorak on or something like that . . .'

'Good thinking, glad someone here's on the ball.'

Kevin watched as Maggi's cheeks flushed with pleasure.

'What was he wearing, Isobel?'

'I'm not sure . . . It would have been his blue fleece, I think, no wait, I told him this morning that would be too hot so he got changed into his T-shirt. A bright orange one, with 57 on the front.'

'Lovely,' murmured Adrian, but Lawrence didn't laugh. 'Not the time, Adrian.'

'Anyone who spots him, call Germaine on her mobile. If we can't find him in half an hour, we'll meet up in front of the clubhouse. Down there' – she pointed – 'where they've put up the display for this year's scarecrow festival.'

Germaine half-expected Dorothy to pull out a whistle and place them all under starter's orders but she didn't need to, they'd all started marching off in their respective directions. The search was on.

'This is all my fault,' Isobel was whining again. 'I should never have left him and gone out for the day. Stanley was right, I shouldn't have been away gallivanting.'

'Stanley? Why does it not surprise me in the least that that old goat would call women going for a swim and a day out "gallivanting" and disapprove?' Dorothy was not going to take that sort of criticism lying down.

Germaine shook her head. 'He's not wrong though, is he? If we'd all stuck with our usual routines doing what we were meant to do, George would be at home now, doing . . . whatever George does in the evening, and I'd be in my own flat watching reruns of *Miss Marple*.'

'Miss Marple wouldn't be told she should stick with her usual routine and put everyone else before herself, I'll tell you that.' Dorothy couldn't quite believe what she was hearing. What chance was there for the next generation of girls if women like Isobel and Germaine were their role models?

'Anyway, if we find him—'

'What do you mean – if?'

'Sorry, when we find him, let this be a lesson to you, Isobel. You can't do this all by yourself any more, you need help. No one can be responsible for another human being twenty-four hours a day.'

'But I love—'

'No matter how much you love them.' Dorothy felt her blood pressure rising and hoped they found George before too long. Otherwise, she feared, the police search would need to be redirected towards the dead bodies of Germaine and Isobel – after she'd killed them.

'What are we even doing here?' Adrian was lifting his ultra-performance trainers, bought especially for tonight's spin class, high up off the mulchy leaves and twigs. 'We're going to miss the best cardio class of the week. And if we go to the later one, we'll never get a parking space when we get home, you can be sure of that. And we don't even know these people.'

'What do you m-m-mean? They're our friends, Adrian. F-f-fellow plot holders.'

'Friends? Simon and Mark are our friends. Jason and Ryan. I'll even concede maybe Marcia and Toni from the gym, but these people? No, I'm sorry, Lawrence, but this is going above and beyond. In any case, the allotments are closing down now, and let's be honest, there's no way we'll be keeping in touch any of this lot, will we?'

'I don't see why not.'

Adrian was too elegant to snort but otherwise he would have done before he said, 'Come off it, we won't be inviting Gorgeous Kevin out with us any time soon, God forbid.'

'Adrian! That's n-n-not n-n— dammit.' Lawrence stamped his foot in frustration at his inability to say what he meant.

Adrian took advantage of the pause and continued, 'You say he's a nice guy and I don't disbelieve you but be honest now, would you really be seen dead with him at one of our usual places – Stravaigin, say, or Stereo?'

'I . . . I . . .' Lawrence didn't know how to respond to what he felt in his heart was a terrible thing to say. He tried to tune Adrian out as he called George's name and turned his head all round hoping to catch sight of a bright orange T-shirt, or hear George replying in his now-jumbled English, letting them know he was fine. Underneath, his mind was whirring. He couldn't understand Adrian's attitude and he didn't like it. Perhaps it was because he'd spent so much more time with the others, especially Kevin, than Adrian had, talking to them, getting to know them as individuals, and becoming part of the allotment community.

Because it was a community, whatever Adrian said. And if there was one thing Lawrence wanted more than anything else, it was to be accepted as part of a community. He realized with a jolt that he was devastated that the allotments were closing. No time to think about that now, though.

'Come on.' He took Adrian by the hand, even though they were close to the clubhouse and he knew Adrian would be on the lookout for the watchful and judgemental eyes of others. For once, Lawrence didn't care. They'd been asked to help, and he was determined to make sure they did.

Kevin could hear the quiet rush of the stream in the distance, the soft rustle of trees. Maggi led the way, her purple Doc boots well-suited to the terrain, even if her red velour skirt, riding up over her thighs, was not. She was breathing heavily with the effort of marching over the uneven ground and a couple of times she slipped and placed her hand on Kevin's arm to steady herself. Kevin started every time he felt her warm palm on his forearm.

'When you think about it, how far can he have gone?' she was saying as she marched. 'These woods can't be that big before they lead out to the open golf course, can they?'

'Sorry, what?' Kevin dragged his attention away from the backs of her thighs and tried to concentrate on what she was saying.

'Do you need a rest?' she said, stopping suddenly. She laughed. 'Really, what I mean is, I need a rest.'

She leaned against the tree whose branches were drooping on to the path and blocking their way. 'Nature, eh? My dad loved it, so I tried to as well so I could spend time with him and get away from Mum.'

'You're hard on your mum,' said Kevin quietly.

'Ha. Everyone takes her side. Try being her child, then you'd know.' She peered further into the wood, where it was growing darker. 'I hope we find George soon though,' she said, changing the subject. 'He is vulnerable.'

Kevin came closer to the tree, wondering aloud whether they should try deeper into the woods and off the path for a bit. 'If he was looking for firewood, he'd have had to go into the thick of the trees, wouldn't he?' he reasoned.

'You're right. Thank goodness you're with me though, I'd never have come this far into the woods on my own.'

Kevin raised his head in surprise. He'd never been anyone's protector before. He stood up a little straighter and pulled in his stomach. 'Don't worry about that,' he said, with a sudden image of himself fighting off lions.

Maggi laughed as though she could read his mind and his chest deflated. 'Let me get this stone out of my boot then we'll carry on.' She reached into her boot with her fingers, lost her balance and fell against Kevin.

'Sorry,' she said, holding the thin cotton of Kevin's T-shirt between her fingers.

Kevin put his hand out to steady her, and felt the solid mass of her upper arm. It occurred to him that he had not eaten since breakfast and he suddenly felt scooped out and weak, not sure if he was the one holding up Maggi, or whether she was keeping him upright.

An image floated to his mind, unbidden. He could see himself reaching over, any awkwardness between them forgotten as he put his hand on the back of her neck. Her hair was scraped up into its purple ribbon and his fingers would reach up to feel the smooth curve of her skull. She wouldn't flinch, wouldn't move, wouldn't breathe hardly, so he would lean his face closer to hers, her mouth would open and he'd catch the scent of her breath, spicy sweet like she'd been eating peppermint chocolate. He imagined how her rib cage would feel, lifting and falling against his chest. He'd be sweating and graceless, but that would be okay because she wouldn't care, she'd want him to kiss her deeply on her mouth, to lean further into the reassuring heft of her body. He stepped forward, breathed her in and—

'Kevin!'

Kevin pulled back immediately. 'I'm so sorr—'

'Never mind that, look, over there by the tree, there's a dead body!'

'What? No!' Kevin turned and saw the man's slumped form on the other side of the tree. As they watched, he slid over to one side, his bulk landing in the slippery wet moss that cloaked the giant tree roots. He made no sound.

'We're coming, George,' shouted Kevin. 'Don't worry, you'll be fine. Call an ambulance,' he shouted back over his shoulder to Maggi as he ran towards the figure on the ground.

The blood was pounding in his head, his heart racing as he reached the tree. 'Oh God, oh God, please let us be on time.' He turned the figure over – and gave a huge sigh of relief, which turned into a strangled sound that passed for laughter.

'Kevin, what is it?' called Maggi, her phone still at her ear as she prayed for the emergency services to answer quickly.

Kevin picked up the pile of rags and old clothes to show Maggi the cause of their distress. 'It's a bloody scarecrow from the scarecrow festival, isn't it?' He checked the outfit on the straw figure more closely. 'Fireman Sam, to be precise.'

'God's sake,' said Maggi, swiping her phone to end the call. 'I nearly had a heart attack.'

A shout rang out from somewhere near the clubhouse. 'He's over here! We've found him, he's okay. George is fine, everyone!'

Maggi raised both hands, her fists punching the air, and then her mouth grew wide with laughter as she watched Kevin slide down to the ground himself in pure relief.

38

The Mercedes drew up to Isobel's house and stopped on the street behind Germaine's Corsa. Kevin got out first and stood uncertainly on the pavement, not sure he was ready to face Maggi again after he'd made an idiot of himself in the woods, almost kissing her like that, what was he thinking? He decided there was nothing else for it and, clutching his bag of Pot Noodles, loped into the house to brazen it out.

'I'm certainly not going in.' Adrian's hands were rigid on the steering wheel. 'Much bigger house than I expected, mind you.' They could see Dorothy and Isobel helping a dishevelled George into the imposing property, its burnished red sandstone glowing in the last of the evening sun.

'Who cares about that? The important thing is, we found George s-s-safe and well, and now we can all have a cup of t-t-tea and relax.' Lawrence was pretending to be a lot calmer than he felt. In fact, when he and Adrian had come upon George, wandering about in the woods, perilously close to the fast-flowing stream that ran behind the golf course, their first thought was how lucky he'd been not to fall in, he seemed so disorientated and lost. Although he clearly had no idea who either of them were, he'd allowed himself to be supported by Adrian on one side and Lawrence on the other, as they led him across to the clubhouse and waited for the others in front of the creepy scarecrow display. 'Who the hell has a festival for scarecrows?' Adrian had said, shaking his head in disbelief, while Lawrence quickly called Germaine to let them know George was safe. She had shouted out to the others who dashed to meet them to see for themselves that George was indeed safe and well. Isobel had hugged him tightly, crying and remonstrating with herself, while Germaine had tried to slip away quietly, satisfied she'd done her bit. Too late, Isobel, still clinging on to George, said, 'Everyone back to mine. I'm going to open the sherry.'

Sitting in their car ten minutes later, Lawrence said to Adrian, 'You can do what you like but I am going in. We've been invited.'

'We've already missed Spin Class but we can still catch Metafit, maybe Circuits too if we're still up for it after.'

Lawrence couldn't think of anything he was up for less. 'You go if you want to. I know it's important for you not to miss a night's training.'

'Important for me? What about you? You had a day off last Tuesday too.'

Lawrence's eyebrows shot up. 'You're keeping track?'

'Someone has to. Left up to you, you'd be back up to . . . well. I'm going anyway.' He waited.

Lawrence made up his mind. He got out the car and leaned back in the window. 'I'm going in to make sure everyone's okay. I'll see you at home. I can walk back.'

'At least that's something,' muttered Adrian as he put the Mercedes into gear and roared off.

'And I might even stop by Enzo's and have chips on my way

home,' whispered Lawrence, in an act of private rebellion, as he watched the car disappear.

The front door was open so Lawrence pushed it and called, 'Hello, where is everyone?' as he walked in. His eyes were all over the place as he entered the big but cluttered hall. As he looked down at the once-beautiful golden oak floorboards scored and marked by years of use and lack of upkeep, a multicoloured dreamcatcher flew into his face and he swiped it away, wondering how anyone could let such a magnificent house go to rack and ruin like this.

He found them all in what he assumed was the main living room. That was a guess as the usual cues of a sofa, some chairs and a coffee table were either missing, or hidden underneath all the junk. The smells of that morning's bacon wafting in from the kitchen, the damp towels piled up on what he assumed was the coffee table, the thick logs beginning to catch and smoulder in the wood burner, and the general underlying neglect, all conspired to create a thick soup of chaos and dilapidation.

'He's fine,' Germaine was saying, as Isobel leaned over George making sure the huge Cadbury's Flake mug full of sweet tea was balanced properly in his hand.

'If you call tired, lost, hungry, *abandoned* fine,' she wailed.

'Don't be so dramatic, woman.' Germaine was itching to leave and eyeing the door like it was a safety hatch.

'George is fine, Isobel,' Dorothy intervened, 'but in any case, none of it was your fault. You can't be everywhere, all of the time. It's time to get some help, I told you that today.'

'Did someone mention sherry?' said Maggi suddenly from across the room, 'because I think we could all do with some.'

Lawrence noticed she was sitting on the same, dipped

down sofa as Kevin, but each was sitting as far away from the other as possible. Kevin was looking straight ahead. Lawrence went and sat in between them, remembering how nasty Adrian had been about Kevin and thinking what a shame it was that people were so freaked out by his face they didn't want to sit next to him. He'd show him he certainly didn't feel that way.

'You're practically on my knee, Lawrence,' said Kevin.

'Oops, s-s-s-sorry.' Lawrence jiggled over closer to Maggi. 'Sherry!' he called in an overly loud voice to mask the awkwardness, as Isobel produced a large dusty bottle of Harvey's Bristol Cream, together with a tray of assorted mugs and glasses.

'Not for me, thanks,' said Germaine. 'In fact I really need to be going soon, I've got . . . things to do.'

The living room door opened a fraction and Lawrence saw Isaac's face appear in the crack. The boy's eyes widened as he saw all the strange adults in his house. 'Is Dad back?' He peered round the room and recognized them from the allotments. 'Is Stanley here?'

'Isaac, there you are. Dad's fine, come and say hello to everyone.' Isobel patted the sofa and, after some hesitation, the boy sloped into the room, mumbling 'excuse me' and 'sorry' as he jumped over all the feet. He sat between his mum and dad and – whether in deference to the unaccustomed company or because he was secretly relieved at his dad's return – he didn't complain when Isobel smoothed down his hair and put her hand on his skinny knee.

'Stanley's not here but you can go and see him at the allotments tomorrow if you like? Dad and I will come too and we'll get back to work. I bet those weeds have missed us.'

'But I thought . . . you said you'd had enough, it was all pointless and you weren't wasting any more time . . .'

'Never mind what I said, you don't usually have any trouble ignoring me.'

Isaac gave a sudden grin. 'True.'

'So – we'll go back tomorrow and get some weeding done. And do you know what else, we are going to show that council we mean business and they're not going to take our allotments away from us.'

Watching her son's face become animated for the first time in weeks, Isobel understood what the allotments meant to him, and how much he valued the time he spent there, with Stanley in particular. George was sitting beside her, clutching his wine glass and swirling the sherry round in the bowl of the glass. He was quiet but happy in the company that had come into their lives as a result of the allotments. She was relieved he was safe, and it could have been so different if the boys hadn't found him before he stumbled any closer to the stream. 'You know,' she said thoughtfully, putting down her cup of sherry. 'If everyone had been at the allotments as normal, digging and planting instead of acting as though it belongs to those developers already, none of this would have happened. I could have had my swim with my friends and George would have been safe, meandering around his allotment, fixing fences and digging up vegetables.'

Germaine squirmed a little at being called Isobel's friend, that was pushing it surely, but she could see her point. And Germaine loved her plot at the allotments, not to mention that when they closed, she'd be out of a job. She really didn't fancy being stuck in her car all day dropping off burgers and smoothies to indolent teenagers but she couldn't see anyone else queuing up to employ a middle-aged ex-alcoholic with limited social skills. For once, Germaine agreed with Isobel.

'I've loved being part of . . . things too,' said Kevin quietly, aware of Maggi sitting at the other side of the sofa but loosened up by Isobel's ancient sweet sherry and determined to speak up. 'I'm still hoping the council changes its mind.'

'M-m-me too,' added Lawrence.

Encouraged, Isobel said in a voice made loud by the sherry, 'Good, because we *need* those allotments. I'm back on board now and I say we don't go down without a fight.'

'That's more like it,' said Dorothy. 'We've still got our big march, remember. We'll show the council what's important to our community. Cheers to that.'

39

It was almost the end of July and the day was already so sticky at ten o'clock that Stanley thought he might even have to dispense with his bunnet.

'All right? That post isn't too heavy for you, is it?' Kevin called over from the other side of the path.

Stanley shook his head and told the boy he was fine. He felt guilty for taking up Kevin's day like this but he'd assured him the day before that he had nothing planned. Stanley believed him. 'Okay,' he'd said. 'If you're sure you don't mind. I'll bring you in a container full of home-made beef stew in payment. Mabel's own recipe.' He tapped the side of his nose. 'Top secret, so don't ask.'

The allotments might or might not be closing but in the meantime, Stanley refused to allow his fruit and veg to be eaten by mice and other rodents, in this case, the family of grey squirrels that he suspected was getting bolder and bolder and coming into the allotments every night. For some reason, Stanley's patch was the one worst affected, either because it was the first plot they hit as they slipped in through the gate or – and this was Stanley's preferred explanation – because his contained the tastiest fresh produce in the place. Whatever the reason, the foraging animals were becoming a huge problem. Kevin had offered to repair the fruit cage on Stanley's allotment so they couldn't get in through the tears in the ancient netting and Stanley was very grateful to him.

Kevin stretched the new netting taut across the ground, ready to cut it to size. He still didn't talk much but it seemed to Stanley the boy's confidence had grown as his allotment had grown and he was a lot more content than he'd been when he'd first come to join them in the spring. Then, he'd seemed afraid of his own shadow, rarely making eye contact and spending most of his time in his shed. But a lot of things were different now, he thought, waving over to Isaac who was helping his dad paint the front door of their shed. The fiery crimson was not to Stanley's taste but each to their own, and it did his heart good to see Isaac and George working side by side.

Dorothy was sitting on the step of her allotment with Isobel, both drinking tea and flicking through magazines. Dorothy's plot was still a crazy assortment of brambles, wild purple pansies shot through with the yellow heads of dandelions, spreading thistle and ivy, and a messy proliferation of bushes, small trees and tender saplings. Stanley, and Mohid, Kevin and Lawrence too, had all offered to help her cut it back into some semblance of order but she'd shaken her head and said no thank you, she loved her wilderness plot just the way it was. And who were they to argue?

'Have you got bigger secateurs than these?' called Kevin. 'This twine's tough.'

'I loaned my pruners to Germaine for those hedges at the entrance, I'll go and get them back,' said Stanley. But he was surprised to find the management shed already locked up for the day. Then he remembered they were all meeting at Germaine's later to finalize plans for the march; she must have gone home to get organized.

'Here, take mine,' called Mohid. 'In fact, I'll come down and give you a hand.'

And the three men worked together under the hot sun, stopping only to slap each other on the back when the job was done.

At six that evening, Kevin was striding along Old Edinburgh Road to Germaine's house. He'd been home and showered and could feel the pleasant ache of well-exercised muscles beneath his fresh cotton shirt. A car horn beeped as he turned to cross the road and Kevin waited for the usual insults to be hurled from car windows rolled down for the purpose. He braced himself — but it was the girl who served him in Greggs. She called to him from the open window, 'It's been a cracker today, hasn't it?' and drove on. Kevin had time to raise his hand as the car disappeared along the road, and she gave him another little toot of the horn as she sped off. Kevin carried on walking, upping his pace. He pushed his bag with the three bottles of Lidl's beer further up his shoulder and swung his arms as he strode on. Like the woman from Greggs perhaps, he'd spent the day with friends and was now headed out on this warm summer's evening to see more friends. Life was good.

By the time he arrived at Germaine's, her small flat was full to bursting with all the other allotment holders. He squeezed on to the end of her beige sofa, next to Farah and Mohid, and waved across the room to Lawrence who was crammed into the opposite sofa between Adrian and George. Stanley was perched on a small stool that had been brought through from the kitchen, his cheeks drawn in as he ate a spicy pickle from the bowl in front of him.

'I love your colour scheme,' said Isobel as she came into the room, followed by Germaine, both carrying trays of glasses and bowls of Pringles. 'Everything's so clean and neutral and . . . beige.'

'Indeed. Just the wrong side of institutional,' whispered Adrian to Lawrence, wondering how on earth he'd allowed himself to be talked into coming here.

'Sshh,' said Lawrence. 'She'll hear you.'

The door opened again and Maggi and Dorothy came in, providing a riot of colour between them.

'Here, sit on the end, Maggi, we'll squeeze up,' said Farah. 'Scoot along a bit, Kevin.'

'Hi.'

'Hi, Kevin.' Maggi was acutely aware of her plump thigh squashing against Kevin's leg.

Kevin was looking straight ahead, his leg on fire, wishing desperately that he'd chosen the opposite couch, or at least that Maggi had sat on the other side of him so that his good cheek was facing her. He was conscious that his bad side was inches away from her own unmarred, perfect face.

'Sorry,' she said. 'Not much room.'

Kevin raised a bottle of beer to his mouth nonchalantly, and both he and Maggi pretended not to notice when most of it frothed over the open bottle before it reached his mouth and spilled on to their clamped-together thighs.

Lawrence watched from across the room, a small smile dancing on his lips.

'Sorry we're late, everyone, we stopped off to buy copies of the paper.' Dorothy stood in the middle of the room, commanding their attention as she held up a pile of a dozen or so copies of the *Lanarkshire Courier*. 'Before we discuss the details of the march, let's enjoy our fifteen minutes of fame. Here, Maggi, get off your backside and help me hand these out.'

As a copy of the *Courier* landed on his lap, it flapped open to the page with the photograph so that Kevin saw it before anyone else. Blood rushed to his face as he scanned the image and, heart pounding, he got up from the sofa and slipped out of the flat, clicking the front door quietly behind him.

'For God's sake, half of this is wrong,' Dorothy shouted over the din. 'The McKie I can just about live with, but Dot? I've never been called that in my life.'

'Never mind that, they're saying we've got 250 signatures when we've got loads more than that. Did no one check the facts before they printed this?'

'It's the local rag, hardly Fleet Street,' said Adrian snidely, and Lawrence glared at him.

'At least they got your age right, Stanley,' said Germaine.

'Ninety-five? Who told them—'

'There's a nice photo of us all,' said Farah. 'That's something we can cut out and hang in our sheds.'

'Wait a minute,' said Stanley. 'I know my eyes are bad but even I can see they've missed someone out. Where's Kevin?'

'Maybe he wasn't there when the photo was being taken,' said Germaine.

'No, he was standing at the end beside me. Let me see.' Mohid took the paper from Stanley and examined the grainy image. 'You're right, Stanley, where's Kevin?'

He looked up and round the room to ask Kevin if he'd moved

out of shot at the last minute. 'Where's Kevin?' he said, putting the paper back on Germaine's coffee table.

'Exactly,' said Lawrence. 'Where *is* Kevin?'

They all looked at Maggi. She blushed and shrugged her shoulders.

Kevin had slipped away and no one had noticed.

40

Lawrence stepped over the grass and on to the path leading to Kevin's shed, careful not to get any mud on his new white Nikes. He chapped the door softly. No answer. He raised his hand to chap again but as he did so, the door opened a fraction, the unscarred side of Kevin's face peeking through the crack.

Lawrence raised his hand in greeting rather than saying hello. He knew the nerves he felt at what he was going to suggest would make his stutter worse.

Kevin didn't reply but raised his eyebrows slightly.

Lawrence noticed that the half-there one on his bad side remained in the same place. He tried to keep his eyes on Kevin's mouth while he spoke. 'Can I come in? I've got s-s-s-something for you.' Frustrated at his inability to say something so simple, but determined to stay calm, he raised the white leather vanity case in his hand instead to show Kevin what he'd brought.

Silently, Kevin stood aside and opened the door wide enough for Lawrence to shimmy through.

This was the first time Lawrence had ever been in Kevin's shed and as he took in the neat shelving and the stacked and labelled storage boxes, he was filled with admiration for his friend's excellent use of space. Kevin, smarting from the newspaper article and questioning his place in the group all over again, misinterpreted his silence as reflecting a rush of revulsion at being alone with him in the enclosed space. He stepped so far back he was almost pinned against the wall of the shed.

'May I . . . ?' Lawrence indicated the garden chair underneath the print headed 'EDIBLE MUSHROOMS and those you must NEVER eat'.

Kevin nodded, but stayed where he was.

Lawrence crossed then uncrossed his legs. Kevin's silence was unnerving him. 'Look, I might as well come out and say it. We all noticed you'd been cut out of the picture in the p-p-paper. Well, S-S-Stanley noticed first and then we all did, and . . . I'm s-s-so sorry, Kevin, that can't have been very nice for you at all.'

Kevin switched on the kettle. 'Tea?' It was the first word he'd spoken.

'Yes please, if you're making some?'

They were both silent as Kevin moved around the neat and well-ordered shed, fetching two matching mugs and filling them with tea. He placed the mugs on the little aluminium camping table between the two seats and handed a pint carton of milk to Lawrence, and a spoon.

When they both had a mug of tea in their hands, Kevin spoke again. 'I'd be lying if I said I wasn't a bit taken aback when I first saw the picture. Like . . . my face would offend readers or something.'

'Oh no, Kevin, I'm sure—' began Lawrence, but Kevin brushed aside his excuses.

'We both know something of that sort must have been said, otherwise why would they have cut me out? You've always been very careful not to mention my face— No don't apologize, I completely understand. Most people don't mention it. It's like the elephant in the room – *I'm* the elephant in the room.' He laughed at Lawrence's aghast look and carried on. 'But really, it's just my face. I know people don't believe me but it's true – I don't mind any more. I wouldn't even think about it if I didn't have to worry about other people's reactions to it every single day.'

Lawrence hesitated but he wanted to get everything off his chest. 'There's something else I've felt bad about for weeks now. I s-s-saw . . . on the Main Street one lunchtime, I saw those k-k-k-kids shouting at you, chasing after you when you left the chip shop.' He bit his lip. 'I w-w-wanted to s-s-s – shit – *say* . . .' Lawrence paused and took a deep breath, trying again. It helped. 'I wanted to say I'm sorry for not doing anything. Not saying anything. I hope . . . you can s-s-see how hard it is for m-m-me to say anything.' He sat back, exhausted. 'But . . . that's no excuse. I should have made myself s-s-speak up.'

'But that happens all the time with those kids. You can't be there to defend me every day. And there's worse names to be called than Gorgeous Kevin.' He raised his mug at Lawrence. 'I'm sure you know that.'

'Yes, I suppose you're right.' Now that Lawrence had managed to get the confession off his chest and Kevin had reassured him there was nothing he could have done to help, he was able to enjoy his tea and relax a little. In fact, with that revelation out of the way, Lawrence couldn't remember the last time he'd felt so at ease in anyone's company – when he hadn't felt the need to censor himself in case he hissed his s's or cackled out the c's, or worse, had to give up completely on the m's and suffer the humiliation of the other person finishing his sentence for him, probably even more embarrassed about the exchange than him. It was different with Kevin. He felt as comfortable as he did chatting to his beloved granddad who judged him for nothing and loved him without limits.

'It's true,' he said. 'I've been called all sorts. Ever since school when it was clear I was . . . different. My voice has always been this high, you know, I'm not putting it on, and I've always been, well, pretty, I suppose.' He raised his hands apologetically.

'I know what you mean.' Kevin held up one hand to the side of his face and the other below his chin, like he was voguing. 'It's a struggle being this pretty, isn't it?' He laughed again and raised his hand to his hair, ruffling the blond curls so they stood up even more on his head.

It took Lawrence a moment to register that Kevin was joking. When he did, he raised his cup towards him and they cheersed.

'That's how I got this stutter, my pretty pathetic response to all the bullying. But no one at home ever mentioned it. Same as they never mentioned the fact I was gay.' He paused. 'I thought you must have known that, that day you . . . rescued me, at the top of the gulley.'

'I honestly can't—'

'It doesn't matter, I remember. And that's why I've felt so bad about that day, not helping you with those pathetic wee morons with the morals of . . . of . . . Peter Sutcliffe.'

'I wouldn't go that far. And at least kids say it to your face.'

'Still . . .'

'Listen, Lawrence, I appreciate the sentiment but don't stress over it too much. I'm already over yesterday and that business with the photo, honestly. I know I've got good friends at the allotments – you all noticed I'd been missed out and you're here now, aren't you? – that's what matters to me, not being cut out of a photograph.'

'How can you be so forgiving?'

Kevin shrugged. 'What I know is, most people are good and they don't want to hurt others intentionally.'

'What about those kids on the street every time you go out? They must make your life a misery.'

Kevin shook his head. 'Tsk, they're only kids. I'll tell you something, when they grow up and think back to the stuff they shouted at me, they'll suffer for it more than me. They'll wonder how they could have done it, and they won't be doing it when they're forty, I guarantee it.'

Lawrence was about to say more when his stomach gurgled and he patted his midriff with the palm of his hand. 'Sorry, I skipped lunch, trying to save a few calories.'

'I'd offer you a Pot Noodle but as you can see, I've finished my last one.' Kevin indicated the empty, washed-out cartons, lined up beside his kettle.

Lawrence thought longingly about a hot and spicy plastic bowl full of salt and additives, and other such treats he hadn't had for years. 'Thanks, but Adrian doesn't let me— I don't eat stuff like Pot Noodles, you know fast food, junk.'

'What do you mean, he doesn't let you?'

'I used to be fat, you see. Then I got' – he indicated his buff body – 'like this. It's a choice,' he said, suddenly remembering Adrian's mantra. 'We can all choose to be fat or thin, unfit or fit. There's no secret to it.'

'But . . . he must have liked the way you looked when he met you?'

'Yes, but that was after I'd lost most of the weight. He wouldn't have been interested in me when I was f-f-fat!'

'Why not?'

'What do you mean, why not? Because . . . because . . .' But he stopped because it was clear to him, as it had been when he'd spoken about this with Mohid, that there was no justifiable reason why not.

'It's like my face,' said Kevin. 'No, don't apologize again, I'm not mentioning my face for you to pity me, I don't need that. Just what you're saying about Adrian not liking the way you looked . . . I really wish people would understand the last thing that's important about us is what we look like, especially when it can change in an instant.' Kevin snapped his fingers. 'I know that's not how the world works, but there's nothing I can do to change what's happened to my face.'

'Actually,' said Lawrence, 'that's partly why I came to see you today. I don't know if I've ever told you this but I'm a make-up artist. That's my job, to improve people's appearance.'

'Nice.' Kevin frowned slightly, unsure of the right response.

'No, I mean . . . I could help you. I know you're right that our appearance shouldn't matter but the way I see it, we all feel better when we make the most of ourselves and if we can do something to improve the way we look, why not do it? What I mean is, I could cover . . . you know, your scar tissue for you.'

Kevin's hand moved to his face instantly, his palm not quite big enough to cover the scarring over his cheek and across his forehead. His eye was dragged down even further by the pressure of his hand.

'That is, if you wanted me to?'

There was a silence. Kevin knew it shouldn't matter what

he looked like, and most of the time, it was true, he really didn't care what strangers thought about his face. But. Kevin was remembering how it had felt, Maggi pressed up close to him in Bothwell Woods, her face a handspan away from his, her breath on his cheek. His heart had been beating fast, his jaw trembling almost at the thought of kissing her, but then – he remembered his face, the rough feel of the skin down his cheek, and his eye, how could anyone ever gaze lovingly into that eye? He'd been kidding himself, he realized later, and he could imagine her relief at being called over to join the others when George had been found.

But maybe, with what Lawrence was suggesting, he could look more . . . appealing?

'What sort of thing were you thinking?' he asked, eyeing Lawrence nervously as he opened his make-up case.

'Cover-up,' said Lawrence simply. 'We'd start with this primer to make sure the make-up sticks to your skin' – he held up an aerosol can like Kevin's deodorant – 'then add a layer of pressed mineral foundation, that's this' – he held up a thick beige-coloured tube – 'and then finish it off with the some high performance setting spray, and Bob's your uncle. Nothing to change you too drastically, just enough to cover up this part.' Lawrence leaned across the table and touched Kevin's cheek with the tips of his fingers. Kevin froze but Lawrence appeared not to notice and kept stroking his cheek lightly with his fingertips.

'You know, Kevin, you've got great bone structure. I could put some darker blusher on here' – he stroked the indent of Kevin's cheek – 'and some highlighter, not too shimmery, along here' – he touched the tip of Kevin's cheekbone. 'Honestly, there's a lot we could do to improve things.' He paused. 'Not that you look that bad, obviously . . .' He trailed off, wondering if he'd said too much.

Kevin felt sorry for him and said in a bright voice, 'Oh no, I'm actually gorgeous, you know' and the tension was broken as they both laughed.

'Come on then, let me see what I can do. Oh.' Lawrence stopped and sat back suddenly.

'What?' said Kevin. 'It's okay, you don't have to.'

'No.' Lawrence's eyes were shining. 'I've just noticed. I haven't stuttered once since we started talking properly. You're so easy to be with, Kevin. You . . . make it easy to talk.'

His mind made up, Kevin moved the table out of the way and shuffled his chair a little closer to Lawrence.

Lawrence said, 'Now then,' and set to work transforming Kevin's face.

Half an hour later, Lawrence handed Kevin the mirror and sat back while he looked at his new face. 'What do you think?'

Kevin inspected himself in the mirror and took in his almost restored face. With the magic of the make-up, he glimpsed the shadows of his former self – the thirteen-year-old Kevin who loved football, and his fifteen-year-old self who was into anime and manga but pretended to like Slipknot instead; a fleeting image of himself at sixteen, the young boy who asked Charlotte McNair, the cleverest girl in their year, out for a Costa as a dare – and she'd said yes! He couldn't believe his previous selves were still there – confident, handsome and unscarred. He touched his face with the pads of his fingers. 'It feels . . . soft.'

'Told you. Maggi won't be able to resist you now.'

Kevin put the mirror down quickly. 'What do you mean? Why do you say that?'

'You must have noticed the way she looks at you?'

'Everyone looks at me,' said Kevin.

'But not like— She definitely fancies you.'

'Don't,' said Kevin tersely.

'Sorry, I didn't know it was a touchy subject.'

'It's not, it's just . . . she's not interested in me. Not like that.'

'She is—'

'Don't,' Kevin repeated.

'I'm right though,' Lawrence persisted. 'She does like you but I won't say any more.'

'Good.'

'But let's see what happens at the march.'

'Lawrence.'

'But—'

'You said you wouldn't say any more.'

'I won't' – he paused – 'but I bet she comes over to speak to you' and ducked before Kevin's well-aimed empty Pot Noodle tub could hit him.

41

THE MORNING OF THE MARCH dawned. Kevin and Lawrence stood together at the entrance to the allotments, their faces raised to a sky that was blue as the Mediterranean sea, the sun only partly hidden by barely-there clouds. After a few moments, Kevin turned back to the allotments, wondering what was taking the others so long. Lawrence cast a furtive glance at his friend's face while he was looking the other way. 'We could have put a little concealer on today, you know.' He patted his fingers against his own smooth cheek to indicate where he meant.

To Kevin's surprise, he hadn't hated the effect Lawrence had created with his magical brushes and potions a few days earlier and indeed had spent quite a pleasant evening in front of his bathroom mirror, turning his face this way and that, marvelling at how smooth Lawrence had managed to make the normally ruched and leathery skin. But he wasn't quite ready to show it to the world yet. 'Let me get used to it a bit first,' he said. 'Thanks though, I can tell you're good at your job.'

Lawrence gave a deep exaggerated curtsy, and pouted, 'Ah merci, monsieur.'

'Are you sure you were bullied at school?' said Kevin. 'I can't think why.'

They were still laughing when Maggi appeared suddenly from along New Edinburgh Road.

'Love the T-T-T-shirt,' said Lawrence, gesturing towards Maggi's red and white striped top, with a picture of Beryl the Peril emblazoned across her chest. She'd paired that with deep navy jeans which clung to her rounded hips and a little red baker boy hat. 'Maggi l-l-looks l-l-lovely, doesn't she, Kevin?'

Kevin glared at him.

'Thanks,' she said. 'Kevin,' and bobbed her head to him as she passed through the gates and up to the fairy garden where her mum and the other allotment holders were gathering.

Lawrence watched Maggi's retreating back then turned back to Kevin. 'What was that for?'

'What?'

'Would it have killed you to tell her she looked nice? She came over to speak to you, Kevin, not m-m-me.'

'Don't know what you mean,' murmured Kevin, pushing out his bottom lip on his good side.

Lawrence was shaking his head. 'I'm telling you, Kevin, she's giving you the s-s-signals and you keep blowing her off. Trust me.'

Kevin's face lightened at last. 'You'll forgive me if I don't trust you on that, since you have to be the only person I know who knows less about women's signals than me.'

'You have a point there,' Lawrence conceded. 'Ah, looks like things are kicking off at last.'

The boys turned to see a small crowd coming towards them, led by Dorothy in tartan dungarees. She was holding a large sign that said 'Kenmar IS Community' and leading a group of about thirty people, all holding similar, hand-painted signs. Kevin could see Germaine bringing up the stragglers, including George and Isobel at the rear. In between were lots of people Kevin didn't know who must have seen the Facebook and Twitter posts and had come along to lend their support. Some kids at the back were holding a long banner between them. Kevin didn't recognize them and they clearly didn't know him as they couldn't stop gawking at his face. He stepped slightly behind Lawrence and held his own placard in front of him so he was half-covered. He could see a pretty girl who looked to be in her late teens whispering something behind her hand to the equally attractive one next to her and squirmed as they both laughed. He dug his foot further into the loose earth and wished he'd stayed home.

'Where are the other allotment holders?' Lawrence asked Dorothy.

'Stanley's taking Isaac by taxi to the council buildings and meeting us there. That's right, isn't it, Isobel?'

Isobel had stepped forward to join them at the front of the group. 'Yeah, not that it was easy, mind.'

There was no way Stanley could have walked from Uddingston to Hamilton but he would never have admitted that. Instead, and following consultation with Dorothy and Germaine, they'd hit upon the idea of asking him if he would forego the march in order to look after Isaac.

'You'd be doing me an enormous favour,' said Isobel to Stanley. 'And George, because that would mean he could walk along with me and he'd love that.'

'Wouldn't the boy enjoy that too?'

'There's no way a lad that size could walk from here to Hamilton, Stanley. Have you seen the boy's legs? They're like those whaddyamacall it – alfafaffy sprouts.'

'Alfalfa sprouts,' corrected Isobel, 'and they are not, thanks very much, Dorothy Mackie. But listen, Stanley, I'm paying for you both to take a taxi there and you can meet up with us at the bottom of Almada Street, okay?'

'You'll do no such thing,' said Stanley. 'That's one of many things Mabel was right about. Bloody taxis. They take you all round the houses making sure they get their money's worth. Me and Mabel never got a taxi in the whole of our married lives. We'll get the bus, won't we, lad?'

'You will not.' Isobel pressed the money into Stanley's reluctant hands. 'And mind, Stanley, I'm relying on you to make sure Isaac's okay.'

Stanley had pouted a little, but inside he was delighted to be needed. 'Don't you worry about us, we'll be fine, won't we?' He turned to pat Isaac on the head. 'Keep your fingers out your nose, son, there's a good boy.'

Dorothy blew on a bright orange whistle she'd picked up at Scotmid that morning for the purpose. The assembled crowd went quiet and awaited their instructions.

'So you all know the drill. We're going to march from these allotments all the way to the council headquarters on Almada Street. We'll take the Bothwell route and that way, we'll pass plenty of people in and out the shops on both main streets – Uddingston and Bothwell. On the way, I want you all handing out as many of these leaflets as you can, oh, and shouting and causing as much rumpus as possible.'

This drew a cheer from the demonstrators.

'Exactly like that.' Dorothy raised a fist in the air and was rewarded with more cheers. 'Are we heading?' shouted someone from the middle of the group. Dorothy glanced at Germaine who'd made her way up to the front to join her. 'It is half ten, are we all ready?'

'Yup. Farah and Mohid would appear to be no-shows, which is surprising. They were such a help printing off all the leaflets and they seemed so—'

From the end of New Edinburgh Road came the unmistakable sound of bagpipes.

'What the—?'

Germaine, Dorothy and the others filed to the edge of the pavement, and looked along in the direction of the Holmbrae. Dorothy started to laugh, Germaine couldn't believe what she was seeing.

Marching towards them, in the middle of the road so that the traffic behind them was at a standstill, was an army of at least a hundred people, led by two young men in kilts, one rapping hard on a bass drum, the other blowing mightily on a set of massive bagpipes. Next to them were Farah and Mohid, holding hands loosely on one side while they each held up a brightly coloured placard in the other. Behind them were rows and rows of people, many in white coats and navy blue tunics, carrying Save Our Allotments placards and a huge red banner on which was painted in clear white capitals:

TEACHERS AND HEALTH PROFESSIONALS MARCH WITH THE RESIDENTS OF VIEWPARK
SAVE KENMAR ALLOTMENTS #

'How did—' Dorothy could feel tears welling up at the

support. Germaine started clapping, and Lawrence and Kevin joined in the little group behind them in a hip hip hooray.

When they reached the allotments, Mohid said, 'Sorry we're late, everyone. This took a bit of organizing. Everyone – please say hello to my colleagues from the Monklands, and Farah's teaching colleagues. They're all here to lend their support.'

'Thank you.' Dorothy stepped forward and shook hands with some of the people on the front row. 'Thank you so much!'

'Not a problem at all,' said a round, freckle-faced man in tweed, holding a 'THREE CHEERS FOR KENMAR' placard. 'Me and my colleagues know something about cuts and marches and fighting back, don't you worry. We'll let them know you have our full support. Let's see them trying to shut us all down. Now – where is this demo?'

The sun was high in the sky as the now much larger group made their way along Uddingston Main Street towards the cross. There were enough of them that they were a problem for the traffic and their marching was accompanied by the sounds of horns honking and frustrated jeers from the cars that were being forced to crawl along behind them.

'Ignore them,' Dorothy instructed, throwing her arm up and directing them towards the route ahead with her hand. 'We're entitled to use the roads too.'

'Perhaps not for walking on and holding up all the traffic, mind you,' said Lawrence to Kevin, in the middle of the crowd.

'What would Adrian and his huge Mercedes have to say about that?' said Kevin. When he turned and saw the other man's crestfallen face, he added quickly, 'Oh sorry, was that out of turn?'

Lawrence shook his head. 'No, n-n-not at all.' He noticed his stutter returned when he talked about Adrian. 'It's just . . .'

Kevin waited, trying not to heed the attention he was drawing from folk who'd gathered on the pavements to watch as they marched by, reminding himself it was the spectacle of the march they were staring at and not the spectacle of his face. He pulled his attention back to Lawrence.

'I was thinking a lot about what you said the other day. You know, about being happy with who you are, and all that sort of stuff?'

'Yes, I remember.'

'I realized Adrian wasn't making me happy. Or maybe he wasn't happy with me' – he turned to Kevin – 'me as I am, not the version of myself he wanted me to be. We've split up. Maybe temporary, I don't know, but I've moved back home with my granddad for now.'

'I'm sorry to hear that,' said Kevin. 'Sounds like you've been having a hard time.'

'Don't worry, it's fine. And Granddad's glad of the company. He's finally got someone to cook his famous leftovers risotto for.'

'Is that . . . Please tell me that's not rice mixed with leftovers?'

'I'm afraid so. Sausages in rice for breakfast, rice with crumbled Scotch egg the other day served up to me for lunch, and last night, so many leftover chopped mushrooms through rice, the whole thing resembled a bowl of grey porridge. You should come for dinner some time.'

'Tempting, but I might stick with my Pot Noodles, thanks.'

'Very wise. It's not all bad though, I'm hitting the scales at less than eighty kilograms for the first time in my adult life. No effort required at all.'

'Apart from eating the leftovers risotto.'

'That is the downside, yes.'

Kevin hesitated, then put his hand on his friend's shoulder. 'But seriously, I am sorry about you and Adrian. I hope I didn't—'

'Nothing you said, Kevin.' Lawrence considered. 'Maybe it was a bit. You and Mohid, in fact, you both told me things I should have been telling myself these last few months. That no one's perfect. But I was also thinking back to that night at the allotments we had the party, remember, when we thought the allotments were safe?'

Since it was the only party Kevin had been to in the last decade, he remembered it pretty well. 'I think so,' he said, disingenuously, scratching his head as though trying to sort the date from the many other party dates he'd had recently.

'Remember when Maggi was up singing "I Will Survive"?'

Only nightly.

'I was going to get up and dance along with everyone else but Adrian whispered in my ear that everyone would laugh at the way I moved my hips and to stay where I was.'

'What?' Kevin swung round, indignant on his friend's behalf.

'I know. I've been thinking about that a lot since then, and I don't think I'm any w-w-worse a dancer than anyone else.'

'No one could be worse than me, trust me,' laughed Kevin.

'But you were dancing. And enjoying yourself. And that's what I want. To be able to dance however I want, whenever I want, without anyone telling me otherwise. I want to be more like you, Kevin, I've decided.'

Kevin's eyes widened but before he could say anything else, his nose was assaulted by the overpowering scent of blueberries and vanilla as a couple of teenage boys jostled him, vaping close to his face, laughing and saying, 'Dare you, right into him' as they pushed against his shoulder.

Kevin ignored them and kept walking but he heard a commotion behind him and suddenly Mohid and George were on his right-hand side, pushing the boys on to the pavement.

'Fuck's sake . . .' began the smaller boy, before catching sight of George's face, which was stained purple with anger, and Mohid's hands, balled into fists, his shoulders rolling.

'This is a peaceful march for the Kenmar allotments, boys,' Mohid was saying. 'Join in quietly at the back, or get the hell off the road. Got it?'

The stockier of the two, his bottom lip pouting as he considered their options, stood his ground for half a minute before looking round for his backup. The other boy had scarpered.

'All right, mister,' he said. 'We were only walking.'

'Go and walk somewhere else then.' Mohid inclined his head to indicate the boy should beat it.

To the surprise of all four men, he did.

'Right then,' said Mohid, buoyed by his surprisingly successful turn as mob boss. 'Let's get to the council and show them that we're not about to be pushed around.'

In the middle of the group, Isobel was watching her husband laughing and acknowledging the cheers from onlookers who had gathered along the route. Seen from where she was walking, you wouldn't know there was anything wrong with George at all. He was one of the lads, jostling and holding up his placard along with Mohid, Kevin and the others.

'Everything okay?' Farah appeared suddenly beside her, the golden threads of her sari sparkling in the sunlight.

'Yes, I was just thinking how great the allotments have been for George,' Isobel said, indicating her husband twenty feet or so in front of them. 'He's so happy today, like his old self.'

'It's the same for Mohid, you know. He's loving the company of the other men, someone to talk to away from the medical stuff, and our . . . issues.'

Isobel recalled that Farah and Mohid often checked that she and George, and Isaac too, were okay, but she had always assumed they themselves were leading perfect happy lives. She'd never thought to check on how they were doing. 'Is everything okay with *you*?' she asked, aware she hadn't asked Farah that question even once in all the time they'd been seeing each other almost daily at the allotments.

Farah picked up her sari so that it wouldn't get trampled by the ever-increasing throng. 'I am fine, my friend. Mohid and I have been discussing our options and . . . I think things are going to be fine. But thank you for asking.'

'This is all going brilliantly,' said Dorothy to Germaine as they marched behind the piper.

'What? Can't hear you, sorry.' Germaine cupped her hand behind her ear as though that would somehow help her hear over the strains of the bagpipes and drums.

'It's all going great!' Dorothy leaned over to Germaine so that she was shouting in her ear.

'God's sake, woman, I'm not deaf, you know.' Germaine rubbed her ear and looked back at the crowd following them. She could see a sea of placards, all held high with pride, and hear the other marchers chanting, 'Ken. Mar. Ken. Mar. Who do the council think they are?' in time to the beat of the drum.

What a spectacle, what a racket, and what a joy to be part of it all.

'This is down to you, you know,' she said suddenly to Dorothy.

'Oh no, we've all done our bit. That's how campaigns work.'

'Yes, yes, but none of it would be happening without your insisting that we fight.'

Farah and Isobel appeared from nowhere on Dorothy's other side, and Isobel said, 'Germaine's right. You were the one who insisted we could take on the council, and now look!' She gestured towards the people following them, at the sight of them all marching for a common cause.

Dorothy beamed and took the arm of each woman on either side of her, indicating that Farah should loop her arm through Isobel's. 'The best thing about it has been making good friends with all of you lot.'

'Pushing it,' murmured Germaine, but she didn't pull away and the four women marched together, arm in arm along Bothwell Road, acknowledging the cheers of the customers outside the Uddingston Costa like the queens they'd become.

42

STANLEY WAS WATCHING THE TAXI driver like a hawk. His eyes only left the poor man's face to watch the meter or to look out the window to check they were definitely taking the most efficient route to Almada Street.

'Do you not like my driving or something?' The driver could feel Stanley's eyes boring into the back of his head.

'I like your driving fine,' said Stanley briskly. 'Keep your eye on the road and no trying to take us down into some industrial estate or round the back of a scheme so it takes us longer, right?'

'He's been in the war,' piped up Isaac in support.

'Has he indeed?' said the driver, before deciding silence would be the best policy since he was clearly driving a pair of lunatics.

Satisfied, Stanley sat back and watched the road with all the purpose of a sergeant major.

'This is great, isn't it?' Isaac leaned back against the leather of the seat, crossing and uncrossing his skinny legs.

'Is this your first time in a taxi, lad?' said Stanley.

'It is.'

'You sit back and enjoy the ride then. I know what I'm doing. This is my third time.'

At the front of the taxi, the driver tried his best not to laugh. 'Nearly there, squire. Who wants some music?'

It was exactly midday when Stanley and Isaac got out of the taxi at the roundabout at the bottom of Almada Street. The noise was immense and they could not believe the scene that greeted them. There had to be three hundred or so people gathered up and down the street. The pavements weren't wide enough to accommodate them all and everywhere Stanley and Isaac looked, people were spilling onto the road, blowing whistles, holding up placards, laughing, shouting. Police officers were dotted throughout the crowds, talking into mobile phones and directing demonstrators to get off the road, to stay back. A cacophony of car horns could be heard at the top of the street, and beneath it all came the strains of Aztec Camera's 'Somewhere In My Heart', seemingly being blasted from the Water Palace whose doors had been thrown wide open.

'Stanley?' Isaac grabbed the old man's big rough hand and held it tight.

Stanley squeezed the boy's hand. 'Would you look at that? Look what they did, son. That's down to your mum, Germaine, Dorothy, the lot of them.'

Isaac stared at the three boys dancing in a conga line in front of him, arms round each other's waists to form a human train, at the toddler held high on her dad's shoulders, laughing and shouting 'Kenmar, Kenmar!', at the gaggles of schoolchildren, the boys jumping and showing off for the girls who feigned disinterest and chatted to each other in high-pitched excitement, marchers waving at other marchers and standing on their tiptoes to read the multicoloured banners that were everywhere. He looked up at Stanley, his mouth gaping.

'Come on, lad,' laughed Stanley, striding along Almada Street as quickly as his bad knees would allow, all the time maintaining his tight grip on Isaac's hand. 'We're part of this too, don't forget. Let's go and find the others.'

They fought their way through the rabble as they made their way up the packed street to the council building. As they reached the steps, Stanley saw the other allotment holders huddled together outside the main entrance, deep in discussion.

'Isaac,' called Isobel. 'Over here.'

Stanley propelled Isaac in front of him towards his mum.

Dorothy picked up the megaphone one of the well-prepared doctors on the march had given her. Mohid extended his hand to indicate she should make her way to the front and Germaine said, 'Go for it', so she took a deep breath and began to speak.

'Councillor Murray,' her voice boomed through the megaphone and everyone quietened down to listen.

'Councillor Murray,' she repeated. 'We are here representing the people of Viewpark and Uddingston. We will not move until someone from the council comes out to hear the demands of the Kenmar Allotments Campaign Committee.'

The crowd remained silent.

Maggi watched her mum in admiration. 'You tell them, Mum,' she shouted, raising her fist towards the council building.

'I repeat—'

The main door swung open and Councillor Murray, flanked by a police officer on each side, stepped out from the safety of the building till he was inches away from Dorothy. They all stood in silence as he stepped closer towards her.

'What's he doing?' whispered Isaac to Stanley.

'Sshh, let's see.'

The councillor took the megaphone from Dorothy, giving her a glare as he did so, and turned to face the assembly before him.

'Good afternoon, people of Hamilton. And Viewpark,' he added with a sneer. 'I don't know what you've been told or why you think it's a good idea to try and intimidate public officials like this but I can tell you that the police have been called, and anyone on the road, blocking the traffic or otherwise causing public disorder, will have them to answer to.'

Behind him, one of the spotty-faced officers in his too-big uniform rolled his shoulders back and stood taller. The other blushed to the roots of his hair.

The councillor carried on. 'So I suggest you all go about your business now and leave council business to the council. This is not the way to go about things. That is all I have to say.'

The music stopped abruptly, the banners drooped to shoulder height. The crowd murmured, everyone looking at each other uncertainly.

'You can't take that, that's ours,' cried Dorothy. She tried to grab the megaphone back from the councillor but he had slipped it into the waiting hands of one of the policemen so she tried shouting instead.

'Everyone, stay where you are. There are things we need to say. Please—'

It was no good. Mohid watched as the crowds parted and people shrugged their shoulders and returned to whatever they'd been doing before the protest had caught their imagination. No one could hear Dorothy and the councillor's words and the police presence had done their job. He went over and put his hand on Dorothy's arm.

Stanley pushed further to the front and was dismayed to see Dorothy, her head hanging low, her shoulders slumped and her placard trailing on the ground. For the first time throughout the entire campaign, she seemed defeated. Behind her, the councillor was smirking and heading back into the building. Stanley felt his blood rising. How dare that little man, with his rat-like features, his shiny suit, and his puffed-up air of self-importance do that to his friend? He stopped short, realizing suddenly that Dorothy was his friend. In fact, the whole ragtag group of them had become his friends. Without meaning to, he'd done exactly as Mabel had made him promise to do. He'd carried on with his life, tending his plants, getting out there and meeting people. He missed her every day, of course he did! But . . . his days were no longer empty of purpose or structure, he no longer felt surplus to requirements or useless. These people needed him, his friends needed him.

He was not going to let them down.

Grabbing Isaac's hand, he moved closer to Dorothy and Mohid and beckoned the others over to join them. 'Listen,' he said to the huddle. 'If they won't listen to what we've got to say out here, we've no option but to get into the building.'

Farah blanched. 'Wait, what? We can't push our way in.'

'Yes, we can,' said Lawrence, his stutter miraculously non-existent. 'We must, in fact. Kevin?'

'We have come this far . . .'

'You don't think anyone's going to beat Mum down, do you?' added Maggi, coming through the crowd and slipping her arm through her mother's. Dorothy shot her a grateful look.

'That's the spirit,' said Stanley. 'Don't worry about me and Isaac. We'll stay outside and you lot barge your way in. Take some of the protestors with you and stay right there until someone tells us exactly what's going on with our allotments.'

Germaine stepped forward. 'Stanley's right. It's the only way people like them will listen to people like us.'

Dorothy's enthusiasm returned as she considered the determined little group. 'Right, we're doing this. Everybody ready?'

As one, the group turned suddenly and pushed past the councillor, throwing the glass doors open wide. 'Quick, follow us, everyone! If they won't listen to what we've got to say out here, maybe they'll listen to us inside the building.'

Before the two young policemen could stop them, the allotment holders surged into the building, joined by those who were closest to the steps. Councillor Murray was screaming to the policemen, 'Do something, you idiots. Stop— Ow!' George stamped on his foot as he pushed past, adding insult to injury with a wicked grin as he did so.

The noise had become thunderous and Isaac pressed the palms of his hands tight to his ears. Overwhelmed suddenly by the chaos and hubbub that surrounded them, he screwed his face up and started to cry. 'Where's my mum gone now?'

'Oh, Isaac, don't you worry, lad. I've got you.' The need to protect the wee boy came to Stanley like a rush of sugar to his brain. He enveloped the boy's tiny hand in his and ignored his creaky knees to bend down and place his face on the same level as Isaac's. 'Your mum and dad and all the others are going to show that councillor what's what, my boy. And in the meantime, you and I are going to head back to the allotments and make sure there's a warm welcome for them when they get home. How about that?'

The boy sniffed and stretched his arms out to Stanley. Praying his back would stand it, Stanley lifted Isaac up, marvelling at his slightness – he was fragile as the starling that hopped across his allotment in the mornings. 'Everything's going to be fine, Isaac. You stick with old Stanley.'

Screeeeeeeeeee

Inside the council offices, the eighty or so demonstrators who'd flocked in through the glass doors dropped their placards and held their ears.

Screeeeeeeeee

'What the hell . . . ?' cried one of the nurses who worked with Mohid.

'It's the fire alarm,' shouted the receptionist, dipping beneath the main desk to grab her belongings before she ran out to the front of the building. 'And there isn't one scheduled which means there must be a fire in the building.'

'Ladies and gentlemen,' called a deep voice. It was the security guard coming out of the lift with a purposeful stride. 'That's the fire alarm. Start moving out please.'

Suddenly, the crowd started moving again. Mohid felt Farah grip tightly on to his hand and he squeezed her fingers reassuringly. 'Stay here with the others for now till I find out what's going on.'

Kevin came over to join him. 'Fire alarm, my backside. Come on, let's go and see what's happening.'

Council workers in their sky-blue blouses and shirts were teeming out of the lifts behind them, some glancing at the discarded placards on the floor, most standing on them and disregarding them in their rush to be out of the building.

Dorothy and Germaine stood in the centre of the reception area with Lawrence as strangers milled round them, parting and joining again at the front door.

Dorothy watched them all go, disgusted at how little they cared about the allotments or the point of the protest. Okay, they were running in fear for their lives, but still.

Germaine was standing next to Dorothy. 'I wonder if we should follow them. In case there really is a fire?'

'Fire?' George's eyes were wide.

Isobel patted his hand and told him to stay calm till they found out what was happening.

'Now then,' said Mohid to Kevin, wading through the sea of people towards the lifts. 'Let's see if there's anyone in the offices who can tell us what's really going on.'

The lift doors opened and Mohid and Kevin moved to the side so they couldn't be seen.

'That ought to do it,' the councillor was saying to one of his colleagues. 'Did you see them running like rats from a sinking ship? Not that I called these people rats, as if, eh?' He guffawed and was joined by his younger colleague.

'But Mr Murray, what about the alarm, won't it alert the fire station?'

'Don't worry about that, young man, I've already notified them it's a false alarm for security purposes – wink, wink, if you know what I mean.' Another snicker.

Beside the lift, Mohid could hardly contain his anger. So they'd sneaked back into the building and organized this – all that commotion, terrifying people with the fire alarm, how dare they? He watched as the pair from the council barged their way through the crowd, ignoring the jeers and sly pushes from protestors, and made it safely out of the front door. Outside, they were deep in conversation with the security guard, who had his hands on his hips like a superhero waiting to be called into action.

The fire alarm continued to assault their ears and Mohid despaired as more demonstrators fled the building till barely twenty or so remained.

'We didn't make it this far to be beaten by the likes of a local councillor.' Kevin was swinging a set of keys round his index finger like a jailer, his pre-accident character – that of his younger self, brave and irreverent – temporarily reasserting itself in the unusual circumstances. 'What do you say?'

Mohid hesitated. He caught sight of Farah, still holding her 'Save Our Allotments' placard high in the air, her face revealing a steeliness he hadn't known she possessed. Then he noticed her sari was ripped, her best red and gold sari. *These people*, he thought again, *how dare they?* He grabbed the biggest key from Kevin and told him to take a couple of the medics with him and make sure the back door and any fire exits were also locked. He darted towards the two glass doors at the front of the building and stuck the key, large as his palm, into the lock and turned it before he could stop to reconsider. On the other side of the glass, the security guard did a double take as he saw Mohid grinning at him from inside the building.

'What the—?'

Mohid dangled the keys in his face provocatively after he'd locked both doors from the inside, and enjoyed the panic on the faces of those outside. Turning back to the group huddled behind him, he saw Dorothy and Germaine's eyes widen in surprise. Maggi was standing by the desk on her own, saying, 'Now we've done it', and Lawrence put his arm round an anxious George. The twenty or so demonstrators who had stayed with them to show their support looked around them in confusion.

'What on earth is happening now?' said Germaine to Dorothy, as the fire alarm cut out abruptly.

'I don't know for sure' – Dorothy was keeping a close eye on the council employees locked out and furious on the top step – 'but thinking back to my Greenham days, I'd say the Kenmar allotment holders have decided to conduct a sit-in.'

43

THE TAXI DROPPED STANLEY AND Isaac on the pavement on New Edinburgh Road, directly outside the allotments. Excited by another taxi ride, Isaac had recovered his good humour and seemed quite happy at the prospect of spending the afternoon alone at the allotments with Stanley.

After he'd paid the taxi driver, generously telling him to keep the 27p change, Stanley waved at the Skoda until the vehicle was out of sight then looked round for Isaac.

'Careful!' Of course he'd installed himself on top of the front wall, still waving to the taxi driver with one hand, the other in his mouth to make a piercing whistle.

'Oy, Isaac, give the whistling a rest, will you?' Stanley had to flap his arms up and down in front of the boy for him to notice. 'That's got to be one of the loudest noises I've ever heard.' He rubbed his huge ears. 'Almost as loud as that damn fire alarm.'

'Maybe worse for you because your ears are so big,' suggested Isaac, getting on to his feet and wobbling his way along the wall in the opposite direction from where Stanley was standing.

'Nothing wrong with my ears, son,' said Stanley, though Mabel had always called him Sonar Ears, he remembered fondly. 'Careful on that wall!' he shouted again.

'Maybe because you were in the war then,' Isaac called back over his shoulder. 'The tank fire and stuff ruined your hearing.'

'For the last time, I was *not* in the war. How old do you think I am?' but Isaac couldn't hear his reply as he'd jumped off the wall at the other end and landed back in the allotments.

'Wait right where you are till I get back in there,' called Stanley uselessly.

Isaac stood at the bottom of the path between the allotments waiting for Stanley. The place had the air of having been deserted after some major incident had happened and everyone else had left in a hurry to save their lives. In the fairy garden, cardigans and jackets were strewn over the backs of chairs, half-drunk cups of coffee and tipped-over water bottles adorned the picnic tables. After the hullaballoo of the protestors shouting and cheering, and Dorothy shouting directions at everyone, and marchers traipsing in and out for their placards and banners, the silence felt strange to Isaac, the scene was exactly as he imagined a shipwreck would look like, without the water rushing in.

'Looks like the Titanic,' said Stanley, as though he'd read the boy's mind.

'Do you remember the Titanic?' Isaac looked up at Stanley with something like admiration.

'Remember it? Seriously, son, what age do you think I am?'

'I know you're old,' said Isaac, contemplating. 'Maybe like . . . sixty-five or something?'

'I wish, lad, oh aye, I wish. Right, come on, let's get some gardening done while there's no one around to disturb us.'

★

Later, back in the shed, Stanley was making them something to eat and Isaac said again, 'It's weird being here when no one else is around though, isn't it?'

Stanley poured the tomato soup into the pot on his camping stove. He was about to say that's how he preferred it when he realized with a start that wasn't true any more. Since this whole Save the Allotments thing, maybe even before that, when all the new plot holders had started showing up regularly, things had changed. So gradually that none of them had noticed it, certainly not Stanley, but . . . they'd built something together. Isobel relied on Stanley to keep an eye on George on the days he came here when she was at work and Stanley no longer minded that. After all, he wasn't one for talking either; Mabel was always telling him off for being – what was it – taciturn, so who better than George to keep him company while they worked, neither saying much, but quietly turning their plots of land into something useful, that gave them something back for all their hard work. Then there were the early mornings he shared with Mohid. Often, the young doctor would come before an early shift, he'd wave from up the hill as he watered those unfeasibly tall sunflowers his wife was so precious about and amble down for a wee chat before he left for the hospital. He'd given Stanley all sorts of tips on sleeping better, and exercises he could do to sort out his lower back. Stanley appreciated that. And the poor lad with the face. He was starting to loosen up too, helping out the other plot holders, like he had with Stanley's fruit cage. He still didn't talk much but enough to let Stanley know he noticed him, he appreciated his presence maybe, someone who took him for what he was, his face and everything, because it was true, Stanley didn't give two hoots about other people's appearance. Not like that pretty boy at No 5, but then again, Lawrence too had changed recently. He'd been much friendlier since the other guy – Adrian was it, Aiden, some fancy name like that – had stopped coming by, and he'd been spending a lot of time with Kevin. Stanley approved of that, two young lads, digging and planting, did his old soul good to see it. And talking of old souls, Stanley grinned as the image of Dorothy in her dungarees wafted before him, along with Germaine and her brillo-pad hair and complete disregard for the vagaries of fashion. Good for them, these were the kind of women Stanley understood, strong women, mavericks, the ones who stood up for what they believed in and couldn't care less what others thought of them. Now Mabel would have approved of that, he thought, with a chuckle.

He heard the bleeping of Isaac's iPad behind him, and it crossed his mind to wonder what Mabel would make of this friendship – for Stanley, the most important of all the new friends he'd made at the allotments. He thought she'd be pleased that a good mother like Isobel would trust her son to him for the day, knowing he'd be safe and happy. In fact, he thought, as he swirled a spoon round the soup to make sure it was heated through, she might even feel proud.

'Is it nearly ready?' Isaac threw his iPad on to the table and came to stand beside Stanley, his nose in the air. 'Smells good.'

Stanley gave the orange soup one last stir – any connection with tomatoes like the ones he grew on his allotment was purely incidental, he thought, but never mind, kids loved it. He poured the soup into two mismatching bowls and set them down on the low picnic table in front of Isaac, taking his own seat opposite him.

Isaac put the spoon in his mouth, and orange liquid dribbled down his chin. 'Hot,' he said, moving his hand to and fro in front of his face.

'That's good then, soup's supposed to be hot.' Stanley picked up his own spoon. The sweet processed smell of the soup caught him suddenly, and he had a flashback to a night in Ardlui with Brian. Where was Mabel, he couldn't remember, but he knew he and Brian had walked in the hills all day till the mist fell and shrouded the shrubs and rough terrain so that they could hardly see in front of their own faces. Stanley had twisted the little head torch on his hat, and motioned to Brian to do the same. He'd laughed at how ridiculous they looked before they set off, but he wasn't laughing in the dark.

'Glad to have the torch now, aren't you?' Stanley couldn't resist.

They'd set up their camp half a mile or so from Loch Lomond marina and kept their torches on as Stanley fired up the burner. In fact, it was the very same burner he was using today, still working all these years later. They'd heated up soup, chicken it would have been, that was Brian's favourite, and eaten it with Morton's rolls and butter and cheese that Mabel had packed for them that morning. They sat by the shadowy waters of the loch for hours, snapping twigs and swapping stories, till their campfire was nothing but embers and the chill set in. 'This has been brilliant, Dad,' Brian had said, snuggling up to him against the damp night air. And it was.

He was aware of Isaac's hand on his shoulder. 'Don't cry, Stanley.'

'What?' Stanley gave himself a shake. 'Oh, don't worry, son, I wasn't crying. What? I wasn't. You sit down and eat your soup. Don't mind me.'

★

After they'd eaten, Stanley set Isaac to work on weeding that patch round the side of the shed that he'd been putting off for weeks. The weeds were tiny but stubborn, the hardest kind to shift.

'Mind you get them out by the roots now, Isaac,' said Stanley, bending over to inspect the boy's technique.

'I know what I'm doing.'

'I know you do. I'm just saying, there's no point in going fast as you can and leaving half the roots in there. You'll only have to do it all again next week.' He pressed his hand to his lower back and took his time standing up. He squinted at the darkening clouds and sniffed the air. 'Time's getting on,' he said. 'Wonder how the sit-in's going.'

'What is a sit-in?' Isaac sat back on his heels and wiped a smear of freshly turned earth across his cheek.

Stanley took off his bunnet and smoothed what was left of his hair. 'It's a kind of protest, son. You know what a protest is, don't you?'

'Yeah,' he said uncertainly. 'Can my dad do that?'

'Can your dad sit?'

'Yeah.'

'He'll be all right at a sit-in then.'

Isaac thought for a moment. 'And what is it they're protesting for? I thought they were marching today? That's what my mum told me. Where is my mum, will she be much longer?'

'We're protesting for our right to keep this, Isaac.' He motioned to the allotments, glorious in the fading sunlight. Isobel's brambles and Farah's sunflowers, Lawrence's pristine white shed, the scents of mint, chives, sage and thyme blowing on the breeze, and the lights beginning to flicker in the fairy garden. 'This belongs to our community, and we're protesting to let them know they can't take it all away from us without a fight, money or no money. Right, son?' Isaac didn't answer and Stanley saw that the boy was tired. 'But your mum won't be long now. Come on, let's leave the rest for tomorrow, those weeds aren't going anywhere. Time to drink hot chocolate and eat a Tunnock's teacake in the shed. And *that's* what we're protesting for – our right to do that.'

44

AN HOUR AND A HALF after they'd barricaded themselves into the building, Germaine was beginning to wonder if it had been such a good idea after all. She calculated there were about thirty of them altogether, gathered round the reception area, some cross-legged on the floor, others lounging against the main reception desk, and some folk pacing back and forth, biting their nails or folding their arms and probably wondering what on earth they were doing there.

Outside, the swarm of spectators had mostly given up and gone home when nothing exciting was happening. Germaine could see a couple of pairs of police officers clustered at the bottom of the steps. They didn't seem harassed or even interested in what was going on inside the council headquarters.

Dorothy was still hunched over the phone at the main desk, in case someone contacted them on that. She couldn't understand it. She'd called Councillor Murray first to let him know exactly what they thought of the council and their decision-making processes, and informing him that the protestors would not be leaving the building until someone spoke with them and told them precisely what was planned for the allotments. He had listened to her in silence then simply hung up the phone.

Enraged, she'd called the *Hamilton Advertiser* and that nice wee Julie from the *Lanarkshire Courier*, and then they'd all sat back and waited. That was over an hour ago and still nothing. Dorothy wasn't sure exactly what she'd expected from their sit-in but she supposed she thought it would be more exciting than, well, just sitting there.

'Maybe we need to escalate things?' called one of the trainee teachers from the floor at the other end of the office. He'd picked up some sort of desk ornament and was pushing half a dozen steel balls back and forth as he spoke.

The young man was beginning to get on Dorothy's nerves. 'What do you suggest?' she said.

'No idea.'

'Maybe just keep playing with your balls then.'

'Now wait a min—'

'What about the police liaison people? Did you give them our demands?' asked Isobel from the floor, where she was sitting with a fractious George.

'I couldn't,' said Dorothy. 'They said they wouldn't talk to me unless we unlocked the doors and came out of the building.'

'Perhaps it's time to do that then?' said Lawrence. 'Apart from anything else, I'm s-s-starving.'

'We've got the answer to that,' said one of Mohid's colleagues from the Monklands, leading a small group of people from the lifts back into the reception area. 'Look what we found in the upstairs staffroom.'

They tipped out the contents of the carrier bags they'd been carrying onto the floor between the protestors. The council might have complained of lack of funds but it certainly wasn't stinting on nice lunches for internal meetings. On the packed shelves of the giant fridge, the young doctors had found a selection of thick-cut sandwiches filled with egg mayonnaise, cheddar and pickle, and Dorothy's favourite Coronation chicken, all neatly wrapped in clingfilmed trays. There was a basket of fruit, including apples and bananas and lots of those juicy little tangerines George loved so much, and – joy of joys – most of a sponge cake with the words '... ppy 50th birthday Maureen' still left on the buttercream icing slathered on the top.

'Jackpot,' said Mohid. 'Here's to you, Maureen, whoever you are.'

'Eat up, Kevin.' Lawrence noticed that Kevin, who was sitting beside him on the floor, was not joining in the feast with the rest of them. 'You're miles away there.'

'Yeah, I'm not . . . really hungry.' Kevin didn't think Lawrence needed to know that he didn't eat in public, not in any circumstances, even highly unusual ones like being locked into the council offices for God knows how long. In any case, it would have been impossible to eat when Maggi was sitting a couple of rows along, her back to him and obviously ignoring him, whatever Lawrence said. He couldn't work out what had happened between them, that they weren't friends any more, never mind anything else. Maybe she didn't want any of these handsome young medics to see her talking to him. He'd never felt less hungry, birthday cake or no birthday cake.

Mohid stood up, brushing sandwich crumbs from the front of his shirt. 'Okay, everyone, it seems to me that we need to try a different approach.'

'Go on,' said Dorothy, bristling at having matters taken out of her hands but frankly at this point unable to see what they could do next to get out of this mess.

'The council won't talk to us, right?'

'Not until we vacate the premises,' said Germaine, 'which I, for one, would not mind doing in the slightest.'

Mohid had no time for such dejection. 'Oh no, we've started this now, we need to see it through.'

Revitalized by sandwiches and cake, there was a small cheer from the crowd on the floor.

'What do you suggest then?'

'We need someone to talk to them on our behalf. A go-between. Someone who will advocate for us.'

Dorothy sat back, considering Mohid's suggestion.

Kevin raised his hand hesitantly, cringing as everyone turned round to see who was speaking, but determined to carry on. 'I think I know someone,' he said. 'A lawyer.' He cleared his throat. 'The lawyer who fought the council for me when this happened, got me compensation, for . . . this.' He gestured to his face — some folk looked away, embarrassed, but the medical staff around him willed him on with nods of encouragement. 'I could call her and ask if she would come over. Maybe . . . they'd let her in to speak to us then she could relay our demands to them outside.'

'That sounds like an excellent idea, Kevin,' said Mohid. 'And while Kevin's doing that, let's carry on tucking into this banquet the council has donated to our worthy cause.' There was an outbreak of applause as the demonstrators' spirits were lifted again by this new plan of action. Isobel peeled another tangerine for George, Lawrence cut himself a colossal chunk of cake, and Dorothy and Germaine saluted each other with a cheese and pickle sandwich and an egg mayonnaise finger roll respectively.

Kevin took out his phone and called his lawyer.

45

GERMAINE HAD ARRIVED AT THE allotments before dawn. She'd wanted some time to sit beneath the cloud-free sky and enjoy her first cup of coffee before anyone else came along to spoil her peace. Of course, Stanley hadn't been long behind her but all he needed was a quick wave and he was happy meandering around his allotment on his own, pinching out the tops of his climbing beans which had reached the top of their canes, pulling out his celery and chicory before the young plants could become bitter, and generally reaping the benefits of all the planting and sowing work he'd put in earlier in the year.

The others arrived according to their various timetables and habits. Mohid and Farah had parked their car outside the gates since they were going off to some social services appointment or other after lunch, Farah told her – not that she'd asked. Stopping to soak their three soaring sunflowers with water, they disappeared into their shed almost immediately and busied themselves behind closed doors.

Isobel and George came next, with Isaac in tow, and holding his dad's hand, Germaine noticed. As they passed her shed, she heard Isaac telling his mum she had to keep practising her chess, she'd remember all the moves eventually and then they could have a tournament with Stanley. She noted with satisfaction that all three looked healthy and happy, then she sniffed and shook her head as soon as the thought had entered it. She must be getting soft in her old age.

Next came Kevin, loping on to his allotment as though he hoped no one would spot him, but too bad if he didn't want to make friends because Lawrence appeared ten minutes later and walked straight past his own allotment and on to Kevin's instead, installing himself on the step outside Kevin's shed, the pair of them drinking coffee and talking. What had happened to the other man that used to be with Lawrence, Adrian, was it? She hadn't seen him in weeks. Not that she was interested in the personal arrangements of the other plot holders, she reminded herself.

Lastly came Dorothy, still in those ridiculous dungarees and laden with two large canvas bags full of heaven knows what. Dorothy waved down to her and pulled out a box of Tunnock's teacakes from one of the bags. 'For later,' she shouted, adding, 'See you there' when Germaine gestured towards the picnic tables beside the fairy garden. *Thank God for that*, thought Germaine. She didn't mind a mid-morning coffee break with the woman – in fact she had almost finished that Betty Friedan book she'd given her and was looking forward to giving Dorothy her own views on womanly mystique – but she drew the line at having it in her shed. Plenty of bags of stuff going in, she noticed, but very little coming out again. She dreaded to think what sort of state that shed was in these days. She shook her head, it was none of her business, and anyway, there was more for a woman to be concerned with than keeping things clean and tidy, as Betty herself might have said.

Germaine stood with her hands on her hips and raised her chin proudly as she took in the scene before her. August was a time of plenty at the allotments. Almost everything that had been sown, planted and nurtured through the spring and the early part of summer was now coming into its own. Even the newbies were leaving the allotments every day with barrows full of peas, beans, carrots and sweetcorn. They swapped bags of potatoes for an armful of fennel bulbs, they gave away fat little aubergines, and took home bags of chillies, coming in the following day to tell the others about blistering hot pasta. Dense red cabbages were picked and pickled, garlic was dried and summer squashes grew so quickly they seemed to sprout again almost as soon as they were harvested.

The sun was burning gold, casting its light across the brambles, hollyhocks, hydrangeas and shrubs, and bathing everything in its wake in an orange glow. How beautiful this land was, how lucky they were to have it. Germaine breathed in deeply and turned back to her own plot to lift and clean the last remaining shallots.

Nina arrived with Karen shortly before lunch and, after a brief chat with Germaine in the management office, the three women came out and stood at the bottom of the path.

'Gather round, everyone,' Germaine called out. 'We've got some news.'

Like bees drawn to the hive, everyone approached at once, appearing from their sheds and swarming down the path from their various plots. There was a low hum of expectation in the air as they spotted the young woman in the trouser suit, blonde hair frizzed round her head like a halo, standing between Karen and Germaine. She shouted, 'Hi, how are you doing?' to Kevin and he managed a shy 'Hey' in response, quietly proud that he'd been the one to bring her on board.

'Nina here has got something to tell us.'

It had been almost four weeks since they'd first encountered the whirlwind that was Nina Valente. She'd appeared like an angel on the steps of the council building, together with Karen, nominated as the council spokesperson least likely to annoy the protestors, and two reporters, including young Julie from the *Courier*. She told them in her no-nonsense way that the council had agreed to meet with her and two nominated representatives from the Save the Allotments campaign to discuss possible ways forward and that the allotments would remain open in the meantime. That had seemed like a victory at the time and the group had stood posing happily for the newspaper photographers outside the now-famous council headquarters and given interviews to the press to make sure their side of the story was told.

'What's the verdict then, love?' Stanley called out from the back of the group. 'Are they shafting us after all?'

'Maybe if you give Nina a chance to speak, Stanley, we can all find out,' said Germaine. 'Nina, please.'

Nina stepped forward. 'I am delighted to tell you that after three solid days of talks with Councillor Murray and then his replacement, Councillor McPhee' – a small cheer went up and Karen turned pink and said, 'It's only temporary, just till the elections', and signalled to Nina to continue – 'we have reached a mutually agreeable solution. With continued support from local businesses, and the cash you've already raised from the Save the Allotments campaign, the allotments will remain open and in public hands for the foreseeable future.'

This time, the cheer lasted much longer, with enthusiastic accompaniment from Isaac, the proud recipient of Dorothy's orange whistle from the march. Mohid hugged Farah, and Stanley shook hands with a bewildered but happy George. Kevin held out his hand to Lawrence, who was standing next to him, but Lawrence grabbed him by the shoulders instead and enveloped him in a huge bear hug. 'Well done us, and well done you, Kevin, for bringing in Nina,' he whispered in his ear. Kevin's arms hung limply at his sides for a second then he thought better of it and returned his friend's hug enthusiastically.

'But what does that mean, exactly?' said Dorothy, remembering the last time they had celebrated too soon and it had all been snatched away from them again.

'That's a good question,' said Nina. 'Of course, we're going to have to keep an eye on the council budgets and keep lobbying for our share. The wall at the back remains an issue so we're probably going to have to raise more cash at some point. *But* the takeaway for now is that you don't have to worry about closure for the next year at least, and after that—'

'I'll be dead,' said Stanley, then, seeing Isaac's face, he added quickly, 'I was joking, lad, I'll be working this land for years yet and after that I'll be haunting the place.' Isaac grinned and raised both his thumbs in Stanley's direction.

When they'd quietened down again, Nina placed her hand against her heart and continued in impassioned tones. 'What it really means is that we have to be vigilant of what's ours, all of us. Of the allotments, yes, but also of our public swimming pools, our libraries, our youth clubs, our senior citizens' dance clubs, all of our community spaces. If we want to keep the places we value—'

'Hear hear,' shouted Dorothy then blushed apologetically, but brightened again as Germaine and Isobel called back, 'Too right' and 'These allotments belong to us.'

Nina carried on, undeterred. 'If we want to keep all of these places, we have to keep using them, keep claiming our space. We will not let them take what is rightfully ours!'

This time, the cheers drowned her out completely, and the plot holders high-fived and slapped each others' backs, as they congratulated themselves on their victory.

Later that evening, Germaine sat back in her office, tired but satisfied things had gone their way. Her dad would be proud, she thought, and might even have considered it a day to make some friends rather than enemies. She glanced up at the silent allotments – the others had long gone – and sighed. She was aware of an unsettling but growing desire for the company of friends rather than the silent flat and solitude that she usually craved. As she tidied up her desk and prepared to lock up for the night, she had the sudden realization, *We've won, this time we really have won and we are going to celebrate it properly.* Her mind buzzing with ideas, she picked up her phone and called Dorothy.

46

'Okay, I've got the stuff.' Lawrence entered Kevin's shed, carrying his white leather vanity case.

Kevin's mouth was dry and even his good eye felt twitchy. It seemed like there was a lot riding on this evening, more than just the party. He hated himself for having built it up into something it was probably not going to be.

The anticipation had been building for the last two weeks. Everyone was determined to make this an event to remember, not only for the allotment holders, but for all the local community since so many people had supported them in their campaign. Invitations were sent to nearby nursery groups and schools, Iris at Viewpark Church had told all their regulars, there were notices pinned up at Scotmid and Tesco, and, of course, the message had been put out on Facebook and Twitter. Donations of food and drink had been coming in steadily over the last week and the picnic tables were buckling under the weight of party snacks, bottles of wine, and beers that even Kevin hadn't heard of. An entire table was dedicated to Tunnock's teacakes and caramel wafers.

George and Isaac had painted a huge 'Welcome to the Kenmar Allotments Party' sign for the entrance and Mohid had gone round propping up several of the placards from the demonstration against sheds and fences to remind everyone of what it was they were celebrating. Isobel and Germaine had hung endless strings of fairy lights, bickering constantly over the best way to weave them into trees and bushes without damaging any foliage, but all agreed the effect they'd achieved in the end was magical.

Everything was ready.

Kevin looked over hopefully as Dorothy made her entrance to the party. She was still wearing dungarees, though in a concession to the events of the evening, she had teamed them up with a candy-striped blouse and red platform heels. But as soon as Kevin saw that she was on her own, his shoulders slumped.

Maggi hadn't been to the allotments even once since they'd won the battle to keep them open. Finally, last week Kevin had plucked up the courage to ask Dorothy where she was.

'Did she not tell you before she left? She got a surprise booking on a cruise ship as part of a tributes show. She's sailing across the Med pretending to be Beyoncé as we speak.'

She must have seen his face fall because she added, 'Don't worry, Kevin, she'll be back in time for the party. She promised me she'd come and sing for us.'

Kevin wasn't sure if he believed her or not, but he couldn't come up with a convincing reason to ask for Maggi's phone number so he had no way of contacting her to find out.

Lawrence tapped him on the shoulder. 'Come on, Kevin, let's have a beer. It's party time.' He decided not to mention whatever it was that was going on with Kevin's good eye. He knew he had to get him more relaxed or he'd blow off the party altogether. 'Drink up. And shall we have some music, maybe? Get us in the mood to party?'

'Okay,' said Kevin. 'Good idea.' He flicked through the pile of CDs and found the one he was looking for.

'Oh, I love this one.' Lawrence jumped up and moved the folding table out of the way so they had room to dance. 'Come on, Kevin' – he started to sing in a loud falsetto – 'show us how you use your walk, you're a woman's man, no time to talk.'

Kevin bit his lip and started to sway slightly in front of the door.

Lawrence laughed. 'Is that it? Come on.'

His enthusiasm was infectious, and Kevin's face brightened as he stuck out one foot and started tapping the wooden floor. Slowly, he began to click the finger and thumb of his left hand and raise and drop his shoulder in time to Barry's soprano.

'That's it.' Lawrence pranced over to Kevin. 'Now, pretend I'm Maggi—'

'Aw no, Lawrence . . .'

'Come on, we've talked about this – you can do it, follow me. Ha ha ha ha, stayin' alive, stayin' alive . . . Come on, Kevin!'

Kevin put his hands on Lawrence's shoulders, and Lawrence had his hands on Kevin's hips. Together they danced round the shed, singing along with the Bee Gees. On the chorus, Lawrence drew back, wiggling his fingers and shouting, 'Jazz hands, Kevin, jazz hands, come on.' Kevin did his best to oblige.

The track ended and Kevin fell into his old gardening chair, laughing and wiping the sweat off his forehead with the back of his hand.

'Right,' said Lawrence as a slower track began, 'now you've got the moves, time to get the looks. You want to look your best for Maggi, don't you?'

Kevin tutted. 'She's not even coming, Lawrence.'

'Dorothy said she was. Keep the faith.'

He put the table back up and sat the white vanity case on top and Kevin watched as Lawrence lined up the bottles and tubes on the aluminium table and pushed up his sleeves. 'Okay then. Lean over to me and I'll do the base coat.'

Kevin hesitated.

'What?' Lawrence stood with one hand on his hip, the other holding a spray can high in the air.

'I've been thinking about what you were saying that day you were here, doing the make-up for me the first time. Do you remember what you said?'

'About Maggi?'

'Yeah – about how she might . . . like me.'

'She does, Kevin, and wait till she sees you when I'm finished with you.'

'That's just it.'

'What is? I don't understand – are you not going to s-s-speak to her?'

'No, I am. Maybe. But . . . the thing is, *if* she likes me—'

'She does!'

'Then if she likes me, she'll like me as I am. This is me.'

'But—'

'No buts. This is me, Lawrence.' Kevin touched his fingers to his scarred cheek. 'What is it they say about Marmite – you either love it or hate it? I'm a Marmite sort of person.'

Lawrence put down the spray can and reached across to Kevin, putting his hand on his friend's shoulder. 'She'd be mad not to love you, Kevin.'

'Well . . .' Kevin looked away for a moment, his unscarred cheek flushed. Then he swept his hands up and down his loose blue T-shirt which had a picture of a mushroom on it and the words, 'I'M A FUNGI', especially washed and ironed for the occasion. 'How could she say no to this, right?'

He drained his beer in one last gulp and left the shed, holding up both hands to show Lawrence two sets of crossed fingers. 'Good luck, Kevin,' said Lawrence to himself softly, praying that his friend was right and Maggi was the woman he deserved.

47

Germaine wasn't sure why she felt so nervous about this evening. After all, the whole thing had been her idea and she'd been helping the others get ready for the party for the last two weeks. She stood outside her shed, watching the crowds stream in, in pairs and family groups of three or four. And it dawned on her what had been bothering her – she was on her own. There was no one helping her to choose an outfit, or decide what time they should leave for the party, or even to share in the excitement of going to a party. Perhaps she'd taken the family motto of an enemy a day too literally, she thought ruefully, wondering if anyone would notice if she skipped the party altogether and went home.

'There she is,' called Dorothy from across the path. 'Come on, girls, come and meet my friend Germaine.'

Germaine watched as Dorothy picked her way unsteadily across the allotments in ridiculous red shoes, a group of three older women Germaine didn't recognize following on closely behind, all waving as they came towards her.

'These are my friends from my dance class – Irish Mary, Terry and Myra. They've been dying to meet you.'

'Irish Mary.' The woman closest to her held out her hand. 'Pleasure to meet you at last, we've heard so much about you.'

Germaine narrowed her eyes as she took in the woman's thick black eyeliner and backcombed hair. She looked like she'd stepped off the set of an eighties rock video, possibly backing up Bonnie Tyler.

'Lovely to meet you too,' was all she said, proud of herself.

'And Dorothy tells us you're a dancer as well?' said the smaller woman who introduced herself as Terry.

'Line dancing,' said Dorothy. 'Your neighbour up there' – Germaine's heart sank as Sue from next door grinned and waved at her enthusiastically from the top of the path – 'was telling us you're practically a pro. You kept that quiet.'

'Yeah, about that . . .'

The twin toddlers were adorable in their matching pale green cotton thobes. They were giggling uncontrollably as Mohid chased and caught one then the other, throwing them up in the air and catching them again. His brother Mustafa watched proudly, saying, 'Careful, careful now, brother,' reminding everyone the boys belonged to him.

Priya put her hand on Farah's arm. 'Thank you for inviting us. It's good to leave the house occasionally. You were right' – she glanced over at her children – 'I do need to make time for myself, to get out and see other people.'

'You're doing a brilliant job with those boys, Priya. Anyone can see how happy they are so take some time for yourself too. You deserve it.'

'Thank you, Farah, always so kind. You'd be such a good mum . . .'

Mohid came over to join them as Mustafa took the boys by the hand and led them down to explore the fairy garden.

He heard Priya say, 'Your time will come, my sister, I am sure of it.'

He put his arm round Farah. 'Would this be a good time to start telling people?'

Farah took out the picture she'd been carrying around with her for weeks now. The little girl staring out at them had a thin, freckled face, ginger pigtails and a green hoodie zipped up to her pointy chin. There was a hint of sadness, perhaps, behind her eyes, things seen that shouldn't have been seen by a child of four, but Farah was confident she and Mohid would soon dispel that and give her the life she deserved.

'This is Suzie,' she said proudly. 'Our daughter.'

Kevin spotted Maggi before she saw him. Clutching a large glass of red wine, she was wearing a crisp white shirt, open at the neck, and a pair of pinstriped trousers like the best man at a wedding, just lacking the top hat and tails. For the first time since Kevin had known her, her mouth was free of lipstick, her hair worn in loose, sun-lightened curls round her shoulders. Kevin stared. When she saw Kevin, she smoothed her hair and gave him a shy smile.

'Hi, Maggi.' Before he knew it, both his hands were moving high in the air, fingers splayed. *Jazz hands? Really, Kevin?*

'Hey, Kevin. Whoa, jazz hands, okay.' Maggi copied Kevin and raised her own hands in the air, careful not to spill her wine.

'Sorry about that, we've been . . . dancing.'

'Who were you dancing with?' asked Maggi quickly, scanning the party guests.

'Lawrence.'

'Oh, okay.' Maggi relaxed. 'How have you been?'

'Fine.'

There was a pause then they both spoke at the same time.

'The allotments are—'

'You look—'

Maggi laughed. 'Sorry, I'm still talking too much, you first.'

Kevin wiped his palms down his jeans. He pulled at one of his long blond curls then let it spring back. 'You look lovely. Your mum said you'd been away singing? On a cruise ship?'

'Yeah.'

'Sounds like a fantastic opportunity for you, Maggi.' He took a deep breath. 'Although I wanted to tell you that I missed—'

'Gorgeous Kevin!'

Kevin paled.

'You look great! Jay, doesn't Gorgeous Kevin look great?'

Kevin turned and said, 'It's just . . . Kevin,' not daring to check Maggi's reaction to hearing him being called by that ridiculous name. 'Wendy, isn't it?'

'It is.' Wendy shook his hand. 'I'm sorry I got your name wrong. I didn't know you knew mine?'

'From the bus?' said Kevin. 'I see you most days on the 255. I always wanted to say . . . I was sorry about your friend. The one who used to sit with you on the bus.'

Wendy's expression softened. 'Thank you.'

'She seemed like a very nice person. Funny.'

'She really was. It's nice to know other people miss her too. She was brilliant, my first ever best friend.' Wendy turned to Jay and said, 'Ginger, that I told you about.'

Jay put her arm round Wendy. 'I know. Isn't it lovely that people still ask after her?'

Wendy turned back to Maggi, appraising her without a

trace of self-consciousness. 'Jay's my friend now. She's a fitness instructor. She does personal training as well, and she can help everybody, even really fa—'

'I have loads of different clients, that's right, Wendy,' Jay interrupted quickly. 'But we're not here to talk about jobs are we, we—'

'No,' said Wendy, 'but I was thinking you could help with . . .' She swept her hand up and down in front of Maggi's body to make her point.

Jay shook her head, trying not to laugh. 'I think you must be Maggi? We were talking to your mum before we came over. Hopefully we'll get the chance to hear you sing later? Dorothy told us you were the entertainment tonight.'

'Maybe,' said Maggi darkly, not sure whether to give her mum or this Wendy person the evil eye first.

'We'll look forward to that.' Jay led Wendy away by the hand, saying, 'God's sake, Wendy, what have I told you about being more diplomatic? Come on, let's get a drink.'

Maggi looked at Kevin, open-mouthed. 'Who on earth . . . ?'

'Oh, don't worry about Wendy. She doesn't mean anything by it. You'll love her when you get to know her.'

Maggi was not convinced but she had other things on her mind. 'Before she came over, you were saying . . . ?'

'Ahh. That is to say . . . I've been wanting—'

'Okay, everyone,' called Dorothy from the picnic area. 'I am happy to announce . . . the buffet is open!'

Children came pelting down the path, their parents shouting, 'Careful' as they made a beeline for the Tunnock's. Groups of adults, famished after the alcohol and fresh air, weren't far behind and partygoers swarmed round Kevin and Maggi. The noise reached carnival levels, making it impossible to continue their conversation. 'Maybe we can speak later,' said Kevin and dashed back to his shed to recover.

Once the buffet tables had been desecrated, it was time to dance. 'Music please,' shouted Dorothy to Mohid who was nominated DJ for the evening. Some young gun in desert boots and hair knotted like a rug shouted out, 'Taylor Swift' before turning to his pal and saying, 'If she isn't the best female vocalist of all time, I don't know who is.' Maggi and Dorothy both shouted at the same time, 'Patti Smith' then turned to each other and said, 'Am I right?' at the same time, then 'Jinx' together. They caught each other's eye, laughing, as the boy turned to them and said, 'Patti Who?'

'Maybe we've got more in common than we think?' Dorothy put her arm round her daughter and touched her forehead to hers.

'You wish,' said Maggi, but she hadn't moved her head away, Dorothy noticed, as Mohid blasted 'You Belong With Me' into the warm evening air.

Half an hour later, Lawrence was searching through the crowd for Kevin and feared the worst when he saw Maggi wandering around forlornly on her own. At least it wasn't just him that was feeling lonely.

There was a tap on his shoulder. 'Penny for them.'

'Adrian! What . . . what are you d-d-doing here?' His stutter was back.

'Everyone in Viewpark and Uddingston is here. It's the place to be, isn't it?' He met Lawrence's eyes and didn't look away.

Lawrence faltered but he was determined not to give in to him. Damn, he looked good though. But different.

'Do you like it?' Adrian twirled round in his multicoloured floral Ted Baker shirt, almost exactly the same as the one Lawrence himself was wearing.

'I don't think I've ever seen you in anything like that. You're usually so—'

'Boring?' supplied Adrian with a laugh.

'I wasn't going to say that.'

'You were thinking it though, and you were right.' When Lawrence didn't reply, he added in a rush, 'You were right about a lot of things, as it turns out. I have been too focused on work, the gym, the superficial stuff that doesn't really matter. Look, I might as well be upfront and say it – I miss you and I want you to come home.'

Lawrence took in Adrian's tight shirt and deep blue jeans that clung to his hips, and breathed in the familiar scent of his expensively creamed and perfumed skin.

Sensing his advantage, Adrian reached over and pushed some hair back from Lawrence's face and stroked his cheek. 'You look great,' he said. 'Have you lost weight? Not that it matters what you look like, of course,' he added quickly, biting the edge of his lip, and Lawrence suddenly remembered why he'd fallen for him in the first place.

'Thank you. I am glad you're here,' he said carefully.

'But?'

'But I think I'm better staying at Granddad's for now. I need to figure out who I am, what I want, rather than trying to be what you or anyone else wants me to be.'

Adrian's unshakable self-assurance grappled with what

Lawrence was telling him and his sceptical 'Are you sure that's what best for you?' confirmed Lawrence's decision.

'Yes,' he said, more firmly now. 'I am sure. I'm not saying we won't get back together at some point, maybe we will, who knows? But . . . not yet.'

'I see.'

Revellers thronged on all sides, their high spirits and laughter parting round the silence between the two men, as Adrian took in Lawrence's words and Lawrence stood his ground.

'Well . . . you know where I am,' said Adrian eventually, in a quieter voice. He turned to leave.

'Wait a minute, where do you think you're going? This is a party, the least you can do is help us celebrate. Starting with' – he put down his rosé – 'a dance.' Lawrence took Adrian by the hand and pulled him towards the makeshift dance floor in the fairy garden.

'Is this a test? Because I draw the line at ABBA, Lawrence, we are definitely not dancing queens – I mean, maybe you are but . . . Lawrence, please, no . . . Oh, go on then. But no jazz hands, promise me?'

48

It was getting late, the evening was still dusty hot, and Isobel helped George slide his arms out of the chunky Aran knit he'd insisted on wearing to the party.

'That's better,' she said when he sat back down on one of the picnic benches, his T-shirt revealing tanned upper arms, strong and muscular with all the lifting and digging, a life lived outdoors. He was still her George in some respects, it was so easy to forget that. She reached over to touch his shoulder when he broke the spell.

'Ppppgggg.' He tutted. 'Ffffuit.'

'What is it? Say it again, George.' She tried to soften her response. 'Please.'

This time he pointed, his hand stretched towards the giant fruit bowl, filled with shiny red apples grown right here on the allotments, what a joy this place was. She reached for one but he shook his head and pointed again.

Isobel looked across the table. 'Peaches? Is it a peach you want?' She grabbed two peaches – Tesco's finest, the sun had shown its face a few times over the summer but not often enough for anyone, even a maestro like Stanley, to grow big smooth-skinned peaches like these in Scotland.

George and Isobel ate their peaches, juice dripping, sticky fingers wiping their chins. As the sweetness hit the back of her throat, Isobel remembered their honeymoon in Tuscany. They'd been on the beach in Porto Santo Stefano, the rocky coastline behind them disappearing in the low clouds as they watched the swollen sunset. They ate peaches smooth and perfect as Fabergé eggs, before lying back in the swell, the white tips of the waves tickling their sun-reddened Scottish limbs. How she'd loved him—

'Stereo,' said George suddenly. He slapped his mouth in frustration. 'Ste— Stefano,' he said finally, and Isobel could sense his delight at pinning down the word he'd been searching for.

'Santo Stefano? George, do you remember? How we were? How happy we were?'

'How we were,' George repeated, each word enunciated perfectly.

Isobel held her breath but he said nothing more, instead sinking his teeth into the flesh of his peach, shaking his head and chuckling to himself.

'Santo Stefano,' Isobel whispered to herself and leaned her head on George's shoulder, remembering the warmth of the sun on her back and the fine sand between her toes.

STANLEY SAW ISAAC'S FACE LIGHT up as the boy watched his mum and dad cuddle closer on the bench at the bottom of the path. He and Isaac were sitting on deckchairs outside Stanley's shed, watching the party swirling around them. He noticed the boy no longer clutched his iPad to his chest wherever he went, clearly no longer requiring whatever comfort it had given him.

'Things are going to be all right, son, and I don't want to say I told you so but . . .'

Isaac said nothing, but grinned. Stanley was pleased to see how his scooped-out cheeks had grown fuller, the colour high on each cheek. His hair was freshly washed and he was wearing his best cargo shorts – a smaller version of George's own – in honour of the party. He was about to tell the boy how well he looked when Germaine appeared at the bottom of the path, carrying two plates piled high with party food.

'I brought you some sandwiches and sausage rolls from the buffet. I noticed you were avoiding the crush earlier.'

Stanley was touched she'd noticed and offered her a deckchair while Isaac grabbed a sandwich in each hand and alternated between bites of cheese and ham, and egg salad.

Kevin walked past on his own, heading up to the top of the hill.

Germaine watched him and shook her head sadly.

'He will find love, you know,' said Stanley. 'He will because we all do. Most of us.'

Germaine looked at him sharply. 'Some of us don't want to find love, not that sort of love. But I hope you're right about Kevin. He's a nice boy.' She sniffed. 'Friendship, mind, that's different . . .'

Stanley thought for a second, wondering if he was getting this right and wishing Mabel was here to help him. 'We could make a project out of redoing that patch at the front of the fairy garden together. If . . . you like, that is?' She said nothing so he stumbled on. 'I mean, we are always here, aren't we? Maybe we could work on something together?'

The corners of Germaine's mouth flicked upwards. 'Maybe. Yes, I think we should do that. None of your damned pansies and primroses, mind you!'

Stanley laughed and Isaac piped up, 'We could teach you to play chess if you like?'

'For your information, son, I was the chess player of the year for Aberdeen School District in 1982.' And she was, she'd forgotten all about that. 'So I think it'll be me that's teaching you a thing or two, don't you?'

Isaac tapped a finger against his nose – a habit he'd picked up from Stanley, the old man realized with pride – and reached into his pocket. 'In that case, you'd better have one of my special badges that only me and Stanley know about—'

'Oh Isaac, no—' began Stanley but he was too late, Isaac had proudly handed over one of his special handmade badges to Germaine and was awaiting praise for his artwork.

'Oh my.' Germaine took in the three large black Ks daubed across the badge. Catching Stanley's eye, and trying hard not to laugh, she said they should probably wear the badges exclusively in their secret chess club and keep them secret from the others.

'Wow!' said Isaac. 'A secret club,' and he and Stanley both tapped their noses at the same time, Isaac's eyes shining.

An hour or so later, Dorothy gave a deep sigh of satisfaction as she watched the last of the party guests drifting round what was left of the buffet and the tired dancers propping each other up on the dance floor as they swayed to the soft music. Isobel and Farah joined her, closely followed by Germaine.

'It's been a great success, ladies.' She poured them all a last glass of the now warm white wine, and handed Germaine a diet Coke.

'Though I do think you could have worn something other than your dungarees,' said Germaine, unable to help herself. 'Even I put a skirt on.'

'Funny you should say that. Here, I've got a wee something for all of you.' Dorothy handed round the packages she'd been waiting all night to give them.

'Dungarees?' said Farah. 'Thank you, my friend, I've never had a pair before.'

'You got us all dungarees?' laughed Isobel. 'Excellent!'

'Excellent for you, maybe,' said Germaine, holding up the light denim dungarees and inspecting them. 'You know I'm going to look like Dolly Parton working a shift at the garage in these, don't you?'

'Stop boasting,' said Dorothy, and they all laughed.

'Here's to us, the four musketeers. Good friends.' She nudged Germaine with her shoulder.

'Pushing it again,' said Germaine but she was laughing too as she raised her diet Coke along with the others.

'Now – where's Maggi?' Dorothy looked round for her daughter. 'I wonder if we can persuade her to do one last song for us before everyone goes home.'

The luminous hands on Maggi's watch in the shape of a red mushroom cap told her that despite the continued warmth of the evening, it was half past ten. She'd waited long enough, and climbed over the tumbledown wall, jumping on to the unkempt field behind.

'I knew you'd be here,' she said. 'Away from all the fuss and noise.'

Kevin propped himself up on his elbows, watching as Maggi joined him in the long grass, stretching her legs out in front of her.

'What's your excuse this time then, are you out here watching the stars again?'

'You remember that?' A smile hovered round Kevin's lips as he took that in.

'Of course.' Maggi looked straight ahead as she spoke. 'One of the highlights of my summer.'

'Really? I . . .' Kevin didn't know what to say. He bit the right side of his bottom lip and suddenly thought about the raspberries he'd picked. 'Want some?' He offered Maggi the chipped blue bowl filled to the brim with juicy, ripe fruit, already starting to soften in the last of the evening sun.

'Ooh, raspberries, I can have them.'

'What do you mean? Have you got allergies?'

'Yeah, I'm allergic to anything that's slimming.' She laughed. 'No, what I mean is I'm on a diet. Not before time,' she said ruefully, clutching a handful of flesh from her thigh, and rolling her eyes.

'Why? You're perfect the way you are.' Kevin put his hand to his mouth but it was too late, the words were already out there.

Maggi didn't turn round but spoke with uncharacteristic slow determination. 'Why have you been avoiding me then?'

'*Me?* Avoiding *you?*'

'Yes. Ever since that day we spent together in Blantyre, when I thought we were getting on so well . . . and then again after that time in Bothwell woods – when you almost . . . when we almost . . .' She turned to him suddenly, making up her mind. 'Am I imagining this, Kevin?'

'What?'

'This.' She waved her hand at the two of them lying on the grass, the shared raspberries, the almost palpable tension in the sultry evening air. 'Because honestly, you're the best person I've ever met – the kindest, wisest, funniest, best person I know, and . . . and I'd really like to know how you feel about that.'

Kevin hastily swallowed the raspberry he'd been holding in his mouth while Maggi spoke, forgetting how he must look to her as he ate, and anyway it seemed – somehow – that she didn't care about that, she *liked* him in spite of it all.

'Maggi, Maaaggi!' Dorothy was calling from somewhere in the background.

Maggi and Kevin looked at each other and laughed.

'Every time. Every single time without fail. I'd better go and see what she wants.' Maggi started to get up but Kevin reached out his hand and stopped her. Keeping one hand on her arm, he moved the bowl of raspberries from between them in the grass and leaned towards her. She held her breath.

Kevin opened his mouth but no words came, so he kissed her instead. A soft kiss, from the right-hand side of his mouth, conscious not to let her beautiful, perfect lips connect with his corrugated skin, the patchwork of scarring, the left-hand side of his face. She didn't pull away so he closed his eyes and let out a tiny gasp when he felt her hand cupping his damaged cheek gently and completely. He drew her closer towards him so that they were kissing properly, deeply, and he forgot about his face and thought only of the kiss.

'Maggi, where are you? Come and do another song for us before things finish up.' Dorothy's high-pitched call broke the spell.

Maggi pulled away from him gently. 'Stay here. I'll be back.'

Kevin watched as she ran down the hill to speak to her mother, stopping at the bottom to turn round and gesture to him that he should stay where he was.

He wasn't going anywhere! He looked at the wide, deep imprint she'd left on the grass and smoothed it over with his hand. He felt different, like she'd peeled back some protective layer and touched the fresh new unblemished skin hidden beneath. He touched his scarred cheek and felt the ridges – still there and yet . . . He brought both hands together and covered his mouth, the smile beneath his fingers spreading across his whole face and pushing the webbed skin of his eyelid upwards. The bowl of fruit fell over and the fresh raspberries tumbled down the hill. It didn't matter, he could pick plenty more with Maggi and they could eat them together later, with cream maybe. He set the bowl upright and ran his fingers through the tender young stalks of grass breaking through the soft earth. New things were coming, new things, he'd been patient and now was the time. His time was now.

Acknowledgements

SINCERE THANKS TO MY BRILLIANT editor, Clare Gordon, who continues to provide insightful feedback on my writing and pushes me to get the best out of every character; to copyeditor, Liz Hatherell, who worries about being picky which is exactly why I value her input; to eagle-eyed proofreader, Sally Partington; to publicist, Isabel Williams, whose organizational skills I covet and for whom no request is too much trouble; and to all the team at HQ, especially Rachel Quin, Francesca von Krauland, Grace Marshall, Sarah Renwick, Angie Dobbs, Halema Begum, Ellen Rockell and Stephanie Heathcote. Thanks, of course, to the captain of the ship, Lisa Milton, and to agent extraordinaire, Cath Summerhayes. Special thanks are due to Mr John Connor Senior for being so willing to share his many years of gardening experience and vast horticultural knowledge with me.

ONE PLACE. MANY STORIES

Bold, innovative and empowering publishing.

FOLLOW US ON:

@HQStories